THE BOOK
SUPREMACY

A Bibliophile Mystery

Kate Carlisle

BERKLEY PRIME CRIME
New York

BERKLEY PRIME CRIME
Published by Berkley
An imprint of Penguin Random House LLC
penguinrandomhouse.com

ISBN: 9780451491411

Berkley Prime Crime hardcover edition / June 2019
Berkley Prime Crime mass-market edition / April 2020

Printed in the United States of America
3   5   7   9   10   8   6   4

Cover art by Dan Craig Inc.
Cover design by Steve Meditz

This book is dedicated with love and gratitude to Jenn McKinlay and Paige Shelton, both brilliant writers and great friends. I pinch myself daily because I can't believe how lucky I am to have you as my coconspirators and plot partners. Thanks so much for this one, and for many, many more.

ACKNOWLEDGMENTS

I want to thank everyone at Berkley for always supporting me and my books. I'm so grateful to have the absolute best team in the world, starting with senior editor Michelle Vega and associate editor Jen Monroe; production editor Megha Jain; marketing coordinator Jessica Mangicaro and the entire Marketing department; associate publicist Tara O'Connor and everyone in Publicity; an amazing sales team; and my brilliant cover artist, Dan Craig, along with senior designer Steve Meditz and the entire Art department, who create magic with every book.

Many thanks to my review crew and all of my readers and Facebook friends for taking Brooklyn and me into their hearts and seeing us through a baker's dozen books—and many more!

Merci beaucoup to my superhero agent Christina Hogrebe and to the uber-talented Jenel Looney. Thanks to you both for always having my back.

Finally, a true confession: I dreamed up Brooklyn's escape room scene before ever experiencing one in person. Now that I have, I must give a shout-out to Escape Room Palm Springs for showing us a crazy good time with the lonely vampire and the evil witch.

Chapter 1

It was our last day in Paris.

My husband (and yes, I was really loving that word—a lot) Derek and I had breakfast on the private terrace of the hotel suite, enjoying the spectacular view of the city that was spread out before us. Nearby, the tall, thin spire of the American Cathedral speared up into the sky like a javelin. The immense Eiffel Tower loomed impressively in the distance. There was a smattering of fluffy white clouds dotting the blue sky, and the early-morning sunshine reflected brightly off the windows of the surrounding buildings. The air was still cool, but I could already feel it beginning to warm up. Lovely Paris was pulling out all the stops for our last day.

Derek watched me grab a thin slice of delectable Iberico ham from the small plate of charcuterie, and I couldn't help but smile. Not because of the ham, which was utterly delicious and melted in my mouth, but because it had been three weeks since our wedding and I still felt a tingle up my spine whenever I saw his stunning face and thought about those three little words: *my husband Derek*.

I shook my head. Honestly, on any normal day I

wouldn't be so consumed by such sappy, besotted thoughts. But who could blame me? *He's so gorgeous*, I thought. With those dark blue eyes, so intense, so intelligent. And his mouth, whew. His lips could twist into a sensual, roguish smile when least expected. He was tall, dark, and dangerous, and he was all mine.

Maybe I was suffering from some kind of honeymoon fever, because lately, with just the right look or tilt of his head, Derek could render me light-headed and woozy.

Who was I kidding? I'd been ridiculously smitten from the very first time we met. And oddly enough, according to Derek, the feeling was entirely mutual.

That first time had occurred about two years ago during a fancy charity gala at the Covington Library. It was the night my mentor was found—by me—dying in a pool of his own blood. Murdered. Derek had been in charge of a security detail guarding the priceless books and antiquities on display. I had seen him stalking the crowded floor, studying faces, observing body language, watching reactions, looking completely isolated despite the crowd. He was lean and muscular in a gazillion-dollar charcoal suit; his eyes were darkly compelling as he scanned the room. And when our gazes met, he frowned at me. Frowned! It was annoying, to say the least.

Days later, though, he had explained his reaction by saying that I had taken him by surprise.

"What's that supposed to mean?" I'd asked, still a little put out.

He had shaken his head, then grabbed hold of my arms and kissed me. "That's what it means," he had murmured.

"Ah."

I exhaled slowly at the memory of that first kiss and, still a little dizzy, reached for a slim slice of buttery Brie and a chunk of fresh baguette. Gazing around the terrace, enjoying the sight of dozens of cascading purple orchids trailing over the wrought iron railings, I sighed. Honeymoon fever or not, the man could still turn my insides to jelly.

Derek touched my arm. "What shall we do today?" With a grin, he added, "As if I didn't know."

"I'm so predictable," I said, smiling self-consciously. "But yes, I'd really like to visit the Bouquinistes one more time. I have a feeling that there's a fabulous old book just waiting for me to pluck it out of obscurity and make it my own."

The Bouquinistes were the bookstalls that lined both sides of the Seine River for several miles. And when your life revolved around old books as mine did, those bookstalls were like a siren song. I had to pay them one last visit before I left Paris.

My name is Brooklyn Wainwright and I'm a bookbinder specializing in rare-book restoration. I considered the bookstalls my own version of panning for gold.

"I'm in the mood to do some browsing as well," Derek said, his normally clipped British accent sounding sexy and mellow in the morning sunlight. "Perhaps I can find more of those tacky souvenirs you discovered. I'd like to bring some back to the office."

"Ooh, good idea. I'll need more of those, too." As if I hadn't already collected a few dozen, I thought.

He took a last sip of his café au lait. "We can walk along the river, hold hands, and watch the world go by. We don't have to be anywhere until dinnertime."

"That sounds wonderful." I reached my arms out in a big, lazy stretch, then relaxed and smiled at the man sitting across the breakfast table from me. "I love my life. And I love you."

"And I love you, too." He leaned over and kissed me, then ran his fingers along my cheek. "I see you also loved your French toast."

"It was delicious." I popped the last bit of Brie and baguette into my mouth, then rubbed my full stomach and frowned at all the empty plates on the table. "I can't believe we ate so much. But this was my last chance to try the French toast. I've been craving it for weeks, but I never saw it on a menu until, well, you know."

I'd had to learn the hard way that the French referred to French toast as something entirely different. Derek had taken pity on me yesterday morning and revealed the secret French code.

"They call it *pain perdu*," he had said. "Or 'lost toast,' because it's made with very dry bread."

It was mortifying to have made that typically American mistake. After all, I had visited Paris at least four times before this and naturally thought I knew everything. One of those visits had been to see my sister Savannah, who had been studying at the famous Cordon Bleu cooking school. With a fancy chef in the family, you would've thought I would know what *pain perdu* was.

But no. I sighed again. You learn something new every day, as my father always said.

We strolled down Avenue George V to the Pont de l'Alma, stopped to marvel at the Flame of Liberty monument and check out the lingering tributes to Princess

Diana—who was killed in the tunnel under that very bridge—and then crossed over the Seine to the Left Bank. Staring down at the water, watching the tourist-filled Batobus cruise near the shore, I was surprised at how cold the river looked and how fast the current traveled.

The sudden chill had me rubbing my arms briskly. Despite the sunny skies, the air was cooler and breezier here by the river, and I snuggled up close to Derek for warmth. He didn't mind, and wrapped his arm around me. We walked a little more quickly until I adjusted to the crisp, clear air.

We ambled along for another mile, maybe two, gazing at shop windows and chatting easily about everything we had seen and done over the past three weeks. We had originally planned to spend only two weeks away, but as friends and family learned of our honeymoon destination, we began receiving requests to run an errand here, or pick up or deliver an item there, or look up someone of importance elsewhere. One or two requests turned into four or five. But only if we had time, everyone insisted, or only if we were in the area. No big deal. Except several of the requests turned out to be quite a big deal. So we extended the trip for a week. I couldn't say that I minded very much.

Walking along the river, we gazed at the expansive grassy park that led up to the imposing Hôtel des Invalides, where Napoleon was entombed in stately splendor under the grand Dôme des Invalides. I had been inside on a previous trip and had to admit that it was the most spectacular setting for a tomb I'd ever seen. Set on a green granite pedestal and placed on a mosaic tile floor that illustrated the main battles of the

Empire, the highly polished red stone sarcophagus
was surrounded by marble columns, statuary, and bas-
relief sculptures that told the story of his many achieve-
ments. Years ago, one of my tour guides had called it "a
simple soldier's tomb." They couldn't have been more
wrong.

On the next block we passed the stately Palais Bour-
bon, constructed for one of Louis XIV's daughters and
now the home of the National Assembly; and then the
Musée d'Orsay, an old train station transformed into a
popular art museum. On the opposite side of the river
were the pretty trees of the Jardin des Tuileries, which
led up to the impressive and historic buildings of the
Louvre.

"If you'd like, we can stop for a light lunch at Coco-
rico." Derek pointed toward the next street. "They're
right around the corner."

"I'd love to." I had fallen for the quirky little bistro
the other day. Their onion soup was positively addictive.

Finally we came to the place on the Quai Voltaire
where the Bouquinistes, or bookstalls, began. The tingle I felt was the same one I experienced whenever I
got up close and personal with old books and the people who loved them.

"You know I'm going to look at everything," I confessed to Derek.

"Of course you are," he said lightly. "I'll move along
at a faster pace, but I'll wait for you at the next corner."

"Is that Rue Bonaparte?" I asked, taking a quick
glance at my foldout street map.

"Yes." He ran his hand across the back of my neck
and kissed me. "Take your time."

Watching him walk away, tall and lean and confident, I let out a jagged breath. The man was compelling, no doubt about it.

Each of the bookstalls—as well as their owners—had their own personality and style. Some of them specialized in older classics with worn leather covers, their gilded titles fading but still readable. Other stalls were dedicated to paperbacks, many of them pulp fiction and noir mysteries with fabulously garish covers. Some owners sold wonderful posters that they clipped to their roofs and allowed to blow in the breeze. These mainly featured those familiar French art deco ad campaigns hocking everything from milk to gin, but there were also lots of stock studio photographs of famous movie stars. Marilyn Monroe was still especially popular.

The bookstalls were uniformly dark green in color and were highly regulated in terms of size, shape, hours of operation, and occasionally, content. Some historians claimed that they had been in existence since the seventeenth century, and some of the stalls—and the merchandise—appeared to be about that old. When the simple green boxes were closed up at night and chained to the stone walls that overlooked the river, they looked almost coffin-like.

But for now, the bookstalls were very much alive and open for business. The avenue was crowded with cars, and the traffic noises mixed with the pedestrians' shouts and murmurs in French. The sounds made me smile with fondness. I loved this city. And I absolutely adored the Bouquinistes. After all, books are my life.

I stopped at the very first bookstall and began to browse through the rows and rows of books on every subject known to man. I glanced up and noticed Derek moving down the sidewalk. He turned and I waved, knowing I would catch up eventually.

I was captivated by the collection of classic mysteries on display in the second stall. Most were written in French, but I still checked every title, hoping to be inspired, hoping to find just the right little treasure to take home with me. Every so often I would pull a book out from the stack to examine the cover and see what sort of condition it was in. These were mostly used paperbacks, but each had been carefully wrapped in plastic, so their condition remained fairly decent. There was also the occasional hardcover, and I examined those even more closely.

The bookseller approached after having allowed me to peruse on my own for a while. "*Bonjour, madame.*"

"*Bonjour, madame,*" I replied in kind, and took a quick look at her. She was probably fifty, wore a thin white sweater over black pants with little black flats. Her dark hair was short and straight. To me, she was quintessentially French.

"Ah," she said. "You are American."

I gave her a rueful grin. "*Oui, madame.*" Even the best French accent couldn't fool a French person, and mine was so far from being the best as to be laughable. Or as the French would say, *ridicule*.

She gazed at the row of books I was going through. "You like the detective stories," she said in her thick accent.

"Yes." I liked them as much as the next person, I supposed. The fact that they were simply *books* had been enough to snag my attention. But to be honest, the long row of Agatha Christies had definitely perked me up.

"I don't know quite what I'm looking for," I explained lamely, "but I'll know it when I see it."

"Ah." She nodded in understanding and brought a little stepstool out from under the stall. "You will stand on this. You can see the books more easily from above."

I was touched by her thoughtfulness. "*Merci.*"

She waved her hand at the books. "Please enjoy your search."

The stalls were high enough that the stepstool did make it much easier to look down and see the titles. I started on the next row and was intrigued to find several James Bond books written in French. I picked one up.

"*Vivre et Laisser Mourir,*" I murmured. I had a feeling I knew what it meant, but just to be sure, I pulled out my cell phone to use my translator app.

"*Live and Let Die,*" I said, delighted. "Cool."

The book next to that one was *Casino Royale*. No translation necessary, although the French version spelled it *Royal*, minus the *e* on the end.

I glanced around to see how far Derek had wandered. Much like the fictional James Bond, Derek had been a commander in the Royal Navy and had gone on to work for British military intelligence before opening his own security company. Also like James Bond, Derek was dashing, sexy, brave, and daring. One of these books would make a perfect, slightly silly gift to give him as a memento of our time in Paris.

But which one? I continued to skim through the books, trying to figure out which title would be best. I leaned farther over to catch a glimpse of the books stacked near the back of the stall. There were hardcovers back there, and it was always exciting to discover a hardcover gem.

And that was when I saw it. I reached out, lifted the book gingerly, and stared at it. I had to admit I was shaking with excitement. "It's too perfect."

The book was a hardcover English edition of *The Spy Who Loved Me*. Many years ago, I had stolen my brother's cache of Bond books and read them all. Since I was only about twelve years old at the time, I probably missed some of the nuances, but I distinctly remembered that this one had been one of my favorites. I vaguely recalled that it had been different from the others because it was told partly from the woman's point of view. I would have to look that up, though, because I couldn't be sure if I was recalling it correctly.

If nothing else, the title of the book made it the perfect choice for Derek. But as I examined the book, I was pleased that its dust jacket was still intact, although there was one small tear along the fold. The cover showed a red carnation, and the book title was written cryptically on a burned note with a stiletto stuck in it. The book itself was a bit cattywampus due to a weakened inner front hinge, a common problem in beloved, well-read books where the front cover had been opened and closed often enough to separate it from the spine. It would be easy enough to fix.

I opened the book to check out the title page. Published in 1962. I wondered briefly if it was a first edition. Probably not. The price, written in pencil on the flyleaf, was only seven euros.

Still, I was thrilled that I'd found it. I stepped down off the stool and found the woman who ran the stall. I smiled and held it up to her. "Perfect," I said. "*Parfait.*"

"*Très bon!*" She clapped a few times, sharing my happiness. "It is a good find."

"*Oui*. Yes, it is." I handed her a five-euro note along with a heavy coin worth two euros. She slipped the book into a small white paper bag and thanked me.

"*Merci, madame*," I said. "*Au revoir.*"

"*Merci. Au revoir*," she said cheerfully.

I spotted Derek farther down the Quai. He stood near another bookstall, and I wondered if he had found his own little treasure as I had. I headed his way, but slowed down when I noticed that he was talking to another man. I didn't recognize the man but I was pretty sure he wasn't a bookseller. He sure didn't look like it anyway. This man wore a snazzy tweed jacket and khakis and appeared almost as tall as Derek. He had bushy gray hair that he covered with a sporty driver's cap. His wardrobe, body type, and gestures said "jolly old England" to me. The two men spoke to each other as though they were old friends. Derek patted him on the shoulder and said something, and the other man threw his head back and laughed.

Derek clearly knew him well. It had to be an old friend. Or at least a friendly acquaintance.

I was still a short distance away when I felt a shiver creep up my spine. I glanced around, trying to figure out where the vibe had come from, then stopped abruptly. Someone else on the street was staring at Derek and the other man. The stranger stood near the curb, about halfway between me and the spot where Derek and his friend stood talking.

The guy wore an olive green hooded sweatshirt with the hood pulled completely over his head so that it obscured the outline of his face. He was probably completely harmless, I thought, but he was staring so intently at the two men. It made me nervous.

I continued to make my way toward Derek, pretending to check out the books in the stalls as I went so I could keep a surreptitious eye on the hooded man. He stayed in the same spot, still staring at Derek and the other man. I began to question whether I was right about him. Maybe he was gazing at something on the other side of the river. But then Derek glanced my way and waved. The hooded man quickly bent down to tie his shoe, almost as though he didn't want Derek to see him.

Definitely suspicious, I thought. But I was diverted when I noticed a small hardcover book resting against the back wall of the stall I was just passing. It caught my eye because of its unusual size and style. It was about the size of a small photo album with Chinese writing and characters brushed onto the cover. I reached for the book, opened it, and saw that it was written in French, but there were Chinese characters on each page. I thought it might be a book of medicinal herbs because there were pretty paintings of flowers and herbs on every page as well.

It was mainly the Coptic binding that appealed to me because I'd never seen anything like it in any of the bookstalls I'd visited. The Coptic binding style was named for the Copts, the early Christians living in Egypt, who were known for binding books by knotting thread or twine on the outside of the spine. The technique allowed the book to lie flat and required no glue in its construction.

I had promised to bring something back from Paris for Inspector Janice Lee, SFPD homicide detective and my good friend. She was a beautiful Chinese American woman with great hair, a fabulous ward-

robe, and a no-nonsense attitude. But it was her mother
who would really love this book, I thought, and that
meant that Janice would love it, too. And thinking of
Janice Lee, I was reminded of my wedding day.

"What would you like from Paris?" I'd asked Inspector Lee that afternoon. It was a short time after
the wedding ceremony, and Derek and I were finally
able to relax and enjoy our guests—along with a glass
of champagne.

"Bring me something interesting," she'd said.

Now as I gazed at the odd little French-Chinese
book of herbs, I was pretty sure that this would qualify.

I held the book up for the clerk to see. "*Qu'est-ce que
ça veut dire?*" I said, and repeated the question in
English, just to cover my bases. "What does this mean?"

She gazed at the book cover and smiled. "*Le Lan-
gage des Fleurs.* How you say, *Language of Fleurs*?"

"*Flowers*," I guessed.

"*Oui!*"

We both grinned at our bumbling method of com-
munication. Feeling emboldened, I stumbled through
another question. "*Il est écrit en français mais il y a
aussi des caractères chinois?*" Once again I repeated
the same thing in English. "It is written in French, but
there are Chinese characters as well?"

"*Oui,*" she exclaimed. "*C'est un livre sur les herbes
chinoises, mais bien sûr pour un lecteur français.*"

"Ah." If I was understanding her correctly, she'd
said something like, "The book is about Chinese herbs,
but of course it is written for a French reader."

"I see," I said. "I will take it."

"*Très bon! Quatorze euros.*"

Fourteen euros? I frowned at her and glanced at the

book. The cover was ready to fall off, and while the pages were fine linen, they were old and dirty. But was I really going to haggle in bad French? And did it matter how much it cost? No, it did not. I started to reach for my wallet.

But Madame had noticed my hesitation and immediately spoke up. "*Douze euros.*" She gave a short, brusque chop with her hand, as if to say, *And that's my final offer.*

"Okay," I said quickly. "I mean, *oui. Merci.*" I hadn't expected her to lower the price, so I smiled broadly as I handed her a ten-euro note and a two-euro coin.

She pocketed the money, slid the book into a small plastic bag, and handed it to me. "*Merci, madame.*"

"*Très bien,*" I said with a short nod. "*Merci, madame.*" Ridiculously pleased with my purchases, I glanced down the row of stalls to find Derek.

The man in the olive green hoodie was still standing on the curb, still staring in Derek's direction.

Maybe he was waiting for the bus or a ride, but I didn't think so. He was staring too keenly at Derek and his friend and not giving the traffic a second thought. The hooded observer wore a pair of baggy denim jeans and white sneakers. He was average height, maybe an inch or two less than six feet tall, and slim.

Not sure exactly what to do, I stopped at the nearest bookstall and pretended to browse, but I was watching the hooded man's every move. His shoulders were tense and his hands were fisted in his pockets. The guy was freaking me out. Maybe he was just hanging out on the sidewalk, minding his own business. Or maybe he was only gazing at the stately buildings on the other side of the Seine. The beautiful trees lining the river.

Those silvery leaves shimmering in the breeze. Anyone could be mesmerized by all that beauty. But I didn't think the hooded man was one of them.

I decided to ignore the man and concentrate on the views. Pulling my phone from my pocket, I took a few photos of the trees and the bridge over the river. And then I aimed the lens at the hooded man and snapped a few more shots, just in case Derek recognized the guy. Not that he would see his face, but it couldn't hurt to capture the moment. And if the guy was harmless, I would have a silly story to tell when I showed off my photos of our honeymoon.

I continued walking toward Derek, and when I got within the hooded man's line of sight, I didn't make eye contact, but kept walking with a casual air, ruffling my hair and letting it be tossed by the breeze. And then, from the corner of my eye, I saw the guy turn and notice me—and quickly walk away.

Why? Did he know me? Did he know I was with Derek? Had he been watching us before? Now I was completely paranoid. I wanted to chase after him and insist that he tell me what he was doing. But that was crazy. Wasn't it?

"Derek," I called, and waved.

"Darling," he said jovially. As I approached, he added, "Come meet Ned Davies."

I walked a little faster, pasted a smile on my face, and when I got close enough, extended my hand. "Hello, Ned."

"So this is the girl who stole your heart," Ned said, grinning as he gave me a hearty handshake.

"This is she," Derek said.

"Aren't you a lucky man?" he said fondly, gazing with interest from Derek to me. With a wink at me, he said, "This bloke here has the luck of the devil. He's pretended to be my friend for years, but has actually been the bane of my existence."

I gave Derek a quizzical look. "How's that?"

Derek grinned as Ned clarified. "We had a weekly poker game going for years. And I couldn't beat him. Not once. Bugger it. He's a shark, I tell you."

"He's pretty good," I admitted with a weak smile. I'd seen him play cards with my brothers. He might've been a shark, but he was a really good-looking shark.

"And now he's managed to meet and marry this beauty." Ned slapped his heart dramatically, causing Derek to laugh merrily.

I wasn't quite ready to be merry, but I managed to keep smiling.

"In case it wasn't clear," Derek explained, "Ned and I used to work together." But then he briskly changed the subject, asking, "Did you buy something special?"

"Oh." I held up the bag. "Yes, wait till you see it. It's kind of perfect."

"Well, let's have a look then," Derek said.

"Um." I flashed him an awkward smile. "Actually, it's a gift. For you."

"For me?" His voice softened and he smoothed his hand over my hair. "You got me something?"

"Well, now we must see it," Ned said.

"Okay." I glanced around, checking up and down the sidewalk. "By the way, did either of you see that guy in the green hoodie? He was standing about a block away and he kept staring at you. When I got close, he turned and hurried off in the opposite direction."

Derek's eyes narrowed and he shot Ned a cautionary look before both men scanned the street.

"Don't see him," Ned said with a casual shrug. But I noticed that his shoulders were rigid and his gaze had sharpened. Did he know the guy?

"Probably nothing," I said quietly, but I frowned as I looked back at the spot where I'd last seen the hooded man. Shaking off the weird vibe, I handed Derek the little bag. "Anyway, here's what I found."

Derek took the bag and slid the book out.

"Well, now," Ned said, and started to laugh. "Isn't that interesting?"

Derek stared at the cover and chuckled as well. He glanced at me and sobered. "Darling Brooklyn, it's perfect. But what made you buy this for me?"

"Well." I was suddenly unsure of myself and began waving my hands as I spoke. "Because, you know. You worked at MI6 and you do all that security stuff. And you know the way Inspector Lee always calls you 'Commander.'"

"I'm not exactly a spy, darling," he said lightly.

"The rest could apply, though," Ned said, still grinning.

"Thank you," I said to Ned. I wasn't about to start arguing with Derek in front of his friend, but come on, I wasn't born yesterday. Derek had worked for Britain's MI6 for ten years. Now his own company handled security for exceedingly wealthy clients and extremely valuable artwork. So maybe his job description at MI6 had been something other than "spy," but he still qualified as an international man of mystery.

I lifted my shoulders and gave Derek a little smile. "I just thought it would make you happy."

"It does, and so do you," he murmured, and proved it by leaning in to give me a soft kiss. "I love it, and I love you."

I breathed a sigh of relief. "Back at you."

"Well, I know you two have big plans for the rest of the day." Ned gave Derek a manly slap on the back. "It was marvelous running into you, Derek. And lovely to meet you, Brooklyn."

"Nice to meet you, too."

"Next time you must tell me you're coming," he added. "I know Patsy would love to meet you. She's an excellent cook and would insist on treating you to a home-cooked meal."

"That sounds wonderful," I said.

"Good to see you, Ned," Derek said. "Take good care. And give me a call sometime. Let me know how you're doing."

"I will. And go see Owen." Ned gripped Derek's arm. "Tell him I send my best. Will you tell him that for me?"

"Of course," Derek said.

The two men shook hands enthusiastically and then Ned took my hand and gave it an affectionate squeeze. He waved to us and walked away, up the Rue Bonaparte toward the Luxembourg Gardens.

Derek watched him go, then turned to me. "Well, are you ready for a bit of lunch? Or would you rather make our way back to the hotel?"

"After that huge breakfast, I think I'd like to save myself for dinner."

He squeezed my hand. "Our last meal in Paris."

"I hate to see it all end." I glanced around. "But I guess I'm just about ready to go home."

"I feel the same, love." He tucked the book under his arm, held on to my hand, and we headed back to the hotel.

We had become used to dining later in the evening as the French do, but that night we took the earliest reservation we could get, knowing that we still had to finish packing and wake up early the next day to catch a plane. We arrived at the little bistro in the heart of Saint-Germain-des-Prés just as they were opening the doors at seven o'clock, and our promptness was rewarded when they led us to a round corner table that allowed us to observe the entire room as waiters bustled by and the place slowly filled with other guests.

While we waited for the waiter to bring us the half bottle of champagne we'd ordered, I took the opportunity to tell Derek a little more about the hooded man. "I wasn't sure he was watching you until you turned and looked his way and he instantly bent down to tie his shoe."

"You have excellent instincts, darling," Derek said. "That does sound suspicious."

"Thank you." I reached for my purse. "And I took some photos."

The waiter arrived just then and poured us each a glass of champagne. When he walked away, Derek said, "In honor of our honeymoon, let's put this mysterious man out of our minds and simply enjoy our last evening in Paris."

"Good idea." I put my purse away and we clinked our glasses, then took our first sips of the delectable golden liquid.

"Darling," Derek said, after setting his glass down.

"I found a little something for you while browsing the bookstalls."

"You did? How? I thought you were talking to Ned the whole time."

"Not quite," he said. Smiling, he pulled a small wrapped package from his jacket pocket and set it on the table in front of me.

"What is this?" I asked, shocked that he had found a book for me.

"You'll be surprised to learn it's a book."

I laughed. "Yes, I figured out that much." I opened the package and found a darling little book with a pink-and-white slipcover. There was a brushed painting in pink of a stylish young lady from an earlier era. I had to open the book to find the title.

"Oh, it's *Gigi*." I was blown away with delight. I looked at Derek and beamed. "It's so sweet. Thank you."

"A small token to remind you of our time in France."

"I'll never forget our time in France," I assured him, and gave him a kiss. Then we lifted our glasses once more and toasted to a wonderful honeymoon.

Although the food was fabulous, Allard was not a fancy Michelin-starred restaurant like some of the others we'd enjoyed on our trip. I didn't care. It was obvious that diners came here to experience comfort, tradition, and a touch of romance, but not fireworks. The old-world bistro furnishings were subtle to the point of being demure: dark wood wainscoting, tiny-flowered wallpaper liberally dotted with eclectic, wood-framed artwork, red cloth banquettes, crisp white tablecloths. In one corner, a zinc-topped service bar held bottles of wine and glassware ready to be dispatched to the tables.

I had always been open to trying new foods, but after three weeks in France, where food was revered like nowhere else on earth, I was frankly ready for a good old American burger and fries. Despite that, when I saw "tender ox cheek" on the menu, I knew I had to order it. It turned out to be a generous hunk of meat as large as my fist and truly so tender it melted in my mouth.

Tastes like short ribs, I thought with relief. Our server brought it to the table in a mini-pot, drenched in its own dark, rich gravy and served with wonderful chunks of buttery carrots. Derek ordered the famous roasted Challans duck served with dozens of rich, slightly tart, Sicilian green olives. The combination was incongruous to me, but it looked delicious.

We didn't speak for several long minutes while we both stuffed ourselves with indescribably yummy tastes and textures.

We had started the meal by sharing two appetizers— escargot and a curly endive salad with huge chucks of *lardons* (bacon) and freshly made croutons—and a crisp white wine. With our entrées we had an excellent Saint-Émilion Grand Cru in honor of our quick visit to the charming village of Saint-Émilion the week before.

For my very last dessert in Paris, how could I not order the puffy profiteroles stuffed with vanilla ice cream, accompanied by a quart-size serving of warm, thick chocolate syrup? *C'est impossible.*

After dinner we strolled along the narrow Rue Saint-André des Arts and down to Rue de Buci to enjoy the lively crowds still dining at the many outdoor cafés and bistros that lined the pretty market street. Then we walked a few blocks up to the fashionable Boulevard Saint-Germain, window-shopping along the way, and finally reached the taxi stand, where we caught a cab back to the Hotel George V. Once we'd greeted the hotel doorman and the concierge, we crossed the lobby and took the elevator up to our suite.

I was looking forward to spending the rest of the evening in our rooms with their pale blue walls and softly lit coffered ceilings. There were beautiful antique furnishings and lovely paintings, and the bathroom was a luxurious marble palace. I had never felt more pampered in my life.

As soon as we walked into our room, Derek grabbed my arm and whispered, "Stay out here."

"What is it?" But I didn't hesitate to do exactly what he'd advised. I watched him bend over and pull a mean-looking pistol from a holster strapped to his calf.

Oh. My. God. I didn't say it out loud. I couldn't speak. I had no more breath left in me. I stood as still as a statue as he prowled across the living area. Then, leaning against the doorjamb, he took a quick peek left and right and crept silently into the bedroom.

Several excruciatingly long moments later, he came back into the living room. He crossed the room and wrapped his arms around me. "Everything is fine," he whispered. "I'm sorry I frightened you."

"That's okay." Frankly, I'd seen him carry a gun before. Through no fault of our own, we had the kind of lifestyle that demanded it once in a while. You know how sometimes you just might stumble across the occasional dead body? And then follow it up with your basic showdown with a vicious killer? Yeah, that was the lifestyle I was talking about.

"What made you think someone was in here?" I asked, leaning against him.

"I took precautions before we left for dinner," he said cryptically.

"Okay." I breathed in and exhaled slowly. "Well, maybe it was Housekeeping."

"Maybe."

"But no one is here now, right?"

"That's right. But just to be certain, let's check to make sure nothing is missing."

"Good idea." Since we were leaving in the morning, our suitcases were almost completely packed. Still, we searched the entire suite to make sure everything was just as we'd left it. I even emptied my suitcase, then repacked, just in case, and double-checked that the James Bond book, the Chinese herb book, and the pretty little copy of *Gigi* were securely tucked away.

And then I remembered one more thing.

"Oh no!" I ran to the closet safe, opened it, and was relieved to find my jewelry still locked inside. It wasn't that I had anything particularly precious or rare, but there were a few sentimental pieces that I would've hated to lose. "It's all here."

"Good." He nodded, then smiled tightly. "So it must've been a false alarm. Everything is fine."

"Everything is fine," I echoed quietly. But I recognized that edgy tone in his voice. And I knew that everything was definitely *not* fine.

Chapter 2

We were halfway through our flight home when I remembered something and turned to Derek. "Who's Owen?"

His mouth twisted thoughtfully. "I was wondering if you'd heard that part of the conversation."

"All I heard was Ned telling you to say hello to Owen. It was just before he walked away. So who is he?"

"Owen Gibbons is a mutual friend of Ned's and mine. Another chap from the old days. He was older than me, closer in age and temperament to Ned, but we knew each other well enough."

"Was he with MI6?"

"No, no. Different agency. American."

"So . . . which one?" I took a look around, as though someone on the plane might be listening in. It could happen. "CIA? NSA? FBI?"

He grinned at me. "Are you checking for eavesdroppers?"

I shrugged, feeling only slightly sheepish. "You never know. The thermoplastic walls have ears."

He leaned in close and planted a kiss on my cheek. "Thank you for looking out for me."

"Someone has to," I muttered.

The sound of his quiet laughter resonating against my skin caused my heart to melt like marshmallow goo. Which was a ridiculous image, but there you had it.

"I was mentioning to Ned that I'd moved to San Francisco," Derek explained. "He reminded me that our old friend Owen owns the spy shop along the Embarcadero. Ned suggested that I swing by sometime and explain the finer points of espionage to Owen, and we had a good chuckle over it."

"A spy shop?" I was stymied. "What do they sell? Trench coats? Magnifying glasses?"

Derek grinned. "It would be very clever of him to sell those items. But no, they sell things like nanny cams, two-way mirrors, GPS trackers, dash cams, lockpicks, all sorts of electronic gadgets. Apparently Owen's shop even features a café and bookshop as well."

"I love the idea of a bookshop. They must sell lots of spy thrillers in there. And the café idea is brilliant, isn't it?"

"I think so. Because nothing goes better after picking a few locks than a nice cup of tea and a scone."

"Exactly."

"And you'll love this," he said. "The name of the shop is SPECTRE."

"SPECTRE." I choked back a laugh. "That's awesome. Very James Bond of him. Owen's last name isn't Blofeld, is it?"

Derek snickered. "No. And let's hope his shop isn't a front for any terrorist groups."

I knew from my preteen glomming of the Bond books that SPECTRE was short for *Special Executive for Counterintelligence, Terrorism, Revenge and Ex-*

tortion. Criminal mastermind Ernst Blofeld ran the organization and enlisted all the worst villains in the world to help him do his dirty work.

"Have you ever gone into the shop?" I asked.

"Never. I was vaguely aware of the shop, but until Ned said something, I had no idea that our old pal Owen is the owner."

"We should go there. It might be fun." I thought about it for a minute, then elbowed him. "Is that why you and Ned laughed when you saw the book I bought you?"

He chuckled. "Darling, you must admit your timing was impeccable."

"Yeah." I sighed. "I get that a lot."

The flight home was interminable, but we were lucky enough to sit in business class, where the seats reclined all the way. I was rarely able to sleep on planes, but I was so thoroughly exhausted from three weeks away from home, I did manage a few short catnaps. I spent the rest of the trip reminiscing, jotting down notes, making lists of things to do once we got home, and writing out all of the special moments I wanted to remember. There were too many to recall, so I just wrote down a few highlights. I would fill in the dozens of little details when I was able to take the time to go through the six billion photos I'd taken on the trip.

Visiting my dear friends Ariel and Pascal in Lyon was definitely one of those highlights. I couldn't wait to introduce them to Derek.

When I was in high school, my bookbinding mentor Abraham Karastovsky had invited famed book artist and historian Ariel Hodges to Dharma to work on a major book-restoration project. She lived with my family for a year and we became like sisters. When the project was finished, Ariel was hired by the Institut d'Histoire du Livre in Lyon to run their annual book history project. While there, she met and fell in love with the handsome and wonderful Pascal, a curator at the printing museum.

I considered Lyon the heart and soul of bookbinding and all things book related, so I soaked it all up. We toured the museums for a few hours and then spent the rest of our time in Lyon eating amazing food and drinking exquisite wines, laughing, and catching up with our friends.

From Lyon we drove west to Bordeaux for a few days, where we relaxed in a spectacular château overlooking the River Gironde in the Margaux wine region. From there we traveled inland to Périgueux and stayed overnight in an ancient farmhouse belonging to Derek's old friend Pierre, a world-renowned truffle expert, and his wife, Marie.

Who knew that there were such experts in the world? But Pierre and his adorable dog, Sadie, gave us a wonderful demonstration of their truffle-hunting ability and actually dug up two big, beautiful truffles. Pierre generously gave me one to take home to my sister Savannah, the chef, who would owe me forever.

Pierre was kind enough to clean and pack the truffle properly. And he warned me that even though we were allowed to bring truffles into the country, it was important to declare it on our customs form. Because the last place I wanted to go was truffle jail.

Our final stop before returning to Paris was the tiny village of La Croix Saint-Just. It was the ancestral home of Robson Benedict's family. Robson—otherwise known as Guru Bob—had asked us to visit as a gesture of goodwill after we had discovered many of the village's treasures sealed away in a hidden cave in the Dharma winery.

Because it was so close, we drove to Oradour-sur-Glane, the small town that was destroyed by the Nazis in World War II. The town played a role in Robson's family history, and I wanted to see it for myself.

Somewhere over the Atlantic Ocean, I reached my limit of reminiscing and was finally able to drift off to sleep with my hand tucked inside Derek's. It was a sweet ending to a beautiful trip.

"Home at last," I said as we stepped inside our quiet apartment.

Derek parked the last piece of luggage just inside the door and glanced around. "Be it ever so humble."

When I shot him an amused look, he managed a weary smile. "We're both blathering clichés."

"I'm too exhausted to come up with something original."

He wrapped his arms around me. "But it is good to be home."

It had taken us several trips from the taxi to get all of our bags and suitcases into the old freight elevator of our building. Once upstairs, it was a real accomplishment to get them all from the elevator into our apartment. I had begun to work up a sweat when we finally closed the door. It was only two o'clock in the afternoon on Tuesday, but my body clock felt like it was midnight. I just wanted to take a nap.

After a slow perusal of the living and dining rooms,

I let go of the breath I'd been holding. Everything appeared to be exactly as we'd left it three weeks earlier. Not that we'd expected problems, but I had trained myself to be wary whenever I walked back into our home since it had been broken into a few times in the past. It didn't seem to matter that Derek had upgraded the security system to the point where our building was about as impenetrable as Fort Knox. I still had to take precautions.

I walked the perimeter of our wide-open living room space, enjoying the brick walls, high ceiling, massive industrial windows, and hardwood floors of our loft-style home. I smiled at the kitchen island that was completely free of newspapers and mail, knowing it wouldn't remain that way for long.

Two years ago, after Derek moved in, we bought the apartment next door and joined the two in order to give him a home office and still have an extra bedroom or two to accommodate visiting friends and family.

"Nothing appears to be missing," he said, walking from the dining room into the living room and gazing through the short hall that led to my workshop. "The plants still look healthy."

"Thanks to Alex," I said. Our down-the-hall neighbor not only was an excellent cupcake baker but also had a green thumb—and a black belt in every martial art known to man. When you put those qualities together, Alex Monroe was the perfect neighbor.

She had even been generous enough to take care of our darling cat, Charlie, for three weeks. We owed her big-time.

That was when I noticed something odd on the kitchen counter. It was more than a foot wide and equally tall, covered in aluminum foil. "Oh my God. Is that what I think it is?"

Derek approached and unpeeled the foil to reveal a three-tiered tray of cupcakes. "Yes."

Alex had made a batch of cupcakes to welcome us home.

"God, I love her," I whispered, taking in the sight of the twelve beautifully decorated treats. There were lemon, red velvet, and chocolate mint. The big puffy mounds of silky frosting glistened in the sunlight pouring in from the windows.

"She's a peach," he said, grinning.

"I want one right now," I said, but a moment later I was scowling. "That's just obnoxious. I've spent the last three weeks eating my way through France. I shouldn't be allowed to eat anything for the next month."

"More for me," Derek declared.

"What?" I was outraged! "No way, pal. Alex went to a lot of trouble to bake these. It would be downright impolite not to eat them."

He laughed. "You stick with that story."

A few minutes later, after we had split one red velvet cupcake—just to be polite—we ran down the hall to let Alex know we were home. We gathered up Charlie and all of her kitty accoutrements—toys, food, cuddly bed, litter box—and proceeded to gush and moan over Alex's generous cupcake making.

Alex assured us that nothing had gone wrong while we were gone. She could tell we were jet-lagged so she promised to come by sometime after work tomorrow to say hello properly and have a glass of wine.

Once we were back home with Charlie, Derek and I spent a few minutes cuddling with her on the couch.

The tabby allowed us a good five minutes before she jumped down and started prowling the apartment, making sure that everything was as she had left it. Derek and I remained on the couch for another moment, silently taking in our comfortable surroundings, then we gazed at each other.

I closed my eyes. "I love you, but I'm starting to feel like death warmed over."

Derek took me in his arms and kissed me sweetly, softly. "You look beautiful to me."

"God, I really do love you."

He pressed his forehead against mine. "I know we had a fantastic time and we'll talk about it forever, but I'm so glad to be home."

"Home with you."

Charlie was winding her soft, furry self in between and around our ankles, purring and meowing with excitement.

Derek and I kissed again and then reluctantly parted. "I really want to take a nap, but I think I'd better unpack and start some laundry. I'll feel better if I get that done."

"And I need to check in with my office," he admitted.

"Why don't you go ahead and do that while I start unpacking?"

He squeezed my hand. "I owe you."

"I'll remind you."

I stared at the huge piles and wondered how two obsessively tidy people could possibly generate so much dirty laundry. Yes, we'd been gone three long weeks, but we had worn a lot of outfits more than once, and we had even used the hotel laundry service twice. It was a mystery.

I started the first load and then turned to face the plethora of books, souvenirs, gifts, and goodies that we'd absolutely had to buy. For instance, my beautiful green cashmere beret. The moment I'd seen it in the window of the small shop on the Île Saint-Louis, I knew I couldn't live without it. It was a dark, rich forest green, and the cashmere wool was thick and warm.

Now, I wondered what I was going to do with it. Would I ever wear it? I doubted it. It was one of those singularly French items that I could no longer picture myself wearing now that I was back home. I'd never been a hat person. But somehow, in France, I'd pictured myself walking around with a beret on my head.

I suppose if we ever vacationed in Hawaii, I would be compelled to bring back a grass skirt. Because who didn't need one of those?

On the other hand, I definitely needed all of the art and research books I had bought. At least I still felt good about them. And as a bookbinder specializing in rare-book restoration, I would definitely use the books. And hello, I could write them off as a business expense on my taxes. So my conscience was clear on those purchases.

But the beret? I stared at the lush forest green and shook my head. No write-off there. And as cute as it was, it wasn't for me. But then I smiled. It would make a perfect early Christmas present for one of my sisters. In fact, my sister Savannah would love it. And why hadn't I thought of that when I was in Paris? Savannah wore berets all the time, especially when she cooked. They seemed to suit her gorgeous bald head.

I would deal with the Eiffel Tower key chains later.

Maybe we could use them as ornaments on our Christmas tree this year.

I gathered up all of my new books to take them to my workshop. As I passed Derek's office, I could hear him talking on the speakerphone to his assistant, Corinne. It sounded as though she was filling him in on the latest office gossip. But not in a funny, laughing way. I heard the concern in her voice as she mentioned several employees causing some sort of trouble. That couldn't be good.

I assumed Derek would tell me about it later, and so I continued to my workshop at the front of our apartment. I found places for the research books in the bookshelf, then placed the James Bond and the Colette books on my workshop table. I wanted to examine them more closely and also wanted to find out what they might be worth on the rare-book sites. Not that I would ever consider selling the books, but I did want to know exactly what they were worth for insurance purposes. Besides, I was curious. One never knew when one might stumble across a hidden treasure.

Pulling my computer from my desk, I set it up on my worktable, turned it on, and went to my favorite online site for evaluating and appraising rare and unusual books. I typed *The Spy Who Loved Me* in the search line, and within seconds a list of available books appeared, along with information and a detailed description of the book, as well as its appraised value. The most expensive edition was at the top of the list, and I almost laughed out loud at the amount of money the bookseller was asking for a first-edition copy of *The Spy Who Loved Me*.

"Twenty-four thousand dollars?" I shook my head. "Seriously?" It was basically the exact same book I'd bought for Derek, but the online book was inscribed by the author, Ian Fleming, and it came complete with a rich, dark leather slipcase. Naturally, that would make it worth the money to some wealthy Bond fan out there.

I moved down the list, looking for something closer to the book I'd bought for Derek. I found it four books later. It was the exact same cover. Both the dust jacket and the book were in very similar condition to Derek's copy. And the price was a little more reasonable, although it was still crazy compared to the seven measly euros I'd paid for the book. This one was only seven thousand five hundred dollars.

"*Only*," I muttered. Good grief, it was worth thousands! I should've felt exhilaration, knowing what a spectacular deal I'd gotten. But instead I was racked with guilt. That poor bookseller could've made so much more money on the book than seven euros. And it occurred to me that I hadn't even declared the book when we went through customs. I mean, I'd declared "books" in general, but I'd given a total value of only one hundred dollars for all the books I'd brought back.

My mind went into overdrive, imagining the police showing up. I would be arrested and brought back to France to stand trial for book fraud. And lying. And cheating. And thievery.

"It's not my fault," I insisted out loud.

"What isn't your fault?"

I flinched, turning to find Derek leaning against the wall by the archway that led out to the living room.

"The Ian Fleming book I bought you is worth a lot more than I spent."

"So you got a bargain."

"Maybe. Unless they come and arrest me."

He bit back a smile. "What have you done now?"

"Really, it's not my fault," I insisted again, and told him the whole story.

"That's rather exciting," he said, picking up the book from the worktable and taking a closer look at the dust jacket. "Instead of worrying, I think we should celebrate our good fortune and let it go at that."

"I suppose."

He set the book down and gave me a warm hug. "I doubt they'll carry you off to prison, darling. You bought the book fair and square and paid the price that the seller requested. Don't give it another thought."

"All right. But not declaring it . . ."

"You declared what the bookseller charged you."

He was right, of course. Guilt was a powerful motivator, though. "I'm just tired, I guess. I sort of let my imagination run away with me."

His forehead furrowed with concern. "Why, that never happens."

"I know. It's weird."

He laughed and let me go, and I picked up the book again. "Besides, once I fix this hinge, it'll be worth even more. It's already in near-fine condition. And it's unusual to find a dust jacket in such good shape, too."

He wandered around my workshop for a moment, then said, "I was going to stay home tomorrow, but there seems to be some trouble at the office."

"Anything serious?"

"Just employee squabbles. But Corinne is at her wit's end and threatening mutiny if I don't get in there and calm things down."

"That's not good. She's usually so cool and collected."

"My thoughts exactly. I'd better go in and see what's what."

"That's fine. I'll probably spend the day finishing up the laundry and shopping for groceries."

He ran his hands up and down my arms. "And I was going to help you."

I laughed. "I know you're brokenhearted about the laundry."

"It's what I live for," he said, walking with me out to the living room. "I especially enjoy the prewash phase."

"Everyone does."

Charlie saw her opportunity and scurried over to wend her way around and between our ankles. Rather than trip over her, I lifted her into my arms and rubbed my cheek against her soft orange fur. Derek gave her a few scratches, and after a long moment, I set the happy cat down on the floor and watched her toddle off to check out her food bowl while I checked my wristwatch. "I'd better start another load of laundry. And since you live for it, you can help."

He made a face. "I stuck my foot in that one."

Later that afternoon we walked down the street to pick up a pizza and salad from Pietro's. We ate dinner in front of the television, catching up on the news of the day. For dessert we each had a cupcake, and both of us were sound asleep by eight o'clock that night. In our defense, we'd been awake for more than twenty-four hours by then. I figured it would take a few more days to get back on West Coast time.

Sometime in the middle of the night I awoke with a

start, realizing that I hadn't put our two new books in the safe. It wasn't that I expected anyone to break into our house and steal them, but I always felt better knowing that my books were securely hidden away. And now that I knew how much the James Bond book was worth, I was doubly determined to keep it out of harm's way.

I got out of bed and tiptoed out of the bedroom, then padded through the house and into my workshop. Five minutes later, the books were happily tucked away inside the old vault in the closet and I climbed back into bed. And lay there for a full hour before I was ready to admit defeat. I was wide awake and unable to sleep.

"I can hear you thinking," Derek murmured.

"I'm sorry, love. I can't seem to fall back to sleep."

"Nor can I," he admitted. "I'm going to get up and do some work."

"You're going into the office?" I glanced at the clock. It was only 4 a.m.

"No, I'll work here. It's a good time to call the London office."

"That makes sense." I yawned. "I'm going to give myself a few more minutes, and if I still can't fall asleep, I'll get up and make some coffee."

"You might try listening to one of your podcasts."

I smiled. "Good idea." Podcasts were my latest fixation. There were some good ones on rare books and ephemera, and book collecting, with lots of history and interesting anecdotes. The last one I listened to was all about book crimes and rip-offs. Totally enthralling stuff for a book nerd like me.

Derek went off to make his calls and I plugged in my earbuds. I made it through the first five minutes of a fascinating conversation about a newly discovered collection of Cuban books once owned by Ernest Hemingway. And then I dozed off. Worked every time.

It took me two full days to finish the laundry, put clothes away, drop stuff off at the dry cleaners, store the luggage in the guest bedroom closet, restock the house with the essentials of life—wine, coffee, soap, salsa, chips—and go through the piles of mail that had accumulated while we were gone. Derek helped whenever he was home, but the employee brouhaha at his office was taking up a lot of his time and energy.

It wasn't until Thursday morning, after Derek left for the office, that I realized I had been so caught up in the whirlwind of getting our post-honeymoon lives back on track that I had completely neglected to find out exactly what was going on with said brouhaha. I would have to remember to ask Derek about it tonight.

Meanwhile, I was finally ready to get back to work myself. I took the two Paris books out of the closet safe, grabbed another cup of coffee, and went to my workshop. I wanted to get a closer look at the sweet copy of *Gigi* that Derek had bought me. And I also planned to repair the wobbly hinge on *The Spy Who Loved Me*.

I knew that repair would be a fast, easy fix, so I worked on it first. My equipment consisted of a sheet of wax paper; my trusty bonefolder, which was a tongue depressor–sized hand tool that I used for folding and creasing paper and cloth; a thin wooden skewer; and some archival glue, otherwise known as PVA or polyvinyl acetate. The PVA was already mixed and ready to go. It was pH neutral, dried clear and flexible, and didn't dry out or turn yellow over time.

I could be a little obsessive about glue.

I slipped on a pair of thin white gloves to protect the book from any oils that might be transferred from my skin. Then I coated the skewer in glue and slipped it into the weakened space behind the loose endpaper, between the spine and the front cover board. I twirled the skewer a number of times in order to completely coat the interior space with the glue, then removed the skewer.

Picking up my bonefolder, I smoothed the endpaper against the board, running it back and forth several times, and wiped away the tiny bud of glue that had seeped out from the channel. Then I inserted a piece of wax paper between the front cover and the textblock to keep any more glue from sticking to the book.

I closed the cover, then ran my bonefolder along the grooved joint on the outside of the hinge to more firmly secure the cover to the endpaper. Finally I placed a cloth-covered brick on top of the book to keep it firmly in line until it dried completely.

The sense of accomplishment I felt after doing quickie jobs like this one always made me smile. That was why I usually started out with the easy stuff.

I tossed the skewer away, returned the jar of glue to its cupboard, and then turned my attention to *Gigi*. When Derek had surprised me with the book at dinner on our last night in Paris, I'd only had time to give the pretty pink-and-white slipcover box a cursory inspection before the waiter had arrived to take our orders. I had slipped the book into my purse with a promise to take more time with it when we got back to the hotel.

But when we'd entered our suite, we had been so freaked out about the possible break-in that I forgot all about the book. And then we were hurrying to finish packing and rushing to get to the airport the next day. And once we'd arrived home, I got wrapped up in laundry and shopping and reading through the mail and, well, I just dropped the ball.

So now I was eager to check it out and promised to devote as much time as it took to study and appreciate the cute little book.

I took it out of its wrapping and set it on the white cloth. With my magnifying glass, I slowly examined every inch of the pale pink-and-white book box. It was amazing that with just a few strokes of his paintbrush, the artist had managed to depict a lovely young woman all decked out in her fancy hat and frilly blouse with a bow at the neck.

I went online to find out about the talented artist. His name was Emilio Grau Sala, a celebrated Catalan painter and illustrator who moved to Paris in 1932.

The pink-and-white slipcover was in fine condition despite some light scuffing along the edges. There were also some visible smudge marks, but I thought I might be able to bleach them away if I was very careful.

Finally I slid the book out of its slipcover and stared at it for a long moment. It was written in French, naturally, and accompanying Colette's story of *Gigi* were numerous engravings by Grau Sala, who, I was thrilled to see, had signed the justification page.

I had heard of the use of a justification page, but had only seen one once before when I was teaching in Lyon. This was something specific to French publishing and only slightly similar to a limitation page in an English edition. When a publisher released a regular version of a book as well as a limited, more expensive edition, the

author would authenticate the limited edition by sign-
ing and dating each book, making it even more valuable than before. The page with the author's signature
was called the limitation page.

I did my best to translate the words on the justification page from French into English and came up with
these two somewhat mangled sentences: *Limited edition
of 350 numbered copies—this copy #206. Unbound, as
issued in original illustrated wraps. Twenty-five copies
on pure vellum stationery of dreams to which we added
a suite with remarks using a copper ink, an original
drawing.*

So much for my French. But clearly this was a
limited-edition copy printed on beautiful thick vellum,
with the original signature of the artist. As I carefully
turned the pages, it was evident to me that Grau Sala's
charming artwork was a perfect match for Colette's
lighthearted words describing her plucky heroine.

I had to wonder how much Derek had paid for the
little book. Would it be rude to ask him? The various
appraisals online indicated that similar books were
worth between three hundred and seven hundred dollars. No matter the price, I would cherish it always.

That night we invited Alex over for dinner as a way to
thank her for watching our place and for the scrump-
tious welcome-home cupcakes. Our friend—and Alex's
new love—Gabriel came with her, and as soon as they
walked in, Charlie was on the spot, rubbing up against
them and meowing for their attention.

"It looks like she bonded with both of you," I said.
"I'm so glad."

"Me, too," Alex said, crouching down to give Charlie lots of scratches and a belly rub. "She's such a sweetie."

"I never thought I would be a cat person," Gabriel said, joining Alex to give the lucky cat some more love. "But this little girl makes it easy."

After finishing off a meal of grilled salmon, wild rice, endive salad, and a beautiful bottle of wine, they sat and listened politely as Derek and I gushed about our trip and forced them to look at all seventy gazillion photos we'd taken while we were in France.

After they left, Derek and I agreed that there was no better test of friendship than that. It wasn't until we were getting into bed a while later that I realized I hadn't asked about his day at work. *What kind of wife does that make me?* I wondered.

A new one, I assured myself. *And a happy one*, I added with a secret smile.

"I was so wrapped up in house stuff all week," I confessed, "that I completely forgot to ask if you resolved the problem with your employee."

He closed his eyes for a moment and slowly shook his head. "Not yet, but we'll fix it."

I rested my head on his shoulder. "Well, at least Corinne must be happy to have you back every day."

"Yes, and I'm happy to be there, too. But as for the larger issue, I'm not sure my presence is any help at all."

"Of course it is. Everyone loves you."

That brought a smile to his face. He turned and kissed my forehead. Then he sighed and I could tell he was tired. "We'll get it sorted out."

"Is it just one person?" I asked.

"It started with one person, but it quickly escalated," he said. "Now it involves an entire department of subject-matter experts agitating against one of my senior partners. And HR is involved, of course. And to be honest, I can understand both sides of the problem."

Of course he could, I thought. He was one of those people who could see obstacles instantly, quickly sum up a situation, and propose ways to solve the problem. Which made him a really good boss, most of the time. And as a husband, pretty hard to argue with.

"So what are you going to do?"

He scowled. "Right now I'm angry, so I'm going to back off for a day or two. Things have descended into gossip and rumormongering and sniping. Morale has been damaged, people are picking sides. It started with one person in Sales. She seems to pick fights and get people stirred up. It moved into middle management, and then the partners got involved. And now, the secretaries have started sniping at each other."

"Well, that's the worst right there. If the secretaries aren't happy, nobody's going to be happy."

"True enough." He hesitated, then continued. "Believe it or not, there's even been a touch of sabotage."

I sat up straight. "Sabotage? What kind of sabotage? Was someone hurt? Are you in danger?"

"No," he said immediately. "Absolutely not."

"Did you call the police?"

"No. The office handled it internally." But he didn't sound too happy about it. "It happened while we were away. Turned out to be nothing serious. Just . . . messy. And annoying."

"No wonder Corinne's going bonkers."

"Yes. I should be grateful that she was thoughtful enough to keep the news from me while we were gone." But he didn't look grateful at all.

"Is there a possibility that the sabotage could escalate?" I asked. "I mean, you do have a bunch of people with military backgrounds. They probably own weapons and stuff."

"It's not going to get that far, love. This is basic office politics and it'll be easily settled." His lips twisted in a half smile. "Eventually."

"You might consider hiring some kind of mediator or something."

"I'm thinking of doing just that. And my HR team has suggested some sort of team-building seminar." He shook his head and scrunched his pillow to raise himself up a little. "I've asked the partners to meet here on Sunday to discuss the matter. Do you mind? I hope that doesn't throw a spanner into your weekend plans."

"Not at all," I said. "I have plenty of bookbinding work to do. And I can always run across the street to visit the bookshop. Check up on our investment."

Several months ago, Derek and I had taken a chance and invested in the popular Courtyard Shops across the street when the owner of the charming Victorian building ran into trouble. There were eight shops and restaurants on the ground floor, all facing the inner tree-shaded courtyard, with two floors of apartments above. Naturally, the bookshop was one of my favorite places to visit, and the new manager was a true book lover: my favorite kind of person. And there was the pie shop, of course.

I shifted in bed so I was facing him, the better to gauge his reaction. "I know you and your partners will work this out, but if you don't mind my saying so, your meeting sounds too top-heavy. You might think about inviting Corinne and a few of the SMEs to provide some perspective."

He smoothed his hands down my arms. "I called Corinne a while ago to ask her to set up the meeting. As soon as I hung up the phone, I realized the same thing. I called her back immediately to invite her to come, along with a few others. I could hear the relief in her voice over the phone."

I felt the same way Corinne must have felt. "Good. I think that'll make a difference."

"I agree, and thank you for your wise counsel." He yawned and it was infectious.

"And thanks for that," I mumbled, yawning loudly.

He chuckled lightly. Turning off the light, he pulled me up close against him and we dozed off to sleep.

By Saturday morning, we were back to our regular sleeping and waking-up schedule, thank goodness. In the kitchen I poured coffee for both of us and we sat at the center island, indulging in croissants with butter and Brie and apricot preserves. We moaned over the fact that we hadn't yet weaned ourselves away from such a ridiculously indulgent and highly fattening breakfast treat. Derek and I were both in fairly good shape. I had spent months working out in anticipation of looking fabulous in my wedding dress. But after three weeks in France, the food capital of the world, I had noticed that my jeans were getting a little snug.

"Tomorrow we'll have oatmeal," I promised.

"Absolutely. With nonfat milk," Derek added.

"We could take a bike ride," I suggested, trying to come up with an activity that would get us moving. I wasn't too excited about the biking idea because it was a little too dangerous to ride around in the city, so we normally hitched our bikes onto the back of my car and drove across the bridge to Marin County. There were some great off-road bike paths over there, and they came with spectacular views of the bay, the mountains, and the city.

Derek took a long sip of coffee. "I was thinking this would be a good day to visit the spy shop. What do you think? I'll introduce you to Owen and afterward we can take a walk along the Embarcadero."

I brightened up instantly. "That's an even better idea. I'm dying to see what they sell at a spy shop."

The spy shop, SPECTRE, was located in Pier 39 on Fisherman's Wharf, a massive tourist complex of dozens of restaurants, shops, and a number of attractions, including the aquarium, theaters, a mirror maze, and a beautiful carousel.

I was surprised to find that SPECTRE occupied a large refurbished warehouse. It featured brick walls, a high ceiling, exposed ventilation, and huge industrial windows, and it was modern and clean and filled with light. I'd had visions of sneaking down a dark flight of stairs, knocking on a heavily locked door, whispering a password, and then stepping into a dank, musty den of iniquity. But that was just me and my imagination.

"Welcome to SPECTRE," a perky young salesgirl said in greeting. Her badge read, HI, I'M STACY! ASK ME ABOUT AIRSOFT! "Are you looking for something special or would you prefer to browse?"

"I think we'll browse for a while," I said, although I was tempted to ask her about Airsoft.

Derek asked, "By the way, is Owen here?"

"He sure is," she said with a hearty nod. "Let me get him for you." She jogged toward the café in the corner and disappeared through a door with a sign on it that read, STAFF ONLY.

We followed her into the café, where a deli-style counter featured an eclectic menu posted on the wall above. Everything from pastries to quiches to salads and sandwiches, plus every coffee drink known to man. They all had cute spy-related names like Double Agent (double espresso), Enigma (café Americano), Honey Trap (sweet tea), Eyes Only (decaf), and Moneypenny (caramel latte). They even served a number of different beers and wines, which was nice, although it didn't fit in with my image of what a spy shop café should offer. Where was the dry martini, shaken not stirred?

A number of people sat at small tables, drinking from big coffee mugs and staring at computers.

The café led into an area that displayed all sorts of books, from fiction (mostly spy thrillers, of course) to nonfiction Cold War treatises (their covers featuring the infamous Berlin Wall) to high-tech manuals and true crime.

Along the perimeter of the large store were miles of counters displaying all the fun gadgets, such as ballpoint pens with tiny hidden tape recorders and wristwatches that doubled as two-way radios. A bunch of different sunglass styles contained either powerful hidden cameras or sneaky rearview mirrors.

And speaking of hidden cameras, there were a dozen versions of the popular fluffy teddy-bear cam, plus a flowerpot cam, a clock-radio cam, and a half dozen other facades to hide a secret mini-camera.

There was an entire wall of GPS tracker systems along with motion detectors and numerous mini–home security systems. With every type of product there were high-end selections as well as low-cost alternatives. So now anyone at any income level could happily spy on their neighbor, babysitter, or spouse.

And just in case you thought someone was watching *you*, there was all sorts of countersurveillance equipment, like bugs and bug sweepers and GPS tails.

Yet another area of the store featured computer and cell phone spyware.

And just as Derek had mentioned to me, there were lockpick kits, forcible entry tools, and kits for making key molds. Apparently these items required a certificate that proved that the buyer was indeed a duly authorized locksmith or involved in some kind of law enforcement. Call me a cynic, but I was pretty sure there were ways to get around that pesky requirement.

In an alcove behind the bookshop was a section that carried self-defense weapons. In the glass display cabinet were knives and Tasers and a really dangerous-looking claw thing that could be used while out walking alone at night.

There was a small sign by the cash register warning that if you bought a weapon at SPECTRE, you were obligated to register it with the police and also sign up for a training session.

While we waited for Owen, I picked up a trifold color brochure and learned that SPECTRE also provided lie detector services. For fun, they featured virtual reality games and several escape rooms.

Escape rooms, I thought. That sounded intriguing. The brochure read, "For Parties, a Special Date

Night, or Office Team Building, Rent One of Our Escape Rooms!"

"Look," I said to Derek. "They have escape rooms."

"What is an escape room?"

"Some kind of party thing." I scanned the brochure. "It's a locked room and you have a certain amount of time to escape. They give you clues and riddles and puzzles and stuff and you have to work together to solve them, and they lead you to other items hidden around the room, like keys and messages and things. Eventually you find the way out. Or you die, I guess."

"That does sound like fun," he said dryly.

I kept reading. "They have eight different rooms, all with different themes. There's a zombie death trap, a cursed kindergarten, a bank heist, a mummy's tomb, the *Titanic*."

"How does one escape the *Titanic*?" Derek wondered.

"You have to find the lifeboat within sixty minutes." I frowned. "I don't think the losers actually drown."

"Let's hope not," Derek muttered.

"Oh hey," I continued, "they have an espionage room. It says, 'You have one hour to find the documents to prove you're not a spy before your guards transfer you to a maximum-security prison, where you will be tortured.'"

"I hate when that happens."

"And there's a slaughterhouse," I said.

"Who thinks of these things?"

"I don't know," I said, smiling. "But the pictures make it look pretty realistic. And the sound effects are supposed to be impressive." I shrugged. "It might be fun if you have the right group of people. Like if your brothers came to visit with their wives. Or if you wanted to do a team-building exercise for your office."

His eyes narrowed as he considered it. "Let's take a look at it."

I handed him the brochure just as a set of quick footsteps approached from behind us.

"Hello. May I help you?"

We both turned and watched the man's eyes grow almost comically wide. I presumed this was Owen Gibbons. He was taller than Derek, and heavier. Not fat, but solid, like a tank. Or a barrel. His salt-and-pepper hair hadn't seen a barber in a few months, and his bright green eyes sparkled with humor.

"Hello, Owen," Derek said with a grin. "How are you, you old goat?"

"Derek? Derek Stone?" he said and thrust his hand out. They shook hands so forcefully, I thought one of their arms would break off. "Holy hell, man. What are you doing here?"

"I ran into Ned Davies in Paris last week and he told me that you're running a spy shop."

"And you had a good laugh about it," Owen said with a smile, his tone self-deprecating.

"A bit," Derek admitted with a grin. "Anyway, we were in the neighborhood and thought we'd come in, say hello, and take a look around."

"Of all the gin joints," Owen said, still gripping Derek's hand and shaking. I figured it was a guy thing. I'd seen my brothers do the same manic handshaking thing with their friends. Sure enough, Derek and Owen were chuckling as they moved on from shaking hands to smacking each other on the back a few times.

"Ned told me to tell you that he sends his best," Derek said, repeating Ned's wish.

Owen's eyebrows shot up, then he smiled sentimentally. "Did he? Ned Davies. There's a name I haven't heard in a while. How is old Ned?"

"He seems to be doing quite well."

"Good, good," Owen said, and then spread his arms grandly. "Well. Welcome to SPECTRE."

"I'm impressed," Derek said, looking around with interest. "What made you decide to open a store in San Francisco?"

"I did a job here six years ago," Owen replied. "Fell in love with the place. So when I decided to retire from the biz, I couldn't think of anywhere else I'd rather live and work. You?"

"Love brought me here, too," Derek said, with a fond look in my direction. He introduced me as his wife (happy sigh), and I carefully extended my hand to shake Owen's. He wasn't quite as ferocious with me and just politely squeezed my hand, thank goodness.

"Hello, Brooklyn."

"It's nice to meet you, Owen," I said.

"What a delight," he said. "Let me buy you both a café latte and we can catch up." Without waiting for a response, he walked up to the counter of the café.

"Sounds good to me," I said, and Derek nodded.

"Grab a table," Owen said, and began to order drinks.

Derek and I sat down at a small table and pulled a third chair over. As soon as I was settled, I happened to glance down and saw an elegant Siamese cat staring up at me.

"Hello," I said. "Who are you?"

Without answering, the cat jumped up onto my lap and made herself comfortable.

"Wow," I said. "Make yourself at home, why don't you?"

"Must be your lucky day," Derek said, reaching over to give the pretty cat a few scratches around her ears.

"She's beautiful." I stroked her velvety-soft fur as I looked around.

The café was definitely a popular place, I thought, since most of the tables were occupied. There was a low buzz of conversation, except for the corner table right next to us, where three young guys and a woman chatted and laughed loudly enough to be overheard by most of the other customers. They all appeared to be about the same age, probably midtwenties. They had their computers open although they barely looked at their screens. When they all lowered their voices, I had to strain to continue eavesdropping on them while Derek read the escape room brochure.

I had to be mistaken, but it sounded as if the four friends were debating the best way to strangle someone.

The cute blond guy in the horn-rimmed glasses whispered, "But a wire can cut your hands if you're not careful."

Next to him, a skinny fellow with dark hair rolled his eyes. "That's why you wear gloves, moron. You don't cut your hands and you don't leave fingerprints."

"Stabbing would be better and faster," the petite redhead insisted, and jumped up to act out the motion. "One swift thrust, right in the gut."

"But the blood," the blond said, looking vaguely queasy.

I could so relate to that, I thought, since I tended to faint at the sight of blood myself.

"Occupational hazard, man." This from the fourth guy, who was tall and muscular with close-cropped sandy hair. He had excellent posture and looked as though he might have been in the military at one time. "If you're going to do this job, you're going to have to deal with the blood."

"Look, Tinker," the skinny guy said, lowering his voice. "I killed a guy with a steel guitar string and it worked like magic. Just don't forget to wear gloves."

Were they kidding? Were they comedians? They couldn't actually be talking about murder, could they? I was a little sensitive about the topic, having run across my share of dead bodies. It wasn't something I cared to joke about.

Owen approached our table, carrying a small tray with our three coffee cups and a plate of madeleines.

"Here we go." He set the tray down and then sat.

"This looks wonderful," I said, taking a cookie.

Derek smiled. "Thank you, Owen."

"It's my pleasure," he said. "It's just so damn good to see you." He turned to me and then noticed the cat. "Well, you must be very special. Miss Moneypenny is quite particular. I'll have you know she doesn't just jump into anyone's lap."

"Moneypenny?" I said, and laughed, charmed by the name. I gave a few more strokes to the cat's soft furry back. "I love it." But the more conversation I heard from the table of would-be killers nearby, the more concerned I grew.

I took a bite of my cookie and briefly considered whether to say something or not. Finally I leaned forward and pointed subtly toward the group. "Owen, do you know those people sitting next to us in the corner?"

He shifted in his chair to get a look. "Ah, the boys,"

he said with a certain fondness. "And the girl," he added. "My very best customers. They meet here twice a week to talk shop and shoot the breeze."

Talk shop? Was SPECTRE a hangout for contract killers after all? I frowned at Derek, then whispered, "But they're talking about killing someone."

"Of course they are," Owen said jovially. "They're writers."

Chapter 3

Writers?

I felt like an idiot. Of course they were writers. People didn't generally chitchat over lattes about how to murder someone. And if I weren't so gun-shy on the subject, I probably would've realized that instantly.

"I call them the Wannabes," Owen said softly, chuckling as he gazed warmly at the four writers at the next table. "They would all love to be the next Ian Fleming or Lee Child, but they're not quite there yet."

"It's a worthy goal," Derek allowed.

"Oh, absolutely. They're all quite clever. One of them might actually get there someday. We let them meet here regularly because they always take our classes. And two of the boys work here part-time."

"You give classes?" I asked.

"Oh yes. On lots of topics, all having to do with security and spy technology. They're awfully interesting." He gazed at Derek thoughtfully. "You should consider teaching something."

"That's a great idea." I smiled at Derek. "You have plenty to talk about."

"I'm not sure about that," he said, and turned to Owen. "But we can discuss it sometime."

Owen smiled. "Gladly."

"Tell us more about the writers," I said, still fascinated by the group at the next table.

"They've given themselves a name, but I can't remember it. They keep changing it. Last week they were the Irregulars." His forehead creased in a frown. "I don't see why they need a name for their group, but what do I know? Must be part of the creative process."

Owen leaned toward the group and raised his voice. "Hello, Tinker. Tailor. Everyone."

The scruffy blond guy adjusted his glasses. "Hey, Spy Man."

"Have you settled on a permanent name for your writers' group?" Owen asked.

"Yeah." Tinker glanced at his mates as if to make sure, then back over at us. "We're the Jackals now."

"Oh, that's bloody brilliant," Owen said. "Well done."

Tinker pressed his lips together in a semblance of a smile, looking relieved that the new name had passed some sort of test. "Drummer came up with it."

"Thumbs up, Drummer," Owen praised.

The redheaded girl's smile managed to be both bashful and a touch shrewd. "*Day of the Jackal*'s my all-time fave thriller."

"It's a good one," Derek said. "Very dog-eat-dog."

"You're English," she whispered respectfully.

"Indeed I am."

"Drummer Girl and fellows," Owen said formally, "may I present my friends Derek and Brooklyn?" He turned to us. "And these fervent young people are the

Jackals. That's Tinker, Tailor, Soldier, and Drummer Girl."

I raised both eyebrows. "Not your real names, I take it?"

Tinker chuckled. "Not exactly."

"And you named yourselves after John le Carré novels."

The skinny guy nodded enthusiastically and jabbed his thumb toward the blond fellow. "Yeah. This guy with the glasses slipping down his nose is Tinker. I'm Tailor." Then he jabbed his thumb toward the buff guy sitting next to him. "This here's Soldier."

Soldier nodded briefly. "I was in the Army, so it works for me." He was a few years older than the others and seemed more mature. He was better dressed, too, and held himself straighter. And he was very much aware of his surroundings. Just since we'd been talking, he had taken a less-than-casual scan of the store at least three times, and not in a happy, hey-what's-happening type of way. More like a grim, who's-a-potential-killer type of way.

I tried to ignore the chill that flitted down my arms. Focusing on the redhead, I said, "I loved *The Little Drummer Girl*."

She beamed at me. "Me, too. And I wanted my name to be something different than the guys."

"It's a great book," I said, then grinned. "And the character has red hair, too."

"Nobody ever makes that connection," Drummer Girl said in amazement, and fiddled with the curly ends of her hair.

"So, guys," Owen said, his tone provocative. "Derek used to work for MI6."

"No way." They all turned and homed in on Derek, their eyes huge.

I caught the tiniest flicker of irritation from Derek. He rarely mentioned his background in MI6. But just as quickly, his features evened out and he was smiling again.

Tinker's mouth hung open. "You were a spy? For real? Can I interview you?"

Tailor piped up. "I've always wondered, is there really an M?"

"What about Q?" Soldier asked. "He's my favorite. Is he real? His character is ingenious. He foreshadows doom while adding comic relief." He paused, looked thoughtful. "And yet he's almost a father figure to James."

"I have no idea about any of that." Derek looked mildly amused. "I'm a businessman."

Tinker nodded wisely. "Perfect cover."

I chuckled and changed the topic. "So what are you all writing?"

"Spy thriller with doomsday overtones," Soldier replied decisively.

Tinker said, "I'm doing a spy thriller, too, with a dyslexic protagonist."

Tailor raised his hand. "I've got a spy thriller with paranormal overtones."

"Interesting," I said. "How is it paranormal?"

He frowned and avoided eye contact. "There's a talking horse. But it's not supposed to be funny."

"Ah. But it's unexpected," I managed after almost choking on my drink. Far be it from me to stomp on a young writer's hopes and dreams. "What about you, Drummer?"

"Yeah, Drummer," Tailor drawled. "What about you?"

Her pretty face instantly flushed a bright pink. I had a feeling that her pale, freckled skin would turn red if someone breathed the wrong way. And it sounded as if the boys enjoyed teasing her, but she could probably hold her own. She huffed out a breath. "I'm writing a really dark romantic suspense. Serial killer, lots of bodies buried under the basement floor, kick-ass protagonist with a troubled past."

"Cool." I gave her an encouraging nod. "I read a lot of romantic suspense. I like it."

"You do?" She smiled gratefully. "I've only written two chapters, but I feel good about it. Lots of blood and gore so far."

"Sounds like a winner."

"Listen, guys." Owen leaned forward, resting his elbows on his knees. "I've asked Derek to teach one of our expert classes. What do you think?"

"Awesome idea," Drummer Girl cried.

"Sign me up," Tinker said.

Tailor, the skinny one, blinked a few times. "A real spy teaching a class? Hell, yeah."

"He's not a real spy," I said, even though I didn't believe it. But I knew Derek would appreciate my jumping in.

"Do you have any words of wisdom for us?" Tinker leaned forward. "We're all writing thrillers, or suspense, I guess. Any thoughts?"

Derek frowned, took a breath, and exhaled slowly. "I suppose if I were writing a thriller, I would want to make it . . . thrilling." He shrugged. "You know, raise the stakes. Feel the clock ticking constantly. On every page. The world is at risk, isn't that right?" He glanced around at their faces. "And your main character will often have a very dark backstory. They'll have to overcome a huge amount in order to earn some sort of peace and happiness in the end."

I smiled at the sight of Tailor's mouth hanging open. He probably hadn't expected Derek to say much. Neither had I, frankly, but I couldn't have been prouder of him at that moment. My husband.

I watched Drummer Girl scrutinize Derek some more. Not that I blamed her. I could vouch for the fact that the man was gorgeous as sin. But I wondered why she was frowning.

"Are you sure you're not a spy?" she asked finally.

"Businessman," Derek maintained with an easy smile.

"If you say so," Tailor said, and glanced at Owen. "Anyway, count me in if you're giving a class."

"Me, too," Drummer Girl chimed. "So what do you teach exactly?"

Derek gave Owen a pointed look. "Owen and I will discuss it."

Owen's laugh was a deep, rich sound. "We'll work it out and let you know."

"Sounds good, Spy Man," Tinker said amiably.

Owen radiated joy at hearing his own nickname. I wondered again which intelligence agency the man had worked for. Derek had never told me.

I was growing to like Owen a lot in the few minutes I'd known him. I especially appreciated that he was so encouraging with his young writers.

"Your store is fascinating," I said, looking to change the subject again. "Will you show us around?"

"I'd be glad to." He stood and picked up the tray of empty coffee mugs. "Let's leave these geniuses to their work."

I stood and waved at the group. "Nice meeting you."

"You, too," Drummer Girl said.

We were forgotten as she and the others huddled together and began a very quiet, intense conversation. And I had a brief moment to wonder again if they really were plotting a murder.

Owen set the tray on the café counter and walked with us into the bookshop area.

"Owen," Derek said as I studied a shelf filled with spy novels. "How in the world did you ever decide to open a spy shop?"

"It sort of fell into my lap. I have a business partner, Richie Sylvestri. Do you know him?"

"I don't believe so."

"He was part of that group that came to the agency out of Texas. We worked together on a few assignments and hit it off. And last year after his wife left him, he was looking for a business investment, and by then I was itching to open this place. I wanted to do it up big and I think I've succeeded."

Derek glanced around. "I would say so."

Owen laughed. "We've got everything going for us. Every gadget you can think of, plus escape rooms, shooting range, you name it. It's like a playground for grown-ups. And Richie thought it sounded like a kick in the pants, so he jumped on board. He's more of a silent partner really, and the moneyman. I run the day-to-day operation."

"Congratulations," Derek said. "I wish you a lot of success."

"Thank you, Derek. It means a lot." Owen beamed. "We're about to celebrate our one-year anniversary and everything is looking up."

"I love that you have a bookshop in the middle of everything," I said.

He spread his arms wide. "Yes, we do, and here's where the tour begins. This is our bookstore."

I laughed. "I figured that much."

"We carry new and used books, mostly spy-thriller titles, although we have a good selection of histories and biographies as well. We have children's books, too, and some Sherlock Holmes and Agatha Christie thrown in for good measure. But we're mainly all about the spies."

"Of course you are," Derek said, smiling.

"We also carry note cards and knickknacks and bits of jewelry and such." Wiggling his eyebrows, he picked up a pair of earrings that had tiny bejeweled daggers hanging from them. "Aren't these wonderful? You can find a gift for almost any occasion here."

Surrounded by books, I was in my element now. I walked up and down the three short aisles, picking up a book here and there. The blond-wood shelves were counter height, and on top of each were smaller book racks that contained individual authors' works. It was an attractive, efficient setup, mainly because the bookshelves didn't block the view of the rest of the store.

The used books on the back shelves were all paperbacks, and most of them were priced at one dollar. One wide shelf was completely filled with books by Ian Fleming. On the next shelf down were another dozen Bond books written by other authors. "Do you have all the James Bond titles?"

"Absolutely. They're our biggest seller. Are you familiar with the books?"

"I am," I said, nodding. "I read all of Ian Fleming's novels years ago. Stole them from my big brother."

"Then you can appreciate why I named the shop SPECTRE."

I smiled at him. "I thought it was very clever of you."

"I think so, too, and thank you," he said, his eyes gleaming with humor.

I flinched when another cat suddenly jumped up onto the top of the bookshelf. Feeling a little silly, I gave her ear an easy scratch. "Now who's this?"

"This is my darling tabby cat. Isn't she pretty? Her name is Octo."

"Octo," I repeated, reaching out tentatively to pet her. "That's an interesting name."

"Yes, she's named after one of the James Bond titles."

"She is?" I frowned. "Octo? Really?"

"Darling," Derek said, and laughed.

It took me another five seconds before it hit me. "*Octopussy!* Oh, that's crazy!"

"We like it," Owen said, wearing a broad grin. He gave Octo a few more rubs before the cat jumped off the counter and dashed away.

Having recovered from the joke, I wandered the next aisle and pulled a used paperback version of *The Spy Who Loved Me* from the shelf. I waved it at Derek, who grinned. Turning to Owen, I said, "I bought a hardcover of this one when we were in Paris. Turned out to be a first edition in really good shape."

His eyes immediately sharpened. "A first edition? Hardcover?"

"Yes."

"In English?"

"Yes."

"Published in 1962?"

I blinked. "Yes."

He leaned against a counter, folded his arms across his chest, and thought for a moment. "Original dust jacket?"

"Yes." I laughed at the mini-interrogation. Of course, I probably sounded just like Owen whenever I asked someone about their books. "I paid seven euros for it in one of the bookstalls, but came to find out it's worth about a thousand times more than that."

He sucked in a deep breath. "Dear lord. My customers would love to see that book. And so would I."

"I don't blame you," I said lightly, returning the paperback to its place on the shelf.

"No. I'm serious." His gaze was intent. "We're having a huge celebration over the next two weeks for the store's first anniversary. It's going to be a blowout party with special displays in each department and lots of treats for our customers. In the bookshop we were going to pull out every James Bond book in stock to create an elaborate centerpiece that will draw the type of person into the store who might not ordinarily shop here. Readers and locals, mainly. That book of yours would be the icing on the cake. What do you think? I wouldn't ask, but then I'd hate myself if I didn't."

He was talking so fast, he lost me. "You wouldn't ask . . . what?"

The sound he made was a cross between a laugh and a sigh. "Sorry. I'm getting ahead of myself. I would love to borrow your book for a week. *The Spy Who Loved Me.* It would be perfect. The anniversary celebration goes from one weekend to the next, so we would actually want to have it for ten days."

"Oh." I blinked. The man spoke at the speed of a few hundred miles an hour.

He continued in a rush. "I'll put it on display right here in the bookshop. You don't know our customers, but a book like that will knock their socks off."

I shot Derek a worried frown. "I don't think that's a good idea."

"We'll take precautions," Owen insisted. "Wait, I know. We can do the entire centerpiece inside one of our glass display counters. The display cases are all wired to set off an alarm if anything is disturbed." He smiled roguishly. "We are a spy shop after all."

"Of course."

"So we know how to safeguard important things." He waved his hands to show the bigger picture. "We have to wire each of the cabinets because of all the expensive electronics and products we carry." He was walking back and forth as he talked out his plan. "We'll put together several lavish arrangements on the nearby counters to draw people over, and then they'll see your book. Like in a museum. You can look, but you can't touch. It'll be fantastic." He turned to Derek. "I'll personally guarantee that nothing will happen to it."

Derek studied my expression, saying nothing.

"It's *your* book," I reminded him. But I considered it mine, too. I felt that way about most books. Possessive. I had to take a few slow breaths to force myself to let that feeling go.

Derek turned to Owen. "I'll need to look over your security system. And it would only be for that short period of time, correct?"

A sparkle appeared in Owen's eye. He could tell Derek was coming around.

"Ten days at the most," he promised instantly, then spread his arms wide. "Look around. We have the best security money can buy. What could possibly go wrong?"

I really wished he hadn't said that, I thought. Someone always said something like that in horror movies, suspense movies, and yes, spy movies, too. Just before something horrific happened.

Aloud I said, "The book will have to stay locked in the glass case. It's too fragile to be handled by a lot of people."

"Brooklyn is a bookbinder who works with rare books, Owen," Derek explained. "She's an expert in her field and quite aware of the value of this one. And she knows the kind of damage that one thoughtless person can inflict on a book."

"I understand," Owen said. "And I'm so impressed with your background. We must talk books someday."

I smiled now. "I would enjoy that."

He placed his hand over his heart. "I give you my personal guarantee that the book will be untouched by human hands. Except your own."

Derek exchanged a quick glance with me, then said to Owen, "Fine, then. We'll be happy to do it."

"Marvelous." he cried, raising his arms in the air in a sign of victory. "You won't be sorry, I promise you." He let go of a breath and his shoulders seemed to relax. "Thank you. That's brilliant. Very exciting."

"You're welcome," I said.

Owen took another moment to regain his composure, then looked around the store. "So. What can I show you next?"

I gazed around the high-ceilinged space and remembered the name tag of the first girl who'd greeted us. "What's Airsoft?"

"Ah." He strolled out of the bookshop and into the center of the store. "It's a type of weapon used in conjunction with a competitive shooting competition. Airsoft guns look like the real thing, but they shoot pellets. Think of paintball, but much more realistic in terms of equipment and training. The rifles are quite dangerous looking, and they have handguns, too. The guns use compressed air to launch the pellets, so they won't kill you. In theory."

In theory?

"Good to know," I murmured.

"Yes," he said. "It's a competitive sport, but it's also used in training exercises all over the world. People come here to use our shooting range in the back. We have a couple of staff members who monitor the range at all times, plus we have closed-circuit cameras going twenty-four hours a day. We don't want any accidents."

"God forbid," I murmured.

"And we don't sell the guns here," he continued. "You just rent them for a set amount of time. And before we'll let you do anything with the guns, you pretty much have to sign your life away."

"Sounds fascinating."

"If you want to know more about it, you should ask Soldier. He's our resident champion."

That made sense, I thought. "I think I'll pass for now." I had to admit that I had occasionally enjoyed shooting at tin cans while I was growing up. But more recently, I'd seen a few too many guns aimed at *me*. I no longer had any interest in visiting a shooting range. But then I brightened. "But I'd love to see your escape rooms."

His eyes lit up. "They're our most popular attraction. I'll give you a quick tour. Oh, but before I make any promises, I'd better check and see if any of them are unoccupied."

"They looked like a lot of fun in the brochure," I said as he led us toward the far end of the large store.

"They're even better in person," he said over his shoulder. "I was skeptical at first, but now I'm a true believer."

As we moved through the shop, I got a chance to see many of the products up close and personal. The ballpoint pens that hid tiny tape recorders, those wristwatches that doubled as two-way radios. At one counter I tried on several pairs of the sunglasses, each of which contained a powerful hidden camera.

And there were even more versions of the popular teddy bear cam than I'd thought when we first walked in.

We finally reached the back counter, where two cashiers were stationed. On the surrounding walls and inside the glass counters on either side were colorful displays of photos of the various escape rooms. Hanging from the ceiling above the cashiers were two signs. One said, WILL CALL, and the other said, PURCHASE TICKETS.

Several people were already in line to purchase tickets, so Owen rounded the counter to speak to the clerk on the other side. "Any rooms empty right now?"

The will-call cashier gave a quick glance around the shop. "Mummy's Curse is empty right now, but we've got a party going in there in ten minutes. Two of them just checked in and they're browsing while they wait for the rest of their group."

"We'll be fast." Owen waved at us to follow him to a set of double doors across from the ticket counter. "Let's go check it out."

Owen opened the doors and led us into a large, glamorous, yet slightly shabby hotel lobby. The vibe was old-world Hollywood, with overstuffed couches and chairs covered in faded red velvet and gold fringe, with plenty of gilded side tables on which to rest a beverage. A concession stand sold boxes of candy, munchies, and small bottles of water.

Directly in front of us was a hotel check-in counter manned by an odd-looking clerk who stood attentively, waiting to help the next customer. His face was made up to look deathly pale—at least, I thought it was makeup—and his eyes were dark and sunken. The tuxedo he wore was old-fashioned, dusty, and threadbare.

We had stepped into a different world. A fantastical, theatrical display that came across as gaudy, a bit sinister, a bit creepy, and pretty humorous.

"This is amazing," I whispered to Derek.

"Hello, Igor," Owen said pleasantly to the clerk.

"Hiya, boss." Igor flashed us all a big grin—which was just plain weird, given the surroundings and his otherworldly appearance. He was missing several teeth. I almost laughed, but hesitated. I was pretty sure his teeth were blacked out with wax, but you just never knew.

Igor waved us toward a long, wide, carpeted hallway
with four double doors on either side.

I glanced back to see him grinning and still waving.

Above each door in the hall was a small theater mar-
quee announcing which escape room it was.

"Over here," Owen said. He walked quickly down
the hall to the Mummy's Curse, took a set of keys from
his pocket, and unlocked the door. "You won't get the
full effect of the game because we won't actually be
playing, but you'll get a rough idea. Come on in."

We walked inside. And entered the inner sanctum
of an ancient Egyptian pyramid.

"Wow." My voice echoed in the chamber. The room
was dimly lit, but I could see the huge stone blocks that
made up the walls. They were covered in symbols and
animal drawings. Hieroglyphics, I presumed. The
room was square on the floor but the walls leaned in,
rising up until they formed a point at the top of the
ceiling. Like the interior of a pyramid—or what I imagined it would look like. It was claustrophobic, on purpose I assumed. Even in the darkened room you could
see the cobwebs hanging off the ceiling.

"Naturally," Owen said, "all of our rooms revolve
around a spy theme. So while this room appears to be
your basic ancient pyramid, the theme and some of the
riddles have to do with a World War II battle between
the British Army, the Nazis, the Italians, and the Egyp-
tians. We fudge on the details a bit, but it's basically
Spy vs. Spy vs. the Mummy. All very dramatic and
swashbuckle-y."

"It's so clever." I glanced around, did some quick
math, estimated the room was about twenty by twenty
feet square. Against one wall was a fancy armchair up-

holstered in velvet, its elaborate armrests in the shape of undulating brass snakes. There was a small writing desk in the corner with a rickety matching chair. The top drawer of the old desk was pulled out, and I noticed a file folder was placed inside. Two big stone blocks were set down in the middle of the space to provide more seating for the groups that participated in the game. The room could easily accommodate six people, maybe more.

"How does the game work?" I asked.

"I don't want to give too much away, but you're given a series of puzzles and riddles and clues to find things around the room. You solve them all, and you break the Mummy's Curse."

"Or?"

Owen pressed his hands together. "Or you die."

I laughed. "What if you can't figure out the answer?"

He smiled and pointed to the wall. "Every group receives a two-way radio you can use if you get desperate. Igor will answer and give your group a hint. He doesn't make it easy, though. You have to be truly anxious and at your wit's end. He makes you work for it by forcing you to dance or sing or whatever strikes his fancy. His music requests are truly awful for the most part."

"Now that sounds funny," I said, smiling. "Okay, so how do you go from one puzzle and riddle to the next?"

"Again, I don't want to give too much away. But for instance, if you solve one puzzle, it leads you to a hidden spring that triggers a panel in the wall to slide open and reveal, say, a key. You have to solve another riddle to figure out where to put the key. Answering that riddle correctly reveals yet another clue, and so on. Finally, a very large panel slides open, and that's where you find the mummy's casket. Answering the final riddle correctly will cause the casket to open and . . ." He laughed. "No more hints."

I walked over and ran my hand along the wall. "It feels like stone, but I assume it's, what? Drywall? Plaster?"

"My lips are sealed." But his eyes were twinkling.

"Okay, I won't ask any more questions." Instead, I stared at the hieroglyphics. "It's amazing."

"It's out of this world, Owen," Derek said, clearly impressed.

"I know." Owen grinned. "And the other rooms are even better."

"How does it work as a team-building exercise?" I asked.

"Brilliantly," he said immediately. "The team members have to focus on communicating and collaborating. There's no time for arguments because the clock is ticking."

"I see."

"The faster you can solve the riddles," he continued, "the sooner you can break out. The puzzles are creative but logical and fun. And there's a real feeling of accomplishment each time the group solves a riddle." He chuckled. "I sound like an advertisement. But honestly, it's good for morale."

"Especially if everyone makes it out alive."

"That helps. But while you're in the room, you're all completely immersed in the game, and most people get into the spirit of it. By the end, they're all laughing and making plans to do it all over again."

Derek's eyes narrowed as he glanced around the

room once more. "You did mention that next weekend is your big anniversary celebration. What are the chances of renting several of your escape rooms for a few hours each?"

"Your chances are excellent," Owen said.

"Thank you," Derek said with a firm nod. "I want to bring some of my staff here next Saturday. There may be as many as twenty-two people, and I want them all to be scared out of their wits."

Owen's smile grew broader. "We can arrange that."

"Good," Derek said.

Owen walked us out of the Mummy's Curse room and all the way up to the front door. On the way out, we made reservations for four escape rooms for next Saturday. We also arranged a time with Owen to bring him *The Spy Who Loved Me*. As we were saying our good-byes, he gave me a slow smile.

"You know, Brooklyn, we're designing two more escape rooms."

"So you'll have ten altogether?"

"Yes. They are overwhelmingly popular."

"I can see why. And here on the pier is the perfect location."

"Indeed it is," he said with a grin. "But it just occurred to me that you might be able to help us with the design and furnishings of one of the rooms. I would certainly pay you for your time."

"I don't understand," I said, and gave Derek a quick look. "I don't know anything about designing, especially when it comes to escape rooms."

"But you know about books," he said. "And one of the two new rooms is going to be the Scary Library."

"A scary library?" I blinked, then grinned. "Oh, it rhymes."

"Yes," he said with a jovial laugh. "Doesn't it sound like fun?"

"Um, yeah, actually. It does."

"For now, I'm just planting a little bug in your ear," he said. "Think about it. We would love to have the benefit of your experience."

"I . . . Okay, I'll think about it. I appreciate the offer and your confidence in me."

He patted my arm. "We'll talk more about it the next time you come in."

Out on the pier at last, Derek and I both put on sunglasses. We had been inside the store for two hours, and during that time, the sun had burst through the cloud cover. It was turning into a beautiful day and it seemed like half of San Francisco had decided to enjoy it here on the pier. We managed to make our way through the tourist hordes until we reached the sidewalk, where we continued to stroll along the Embarcadero until it ended at Taylor Street. The briny scents of shellfish and lobster bisque filled the air, causing my stomach to grumble. "I'm hungry."

"Me, too," Derek said. "Let's head over to McCormick and Kuleto's for lunch."

"Sounds perfect." The popular seafood restaurant in Ghirardelli Square was perched on the hill and offered a stunning view of the bay from almost every table, along with good seafood and excellent cocktails.

Turning on Taylor Street, we continued our leisurely stroll toward the restaurant. I could tell that Derek was still pondering his office problems, so I gave his arm a light squeeze. "I don't know if the escape rooms will solve all your employee problems, but I do think they'll be fun. And that's a start, right?"

"Right." But then he scowled. "Believe me, darling. If they don't snap out of it, death by the Mummy's Curse will be the very least of their worries."

Chapter 4

After a late breakfast on Sunday, the doorbell rang. I was still cleaning up in the kitchen, so I was close enough to reach for the video screen to see who was at the front door. Two guys from our local deli stood there holding three platters and several bags.

I stared at the screen as I pressed the com button. "Hello?"

The guys lifted their packages. "Deli delivery."

"Great. Come on up," I said, adding, "We're on the sixth floor."

I buzzed them into the building and kept my eye on the screen until they disappeared into the lobby and the door closed securely behind them. Only then did I step away from the security screen. Months ago, after several scary break-ins and the discovery of a dead body in our home, Derek and our friend Gabriel had completely redesigned the security system for our entire building. So now, even though I recognized the guys from the deli, I had trained myself to say hello and hear them talk rather than simply buzzing them into the building. And I always waited until I heard the door lock completely.

Knowing how slow our ancient freight elevator moved, I took my time finishing up in the kitchen and turning on the dishwasher. Then I went into Derek's office to let him know that the deli guys were on their way up with food for his meeting.

"Thanks, love," Derek said, pushing away from the desk. "I'll get the door."

"Okay. I'll be in my workshop." I had already helped him set up the dining room table for the meeting. The kitchen island would be used for the buffet lunch, and there were already platters and utensils set out, along with napkins and glassware. And we had brought in the large cooler from the rooftop patio and filled it with ice for beverages and water bottles.

Seeing that everything was ready for Derek's meeting, I quickly tidied up the living room before wandering into my workshop. I had already decided how I planned to spend the rest of the morning while Derek met with his people.

I pulled the French-Chinese herb book from my desk drawer and set it on top of a smooth white cloth spread out on my worktable. My plan was to take the book apart, brush it down, and clean it completely. I was hopeful that cleaning wouldn't include the need for bleaching in a few spots. Bleaching paper was always risky, so I would have to check each spot closely to see whether or not the paper could withstand the harsh treatment. If not, I still had a few tricks up my sleeve, including a soft eraser and a loaf of white bread. But I would wait and see if the book would require my going there.

After cleaning, I would repair the torn pages, replace the endpapers, and then rebind it using sturdy waxed linen thread so it wouldn't fall apart again. Not for another hundred years or so anyway.

And then I would wrap it up and give it to Inspector Janice Lee, even though it wasn't actually meant for her. It was a gift for her Chinese mother, who, as luck would have it, had a strong interest in books and art and Chinese herbs.

For Inspector Lee, I'd brought back a tacky Eiffel Tower key chain. I was pretty sure it would make her laugh and I smiled at the thought. She wasn't one for a quick laugh.

I recalled our last conversation before Derek and I had left for Paris, when she had asked me to bring her back "something interesting."

"Maybe a snow globe?" I'd said.

Through gritted teeth Lee had said, "No snow globes. No shot glasses."

"Key chain?"

"God, no."

"Corkscrew?"

"Good grief."

"That about covers the list of souvenirs I was planning to bring back."

She had simply rolled her eyes.

Now I thought about the Eiffel Tower key chain I'd brought back and chuckled. Janice would love it.

But since she had saved my life on any number of occasions, including the day of my wedding, I really did owe her "something interesting."

And this Chinese herb book was it. I knew she would be touched to know that I'd seen it in Paris and had thought of her mother. If someone did that for my mother, I would probably be in tears. I didn't expect quite that reaction from the tough-minded detective inspector, but I knew she would be pleased.

Since I was going to take the book apart, I got out my digital camera to memorialize the process. The pictures would provide a photographic reminder of exactly how the book had looked originally as well as my step-by-step process from beginning to end.

Photographing my process was not only smart in an artistic sense but also good business. If an owner wanted a book appraised, before and after photographs of the book would help establish its value. If the provenance of a book was ever in question, photographic evidence of the rebinding process would go a long way toward proving where the book had come from, who had owned it, and what changes it had gone through.

It occurred to me that I might bind the best photos together in their own little book and give them to Janice and her mom as well. I wasn't sure if that would work as part of the gift or if they would even care. Not everyone was a book geek like me. So if they weren't interested, I would keep the little book for my own record. And I would certainly post a few shots on my website.

I grabbed a bag of chocolate-caramel kisses for energy and pulled the high chair up to the worktable. Putting on a pair of white cloth gloves, I slipped on my new magnifying glasses and began to examine the book. This was the first time I was wearing the glasses, having gotten the idea the last time I had visited my dentist's office. The hygienist had worn them, and I'd realized that they would be perfect for the kind of work I did. It made so much more sense than just holding a magnifying glass up to my eyes, especially when I would be working for several hours on any particular project and needed both hands to do the job.

In my work it was important to observe the tiniest details up close: the hairline tears on a fragile page of vellum; a minuscule smudge along the edge of a paste-down; the bits of fraying animal hide on the hinge of an old leather tome; the decomposing threads of a once-colorful headband; the rust-colored stains, called *foxing*, that could devalue the rarest book; even a fraudulent title page sewn into the gutter to defraud an unwary buyer.

I heard voices and stopped to ask myself if I should be out in the dining room, helping Derek set up the lunch we'd ordered. I quickly brushed off the idea, knowing that if he needed me, he would call. And so, back to the book.

After photographing the book from all angles, I took some close-up shots of the binding itself and studied the reedy, knotted string that was barely keeping the book together. Magnified, the thread looked like an ultrathin twine made of jute or sisal. It was definitely some kind of fiber, but not linen or silk. And over the years, it had begun to come unstrung.

Taking out my tape measure, I noted the size of the book. Six and a half inches wide, nine and a half inches tall, and almost one inch thick. It was a pretty good size for a book that was essentially being held together by old, tattered bits of string.

Opening the book, I examined the pages. They were stiff yet fragile, as though the paper might snap or crackle at the slightest bit of pressure. Taking off one of my gloves, I touched the paper, running it gently between my thumb and forefinger. It had the thick feel of handmade paper. This might have been due to the texture of the paper itself, which was fibrous and rough but still beautiful in its own way. The edges were lightly deckled, or feathered, and I could see teensy individual fibers in every color of the rainbow woven into the paper's grain.

I had seen a few woodcut prints when I first bought the book, but paging through now, I found color woodcut prints of a flower or an herb on at least half of the pages. Each woodcut included a Chinese word or symbol, which I figured was the name of the plant. The rest of the text, having to do with the medicinal value or healing properties of each plant, was written in French.

I put my glove back on and picked up my X-Acto knife. I began sawing at the ties, carving around the knots, and slicing the threads one strand at a time until the ties came apart. The back and front covers loosened and fell away from the thick block of pages in between.

After gathering all of the clumps and bits of thread, I lined up the remnants and laid them out on the cloth. I was determined to save all of the old materials and package them within the newly bound book. This would lend weight to its provenance and thus give it more value.

I snapped a few more photographs, then stared at the parts of the book laid out on the white cloth. I was ready to move on to a new phase in the deconstruction of the book, but for a moment, I relaxed, popped another kiss into my mouth, and listened to the sounds coming from Derek's meeting.

The doorbell had been ringing for the last half hour, and now I imagined everyone had arrived and people were gathered around the kitchen island, grabbing sandwiches and spooning the various salads onto their plates. There were cookies and brownies for dessert, and I hoped they would all grab a few of each. The better to lighten the mood.

With a sigh, I stepped down from the high chair and hustled out to greet everyone.

"Darling, there you are." Derek met me halfway, took my hand, and walked with me across the room.

A woman in her midfifties broke away from the crowd to join me. "It's herself then, is it?"

"Corinne." I gave Derek's beloved assistant a big hug. "How are you?"

She smiled. "I'm dandy as dumplings and happy to see you." Her voice contained the lilting tones of Devonshire and brought to mind the medieval towns and mystical moors I'd visited ages ago. She had a softness to her appearance that was completely belied by her steely resolve and whip-smart intelligence. With a private wink, she said, "Let's try to catch up after."

"It's a date." I greeted the rest of the group, hugging the ones I knew well and shaking hands with the others. They all asked about the honeymoon, and I gave the world's quickest rave review of the entire trip.

"I'd better let you get started with your meeting," I said after another minute. "But I'll see you all before you leave."

I heard murmurs of "Great" and "See you soon" before they returned to the task of piling their plates high.

"I'll walk you back to your office," Corinne said, and wove her arm through mine. She glanced around, careful that she wasn't overheard. "I understand we'll be seeing you next weekend."

For a moment my mind went blank, then I remembered. "You mean, the team-building thing? At the spy shop?"

"Yes, the escape room. I think it's a brilliant idea. Only the partners know about it right now, but we'll talk about it with everyone who's here today. Derek plans to make the official announcement at the office tomorrow."

"Should be interesting."

"Yes," she said. "Especially because he plans to make it mandatory."

My smile was all innocence. "Won't that be fun?"

Her face crinkled in silent laughter. "I'll keep you posted."

"We saw one of the rooms and I think everyone really will have fun." I smiled. "As soon as I saw that brochure, I thought I'd better suggest it to Derek."

Her smile tightened. "*Fun* is something we're not having a lot of these days, so I thank you for bringing it up." She patted my arm. "I'd better join the group."

I glanced over her shoulder. "I hope you all work everything out."

"We will. Dialogue is good." She gave me a brave smile. "See you later."

Back in my workshop, I pulled my high chair up to the table and continued working. The sounds from the dining room died down to almost nothing, which meant that everyone was eating. Within a few minutes, though, I heard Derek's clear voice and knew the discussion had begun. There were low-pitched tones as someone else spoke, punctuated by the occasional burst of laughter or griping as Derek went around the table, asking each person for their own version of what had caused the rift to occur at the office.

I didn't have to be in the room to know what was happening; Derek had revealed his plan to me at breakfast earlier. I'd told him it was a good idea and hoped the discussion would make it all the way around the table before the meeting dissolved into bedlam.

Derek's voice had been filled with humor as he called me a cynic. He assured me in that deceptively soft tone of his that he wouldn't allow that to happen. And I believed him.

I tuned out the sounds of the meeting and concentrated on the book. Using my X-Acto knife, I picked and nipped at the pastedown inside the front cover until I was able to pry it far enough away to reach the edges of the book's cloth cover. I intended to keep the same cover because it was so pretty, but I had to carefully remove it first because it was buckled and worn. My plan was to iron or steam the cover to smooth out the wrinkles and bends in the cloth before pasting it back onto a smooth new board.

"Probably have to iron it," I mumbled absently. Steam involved moisture, which was rarely a good thing for paper. But ironing would be tricky. I didn't want to damage the fragile cloth. After all, the book was close to sixty years old. Yes, parts of it were still strong, but overall it wasn't in the best of health.

"Brooklyn to the rescue," I said with a determined grin. Fix the tears and wrinkles; brush away the dust and grit from every page and gutter; add new boards and newer, stronger thread and knots to keep the signatures—the folded pieces of paper that made up the pages of a book—more tightly bound together; use my beautiful Chinese-inspired tissue paper from Paris for the new pastedowns; sew on a new, colorful head-band; then add a little bit of magical bookbinder love, and this baby would be healthy and happy again.

"You're being ridiculous!" a woman shouted from the dining room.

A chair screeched and scraped across the hardwood floor. I flinched and imagined the gouge left from that chair being yanked across the floor. But more impor-tantly, some very angry woman was confronting my husband. Was she leaving? I didn't hear footsteps pounding across to the door, but maybe they were wearing rubber soles.

I had to take a few deep breaths in and out. I really didn't like to hear people shouting at Derek. It tended to cause my blood to boil. My teeth clenched in righ-teous anger. How dare they bellow at my husband in our own house?

"You're out of line. Sit down, please." That was Der-ek's low-key voice, and it caused more chills to gather across my shoulders. He rarely used that cold, clipped tone, but I'd heard it more than once in my life. It was the way he spoke just before he went ballistic and tore into someone. The only times I'd ever seen him actually hit someone were the few instances when I had been at-tacked. Most often he simply exuded this subtle anger, and I had to admit, it was kind of awesome. With little more than a whisper, he could bring a grown man to tears.

Against my better judgment, I tiptoed through the short hallway to the edge of the living room. I just had to listen in.

"But Derek," the woman argued, "you can't just demand that everyone in the company show up next Saturday afternoon and play games."

"Actually, Jocelyn, I can," Derek countered. "Especially when it's for the good of the company."

I had met Jocelyn before. She was one of the newer partners in the company. I had liked her immediately, and I knew that Derek respected her business acumen and her keen sense of humor. So why was she so angry? Why was she yelling at him? I didn't care for the sound of her ranting voice aimed at my husband. Maybe there was something else going on below the surface.

Derek paused for a long moment, and I imagined him scanning the table, meeting each person's gaze. "While I expect that your people will have fun in spite of themselves, these aren't games. They're team-building exercises that everyone will benefit from."

"Escape rooms," the woman muttered.

"Yes," Derek said with deadly calm. "We could employ an outside company who would happily put us through any number of these so-called team-building exercises. But why should we when there's a perfectly entertaining way to accomplish the same thing on our own?"

"Not sure how this is going to go over," one of the men said.

"I will make the general announcement tomorrow. After that, I would like each of you to explain to your group that they will all be paid time and a half for their participation. And unless they have a very good reason not to attend this official team-building event, I will consider them effectively resigned from the company."

"Damn it, Derek," the same woman—Jocelyn— whined. "That's not fair."

"Yes, it is," he snapped. "I won't have the welfare of the entire company and our other employees threatened like this. Simple as that."

"Johnson in my department is leaving on vacation Friday."

"If he can show me his nonrefundable airline tickets to Mozambique or wherever," Derek drawled, "I'll consider letting him slide."

That earned him a few chuckles. I smiled, too. He wasn't quite as hard-assed as he sometimes seemed. On the other hand, he could be just that hard-assed when the situation called for it.

"I think the escape rooms will be jolly fun," Corinne said cheerfully.

I pressed my hands to my chest. I loved her so much at that moment. A few more people managed to chuckle, although I imagined several others were rolling their eyes. But the comment seemed to break the tension for the moment.

"It *will* be fun," Derek reiterated. "And the team-building aspect is important. I'm willing to try anything to bring our people together and get beyond this idiotic impasse."

Leo, one of Derek's closest friends from their early days in the London office, muttered, "The woman thrives on impasses."

"True," Jocelyn grumbled. "*She* is, after all, the reason we're jumping through hoops like this."

"No comment," Derek muttered.

I tiptoed back to my worktable, Charlie following briskly behind me. I sat down and stared at nothing while the cat curled up on her little cat pillow.

I thought about what I'd overheard. *She* thrives on impasses? *She* is the reason we're jumping through hoops? It seemed that no one at the table liked *her*— whoever she was.

Who is she? I wondered. What did the partners mean by that? It made me wonder if there really was just *one* person who had started all the trouble. I knew Derek didn't like to burden me with all the gossip and drama from the office, but this was important. I didn't consider it a burden. I wanted to know who *she* was. How could I offer advice if I didn't know what I was dealing with? And I had every intention of offering advice. That's how I rolled.

Derek's meeting finally broke up over an hour later, and some of the people stayed to chitchat for a while. Happily, I had managed to get back into my bookbinding work and was so wrapped up in cutting the endpapers that I almost missed it. But then my attention was caught by the loud, barking laughter of one of the women as she was saying her good-byes.

I stared at all the parts of the book spread across the white cloth and sighed. Knowing I was too distracted to do anything else, I covered everything with another clean white cloth, jumped down from my chair, and walked into the dining room to say good-bye to everyone. There were more hugs and many thanks for setting up the fabulous lunch—which I accepted, even though I hadn't done anything except buzz in the caterers.

"Have a good afternoon," I said, waving to the last

two people as Derek walked with them down the hallway to the elevator. I realized he was taking the moment to have a private conversation with those two, so I closed the door.

I started clearing the lunch buffet. Charlie followed me in and out of the kitchen as I moved around the island, carrying the larger platters to the sink.

I had counted five women at the meeting, but whoever the unknown *she* was, she wasn't one of the women in attendance today. Derek had at least seventy employees working in the San Francisco office and another eighty-five in London. He had told Owen that he'd be bringing twenty-two people to the escape rooms on Saturday, so I guessed that would encompass one good-sized department, plus a few partners and some people from Human Resources.

Each of Derek's partners held the title of vice president of their department: Accounting, Sales, Marketing, Management, Security, Human Resources. Within each department there were executives, supervisors, assistants, clerks, and other entry-level employees. Unlike the others, the Security department had three vice presidents running it, plus a dozen investigators, logistics experts, field agents, and a highly specialized strike force of at least ten people. Derek's company handled security for people, for buildings, for artwork. People, places, and things. His Security department had the biggest number of people, and I'd met many of them. I couldn't imagine any of them being the source of the trouble.

So who was wreaking havoc? In which department?

I shook my head and carried a few stacked plates into the kitchen. I would just have to ask Derek as soon as he returned from walking his people to the elevator.

I almost didn't want to know. I hated to think that my husband had enemies, but since he owned the company, I supposed it came with the territory. He was in charge of these people's livelihoods. Some of his employees might take that personally and would get defensive if things didn't go their way. It could cause a major rift if their loyalties weren't in line with his. And after overhearing that very short confrontation a while ago, I wondered if a major rift had occurred right here in our home. It felt major to me, but that was because Derek was involved. Maybe it was just a blip, but I knew it was bugging the heck out of Derek. And therefore, me.

He had created this company and I knew he loved it, loved the work that he did, loved that everyone had always gotten along and worked well together. He'd made sure to hire the best people and he took good care of his employees, so I knew that the rift was hurting him. And that made me hurt, too.

I heard the door open and close and I watched him walk toward me. He gave a humorless chuckle. "You must've heard some of that."

"Just the yelling part."

"There was very little yelling, all in all."

"Only enough to make me worry about you."

He walked over to the kitchen island to survey what needed to be cleaned up. "You needn't worry."

"But that's my job." I walked closer and slipped my arms around his waist. "Someone's causing you trouble."

"Yes."

"Who is she?"

He smiled at me. "How do you know it's a *she*?"

"Seriously?" I drew back far enough to look him in

the eyes. Those gorgeous midnight blue eyes got to me every time. "I have ears."

"Lovely ears." His lips curved into a rueful smile. "So you heard that part."

"Yeah," I said, growing impatient. "Look, whoever she is, why don't you just fire her?"

"It's not that simple." He took a step back, ran his hands down my arms, squeezed my hands, and leaned back against the kitchen island. "Last week she had her lawyer call HR and threaten them with a lawsuit if anything happened to her."

"Oh, for God's sake," I said irritably and asked again. "Who is this snake weasel?"

His eyes narrowed in response. "It's Lark."

Chapter 5

"Of course it's Lark," I muttered, instantly irate. "You should've fired her last year after Crane left town."

"That was the plan." He shook his head in disgust. "My head of Sales was supposed to handle it, but instead of firing her, he gave her a raise for bringing in the most new clients that month."

"Can you fire *him*?"

He laughed. "Bart apologized about it later. He claimed that at the time I asked him to fire her, all he could see were her sales numbers."

"That's not all he saw," I muttered.

"You would think so," he mused. "And it may be true that she has him wrapped around her little finger. But I've known Bart for fifteen years and he's above reproach. Completely trustworthy. He brought Lark into the company a few years ago and took her under his wing. He's convinced that he can moderate her aggressive style, so he's asked for more time."

"What do you think?"

Derek pressed his lips together, so I knew he was frustrated. But he said, "I'm willing to give Bart some space."

I rolled my eyes. I supposed men considered Lark beautiful. Much like a black widow spider was beautiful—if you were a stupid male spider.

I flashed back to the office party last year when I'd first met Lark. The entire company had been invited to a party honoring Derek's best friend, Crane, who had been visiting from China and was bringing several lucrative new accounts to the company.

I had been standing near Derek as he'd introduced Crane to his partners and colleagues. As soon as he finished his speech, the partners gathered around Crane to introduce themselves. There was one woman, however, who sidled up to Derek in a way that caused my jaw to tighten and my blood pressure to spike.

She was beautiful, for sure, tall with gorgeous skin and a model-thin body. She praised Derek to the heavens, calling his speech brilliant, sensational, amazing. Her voice was low and her smile was sultry, and both were aimed directly at my then-fiancé. And when she touched his tie and ran her fingers along the lapel of his jacket, I thought my eyes would bug out of my head. Was she insane? Did she realize I was taking martial arts classes from my friend Alex? I had rarely been jealous of anything ever, but I was seriously *this close* to knocking her on her butt. And that was when Derek had turned and given her a look meant to chill to the bone, silently warning her to get her hands off him and back away.

She had looked completely frazzled by his rebuff, but before she could scamper away, Derek reached out, pulled me closer, and introduced me to her as his fiancée. With his arm firmly wrapped around my waist, I watched her turn a lovely shade of pale green. She had managed a few words and then slunk away.

And if I hadn't already been in love with Derek, that moment would've solidified my feelings.

There had been other incidents, other office parties, where Lark would manage to catch me alone in the hall or the ladies' room or the terrace and make a snide comment or give me a dirty look. She seemed to be carrying out a personal vendetta against me, and I could only conclude that she thought she deserved to have Derek for her very own.

Sadly, she had poisoned several other women against me, too. These were her toadies, and they would rally around her at the parties, enjoying her awful attitude.

Thoroughly annoyed now, I paced back and forth, pounding my palm with my fist. "I hope she's bringing in some huge clients for you because she's nothing but trouble as far as I'm concerned."

I confess that except for that first office party I attended, I had never told Derek about the many awful things she'd said to me or how she had turned her little group of friends—the mean girls, as I called them—against me. So Derek had no way of knowing just how vicious Lark could be. But it had become a matter of pride that I refused to have him fight my battles for me. I could handle her vitriol. I just didn't like it.

"I should've known she was the one causing you problems," I said. "And by the way, what was Jocelyn's problem? She seemed so angry. Is something else going on?"

"She's had a run-in or two with Lark, so she's on edge as well."

"Lark strikes again," I muttered, still pacing.

He watched me striding back and forth, and when I got closer, he pulled me into his arms. "We'll see how this team-building exercise goes. Frankly, I haven't paid much attention to Lark this past year because she hasn't made any waves and she's brought in so many new clients. Bart's very happy with her work, so I don't want to interfere unless I have to."

"What does Corinne say about it?"

"She's not at all happy. Apparently the problems began while you and I were on our honeymoon. Corinne tried to handle it and it didn't go well. In fact, it got worse. But look, I don't want you to worry. We'll get through it."

"I won't worry," I said, smiling up at him.

But I would, I thought. Maybe I should've told him about Lark's attacks from the very beginning.

"I heard someone at your meeting say that she's the one who's making you all jump through hoops. That's unacceptable."

"You're right," he said. "But Bart insists that he will deal with it."

I spread my arms wide. "And if he doesn't, then you can fire her?"

He smiled. "Darling, I would do it in a heartbeat. But HR insists she would have a viable lawsuit if I did so."

"How so?"

"Bart has given her glowing recommendations and raises each year, plus a big bonus last year. And she's won the award for top sales several months in a row. She could claim bad faith, breach of covenant, lord knows what else."

"I know you think she's a good employee, but she's poison. She's driving you crazy." *And me*, I thought. I couldn't stand the woman, but that was an entirely different issue. I wouldn't bring my own personal feelings into the mix. Not out loud anyway.

I glanced around the kitchen and sighed. "Let's clean up."

"Good idea."

There were four sandwiches left over and we packed them in individual baggies for lunches during the week. The cole slaw, potato salad, and pickles had their own containers, and I put those in the refrigerator.

"Wow, they left two brownies," I said in shock. "I figured they'd gobble them all up."

"I was frankly worried," he admitted, tongue firmly in cheek. "So I hid some away for you. Cookies, too."

I blinked and fake sniffled. "You did that for me?"

He laughed. "Yes, darling. I would do anything for you."

"I'm overwhelmed. Thank you." I broke off a piece of brownie, popped it into my mouth, and then handed him a chunk. "These are so good. They melt in your mouth."

He took the brownie piece and kissed me. "Thank you."

I smiled. "For the brownie?"

"For your love and your support and your good advice. But mostly for the brownie." He kissed me again, slipped his arms around my waist, and managed to reach over and grab the rest of the brownie from the plate on the island.

"Cheater," I said with a laugh, then sobered. "Do you have a strategy going forward? I mean, what good is team building when you know she's never going to be a team player?"

He lifted a shoulder. "Corinne thinks we should

plan these activities every week until she gets with the program. Or gets so annoyed that she quits."

"I'm afraid she'll never quit. She thrives on chaos."

"I'm afraid you're right," Derek said. He added, "But see here. If all else fails, we'll simply pay her to go away."

"She probably wouldn't leave for less than a million dollars."

"You're close."

"Oh my God," I said, angry all over again. "She's already named her price I'll bet. Still, it would almost be worth it to have her gone. But it's infuriating."

I closed the dishwasher and punched the On button a little too vigorously. Feeling bad, I gave the stainless steel surface a little pat of apology.

It was a clear sign of my confusion and annoyance that I was now expressing my regret to a kitchen appliance. No wonder Lark was their top salesperson, I thought. The woman was like a velociraptor. Smart and fast on her feet, she knew when to strike. While others with these traits might actually be admired, I had a feeling that Lark might've crossed a line this time.

I couldn't help but suspect that Lark had deliberately waited for Derek and me to leave on our honeymoon before stirring up trouble for everyone else in the office. Derek never would have put up with her crap if he were there, but some of the other partners were more intimidated by her. Now things were too far gone for Derek to simply walk in and fire her. So for now, he and his partners would pretend that everyone in the department needed to beef up their team-building skills. I had gotten to know and like many of Derek's staff members, and I had a feeling they would enjoy the team-building event. Most of them had always gotten along with each other—until recently, when Lark began to make waves.

It was enough to chap anyone's ass, as my mother used to say.

Derek made it through the week despite Lark continuing to spew her toxic vibes around the office. The good news was that everyone who was required to attend the weekend escape room event had promised to be there, so no resignations would be forthcoming. Some of the staff, as predicted, were actually excited about it and were planning to make a day of it with lunch or shopping down at the Embarcadero.

I planned to be there, too, of course, and had invited Alex to join me. It really did sound like fun, and we'd be supporting Derek at the same time. Alex had good instincts about people, having been a covert operative for many years before starting her own company. Her life had depended on her trusting her first impressions. I couldn't wait to hear her opinion of Lark.

Thursday night, on our way out to dinner, Derek and I stopped at SPECTRE to drop off *The Spy Who Loved Me* for the big party on Saturday.

"Wait until you see the display we've created for the book," Owen gushed as we walked through the store with him. "I'm so excited, I can hardly stand it."

There was definitely a feeling of anticipation coming from the salespeople and customers alike as we crossed into the bookshop area and took a look around. One large round table at the entry held stacks of books, with the top book resting on a mini-easel and facing out to the crowd. The book displays were clever and inviting, with some books stacked up and others fanned out like flowers in a colorful bouquet. Confetti, balloons, and flower arrangements were everywhere. Above our heads, a sturdy wire ran the length of the bookshop, and books were hanging from it. I took a closer look and saw that there were clever cords with little platforms supporting each book, making it easy for a buyer to reach up, unhook the book, and peruse it.

"It looks so festive in here," I said.

"Our design team went wild." He maneuvered his way around to the central display case. "Here's where your book will live for the next ten days."

I gazed into the case and was delighted to see a small vintage bookstand for the book itself to rest upon. The elegance of the bookstand was countered by the dangerous-looking guns, scary knives, scattered bullets, brass knuckles, and even a few hand grenades that surrounded it. All fake, I presumed. There was also a fancy-looking wristwatch, some cool sunglasses, and a black tie suitable for a tuxedo that was draped casually across the bookstand as though James Bond himself had tossed it there after a long night of chemin de fer or baccarat at the local casino. And strewn everywhere else were more colorful streamers and confetti.

"This looks fabulous," I said, smiling at Owen. "I love it."

He pressed his hand against his chest in relief. "I'm so glad you approve." Stooping down, he opened the case and set my book gently on the bookstand. "How does that look?"

"Perfect," I said.

With a broad grin, he stood up and locked the case, slipping the key ring into his pocket. "Now look closely. You can see the wires in the glass, right?"

I nodded. "Yes."

"Those go directly to our alarm system and will alert us if there's any tampering. And of course, we'll keep it locked at all times. Your book will be perfectly safe with us."

I examined the implanted wires and the lock mechanism. "I'm sure it will be. Thanks, Owen."

Derek touched my arm. "Darling, I'm going to check on our escape room reservations for Saturday. Be right back."

"And I've got to check on a delivery," Owen said. "Will you be all right by yourself for a moment?"

"Of course. I'm surrounded by books. I'll be fine."

After talking to Drummer Girl, I had an itch to get back into dark suspense, so I sought out the latest J. D. Robb and a scary new one by Karin Slaughter. I would've loved to have bought a few of the vintage books on display as well, but decided to wait until Saturday when I could spend more time browsing and shopping. I rounded another bookcase, and that was when I saw the Jackals sitting in the café.

I smiled and waved. "Hi, you guys. I was just thinking about you. How's it going?"

Drummer Girl's eyes brightened. "Hey, Brooklyn. We're right in the middle of torturing Soldier's hero."

"Sounds like fun."

"Fun for me," Soldier said, attempting a grin. "But my protagonist just lost his lunch."

"And Tinker's still having problems with his murder scene."

"The strangulation?" I asked. "Or did you go with stabbing?"

He exhaled heavily. "There's just too much blood."

"You're just not committing to the work," Tailor claimed.

"Oh, bite me," Tinker grumbled. The others laughed, including Tailor.

"I've seen someone who was stabbed to death," I murmured. "There's definitely a lot of blood."

Tinker's mouth dropped open. "You've seen it? Can I interview you?"

"Uh." My vision wavered for a moment as I relived it all over again. Stepping inside the flower shop, seeing the woman on the floor with a razor-sharp pair of English garden shears protruding from her stomach, her white blouse stained with blood. I swallowed carefully, unsure why I'd said one freaking word about it. I really hated the sight of blood, even in memory. "I'll think about it."

"So what're you doing here tonight?" Drummer said.

I quickly brushed away the brutal memories. "I brought my book in for the big party this weekend. Owen's got it on display in the center case."

"What's the book?" Tailor asked.

"*The Spy Who Loved Me.* It's a first edition. I bought it for Derek when we were in Paris."

"Seriously?" All four of them jumped up and wound their way over to the center display case.

"That looks so chill," Drummer said. "Like in a museum."

Soldier stared at the display for a long moment. "I wonder whose guns those are."

"As long as they're not real," I muttered. I seriously needed them to be fake.

Soldier snorted, but didn't bother to argue—for which I was thankful, because really? Real guns in a book display? That was carrying the whole spy theme too far. But I was afraid Soldier was probably right to scoff at me.

"I'd love to have that book," Tinker said, bypassing the gun comment as he admired the book.

Tailor agreed. "Completely rad."

Drummer frowned at me. "I thought you said Derek wasn't a spy."

"It's just a book," I said gently. "Not a declaration."

But Tailor's eyes were narrowed in on me. "Right."

"Is he here?" Drummer asked, glancing around.

"Derek? Yes. He went to the back for a minute. We're doing an escape room on Saturday."

"You'll love it," Drummer declared. "It's a blast."

"I work here on Saturdays," Tinker said. "I'll see you around."

"I'll look for you," I said. "What department do you work in?"

He pointed across the room. "I'm in countersurveillance. Hidden cameras, bug sweepers, GPS trackers. All that stuff."

I smiled. "That must be fun."

"It would be more fun if he wasn't so obsessed with all this stuff," Tailor muttered.

"You should talk, dude," Tinker said.

"I know, right?" Drummer grinned. "Tailor buys every new gadget that comes on the market."

Tinker snorted. "I wouldn't say he *buys* them."

"Shut up about that," Tailor said, elbowing Drummer. "I don't need everyone knowing my secrets."

"I promise not to tell," I said lightly.

"And you should talk," Tailor continued, jabbing his finger at Tinker. "You buy more stuff than I do."

"But you're the one who freaks out if someone new walks into the store."

Tailor shrugged. "My mom says I'm suspicious by nature. Besides, it's a spy store. People come in here looking for ways to spy on their neighbors, their friends, their employees. What the heck is that all about?"

"He's got a point," Soldier said. "Some of the people who come in here are seriously paranoid."

"Damn straight they are," Tailor continued. "Don't you wonder what some of these people are doing here? What's happening in their lives that they've got to come to a place like this? Are they just paranoid or are they really being followed?"

"You're such a freak, Tailor," Drummer said, laughing. "But it's okay. You're *our* freak."

"I love this store," I said. "It's got so much going on."

"It really does," Drummer said.

Tinker elbowed Tailor good-naturedly, and I figured their argument was history.

Tailor looked up at me through his eyelashes, suddenly shy. "I work here, too. A couple nights a week."

"Oh, good. Maybe I'll see you in here on Saturday, too."

"Yeah, maybe." He smiled and managed to look even younger than I'd suspected he was.

I was pleased they weren't grousing at each other anymore—then had to smother a laugh. That was me,

I thought. Happy-clappy. I just wanted everyone to get along.

Glancing up, I noticed Derek waving at me. "I've got to go, guys."

"See you around, Brooklyn," Drummer said.

Looking back and forth from Tinker to Tailor, I added, "We'll see you both on Saturday."

"Dig it," Tinker said, while Tailor flashed me the peace sign.

As I approached Derek, my thoughts drifted back to the writing group. They intrigued me. Did they really buy all this surveillance equipment for themselves? And if so, what did they do with it? Spy on their neighbors? Their parents? Their siblings? And what were their real names? Did they all have day jobs? Was there a group leader? If so, I was pretty certain it was Tinker, although Soldier seemed like a born leader. A little too quiet to lead this group, though, I supposed. And what about their writing? Were any of them any good? I figured I could ask Tinker all these questions when I saw him on Saturday. Not that it was any of my business.

"But that's never stopped me before," I murmured with a light shrug, and took Derek's hand in mine as we walked back out to the car.

"I'm glad you were able to come with us," I said to Alex as we walked into SPECTRE Saturday morning.

Alex had pulled her long dark hair back in a casual ponytail, and she wore a slouchy sweater, jeans, and boots. It made me happy to see her looking so relaxed and comfortable. She grabbed my hand. "I wanted some girl time with you and this was the best way to get it."

"And what am I, chopped liver?" Derek asked.

Alex and I laughed, tickled to hear that phrase spoken by a sophisticated Englishman.

"We can all catch up at lunch," Alex said, reaching out to squeeze his arm.

"Good," Derek said. "We'll only be in the room for an hour or so, followed by a few minutes of chatting and commiserating. Then we can go to lunch."

I glanced around. "I wasn't expecting to see so many people in here today."

"I'm happy for Owen," Derek said.

There were people standing at every counter, chatting with salespeople, trying out gadgets, checking out the products on the shelves and tables. Banners hanging from the ceiling announced the various special anniversary deals available in each section. Everyone seemed to be in a cheery mood, despite the crowds.

I headed straight for the bookshop and was thrilled to see the line of people standing around the glass display of *The Spy Who Loved Me*.

"That's your book in there?" Alex said.

"Yes." I couldn't wipe the smile off my face.

"You might be able to get a look at it later," Derek said.

Alex grinned. "I hope so."

"Oh, look." I pointed toward the back counter. "There's Corinne."

"I see some of our other employees are here, too," Derek said, and gave me a resigned smile. "I'd better go greet them. I'll see you as soon as we escape."

"Have fun," I said, chuckling, then gave him a quick kiss and watched him walk away.

"Don't you want to say hello to his people?" Alex asked as I veered off into the bookshop.

"I would love to, but I don't want to run into Lark." I winced. "That makes me sound like a complete wimp."

"No, it doesn't."

I laughed. "Yes, it does, but I don't care. She's so toxic it's scary."

Alex glanced around. "Well, point her out to me so I'll have a frame of reference."

"I will." I scanned the shop. "I don't see her yet, but I'll give you a heads-up when I do."

She gazed around the wide room. "This place is awesome. I have a feeling I could spend a lot of money in here."

"You definitely could. Can we start here in the bookshop?"

"Naturally," she said with a grin.

As we walked around the bookshop, I was able to keep an eye on the activity back by the escape room ticket counter. Derek was dutifully buying all the tickets for his group, and soon they would be herded into the theater lobby.

Besides Derek and Corinne, there were fourteen out of fifteen members of the Sales department, which included the VP, a bunch of salespeople, four assistants, and two clerks. Also attending were two people from Human Resources and three additional VPs from other departments.

I didn't see Lark, but I assumed she would be there any minute. Their escape room appointment was scheduled for ten thirty, and the reservations clerk had been adamant about arriving early in order to start on time. It would be Lark's style to show up at the last minute.

Derek had told me that Corinne had already arranged the teams by drawing names from a hat. One of the HR clerks had witnessed the drawing to make sure everything was fair and impartial. I silently commiserated with whichever team was unlucky enough to include Lark because I knew she would be absolutely no help at all. If she even bothered to show up.

I frowned, wondering if I was being unfair. Too harsh? Too judgmental? Maybe, but I didn't care, not after all the times she'd been such a jerk to me. Was Lark aware that all of this preparation and planning had been done strictly for her? Because she was a freaking nightmare.

I noticed an older gentleman perusing one of the countersurveillance displays and couldn't help but smile. Corinne's husband was one of my favorite people, with his gentle smile and cozy, cuddly style. Sometimes I just wanted to give him a hug. Today he wore a navy cardigan with pockets, worn jeans, and Hush Puppies. Definitely huggable. I walked over to greet him. "Wallace?"

"Brooklyn," he said joyfully, and gave me a light hug. "Isn't it lovely to see a friendly face?"

"Yes, it is. It's very nice to see you."

"Are you going to play the game?"

"No way," I said with a short laugh. "I brought our friend Alex, and the three of us are going out to lunch after everyone escapes."

"Or dies," Wallace said balefully, and we both chuckled.

Alex approached and I introduced the two. "This is Wallace Sterling, Corinne's husband. Corinne is Derek's wonderful administrative assistant. The one who saves his life on a daily basis."

Wallace beamed at the words and the two of them shook hands.

"So nice to meet you, Wallace," Alex said.

"I'm delighted to meet you, too."

"Are you going to do the escape room?" she asked.

"No, no. My son is here somewhere. We're just killing time until Corinne is finished." He gazed around, looking for his son. "Reggie's visiting for the summer. He's normally at university, so we're thrilled that he's taken time to visit."

"Where does he go to school?" Alex asked.

"He's at Oxford."

"I'd love to meet him," I said.

"I'll introduce you. Right now I believe he might be trying out the virtual reality room."

"Virtual reality?" Alex raised an eyebrow. "I've got to check that out."

"It seemed a good day to play tourist," Wallace said. "Reggie wants to tour the submarine after Corinne finishes up, and then we're having lunch at the Slanted Door. We've never been."

"One of the best restaurants in town," Alex said. "And the view is spectacular."

"It's a beautiful day to sit outside," I added.

"I'm looking forward to it."

"The submarine is one of my favorite things to visit," I said. "You'll enjoy it. Unless you're prone to claustrophobia."

He smiled. "That shouldn't be a problem."

The submarine was the USS *Pampanito*, a World War II vessel, part of the maritime museum that included navy ships, schooners, a paddleboat, and others. It was top on my list of places to take visitors when they came to town. Because who didn't want to explore a submarine?

"Yoo-hoo! Derek! Wait for me!"

We turned and watched Lark prance through the store on sparkly five-inch stiletto heels, shaking her hair back as she moved to join the others. She wore skintight tan leather leggings and a matching leather crop top. Granted, she was tall and svelte and beautiful, but this wasn't a nightclub, for Pete's sake. Her outfit was so wildly inappropriate, I had to laugh. Not in a ha-ha-ha sort of way but in more of an OMG-are-you-kidding way.

And there I went, being judgmental again. In my defense, though, there was plenty to be judgmental about. I mean, really? *Yoo-hoo, Derek?*

I was feeling righteously snarky as Lark passed by. Then without warning, she stopped, turned, and looked right at me. Her expression had flipped from flirtatious and flighty to sneeringly contemptuous.

"You." That was all she said, and the deadly chill in her eyes flew right into mine and went straight through to my spine.

"Lark." I kept my response to one syllable. It was all I could do to keep myself upright, but I managed, staring right back at her with the same level of scorn she'd just given me.

After a few seconds of cold silence—it felt like an hour—she flashed a bared-teeth snarl and hissed loudly. Hissed! Like a snake! Her eyes flashed with hostility.

And then she turned and strutted off to join the others.

"Oh my God," I whispered. I was shocked and breathless from the near-silent encounter. I'd been right to call her a snake weasel. The hatred oozing from her made me want to howl and claw her face off. I rubbed my stomach. It was physically painful to feel so disturbed by a person.

"What is wrong with her?" Alex whispered, tugging at my arm. "That was evil."

"That was Lark." Just saying her name out loud sent goose bumps slithering down my back.

"She seriously hates you," Alex said. "Are you all right?"

"Fine and dandy." But I wasn't, especially now that Alex had confirmed my own thoughts. The woman hated me. I suppose it was mutual. A part of me wanted to kill her with my bare hands and then take a long, hot shower to wash off the venom.

What was with the hissing? She was like a combination of snake and wicked witch. Scary and weird.

"Why don't I believe you?" Alex said, studying my expression. I was pretty sure the contempt was written all over my face.

It wasn't easy, but I forced myself to smile. "I'll be okay."

"That's not going to go over well with Corinne," Wallace murmured. He was still staring at Lark as she blithely greeted the crowd at the back of the store.

I turned and saw Corinne's face as Lark approached. *If looks could kill*, I thought, watching the older woman glare at the blasé latecomer with her bad fashion choices.

Derek didn't look too thrilled, either, but he wouldn't care about what she was wearing. No, Derek's displeasure would come from her being so late and holding up the rest of the group. She was rude and thoughtless.

And those were the nicest things I could say about Lark.

If Lark noticed the expressions on Derek's and

Corinne's faces, she didn't seem to give a flying falafel. Instead, she cuddled up to Derek, grabbing hold of his arm and giving him a flirty greeting. She didn't stay with him too long—just long enough to annoy me. Then she sashayed on to someone else and continued around the group, greeting and giggling and fluffing her hair as she went. She paid no attention to Corinne's announcement that it was time to start. But then, why would Lark care what anyone else said?

"I would fire her in a heartbeat," Alex murmured next to me.

"I thought it was just me," I said.

"No, she's dangerous."

I took a deep breath and let it out, trying to calm down as I watched Derek's four groups slowly disappear through the double doors that led into the escape room lobby.

Wallace, Alex, and I stared at each other.

"What shall we do now?" I asked, not quite fully recovered from my staring contest with the evil witch. "We could grab a latte. Or, I don't know. Go shopping."

"There's a Whac-A-Mole game in the arcade next door," Alex suggested. "You might enjoy pounding something."

I had to laugh. "That's not a bad idea." But then I noticed her gazing longingly toward the back of the store.

"You're going to think I'm crazy," Alex said. "But I'd really like to try one of those escape rooms."

"For real?" I asked, but it did sound like fun. I gazed at Wallace.

He looked slightly embarrassed. "I wasn't going to say anything, but I'd love to do it, too. Corinne and I came here earlier this week in anticipation of today's activity and we had a rollicking good time."

Alex watched me. "What do you think, Brooklyn?"

I couldn't think of a reason why not. Maybe it would help some of my irritation and stress fade away. "It sounds like fun."

Alex raised her fist in victory. "Let's do it!"

We rushed over to the ticket counter and I asked the clerk, "Are any of the escape rooms available right now?"

She glanced at her computer screen. "We have the Spooky Circus and the Zombie Death Trap available."

What was more terrifying, I wondered. Clowns or zombies? "Which one is harder to escape?" I asked.

The clerk cast another glance at the computer. "They're both rated four Slashes out of five. That's like four stars."

"Got it."

"Anyway, that means they both have the same level of difficulty." She squinted at the screen. "But it says here that, on average, people have escaped the Spooky Circus six minutes faster than they escaped the zombies."

I took that to mean that the Zombie room was slightly more difficult. I was all for giving myself a challenge. And frankly, the whole idea of terrifying clowns was just wrong. Clowns were supposed to make you laugh, not freak you out. Zombies, on the other hand, were supposed to be scary, supposed to give you nightmares. I could accept creepy zombies as part of the natural order. But not clowns.

I wasn't sure if that made any sense at all, but I'd made up my mind. "I'll take three tickets for the Zombie Death Trap."

She nodded. "Good choice." She punched a button. Three tickets zipped out of a contraption and she handed them to me. "Here you go. We have lockers for your personal items—no cell phones or cameras in the rooms—and I strongly suggest that you use the restrooms before you start the game. Then just let Game Master Igor know you're all ready to go and he'll get you started."

"Thank you." I held up the tickets, and Alex and Wallace grinned. As the three of us pushed through the double doors and walked into the shabby theater lobby, Wallace sent a text message to his son. A few seconds later, he read the response out loud. "Reggie is perfectly happy to have extra time in the VR room."

Alex gazed around the plush yet tattered anteroom. "This looks amazing. Like a film set."

As Alex and I put our purses and phones in one of the lockers, Wallace walked over to the concession stand and bought a few boxes of gummy bears, chocolate-covered almonds, and caramel drops, along with three small water bottles.

"To keep up our strength," he said.

"My hero," Alex said. She took the box of gummy bears, opened it, and shook out a handful.

"Let's go talk to Game Master Igor," I said, and approached the booth where the Game Master held court.

Igor grinned, showing us his blackened teeth. "Welcome to my nightmare." Still grinning, he took our tickets, tore them in half, and handed me the stubs. "Ah, zombies it is. Right this way."

He led the way down the hall to the Zombie Death Trap escape room. I noticed his threadbare tuxedo jacket had moth holes across the back. The frayed front pocket was hanging and flapping, one corner still attached by a few thin threads. And with every step he took, a little cloud of dust fluttered off him.

"Hey, man. Going to lunch."

We all turned and saw Tailor jogging down the aisle toward the back exit.

"You're not supposed to leave this way," Igor said.

Tailor gave him a cocky smile. "But I always do."

Igor pointed a bony finger at him and said, "You're dead."

"You're a freak," Tailor said, laughing. He walked away and disappeared around a corner.

Igor shook his head as he unlocked the zombie door, and we entered an old office that smelled and looked as if it had been closed up for years. It was a decent-sized room, furnished with a battered wood desk and chair and a bookshelf filled with musty old leather-bound books. A small rack held magazines that appeared faded and out-of-date. A broken clock sat on the bookshelf next to a cracked vase. There were two oil paintings of hunting dogs and horses on the walls; scattered across the desk were keys in every color, size, and shape.

A clothing rack held a trench coat, two men's suits, and several vintage dresses from the forties or fifties. On the bottom shelf of the rack were eight pairs of old shoes, both men's and women's. There was also a standing wooden coatrack with different wigs and hats hanging on each rung. A Monopoly game was set up on a side table, and a deck of playing cards sat beside it. Three pieces of worn leather luggage were stacked against a wall.

A faded green velvet loveseat sat against the opposite wall from the desk. An old hope chest was being used as a coffee table. It was buckled and locked with a modern-looking combination lock. On the other side of the short couch was a wooden file cabinet with one drawer open, and a file folder was sticking up with a jumble of pages fanned out in disarray.

Alex looked up and gasped.

I followed her gaze up to the ceiling and saw that one of the acoustic tiles had come loose. A bloody hand and part of an arm were sticking out from the duct. A dozen bloody handprints marked the nearby ceiling tiles.

Unsure whether to laugh or shriek, I whispered, "Oh my God."

"Don't mind him," Igor said. "He's dead. There are other zombies outside, also dead of course, but ready to attack."

Igor stared intently at the three of us. "We usually have more people playing the game, so you three will have to work harder. But you all look like you've got brains."

"We do," Wallace said.

"Good." Igor flashed an evil grin. "Zombies love brains."

We all laughed weakly.

Igor tossed a walkie-talkie on the cushion of the loveseat. "If you get stuck, use the walkie-talkie. It's set on channel four. Maybe I'll answer, maybe I'll help. But you'll have to prove your desperation. And I'll want something in return."

"Such as?" Alex asked.

Igor bared his blackened teeth in a grisly smile. "A song, a dance, a penny for your pants."

I wanted to laugh, but his voice gave me chills. He didn't sound human.

I remembered Owen telling us that Igor would demand a song or a dance, but it had sounded whimsical at the time. Not so much now.

The Game Master began to giggle. His laughter grew louder and louder until he was hysterical.

Abruptly he stopped laughing and headed for the door, then whipped around. "Two rules: Don't break anything. And don't climb on the furniture. You'll hurt yourself. Clues are everywhere." He pointed toward the filing cabinet. "Start over there." He turned to go.

"Beg pardon, Mr. Igor," Wallace said, holding up a finger. "I believe we need a bit more information. Specifically, a backstory."

"I was getting to that." Igor's eyes narrowed in on Wallace. "You look familiar."

"The wife and I were here earlier this week. We had a marvelous time."

"You escaped?"

"Yes, we escaped the *Titanic*."

"Hmm. Good for you. Well, enough with the small talk. Once I'm gone, you're to go and push the black button on the wall over there. That'll activate the monitor and you'll get the whole story."

"Okay, thanks," I said.

"Don't thank me," Igor said, his voice turning even more sinister. He pointed to a digital clock affixed to the wall. "Clock starts now. Good luck, kiddies."

He shut the door firmly and we heard the loud click.

"Okay, let's—"

There was a sudden loud pounding on the door. I swore I must've jumped a foot.

"Open up!" someone screeched. "Let us in!"

There was growling and more shrieks as the pounding continued.

"Holy crap." I quickly backed away from the door.

Wallace gazed from me to Alex. "I believe those are the zombies."

Chapter 6

As we huddled around the TV monitor, the threatening noises outside the door subsided for the moment.

Wallace pushed the black button and the flat-screen television monitor turned on automatically.

The screen was blurry with lots of loud static at first, but it quickly cleared and the camera focused in on a skinny, wild-haired man wearing blue doctor's scrubs and a stethoscope around his neck. His eyeballs moved nervously in their sockets and he occasionally grabbed and pulled at his hair.

Like the trashy theater lobby out front, the laboratory in the background was run-down and cluttered. Rows of beakers and flasks, a Bunsen burner, and other medical equipment were lined up on shelves behind the doctor.

"I'm Dr. Franken," he shouted frantically, "and I need you to listen to me!" In the background, a lab assistant poured some sort of solution into a beaker. The solution began to sputter and foam and overflow. The assistant gave the doctor a quick worried glance, then set the bubbling beaker down on the counter and ran out.

The doctor gestured madly as he spoke. "The world has become a postapocalyptic wasteland! The reason?" He glanced around quickly, then leaned in close. "A spy stole my formula for a brilliant new chemical warfare drug. The drug was accidentally released into the water supply, and thus was created a legion of deadly superzombies. They're everywhere!"

Alex made a *tsk-tsk* sound. "We know that much."

On the screen, Dr. Franken's eyes twitched. "Thankfully my associate Dr. Stein has created an antidote." He swallowed anxiously. "But now he's disappeared. I need that antidote!"

Wallace scanned the office. "So we're looking for a chemical formula."

"Right." I followed Wallace's gaze for a moment, then concentrated on the video and the doctor's words.

"If you're watching this film, then you've found Stein's office." The crazed doctor stared into the camera, and I felt as if he were looking directly at us. "A horde of killer zombies is swarming right outside the door. Can you hear them? They're getting restless! And hungry! You have one hour to find the formula for the antidote and deliver it to the Game Master before the zombies break in and eat your brains for breakfast!"

He stared at us for another long moment, then began to scream, "Hurry up! Hurry up!"

Abruptly the screen went black.

"Jeez Louise." Alex let out a breath. "Why did I think this was a good idea?"

Wallace chuckled. "Gave you the willies, eh?"

"A little bit," she admitted. And the fact that my fearless, multi-black-belted friend was freaking out made me feel a little better.

"Deep breaths," I reminded her.

"Right." Alex sucked in a breath and let it go as she glanced over at Wallace. "You said that you and Corinne have done this before, so you know how it works."

"I do."

I felt a rush of relief. "What do we do first?"

"Divide and conquer is the best strategy," he said, and crossed over to the file cabinet. Grabbing the file folder, he set it down on the hope chest. "These are puzzles and riddles we have to answer. We can each take different ones and work them out. As soon as we solve one, we search the room for the clues that the puzzle revealed."

"Okay, got it," I said.

"And every time one of us solves a puzzle, we let the other two know it. Communicate and collaborate."

Alex nodded. "And if we hit a wall, there's always Igor."

"Hmm," I said. "Something tells me we'll be better off on our own."

She glanced at the digital clock mounted on top of the bookshelf. "We've used up five minutes."

"That's okay. We'll make up the time." I opened the file folder and fanned the laminated puzzle pages across the table. I grabbed the top page. "This one's a cypher puzzle. It's got all those military words. You know, Bravo, Oscar, Tango."

"That's easy," Alex said. "I'll take it."

"Do you think this clock is broken on purpose?" Wallace asked, gazing at the old clock on the bookshelf.

I looked up. "Yes."

"I agree." He took the clock off the shelf and examined it. "I can't open the back. Looks like it needs a little key or a screwdriver."

"There are thirty-seven keys on the desk," Alex said, then shrugged. "I counted."

"That was fast," I said, marveling at her speed.

"I may be a little OCD," she admitted.

Wallace grabbed another puzzle page and read it out loud. "It's a rebus," he murmured. "Very simple. There's a picture of a bed, minus B, plus R, equals?"

I smiled. "I'm guessing the answer is *Red*."

"There's a red key on the desk," Alex suggested.

"Is it that easy?" I asked.

"Not always, but let's try it." Wallace found the key, and glancing around, he murmured, "Now what does this open?"

While he tried every possible lock in the room—there were lots of locks in the room—I continued working the puzzles. They were mostly challenging, but fun, and we were starting to find things. And I was starting to lighten up after my encounter with the snake witch.

We searched the pockets of the trench coats and shook each of the shoes for hidden objects. We checked out the Monopoly game and opened up the deck of cards. And we gobbled up every bit of Wallace's candy as we went along.

"The solution to this puzzle is *Elvis song*," I said a few minutes later. "Any thoughts?"

"'Hound Dog,' perhaps?" Wallace said.

Alex pointed to the painting. "Hounds hunting."

I jumped up, dashed over, and lifted the painting off the wall. Scrawled on the back was a poetic message: *Blue key sets you free.*

"Is there a blue key on the desk?" I asked.

"Yeah," Alex said, then riffled through the odd collection and pulled up a bright blue key. "Right here."

"Yay! Now where does it go?" I wondered.

"Good question."

"Try the hope chest," Wallace said.

"Or the desk drawer."

I tried them both but the key didn't work in either. I did another quick search, but didn't find anything.

"Set it aside," Wallace said. "We'll return to it once we've got a few more clues."

We went on like that for another fifteen minutes, stumbling our way through the puzzles, finding clues, and then searching the room for their meaning. Thanks to Wallace finding the lock that my blue key matched, we discovered the name of the spy who stole the formula, along with some information about the first human who was turned into a zombie. Those details wouldn't get us out of the room, but we knew we were on the right track.

Every few minutes the zombies outside the office would scream, pound on the door, and growl for us to open up. It unnerved me every time, even though it was obviously a recording of some kind. But after the first few screams, we were all able to laugh. In fact, we were having a good time, I realized. I hoped Derek and his contentious colleagues were getting into the spirit of the game, too. There had been so much lingering anger after their meeting last weekend that I'd been afraid that tempers might devolve from there. But who had time to get angry when you were all running around trying to save the world and escape the room?

My last puzzle was the hardest. There were pictures

of seven different flowers: rose, daisy, peony, sunflower, begonia, carnation, and iris. Once again my gaze moved around the room while I tried to connect the flowers to some other object. Or seven objects grouped together.

I tried the flowers' initials: R-D-P-S-B-C-I. Was it a code? Did it correspond to numbers, or names or—what?

Maybe the solution had to do with the colors of the flowers: red, yellow, pink, yellow, pink, red, and blue.

"I hate puzzles," I said out loud. And for just a brief moment I let my mind wander, once again, to Derek. Was he having fun? How was his team doing? Were they collaborating and working together? Or just feeling frustrated and freaked out? And what about Lark? Was she participating? Were her teammates ready to kill her? Oh God, was she on Derek's team? Ugh. Would she still have a job on Monday? Was it wrong of me to hope not?

I shook off those thoughts and forced myself to return to my flower puzzle. Checking the digital clock, I noted that we had twelve minutes to go before the zombies would break in and eat our brains.

"Okay," I murmured. "Seven flowers, so find something with seven . . . somethings."

"I unlocked the desk drawer!" Alex shouted suddenly.

I clapped my hands. "Good girl."

"We're getting there," Wallace said. "Keep going."

"Oh, for Pete's sake," Alex said in disgust. "The only thing in the top drawer are some jigsaw puzzle pieces."

"I'll be able to help you in a minute or two," I said.

"I can do it," she grumbled. "There's only twelve pieces. They're made of wood, like a kid's puzzle."

I smiled and turned back to my own conundrum. *I can do this*, I thought. Scanning the room again, I searched for anything connected with the number seven. And finally my brain clicked on the most glaringly obvious answer of all. For me anyway.

"The books," I whispered. "Idiot!"

In my defense, the bookshelf was filled with all sorts of books. But only seven were matching, beautifully bound editions. The others were all cloth or paper. I'd noticed the leather-bound books earlier, but somehow I'd skipped right past them.

All of the seven were horror stories, naturally, and they ran the gamut from the 1800s to the current day. None of them were about zombies, though, unless you counted the one about the undead pets.

And not only were there seven books, but their titles began with the same letters that the flowers did. So just in case I'd had any worries that this was the connection I'd been looking for, those doubts were erased.

I quickly rearranged the seven books according to the order of flowers on the page. *Rose, daisy, peony, sunflower, begonia, carnation, iris*, I reminded myself. The books were now arranged according to the first letter of each flower: *Rosemary's Baby, Dracula, Pet Sematary, Silence of the Lambs, Blood Meridian, Carrie, It.*

Okay, that was brilliant. So now what? I wondered.

Staring at the spine of each book, it was again obvious. Each book was numbered.

"Of course they're numbered," I groaned. These seven had been culled from a larger set of books. And I knew that because I'd already checked the title pages of the first two. Because that was who I was. A book nerd.

They were part of a collection published in the nineties known as the Great Classics of Horror.

The order of the numbers gilded onto the spines was: 29-10-24-32-5-8-19.

"I got it!" I shouted, but then had to admit, "Sort of. Not sure where to go from here."

"That's okay," Wallace said. "I think I've figured out something as well. There's only one card missing in this deck. It's the king of diamonds."

"Okay, as soon as I finish this, I'll help you look for a diamond."

"Or a king," Wallace mumbled, scratching his forehead. "Hold on now. I thought I saw something . . ." A few seconds later he pulled an old magazine out of the rack, one that featured Martin Luther King Jr. on the cover. When he opened it up to the story, he found a piece of paper.

"It just says, 'TICK-TOCK,'" he muttered. "That's got to refer to the clock, doesn't it? But what about the diamond?"

"Oh. I know this one." Alex rummaged through the keys, found the one she wanted, and handed it to him. "I saw it earlier. It's got a big jewel on the bow."

"'Diamond Keys,' it says," Wallace said, examining it. "Brilliant!" He pulled the broken clock from the shelf and used the key to open up the back. "There's something inside."

I grinned. "Of course there is."

Tucked inside was a piece of cloth. He pulled it out and unfolded it. Wearing a silly grin, he held it up for both of us to see. "It's the formula for the antidote."

"Fantastic," Alex cried. "Now we just need to find the key that will get us out of here."

"I think it's connected to the numbers on these seven books." I stared at the numbers again and explained briefly.

"It's going to be a combination lock," Wallace guessed.

"There's a dozen combination locks around the room," I said. "What about—"

"Okay, wait," Alex said, interrupting my train of thought. "This might be connected, too, but I need some help. It's the jigsaw puzzle."

Wallace and I hurried over to the desk and stared at the puzzle. It was a cute photograph of a duck with its head in the water. All we could see was its tail feathers sticking out of the water.

"All I can think of is, duck tails," Alex said.

"How about, bottoms up?" Wallace said, grinning.

"Oh. Okay, yes," Alex said, then frowned. "But which bottom?"

We all stared at each other, eyes glazing over. We had barely five minutes to escape the zombies, who continued to pound and scream relentlessly outside the door.

"The bottom of one of the shoes?" Wallace suggested. "Perhaps there's a loose heel."

"Or the bottom drawer of the desk?" I said.

Alex gave her head a light slap and grumbled, "I would've checked there eventually." While Wallace rummaged through the shoes, Alex began to try every key left on the desk. The fourth one worked and she yanked the bottom drawer open.

"Eureka!" she said. Flashing a radiant smile, she lifted a small lockbox from the drawer. "It's got a combination lock."

"I'm going to bet that's the one we need," Wallace said, abandoning the shoes.

I stared at the simple combination lock that reminded me of my locker in high school. "This only takes three numbers and I've got seven."

Alex rolled her eyes and glanced up at the digital clock. "Great. We've got about three minutes."

I took a deep breath, stared at the numbers on the book spines, and prayed I'd arranged them in the right order. "Okay, I'll just start guessing. Twenty-nine, ten, twenty-four."

She spun the wheel back and forth on the lock. "Ooh. Twenty-nine sounded like it clicked in, but the others didn't."

"Okay, then try twenty-nine, thirty-two, nineteen. That's every second number."

"Nope."

"Try them backward," Wallace suggested.

"Good idea. Nineteen, thirty-two, twenty-nine."

The lock clicked open.

"Yes! Yes!" Alex pulled off the lock, lifted the top of the lockbox, and pulled out an old, heavy, medieval-looking key.

"No way is that going to open the door," I said, feeling a giant wave of disappointment.

"But it should open the hope chest," Wallace said, his eyes glittering.

"Let's all join hands and pray," I muttered.

Alex snorted as she slipped the key into the big keyhole. The lock snapped open. As Alex unhooked the buckle, I felt a sudden flash of fear that we were going to find a dead body inside the chest. It would be curled into a fetal position, left there for me to find. Because for some reason, the universe insisted on sending dead bodies my way. Guru Bob had a theory that those lost souls knew that my sense of justice wouldn't allow their murders to go unanswered. I got it, sort of, but I still didn't like it.

But when Alex opened the chest, it was empty except for yet another key, all by itself at the bottom. A regular, modern-looking key.

"Oh, hallelujah," I whispered, letting go of the breath I'd been holding.

Alex threw her arms up and wiggled her hips in triumph. "Yee-haw!"

"Before we celebrate, let's make sure it fits the door."

Alex grabbed it and dashed to the door. "It fits," she cried. "We're out of here."

Wallace snatched up the cloth. "We need to bring the formula to Igor."

We ran out the door and up the wide hall to the theater lobby. Wallace handed the formula to Igor and he congratulated all of us. I was beyond exhilarated. It was as if I'd run a hundred-mile marathon. My heart was racing and I couldn't believe I'd survived. Colors were brighter, sounds were louder. I had to breathe slowly to get my system back into gear.

"Can you believe it?" Alex said, grabbing my arms and jumping up and down.

After we'd calmed down, I said, "Good grief, that was grueling."

"Let's do another one!" Alex cried.

I frowned at her. "You're out of your mind."

"Maybe." She did her wiggly happy dance again. "Woohoo! We escaped!"

Wallace came over, and the three of us grabbed each other in a hug. We drew back, laughing. "It's like we survived a flood or something."

"Or something," I said.

"There you are," Corinne said, giving Wallace a light pat on the back. "I was wondering where you disappeared to." She glanced at me and Alex, then studied Wallace's expression. "You played the game again."

"The *game*?" he repeated dramatically. "That was no game. We outwitted a deadly pack of zombies and escaped within an inch of our lives."

She laughed and rested her head on his arm. "Oh, Wally. You're such a noodle."

He closed his eyes and kissed her forehead. When he opened his eyes, he smiled at Alex and me.

It was sweet, I thought. They were so comfortable with each other and still in love after so many years. I could understand, because Corinne was amazing in a hundred different ways. And I was half in love with Wallace Sterling myself.

I wanted that with Derek, I thought. I wanted us to look at each other that way after thirty or forty years together. It was a combination of love and comfort and kindness. I realized that my own parents had that as well. So did Derek's. Maybe it was in the blood. I hoped so.

I wiggled my eyebrows at Corinne and whispered, "How was Lark?"

She glanced around. "I shouldn't talk about it here. Give me a call this week."

"Okay." But I wasn't quite ready to finish gossiping. "I guess she left pretty quickly."

Corinne rolled her eyes in disgust. "She had nothing to say to any of us, just walked away. But I noticed she stopped and talked to that cute salesclerk for ten minutes." She waved her hand in the direction of Tinker, who was alone now.

"He is cute," I said, smiling.

"Yes, he is," she admitted. "But Lark is nothing but a cheap flirt."

"Sweetie," Wallace said, a little shocked.

"I'm sorry, but I'm on my last nerve with that woman."

Wallace gave her shoulders a squeeze. "You need a change of scenery. Let's find Reggie and go see the submarine."

"I might need a beverage first," she said.

"Right there with you," I said. And gazing across the room at Derek, I saw that the rest of his people were starting to leave. Some had broken up into small groups and were chatting happily. I was glad to see it. But more than anything else, I was just relieved that Lark had already left. It made sense. Why would she hang around and pretend to be friendly?

The thought of her being a part of this great group of people really irked me. The sooner Derek got rid of her, the better off everyone would be. Especially Derek. And Corinne. And yeah, me.

On impulse, I turned and grabbed Alex in a big hug. "Thanks for being my friend."

"Back at you, sweetie," she said.

"Did we have fun?" I asked.

She thought for a moment. "I'm not going to say it was fun, per se. But I do feel like I triumphed over adversity and that's a good feeling, no matter what."

"Zombies," I said, grinning. "We triumphed over zombies."

She laughed. "Right. How could I forget?"

"I think this is something we'll enjoy a lot more in retrospect."

"Oh yeah," she agreed. "Especially after we've had a glass or two of wine."

I nodded cheerfully. "Now you're talking." I scanned the cavernous space for Derek and saw him deep in conversation with a couple of his partners. I couldn't gauge his mood from this distance. He wasn't smiling, but he didn't look thunderous. I couldn't wait to get out of here and get debriefed. Over that glass of wine.

"Hey, Brooklyn."

I whipped around and saw Tinker heading toward us. "Hi, Tinker. I saw you earlier, but you were busy."

"Yeah. I'm not at my usual position today. The assistant manager is out sick so I'm filling in for her."

"Assistant manager? Cool."

"I guess." He glanced from me to Alex.

"Oh, sorry," I said. "This is my friend Alex Monroe, and . . ." I frowned at Tinker. "I never asked. What is your real name?"

He grinned. "It's Teddy, but around here everyone calls me Tinker."

"Teddy's a nice name." I completed the introductions and Alex shook his hand.

"Good to meet you, Teddy," she said. "Unless you'd prefer I call you Tinker."

"Umm." Tinker blinked rapidly as if he'd been staring at the sun for too long. "Uh, either. Whatever. I mean, yeah. Call me Teddy. Nice to meet you, too." He pulled his glasses off and wiped them with the tail of his shirt. Putting them back on, he focused on Alex as if he hadn't been sure his first impressions of the woman were real.

I bit back a smile. Alex was gorgeous, tall, and supermodel slim with lustrous black hair and a beautiful smile. No wonder young Teddy was gobsmacked.

"What do you do as assistant manager?" I asked, trying to bring him back down to earth.

"Oh." He blew out a breath. "Well, basically I do everything that needs to be done. I talk to irate customers, try to calm them down. And I approve checks, you know, and give advice on the different products, and well, a little bit of everything." He grinned and his smile held a hint of pride.

"Do you ever do the escape rooms?" I asked.

His smile grew. "I've done them all, a couple of times."

"We just did the Zombie room."

"That's one of my favorites. You need real brainpower for that one. Did you escape in time?"

"Barely," Alex said. "But we made it."

"Good job."

"Tinker is writing a book," I explained to Alex. "A spy thriller, right?"

"Yeah."

"He's part of a writing group that meets in the café a few times a week."

Alex nodded, impressed. "You can certainly get a lot of research done in here. Lots of great spy stuff to play with."

"For sure. Owen lets me try out everything new that comes in. I take it home and figure out how it works. That way, I'm able to recommend the best stuff for our customers."

"That's good to know," Alex said. "I'm interested in beefing up my home security, so I'll come see you next week."

His eyes grew bright with pleasure and he nodded eagerly. "Yes. Yes, I can help with anything you want."

"I'm sure you can," she said with a smile. "Thanks, Teddy."

"You're welcome." His glasses had slipped, so he shoved them up to the bridge of his nose. "See you next week."

"Yes, you will."

"See you later, Teddy," I said with a wave.

"He's adorable," Alex said as soon as Teddy had reached the other side of the store.

"Pretty sure he thinks the same of you."

"Pretty sure I'm twice his age," she drawled, flashing a smile.

"Oh, please," I said. "No more than one and a half."

She smacked me on the arm, then laughed. "But he is sweet. And I'll bet he's equally impressed with you."

I made a face and waved her words away. "Anyway, you should meet the others in his writers' group. They're all great kids."

"Kids?" she repeated.

I shrugged. "They seem so young and innocent."

"Yeah, I get that," she said. "Maybe I'll run into them when I come back during the week."

"Okay, but just a warning," I said. "If they find out you used to work in covert ops, they'll faint in their chairs. And when they come to, they'll want to interview you."

I glanced across the room and caught Derek's gaze. He pointed to his wristwatch, signaling that he would be a few more minutes. "Looks like Derek isn't quite ready to go. Do you want to grab a latte in the café? Or would you rather browse?"

"I'm up for a cup of tea," she said, her forehead furrowed in thought. "And we'll have a few minutes to gossip about Lark."

Over coffee and tea, Alex and I somehow managed to avoid talking about Lark at all. Derek finally joined us, and on our way out, we waved at Tinker and Owen, who were deep in conversation over in the Counterespionage department. Leaving the store, we crossed the street and walked into the Buena Vista.

"I've been dreaming of their Dungeness Crab Melt ever since we got back from Paris," I confessed. "And I think we deserve an Irish coffee after fighting off zombies for the last hour."

"I've never had the crab melt," Alex said. "Is it good?"

I smiled and closed my eyes. "It's heavenly."

"Everything here is good if you're in the mood for comfort food," Derek added.

"Always," Alex said with a grin.

We gave our name to the hostess and were told it would be a twenty-minute wait for a table. Miraculously Derek was able to snag two stools at the bar, so Alex and I sat down and Derek stood behind me. Since this was the Buena Vista, the so-called birthplace of Irish coffee, we all ordered one.

Less than three minutes later, the bartender handed us our drinks. Alex and I swirled our stools around to take in the view through the huge bay windows. We watched tourists stroll past with their shopping bags while cable cars chugged up and down the steep hill. The brisk wind caused whitecaps to form in the sparkling blue water that stretched for miles before meeting the rugged hills and canyons of Marin County. I'd always thought it was interesting that the bartenders who worked here had the best view in town. Gazing out the window, I wondered who would want to work anywhere else.

Alex asked Derek about his escape room experience, and he told us about the Slaughterhouse. "We had to escape the bloody butcher," he said. "It was nip and tuck for a while."

I moaned. "Really? Nip and tuck?"

"Oh, that's bad," Alex said, laughing. Then she and I told Derek all about the zombies.

"I'm glad you had Wallace with you," he said. "Corinne was a bit concerned that he would be bored with waiting, especially since their son was completely wrapped up in the virtual reality experience."

"Wallace was great." Alex sipped her Irish coffee. "So let's hear about your team-building exercise."

"And by *team-building exercise*," I said quickly, "she means *Lark*. So what happened?"

"Yes," Alex said. "How did she handle it?"

I gazed up at Derek. "I hope you don't mind that I told Alex a little about her."

"No, of course not," he said, but his teeth clenched a little at the sound of Lark's name.

"So whose team was she on?" I asked. "Did everyone get along? Did she participate at all? Is she ready to quit yet?" *Please, God*, I added silently.

He tried not to scowl, but I could tell he was still irritated about the woman.

"Sorry," I said. "We don't have to talk about it right now."

"No, I don't mind talking about it. It's just . . . quite annoying. I don't enjoy working like this." He shook his head and took a sip of his drink. "She was a disaster."

"Oh dear," I said.

"She was on Corinne's team," he added.

My mouth opened in surprise, then nodded in realization. "Corinne set that up on purpose."

"Yes," Derek said. "I had no idea she'd arranged it until today. She explained it to me afterward, told me she'd made the decision while she was picking names for each team. She realized that one of us would need to monitor Lark's behavior and actions during the exercise."

"So she put herself in the line of fire." I shook my head. "Poor Corinne."

"But better Corinne than you," Alex said to Derek.

"Selfish of me to say it," Derek said, "but I agree. I wouldn't have been as kind to the woman as Corinne was."

"So what did Corinne tell you? What happened?"

"I think we need more drinks first." He ordered another round of Irish coffees and was silent until they were delivered and he'd taken a long sip.

"That bad, huh?" I said.

He gave a short, rueful laugh. "Lark didn't do one damn thing to help the others. She brought a nail file and sat and worked on her nails while everyone else kicked their butts to escape before the hour was up."

"That can't be true," I whispered.

"You've got to be kidding," Alex said.

"No."

"Wow," Alex marveled. "She really is shameless."

"She's taunting all of you," I said, my anger growing with every second. "Daring you to fire her. She wants that big payoff her lawyer threatened to get her."

"You're right, darling, and I'm not going to let her have it." I rarely saw Derek this annoyed. "Of course, that means she'll probably be around for a little while longer."

"Ugh," I said.

"Don't worry," he said, patting my knee. "I'll take care of it."

"I know you will," I said quietly.

He glanced at Alex, gave her a half smile. "I've faced down thugs on the streets of Marseilles who were easier to deal with than this woman."

"That's because you knew you could kill them," I muttered, then happened to look up and notice their faces. And gulped. "Not that I want you to kill Lark. Or for anyone else to kill her. Cancel, cancel, cancel."

He laughed and wrapped his arms around me.

I had seen too much real-life murder to make light of it. Even in relation to a woman as awful as Lark. So, no, I didn't wish her dead. But I wished her gone. In a nonviolent, non-take-Derek's-money kind of way.

I pressed my lips together in frustration. "I wouldn't be sorry if she disappeared from our lives forever."

He kissed my temple. "I love you."

I rested my head on his muscular arm. "I love you, too. And I promise not to kill her, even though, you know, I'd like to."

"Yes, I know. Thank you for cheering me up."

I shrugged, then smiled. "That's my job."

"I have something to say," Alex said. She took a quick last sip of her drink and glanced around to make sure we weren't being overheard. Then she leaned in close to Derek and spoke quietly. "You've got to fire her, Derek. You didn't see the way she was looking at Brooklyn earlier."

Derek's eyes chilled instantly. "What happened? What did she say?"

"She didn't say a word," Alex said. "She didn't have to. If looks could kill, Brooklyn would be dead. The woman has evil intentions, and I don't say that lightly."

The words carried weight coming from Alex. She had battled her own enemies as a covert operative, president of her own company, and a black belt in any number of martial arts disciplines. She knew what evil looked like.

"I was already planning to have another chat with Bart on Monday," Derek said evenly. "But I've changed my mind."

"But—"

He held up his hand. "I'll talk to him this afternoon."

I mentally said a prayer of thanks.

"I'm sure you have a stable of highly competent lawyers," Alex said. "But I happen to have the world's best employment and labor attorney if you need her."

"I'll take her name."

I finished my drink and set it on the bar, then stood and took hold of Derek's arms. "Let's not talk about this anymore because it'll spoil your appetite. And mine," I added quickly, because there was no way I was passing up that crab melt.

Derek rested his forehead against mine. "Agreed."

As the hostess arrived to take us to our table, I shot

Alex a grateful look. "Thank you for saying that. You rock."

She sidled up next to me. "Hey, it's you and me against the zombies, kiddo."

Two nights later, Derek's cell phone buzzed on his nightstand. It rang twice before he tossed back the covers and grabbed the phone.

"Stone," he said, his voice husky from sleep.

I dragged myself out of a dream and struggled to sit up and check the clock radio. It was three o'clock in the morning, for God's sake. Nothing good happened at three o'clock in the morning. Was there an accident? Was someone in the hospital?

Derek shook his head to rid himself of the fog of sleep. "Say that again."

"Who is it?" I whispered loudly.

He didn't answer. His expression grew hard as he listened, uttered an angry epithet, then said, "All right, Owen. I'll be there in twenty minutes."

Owen? Okay, I hadn't expected that.

As Derek ended the call, I jumped out of bed and slipped into yoga pants, threw on a heavy shirt, and grabbed my windbreaker. Something had to be very wrong for Owen to call Derek at this hour of the night— or morning. "I'm going with you."

"Brooklyn, no," Derek said, tugging on a pair of worn jeans. "You stay here and get some sleep."

"That's not going to happen."

He shook his head as he pulled on a thick sweater. "I didn't think so."

"Is Owen hurt?" I asked, tugging on my running shoes.

"Not physically. But apparently someone broke into SPECTRE."

I gasped and clutched his arm. "The book!"

"That was my first thought, too." He moved fast, grabbing his wallet and keys. "Let's go."

Chapter 7

We made the trip across town in fifteen minutes by taking Brannan straight down to the Embarcadero. As we pulled into the empty parking garage across the street from Pier 39 and stepped out of the car, the darkness enveloped us completely. I felt nothing but chills, and Derek must have seen me shivering because he grabbed my hand. "Come on," he said, and we ran across the darkened street to Owen's shop.

A black-and-white police car was parked at an awkward angle in the No Parking zone in front of the pier. Of course, they could have been called to check out any of the shops or restaurants within the massive tourist attraction, but I was pretty sure they were here because of Owen. Or had a silent alarm alerted them?

As we dashed into the store, I prayed that nothing important had been stolen. Namely, *The Spy Who Loved Me*.

It was a selfish thought, but I couldn't help it. Derek and I hadn't owned the book very long, but I'd already attached a great deal of sentimental value to it. After all, I had found it in Paris during our honeymoon and had bought it for my beloved husband. That made it extra special, and it would break my heart if it was stolen.

Obviously, there were a lot of lucrative items in the store for a thief to steal. Expensive electronics, high-end countersurveillance equipment, exotic weapons, costly cameras. But why would Owen have thought to call Derek if the break-in didn't have something to do with the book?

I should've been counting my blessings that theft was our biggest concern. I'd dealt with worse before. A lot worse. At least tonight, no one had been murdered. Another shiver skated up my spine at the thought, and I felt my hair stand on end.

Owen waved at us from a section near the back, where the most expensive high-tech products were sold. He broke away from the two police officers and scurried forward to meet us, and I tried to brace myself for the inevitable bad news that the book had been stolen. He wore khakis and a windbreaker and his hair was still rumpled from sleep.

We walked quickly toward him, passing a dozen different display counters of various spy gadgets, hidden cameras, and surveillance equipment. Everything looked normal; nothing seemed to be disturbed. Naturally, my worries multiplied. If they hadn't broken in for the sophisticated tech stuff, then it had to be about the book. That was how my mind worked anyway.

"Derek, Brooklyn, thank you so much for coming."

"Owen, are you all right?" I asked, touching his arm in concern.

He waved off my distress. "I'm fine, fine. I wasn't even here." He pounded his fist into his palm, grimacing. "But I wish I had been. I might've prevented this from happening."

"Or you might've been hurt," Derek said flatly.

"Don't blame yourself, Owen," I insisted. "You can always replace merchandise, but not yourself."

"I know, I know. You're both right. But this is intolerable. I feel so helpless." He glanced back at the cops, one of whom had a clipboard and was filling out a form of some kind. Then he edged closer to us. "The police arrived immediately, but I wanted someone with a higher level of security experience to be here. That's why I called you, Derek. I hope you don't mind. I would be very grateful if you'd have a closer look around."

"Have you noticed anything missing or out of place?" Derek asked.

"Honestly, no. But I haven't had a chance to check everywhere." He wiped his forehead. "I'm still a bit frazzled. The alarm woke me up out of a sound sleep, and I drove like a maniac to get here and meet the cops."

We knew the feeling, I thought, but didn't say anything.

"We'll look with you," Derek said calmly. "As soon as you're ready."

There was no way I could wait until Owen announced that he was ready. I needed to see the damage done in the bookshop. I squeezed Derek's arm. "I'm going to go check on . . . you know."

He put his hand over mine and nodded in sympathy. "Yes, love. Go do that now. I'll be there in just a moment. I want to have a word with the police."

My insides were already twisting into knots, and the closer I came to the book display, the worse it got. It wasn't life and death, and I knew I could face the truth, but that didn't mean I wouldn't suffer. For someone like me, losing a book was like being smacked in the head. It was physically painful. I hated the thought that it might be gone, that it might've been stolen by some thief.

I rounded the last shelf and almost collapsed in relief.

"Oh, thank goodness." I stared at the book, still on its bookstand inside the glass display case, undisturbed. It managed to look dignified while embellished by that oddly festive and surreal mix of deadly weapons and confetti.

I absently rubbed my stomach and felt my shoulder muscles relax, then took some deep breaths just to get my wits back into line. I'd been so worried and had been expecting such a negative outcome that I now felt wrung out and exhausted.

I leaned back against the nearest bookshelf. That was when the guilt slithered in and I had to ask myself if I was a terrible person for being so single-minded. For caring only about my book and not about anything else. Where was my humanity? Why did I worry so much about an inanimate object like a book when someone could've been hurt?

But no one had been hurt. And guilt was a stupid reaction, darn it. So I brushed it away with one ruthless swipe, then glanced around, searching for Derek. I spied him halfway across the wide space, talking to Owen and the two police officers. He looked up and saw me watching him, so he broke away and joined me.

"The book is safe," I said, gesturing toward the display case.

"I'm very glad." He wrapped his arm around my shoulder and gave me a warm squeeze.

"Me, too."

Owen was walking with the police toward the front door, so we waited until he was finished with them and made his way back to us.

"They're not leaving, are they?" Derek asked.

"Just for the moment," Owen said. "They're going out to the pier to see if any other stores were broken into. They'll be back later and they're going to want me to give them a list of whatever was stolen."

"Shall we look around then?" Derek asked quietly.

"Yes," Owen said, although he seemed distracted. "Yes, indeed. Thank you, Derek. We must see if anything's been stolen."

"Then let's get started. Brooklyn and I are here to help." Again, Derek's voice was softly casual, almost deferential, as though he didn't want to upset Owen. And wasn't that odd? Was Derek worried that his old friend was on the verge of a breakdown or something? I knew my husband and I recognized that something was going on here, below the surface. I knew Owen had been a government agent like Derek and his friend Ned. And now he owned a *spy* shop, so he must have had some experience in the field. Didn't those covert ops jobs take a lot of intestinal fortitude? I mean, it could get scary out there.

On the other hand, I thought back to our first conversation with Ned Davies in Paris. Ned had suggested that Derek stop by the shop and give Owen some pointers, and the two men had chuckled about it. So maybe Owen wasn't quite as hardened as I had expected someone in his line of work would be. Maybe he'd worked at a desk his whole life.

I gave a mental shrug. I would have to ask Derek about it, but meanwhile, I wanted to get this show on the road, as my father would say. It was the middle of the night and we had work to do.

Owen shoved his hands into his pockets. "It's very strange, Derek. The police told me that the main alarm system hadn't been breached."

"That is strange," Derek mused.

I frowned at them both. "Then why did the police show up? How did they know the store was broken into?"

Owen gestured toward the back of the store. "The double doors leading into the escape room lobby were breached. That set off a separate silent alarm. That's the one the police were responding to."

"So someone was definitely inside the store," Derek reasoned.

"Yes." Owen sighed. He sounded completely exhausted as he raked his fingers through his short-cropped hair. "We really must go through everything."

"We can get a good start on it," Derek said, trying to coax the older man into action.

"But wait." I stared at the double doors in the back. "I don't understand. Once someone steps through the double doors into the store itself, wouldn't the main alarm system be activated, too?"

"Ordinarily, yes," Owen murmured, then gritted his teeth. "The problem is, the main alarm wasn't turned on."

I took a step closer, unsure if I'd heard him correctly. "What did you say?"

"The police checked for me," he said more clearly. "They said that the main alarm wasn't activated." He

shook his head. "But I swear, it was. I turned it on myself. Someone must've shut it off after I left for the
evening."

"Who closed up the store tonight?" Derek asked.

"I did." Owen looked miserable.

"You were the last one to leave?"

"Yes. I punched in the alarm code before I left." His
features were grim. "I never forget. This place is everything to me. I don't take chances."

"Who would've shut it off?" Derek asked, his voice
rising. "Who else has the security code for the alarm?"

He sighed. "Several of the senior clerks, my assistant
manager, the café manager, my accountant."

Derek and I exchanged looks. It must have been one
of those people. But why would any of them break in?
I suppose the answer was obvious: to steal stuff.

"Maybe one of your senior staff forgot something
and came back to the store." I splayed my hands as I
warmed up to the idea. "Maybe they deactivated the
alarm and forgot to reset it when they left."

"It's possible," Owen nodded slowly. "In fact, that
very thing has occurred before. But the person remembered and called to let me know what was happening."

"Okay, so let's say one of your people deactivated
the main alarm," I said, working through another sce-
nario out loud. "But they didn't bother with the secondary alarm. The one for the escape rooms. Because
they didn't need to go back there?"

"It's not that they didn't bother," Owen corrected.
"It's that they don't know about the secondary alarm."

"Wait." Derek's eyes narrowed as he tried to get the
story straight. "Your senior staff members don't know
that you have another alarm on those doors?"

"I never thought it necessary to tell them. None of them go through those doors except Igor."

"Does Igor have access to the secondary security code?"

"Yes, of course. Igor has been with me since my early days at the agency. I trust him with my life."

Curiouser and curiouser, I thought, but was still too baffled to conclude anything. Except I had to wonder. Igor the creepy toothless Game Master had worked for the CIA? Huh?

Derek gazed up at the industrial ventilation as he worked through the problem. "So someone deactivated the main alarm and walked into the store without any resistance."

Owen spread his arms. "That's what I'm saying."

"But then they walked into the escape room lobby, and that's when they set off the alarm that notified the police of the break-in."

"I believe that's what happened," Owen said. "At least, that's the theory I'm going with until further evidence is uncovered."

"Owen, why do you have two separate alarm systems?" I asked.

"It's a bit confusing, I suppose," he admitted. "But the escape room area used to be a separate store. When they lost their lease, we took over that space to build the escape rooms. A good thing, because they have become very popular."

"I believe it."

"So the neighbors' alarm system was under warranty and they still had two years to go on their contract." He shrugged. "It was basically free. And since the escape rooms are a completely different area from the store, I thought it made sense to keep that system running until the contract is up."

I glanced at Derek, whose shoulders lifted in a slight shrug. It still didn't make a lot of sense, but it worked for Owen.

Derek scanned the large open space and I followed his gaze, checking out each of the different departments. From where we stood, everything looked perfectly tidy and undamaged. There were no smashed glass displays, no shelves emptied of the products that lined them. No mess, no fuss.

"Owen," I said. "Is there someone on your staff you can call to come and help you figure out if anything's been stolen? They'll have a better idea of your inventory than we will."

He blinked as if I had awakened him from a dream. Shaking his head, he said, "That's an excellent idea. I don't know why I didn't think of it myself, but the break-in really threw me off. I'll call Tinker and Tailor. They both live within a few blocks, so they can be here in ten or fifteen minutes."

"Good," Derek said. "We can stay and help, but you'll feel better having some of your own people here."

"Of course." He pulled out his cell phone. "I hate to wake them up. But here goes." He punched in some numbers and ambled over to the bookshop area to talk to the two young writers.

I figured it would be rude to remind him that he had awakened Derek and me from a sound sleep just an hour ago. But maybe once Tinker and Tailor arrived, Derek and I could go home. Or maybe not. Owen had specifically requested that Derek help with the security breaches, so chances were good that we wouldn't be going anywhere for a while.

I glanced at Derek and saw him staring up at the ceiling, checking the locations of each of the video surveillance cameras. He wandered over to the front of the store, into the café and bookshop, and then back to Owen and me.

"I count ten cameras altogether," Derek said. "Is that about right?"

"Yes. We've got them in each corner of the store, one in the café and one over the bookshop. And we've got the three larger dome cameras running down the center of the room."

Derek nodded. "Yes, I counted them."

"And there are three more in the escape room lobby and hallway. So thirteen altogether."

"What about the escape rooms themselves?" Derek asked.

Owen shook his head. "We've never installed cameras inside the rooms. It seemed invasive."

I would've thought an escape room would be the perfect place for a camera, but what did I know?

"I suppose," Derek murmured. "Is there a place we can review the security videos? We'll be able to get a better idea of exactly who or what set off the alarm."

"Yes, I have monitors in my office. We can go and watch right now. We're in luck because I just recently upgraded the system and the quality is quite good. We should definitely be able to figure out what happened."

It was a good thing, I thought, since he had promised that his security was top grade. It was the main reason

Derek and I had allowed him to display the book in the first place.

"Were you able to reach Tinker and Tailor?" I asked.

"Oh yes, forgot to tell you." His smile was sheepish. "This break-in has turned my brain to mush. But yes, Tinker's on his way. Tailor didn't answer his phone. I'll call him again in a few minutes."

I really enjoyed hanging out at SPECTRE, but we had been there for almost an hour and done very little to find answers. Maybe if we could get some coffee brewing in the café, I would feel a little perkier. I hated to bring it up to Owen because I had a feeling he wouldn't know the first thing about making coffee in those big industrial-sized coffee urns. Maybe when Tinker got here, he could do it.

"Shouldn't we search the escape rooms?" I said.

"Yes," Derek said. "Right after we view the video."

Owen pointed toward the bookshop. "Let me show you the way to my office."

"Thanks," Derek said, patting his old friend on the back.

"Oh, here's Tinker," Owen said, brightening.

Tinker walked into the store, glanced around, then jogged over to join us.

"Thank you for coming in, Tinker," Owen said. "I'm sorry I had to wake you up."

"No biggie," he said, pushing his glasses up in front of his eyes. His blond hair was tousled from sleep and his sweatshirt was inside out. He didn't seem to notice or care. "What happened?"

"We're not sure," Owen admitted. "The alarm was tripped and the police were here, but I have no idea if anything was taken or not."

Tinker glanced from Derek to me and then back to Owen. "So you want me to check the shelves and the storeroom, see what's missing?"

"If you would," Owen said, clearly relieved. "I've tried to call Tailor to come and help, but he's not answering his phone."

"He must really be snoozing," Tinker said with a grin. "His phone is always in his hand, no matter what."

"I'll try him again in a few minutes."

"We're going to go look at the surveillance tapes," Derek said.

"Okay," Tinker said amiably. "I'll get started in the storeroom."

Owen led the way through the café to his office, which was tucked behind the wall of the bookshop. He powered up his computer and signed on to the security site.

"Here we go," said Owen. "You two should stand over here so you can see the screen."

Derek and I walked around his desk and stood behind him and stared at the picture that filled the computer screen. It showed the front door of the store.

"Here we are," he said.

"The alarm went off at around two fifteen this morning," Derek said. "Can you rewind back to that point on the video?"

"Yes."

He clicked on the back arrow and the picture went away for a minute. Then it came back, looking exactly the same as it had before. But now the digital clock in the corner of the screen showed an earlier time.

"Yes," Derek said. "Start it rolling right there. If you want to speed it up slightly, that would be helpful."

"Yes, of course," Owen murmured, then pointed out a few things. "There are thirteen cameras, counting the ones in the escape room lobby. You can see their pictures all lined up here." He moved his cursor to the top of the screen, where thirteen little squares of video were lined up in a row.

"So we can watch them all at once," I said.

"Exactly," Owen said with a smile. "And you can click on any one of them to enlarge that picture."

He looked up at Derek. "You should sit here and do this. You're the expert."

"All right," Derek said. He wasn't about to say no.

The two men switched places and Derek began to move the cursor, causing the video to fast-forward, but it was slow enough that we could still see the moment when everything changed.

Derek clicked to freeze the video. "Here we go," he muttered.

I knelt down next to Derek's chair and leaned my elbows on the desk so I could get a better look at all the camera views at once.

We watched someone push the front door open and walk into the store as bold as day. The intruder was tall and thin with an athletic gait, but his face was completely hidden from view. He wore black from head to foot, including gloves and a black hooded sweatshirt. It was hard to say for sure, but it looked like he might've also been wearing a ski mask under the hood. He wasn't taking any chances on being identified. Also, he clearly knew where all of the cameras were situated because he ducked his head each time he came into the frame of the next one.

I was instantly transported back to the Paris side-

walk where I had seen another hooded man watching
Derek and Ned. Of course, this wasn't the same person,
but the memory had me rubbing the chills off my arms.

Derek stopped the video. "He walked right in. He
knows the alarm had been deactivated."

"Yes," Owen said, practically shaking with fury.

I pointed to the freeze-frame shot of the intruder
hiding his face from the lens. "Look at him. He knows
where each of the cameras is aimed."

Derek glanced up at Owen. "He's been in here before, probably more than once. He might even be on
your staff," he mused. "Knows too much to be a random burglar."

I felt so sorry for Owen. He looked miserable and
his face had turned pale.

Derek turned back to the video, and we all watched
as the hooded intruder took his time strolling by each
of the display cases in every department. He walked
behind the counters and pulled things off the shelves.
He reached under his sweatshirt and pulled out a shopping bag, unfolded it, and stuck a few small boxes of
merchandise inside. Then he spent a minute straight-
ening up the shelves so that everything was tidily arranged, and moved on.

No wonder Owen couldn't tell if any of his products
were missing. Everything had been organized so carefully by the neat-freak intruder, who would notice
something missing?

"Brazen," Owen whispered.

Derek continued to switch camera views to find the
best angle on the intruder. The hooded guy spent almost ten minutes browsing and occasionally slipping an

item into his bag before he turned and headed straight for the bookshop.

Every muscle in my body tensed as the hooded prowler walked up and down the shelves until he ended up right next to the central display case where *The Spy Who Loved Me* was enclosed in glass. Pulling a tool from his jeans pocket, the intruder moved closer to the glass.

"I can't see what he's doing," Owen griped.

"He's deliberately blocking the view. But you know he's going to break into the cabinet and steal the book." But he was going to fail, I thought, because the book was still there. So what in the world had happened? I would find out soon enough.

"He's holding a glass cutter." Derek said, and glanced over his shoulder. "Owen, do you recognize this person?"

"I can't get a clear look at him. Can't see his face."

I scowled. "I can't even tell if it's a man or a woman."

"I'm assuming it's a man," Owen admitted. "He's quite tall."

Derek asked, "How many of your employees are tall and thin like that?"

"Too many of them," he said glumly. "But I'll make a list."

All of a sudden, the hooded guy whipped around.

"What's going on?" I asked. "What's he looking at?"

"I don't know," Owen said. "There's no sound."

"I'll find a different angle and rewind a few seconds." Derek did it quickly and we watched a newcomer run across the space. "There's someone else in the store."

"Who is that?" Owen demanded.

"Can't see his face either," Derek muttered. He tried another camera angle, but the second guy kept moving.

I scowled. "His face is in shadow from that baseball cap he's wearing." He was also wearing baggy jeans and a long-sleeved T-shirt. I could make out a Giants logo on the front.

"Are they together?" Owen wondered.

"It looks like they're yelling at each other," I said, watching in dismay as an argument broke out. "See how the second guy is pointing and gesturing? He's angry."

All of a sudden the second guy stormed toward the guy wearing the hood. The hooded man pulled a gun from his waistband, aimed, and shot the second guy.

"Oh my God, oh my God," I shouted, and pushed up to a standing position. "He shot him."

"Good lord," Owen whispered. "Someone was shot in my store."

"But where is he?" I wondered. "Where did he go?"

"Perhaps the bullet just grazed him."

"I didn't notice any blood," I said.

"The carpeting is too dark," Derek murmured. "But if there's a drop of blood, a crime scene team will find it." Derek switched to the other camera, and we watched the injured person drag himself to the back of the store. Clutching his stomach, he yanked open the double doors and disappeared into the escape room lobby.

"The bullet didn't graze him," I said. "It looks like he was hit in the stomach."

"What the hell is going on?" Owen cried.

"He activated the secondary alarm when he opened

the double doors," Derek noted, pointing to the time code in the bottom of the video. "That was at two twenty-three a.m."

He switched back to the other view in time to see the gunman running after the injured guy. Derek continued to switch back and forth among the camera views to catch the shooter flinging open the double doors and dashing inside the lobby.

Derek froze the picture for a moment in order to switch over to the lobby cameras. He rewound the video in time for us to watch the injured guy stagger through the lobby to the hallway leading to the escape rooms. And then he disappeared.

"Can you tell which room he went into?" I asked.

"I can't." Owen shook his head. "Can you get a better angle, Derek?"

Derek rewound the picture and tried the other two lobby cameras, but none of us could tell which of the eight escape rooms the second guy had run into.

He rewound once again and let the video play. We watched the intruder sprint through the double doors and into the lobby. He whirled around, looking every which way for the injured person. Then he tore off down the hall toward the escape rooms, grabbed hold of the doorknob of the first room, and pulled. But he couldn't budge it.

"Only Igor and I have keys to the rooms," Owen murmured.

"But how did the injured guy get inside?" I asked. "He had to have a key."

Owen blew out a breath. "I have no idea."

Igor. Derek and I exchanged worried glances. Was

Igor the second person who entered the store? Was he injured and hiding in one of the escape rooms? Was he bleeding? We had to find him.

But in the back of my mind, I had to ask myself different questions: Was *Igor* the hooded shooter? Was he the one trying to steal my book? Had he just shot the other person?

Meanwhile, the hooded man tried three more doors before he got visibly disgusted and dashed back to the lobby and through the double doors. Back in the store, we watched him return to the bookshop. He wasn't strolling and taking his time now but was clearly bent on breaking into the display case. He grabbed the glass cutter tool.

Then his head jerked up.

"He's hearing police sirens," Derek guessed, looking at the digital time readout.

"Good," I said through clenched teeth. "Get away from my book, you jerk."

The intruder's body language showed how furious he was. He shook his fists and pounded on the nearest counter, then grabbed his bag of stolen goods, raced to the front door, and left the store. The camera was able to catch him darting to the right, where a walkway led to a set of wooden stairs that went down to the dock below.

"There's a dock under the pier that leads out to the street," Owen said.

"He's gone," Derek said.

"But the injured guy may still be in here somewhere," I said.

"Maybe he wasn't hit," Owen said, trying for a hopeful note. "Maybe he was able to sneak out before we got here."

Derek rewound the video to the spot where the hooded man shot at the guy. He switched to a different angle, and that's when we saw the second guy spin around from the impact of the bullet.

"Definitely hit him," Derek said. "Not sure where or how badly, but he got hit."

"He's got to be badly injured. We have to find him." I pulled out my phone. "I'll call the police."

"Good. Let's go." Derek pushed his chair back. "Bring your keys, Owen. We'll need to get into those rooms."

"Right." Owen pulled the desk drawer open and grabbed a set of keys. We raced to the back of the store and through the double doors. As we crossed the lobby, I got hold of the emergency operator, who assured me that the police were only minutes away.

Derek headed for the first escape room. "Owen, if you'll just start unlocking doors, I'll check each room as we go."

"Will do." Owen did as Derek instructed, unlocking the first door and moving to the next one.

Once the first door was unlocked, I grabbed the handle and opened it.

"Brooklyn, no!" Derek shouted, and grabbed my arm.

I halted, unnerved by his sudden command. "What?"

"Sorry, love." He gave my arm a hasty squeeze. "We're all a bit jumpy."

"I know I am," I admitted.

"Let me go in first. Please." Derek pulled his gun

from his waistband. "He's injured and he may be armed. He may be willing to do whatever it takes to escape."

After all this time I should've been used to seeing Derek with a gun. He'd used one when we were in Paris, barely two weeks ago. But it was always a shock to see him holding the weapon with such deadly intent, and now I was scared all over again for the reasons he had just mentioned.

"Just be careful," I whispered.

"I will."

He led the way into the room, and after a brief few seconds, I snuck in right behind him. We quickly searched every inch of the space, but there was no one in there.

"Derek," Owen cried. "Come look at this." He was standing at the fourth door down the hall. "There's blood."

We both ran over and saw the blood on the doorknob. It was smeared on the doorjamb, too, and on the wall next to the door. There was probably some on the floor, too, but again, the carpeting was dark enough to prevent us from seeing anything.

"He's in here," Derek murmured.

I saw the blood, too, and my stomach dipped and rolled. I really hated the sight of blood. You would've thought I'd have gotten used to it after all this time, but unfortunately I hadn't.

Derek pulled his handkerchief from his pocket and used it to turn the doorknob. "I'm obliterating some of the bloody fingerprints. But at this point we need to get inside and find the fellow."

"Right." Owen backed away as Derek opened the door.

"We're coming in," Derek shouted. "We don't want any trouble. We know you're injured. The police are on their way."

There was no response.

I stared up at Derek. "Should we wait for the cops to return?"

"I'm going in," Derek said.

I tried to shake away the paralyzing fear I felt. "Watch out, please."

"Of course." Then he called into the room again, "I know you're in there. I know you've been shot. We just want to get you to a hospital."

There was no response. Nothing. Not a sound.

Derek stepped inside the room, and I followed him into what had to be the creepiest, most bone-chilling escape room of them all.

The Cursed Kindergarten. Ugh.

I had chills on top of chills as we tiptoed around, looking for the injured intruder. I had to remind myself to breathe because I was so freaked out, I could barely think. The room was dark and dank and frightening. Something brushed against my pants leg and I jumped and shrieked. I glanced down and saw the cat, Miss Moneypenny, and almost collapsed in relief. It wasn't my finest moment, but I forgave myself. The cat strolled farther into the scary room, and I blew out a breath, then followed her.

A child-sized table and chairs stood in the middle of the room with old-fashioned toys scattered across the surface: a twisted and bent Slinky; a jack-in-the-box toy with a headless clown popping up; a set of pick-up sticks jammed into a primitive cloth doll, looking like some kind of voodoo sacrifice.

I took one look at the giant dollhouse in the corner and had to turn away. There were cobwebs hanging from the eaves, and old dolls were propped up and staring out the windows. Their eyes had been removed from their heads, making them lifeless zombie dolls.

Good grief.

Old lace curtains were draped across the windows. A skeleton was hanging on the wall next to a tiny baby's crib. A broken tricycle was stuck in the middle near a battered baby swing that held another creepy-looking doll.

Someday we would laugh about this, right?

"Brooklyn," Derek said. "Would you go out to the lobby and call the police?"

"The dispatcher said they would be here any minute." I watched Derek shove his gun back into his waistband, a good sign. "I'll run out to the pier and find them."

"No, love," he said quietly. "Call Inspector Lee."

I frowned. "Are you sure?" Did he really think we needed a homicide detective?

Homicide. Oh God.

"I'm sure," he said.

I tried to swallow but my throat was too tight and dry. My heart was beating too fast. I couldn't just walk out and leave Derek. Instead, I crossed the room and came up behind him to see what he had found.

It was the second man, the injured one. I could tell it was him from the bright orange long-sleeved Giants T-shirt he wore. He was on the floor, curled up next to the dollhouse.

Derek held his cell phone with the flashlight app aimed down, illuminating the face of the guy who'd been shot.

I gasped again and tears burned my eyes. "Oh no. Derek, no."

"Yes, love," he whispered, and grabbed my hand. "Let's go call Inspector Lee. We can't do anything for him now."

No, we couldn't do anything for Tailor. He was dead.

Chapter 8

Inspector Janice Lee walked into SPECTRE at five thirty looking more awake and refreshed than anyone had a right to look at that hour of the morning. Her straight black hair framed her pretty face and accentuated her flawless skin. She was Asian American, born and raised in San Francisco.

Normally she was almost as tall as I was. Today, though, she wore black high-heeled boots laced up to her knees, making her an inch or so taller and twice as intimidating. With her dark gray cashmere trench coat, matching gray sweater, and black skirt, she should've been walking the runway instead of investigating a murder.

I itched to touch that cashmere coat. The woman had ridiculously fabulous fashion sense.

"Amazing boots," I said.

She glanced down, nodded. "They're great for kicking ass."

I bit back a grin, since grinning wouldn't be appropriate at the scene of a murder. "It's good to see you."

"Yeah, you, too." She smirked. "I was hoping once you got married, you'd stop seeing dead people."

"I was hoping the same thing," I said, trying for lightness. "But that dream has died."

She shrugged. "Guess we'll have to accept that this is just your thing."

"Please bite your tongue," I said. "We both know it's not my thing."

She chuckled and pulled a small notebook and pen from her snazzy, compact leather cross-body purse. "So how are you, Brooklyn?"

I was momentarily distracted by the sound of her voice. Funny, I had forgotten how deep it was. I chalked it up to her having been a smoker once upon a time. She had quit several years ago and now she was hooked on those little sour lemon drops that came in fancy tins. Whatever got you through the night, I thought.

"I'm good," I said, remembering her question. "Except for, you know. This nightmare." I gestured toward the back room, where we'd found Tailor's lifeless body.

"Except for that," she said soberly, and looked around at the activity inside the store. "Give me the rundown. Who's the victim?"

"His nickname is Tailor. I don't actually know his real name." And wasn't that sad? "He's just a kid, Janice. Midtwenties, but a kid. He hangs out here a lot and he also works here part-time."

"The officers have secured the scene, so I'll see him in a minute." She nudged her chin. "Who are these people?"

I followed her gaze. "The older guy talking to Derek is Owen Gibbons. He's the owner of the store. He and Derek knew each other years ago." I pointed toward the café. "Those three are friends of the victim. One of them works here, too."

"Which one?"

"The cute blond guy wearing glasses. He works in the Countersurveillance department. Over there." I pointed to the area along the wall in the center of the store. "Owen called him to come in and help do an inventory. We weren't sure anything was taken until we saw the surveillance video."

Her eyes narrowed. "I saw all the cameras. So you've already looked at the video."

"Yeah. They've got cameras all over the place." I explained how Owen had called us in the middle of the night and we'd come rushing over. How the two police officers had taken a look around and then left, and how Derek had asked to see the video. And how we'd seen the hooded intruder and then seen Tailor interrupting and getting shot and running to the escape room.

She shook her head in disbelief, still taking notes. "I'll check it all out in a minute." She pointed back to the three writers. "What are their names?"

I gave her an apologetic smile. "I don't know all of their real names. They're a writing group, trying to write spy thrillers, so they call each other Tinker— whose name is actually Teddy—Tailor, Soldier . . ."

"And Spy?" she guessed.

"No, the girl calls herself Drummer Girl."

"Huh." She considered, then nodded. "I like it."

I gazed at the tearful threesome and had to fight to keep my own eyes from watering. "Tailor isn't sitting over there, obviously. He's the victim."

"Spy thrillers, seriously?" Inspector Lee watched the three writers for a long moment, then glanced around. "Guess they meet here to soak up the ambience."

"Right. Plus there're scones."

"And a bookshop," she said dryly. "Please don't tell me this killing has something to do with a book."

I almost laughed, except there was nothing funny about the situation. "Actually, yeah, there's some kind of connection. Except I have no idea what it is."

She glanced up from her notebook. "Care to explain?"

I quickly told her all about the book I'd bought in Paris for Derek and how we'd loaned it to Owen. "The intruder headed right for the glass cabinet where the book was on display and took out a glass cutter. And that's about when Tailor interrupted him."

"What happened then?"

"They started arguing. And suddenly the intruder pulls out a gun and shoots him." I flinched, remembering the moment.

"What were they arguing about?"

"I don't know. There was no sound on the video. But they were definitely arguing; we could tell from their body language."

"Okay." She flipped back through her notes. "So back to the book."

"The book I bought Derek is on display over there as part of the store's anniversary celebration. It's a James Bond novel, so Owen asked if he could display it. And then the killer tried to steal it."

"Tried to?"

"Yeah. He was interrupted, like I said. And then after he chased Tailor and lost him, he raced back to try and steal the book again, but that's when the police showed up. He escaped out the front door without the book." I frowned. "You should probably take a look at the surveillance video."

"I will."

"Inspector Lee." Derek approached, and I could see the tension and strain in his neck and shoulders. He smiled at the inspector, and if we hadn't been at a murder scene, he would've given her a hug and a kiss on the cheek. Given the circumstances, he simply took her hand and shook it warmly. "You look wonderful."

"Thanks, Commander," she said. "Hope you two had fun in Paris."

"It was lovely, thank you. I'm sorry to meet again under such dreadful circumstances."

"Yeah. Me, too." She shoved her notepad into her pocket. "I'd like to see the body."

"And you'll want to take a look at the surveillance footage. It's quite revealing."

"That's what I hear."

He walked her toward the back of the store. "First let me introduce you to the store's owner."

"Thank you," she murmured.

"Owen, I'd like you to meet Inspector Janice Lee." He completed the introductions and the two shook hands.

"I'm sorry for your loss, Mr. Gibbons," Inspector Lee said.

"Thank you so much," Owen said, shaking his head as if he still couldn't quite believe this was happening. "He was a harmless boy. It's a tragedy for all of us."

"Yes. I'll do my best to find out who did this and bring them to justice."

"Thank you," he said quietly. "I can arrange a room if you need to conduct your interviews here. And if I can get you anything, coffee or tea or something to eat, please let me know."

"I appreciate it." She smiled. "There are a few things you could do for me, if you don't mind."

"Anything you want."

"Good. I would like everyone who's here right now to remain inside the store. And if you would please call all of your employees, including your managers. I'll want to interview each of them today."

"Oh dear," Owen said, back to wringing his hands. "Several of them aren't working today. What if they can't come in?"

"If they can't make it, I'd like their names and numbers. I'll call them myself and set up interviews down at the Hall of Justice." She said it with a smile.

"Oh my." Owen's eyes widened as reality set in. "I'll tell them. But I'm sure they'll want to make every effort to come in today."

"I hope so." She glanced up at Derek. "Would you take me to the victim now, Commander?"

"Yes, of course."

Derek and I exchanged a look. "I'll be in the café, talking to the Jackals."

Inspector Lee looked mildly alarmed. "The Jackals?"

"The writing group," I explained. "They gave themselves that name."

She opened her mouth, then shut it. "All righty then."

Derek gestured toward the back of the store. "Shall we?"

"Yeah," she said. "Let's do this."

I waited until I saw them disappear through the double doors, then headed for the café. Ordinarily I would've gone with them to view Tailor's body because, let's face it, I'm nosy. I was always interested in hearing Inspector Lee's thoughts about a crime scene, and I was more than happy to share my own theories. But this time it was just too depressing to revisit that horrible scene. Tailor was so young, and he had died in that disturbing room.

Cursed Kindergarten. Seriously?

I shuddered and rubbed my arms to quell the chills and moved quickly to the café counter. I was grateful that Owen had asked Tinker to make coffee in the café.

But after I placed my order, I realized that I'd left my purse in Owen's office.

"I have to go find my purse so I can pay for the coffee," I said. "I'll be right back."

"That's okay," Tinker said. "Owen told me we're not charging for coffee today."

"Really? That's so nice. Thanks."

While I waited for my coffee, I thought about the crime we'd witnessed on the videotape. Tailor had been shot in the stomach, but he had been strong enough to get away from the shooter and hide. But as soon as he reached the escape room, he must've passed out from the loss of blood and died within minutes.

Derek and I had wondered about the lack of a blood trail through the escape room lobby until we realized that the combination of dim lighting and dark red carpeting had masked it. After I'd called Inspector Lee, Derek had used his flashlight app and we had tracked the trail of blood through the lobby and down the hallway to the escape room where Tailor died.

I figured the crime scene unit would bring their blinding light bars and clip them everywhere so they'd be able to see the blood easily.

And why was I so concerned with the detectives

finding the blood trail? That was their job; it was what they did every day.

I was getting punchy. The coffee would help.

"Coffee's ready," Tinker said. "And here's a mini-scone for you."

I was pitifully grateful. "Thank you. I really needed this."

"We can all use a little extra energy today." He smiled sadly and crossed the café to join Drummer Girl and Soldier at their table.

I grabbed my goodies, then turned to look at the three writers. "Mind if I join you guys for a while?"

"No problem," Tinker said. "Have a seat."

I sat down and looked at them. Tinker's eyes were rimmed in red, and it was obvious that both Drummer Girl and Soldier had been crying, too.

"I'm so sorry, you guys."

"Yeah," Soldier said. "It's a big shock."

"Tinker says you found him."

"Derek and I did." I hesitated. "Did you know we found him in one of the escape rooms?"

"Oh God." The news was too much for Drummer Girl, who dissolved in a flood of tears and loud sobs. Tinker scooted his chair closer and draped his arm across her shoulder.

I couldn't speak for a long moment. Drummer's tears had set off the two guys' tear ducts. And mine, too, darn it.

When the sobs subsided, I gave Tinker a long look. "It happened at two thirty this morning. Do you know what Tailor was doing here at that hour of the night?"

He shook his head, looking miserable. "I have no idea."

"He had a key to the store, right?"

"Yeah. I do, too."

"And he knew the security code."

"Uh, sure. Most of the senior clerks have the code, so he must've let himself in."

A bunch of thoughts flew through my mind. The alarm had already been deactivated when the hooded intruder walked in. Maybe Tailor was the one who had deactivated the alarm. Maybe he had been here all along, long before the first intruder had walked in. Maybe he and the hooded guy were working together. I went back to my earlier theory about Igor. Was Tailor working with Igor to rip off the store? Tailor had shown a keen interest in my book, too.

And that's when I remembered Igor pointing his bony finger at Tailor and saying, "You're dead."

What did that mean?

And here came more chills. Rubbing my arms, I had to force myself to remember the conversation I was having with Tinker. "Did Tailor ever spend the night here?"

Tinker looked uncomfortable.

"Is it a secret?" I asked. "I won't tell Owen."

He let out a heavy breath. "So every once in a while, when we do inventory, we crash on the couches in the back lobby."

"How often do you do inventory?"

"Every two months. It can take all night, and you get wiped out counting merchandise and looking at lists and all that. It gets so your eyes are bugging out of your head. But even so, Owen didn't like us hanging out all night."

"I get it. So do you know if Tailor spent last night here?"

"I don't see why he would."

Soldier looked doubtful. "But he's got a mind of his own."

"The other night," I said. "You were all teasing him about being paranoid."

Drummer piped up. "Well, yeah. He's got cameras everywhere and he records everything he does."

Tinker shot her a narrow look.

"Don't look at me like that," Drummer said mildly, then her bottom lip began to tremble. "He's dead. Nothing can hurt him now. And it might help find his killer."

"Okay, okay." Tinker squeezed her arm. "Don't think about it right now."

Soldier finally spoke up. "Here's the deal. The protagonist in Tailor's book is totally paranoid. He knew he was being followed, so he put hidden cameras everywhere. So Tailor was always testing the cameras in the store. He would set up a hidden camera in an unexpected place and then watch the footage to see how many people noticed it. He had several of the wireless cameras set to feed to his smartphone so he could check them from home."

"And Owen was okay with that?"

Soldier flashed a crooked smile. "Owen was okay with it because the more Tailor learned about the different cameras, the more he could give the customers the benefit of his experience."

"Yeah," Tinker said. "Except that Owen didn't know how much or how often Tailor was recording stuff and where the cameras were hidden."

"Don't get the wrong idea," Drummer said, waving her hands nervously. "He wasn't a pervert or anything. It was research. For his book."

"Yeah," Soldier said. "I hate to admit it, but Tailor was the best of all of us. He was a good writer and he really got into the research. He kept his writing honest and real. And deep."

Deep. And now he was dead. I was sickened by the thought. My mind couldn't help but return to the image of that poor young guy curled up and bleeding out in a corner of the Creepy Kindergarten escape room. I pushed the vision out of my head and concentrated on the three writers in front of me.

And glancing around, I started to grow a little paranoid myself. Cameras everywhere? Not that I was so naïve to think I could walk into any store or gas station in the world and *not* be videotaped. But at least I usually knew where the cameras were. And what their function was.

In this day and age, it was sort of a social contract. Shops always posted a notice that there were cameras surveilling the premises. And once inside, you could look up at the ceiling or in a corner and see the cameras. So if you didn't want to be photographed, you didn't go into that store. It was that simple.

But Tailor had taken the idea of surveillance a step further. His cameras were hidden away in odd and unknown places, and somehow that made it a little creepier. Who knew where he'd put them? There was no disclosure, no sign posted in the bookshop that said, Smile, You're on Candid Camera!

And that brought up another question. Did Tailor's

cameras record sound? Could he listen in on private conversations?

I took a deep breath and let it out. Glancing at each of the writers, I asked, "Do you know where he put the cameras?"

"He changed them up a lot," Tinker explained. "You know, he'd put one in the bookshop, another in the café, then move the next day over to the electronics department, back to the escape room lobby, over by the cash registers. All over the place."

"And different kinds, too," Drummer Girl added. "He liked the tiny ones. But he would try all sorts of different products, different price points. And he'd disguise them in all kinds of ways. Some were pretty funny." She tried for a grin, but it was a little wobbly.

"Yeah, he got really into it," Soldier admitted.

"But he was particular, too." Tinker's glasses had slid down his nose, so he pushed them up. "He was really careful about lighting and angles, too."

"Right," Drummer said. "That's because he went to film school for a semester."

"Ah," I said. *He was a regular auteur*, I thought.

"He checked his recordings every night," Soldier said. "Then he'd adjust the cameras the next day."

"Were they hooked into the store's surveillance system?" I asked. "Did he view them in Owen's office?"

"No way." Tinker shook his head, then glanced around. His voice lowered, he said, "Owen gave him permission to test the cameras, but he never knew the extent of it. Tailor sort of got carried away. He had his own system."

I was getting more worried by the minute. What had

Tailor caught on his recordings? "But if he had all his cameras hidden around the store, where did he monitor the videos?"

Tinker exchanged a hesitant glance with Drummer Girl, who gave a brief nod of consent. "He's kind of a pack rat. His apartment looks like a recording studio, with tons of equipment and old vid discs on all the shelves."

"You call him a pack rat," Soldier said. "But Tailor preferred the term *collector*."

Drummer smiled. "*Hoarder* was more like it."

"Some of that equipment must be obsolete," I said. "I mean, he didn't have a bunch of videocassettes piled up, did he?"

"Oh my God," Drummer said, her eyes wide.

"It wasn't that bad," Tinker said.

"He was just kind of a nut," Soldier said affectionately. "Liked to hold on to stuff."

These three all looked genuinely sad and seemed to truly miss their friend, but I had to remind myself that murder was almost always committed by someone who knew the victim. And Tinker, Soldier, and Drummer knew Tailor well. All three were familiar with the way things worked at the spy shop. So all things considered, they were the most likely suspects. It was a little depressing, but I realized that it would be wise not to take anything they said at face value.

"What about the newer videos?" I asked. "Like, say, from last week. Where did he keep those?"

Once again, Tinker seemed taken aback, as if he couldn't believe I was dumb enough to ask something so elementary. "Everything is saved to the cloud."

I nodded thoughtfully. Hey, I knew about the cloud.

"So he could download them to his computer or his phone anytime he wanted."

Now he beamed at me as if I were a really smart six-year-old. "That's right."

Did someone want those surveillance videos? Was that what the intruder was really after?

I took a deep breath and let it out slowly as I gazed at the walls and shelves nearby. "So, do you think he's still got an active camera or two in place?"

The three of them glanced around, scanning the room. Then they looked at each other for a long moment. Finally, Tinker folded his arms across his chest and nodded. "No doubt about it."

Chapter 9

"I want to find Tailor's hidden cameras," I said, absently pounding my knee with my fist. "I just know there are still a couple in the store."

Derek gave me a glance as he drove out of the parking garage and headed for home. "I notice you didn't mention Tailor's cameras to Inspector Lee."

"I barely got a chance to talk to her," I said in my defense. Although yes, I probably could've made time to tell her. But that wasn't the point, was it? "After you went with her to see Tailor in the escape room, she stopped to talk with the CSI guys for at least fifteen minutes. Then she started watching the surveillance footage."

"You're forgiven," he said, patting my hand, knowing from my tone that I was already guilt-ridden.

"That was about the time I lost my second wind," I confessed, then shot him a quick look. "And that's something I don't like admitting to anyone but you."

When we came to a stoplight at Broadway, he smiled and moved his hand up to rub my arm. "Your secret is safe with me."

I pulled his hand into mine and held on. "I appreciate it."

"It's been a long night," he murmured.

It was almost seven thirty in the morning, so yeah, it had been a long night.

"So anyway," I said, still in defense mode. "Inspector Lee told me that after she finished watching the surveillance video, she was going to start interviewing everyone. That's why I didn't want to hang around just to tell her about any possible hidden cameras."

"Chances are she'll find the cameras on her own," he said. Then he added dryly, "She's fairly competent in her investigating."

"That's putting it mildly." I responded in that same teasing tone, then sobered. "I suppose once she finds his computer, she'll be able to access any extra videos he recorded."

"True."

I closed my eyes and rested for a moment. "I'll check in with her later. I'll tell her about the possible hidden cameras and see if she needs any other info."

He was quiet as he maneuvered his way around an electric trolleybus. "I was thinking I might go back there later today and talk to the kids myself."

"The kids?" I said, smiling.

He smiled. "I've picked up your nickname for the writers. They really are so young."

I shifted in the seat to get a better look at him. "Soldier's a little older, but the others are in their early twenties, which means they're only ten or twelve years younger than me."

"That's a whole generation." He looked over at me.

"Plus you have qualities that are well beyond your years."

"Are you calling me old?"

"Never." He laughed out loud. "You're sophisticated, clever, and mature."

"So I'm old," I said, shaking my head.

Still laughing, he said, "I love you."

"I love you, too." But then I shook my head. "You're right about the kids. I felt so old talking to them today. At one point, I mentioned videocassettes and Tinker looked at me like I was some kind of a dinosaur." Grumbling, I added, "That big, slow one with the tiny brain."

"Did you really ask about videocassettes?" he asked, grinning. "Did they even know what you were talking about?"

"Barely." I sighed.

He grabbed my hand again, holding on to it as he came to a stop at Harrison Street. "That's adorable."

"Oh, shut up," I said, but I was laughing as I said it. After another moment, I said, "I really want to see what's been recorded on those hidden cameras."

"So do I, darling." He pulled my hand up to his mouth and planted a kiss. "But right now I want to go home, take a shower, and get to the office."

"I wish we had time to sleep for a few hours."

"So do I."

I hesitated to mention it, but now I had to know. "I assume Lark is still there?"

"Yes." His eyes grew cold and he huffed out a breath. "Bart insists on waiting until the end of the month to tell her. She has a number of deals ready to close and he doesn't want to take a chance on losing them."

"But—" I stopped talking. Derek was much more patient—mature—than I was. I wanted to go down to his office and fire Lark myself, then walk her out of the building and out of Derek's life. How many times could I say it? The woman was toxic! Why couldn't they just kick her out? Were a couple of new clients worth more than having someone around who continually infected the office with her poisonous personality? Still, when I started speaking again, I really tried to sound like a grown-up about all of it. "But you're the boss. Don't you get to make the final decision?"

He managed a thin smile. "You'd think so. But as you know, I have partners who have almost as much of a stake in the company as I do. And Bart is an old, trusted friend."

"And she's playing him like a cheap guitar."

He smiled at that, but said nothing.

"I don't like it," I said, then sagged into the seat. "God, I sound like a jealous girlfriend, but I swear I'm not. And believe me, I like Bart, too. He's always been really nice to me, so that makes it even worse. I'm furious that she's manipulating him and a little furious that he can't see it. I mean, she's so transparently evil. And I seem to be one of the few people who can see it."

He squeezed my hand again. "Believe me, darling. There are others who see it, too."

"I know," I said, more calmly now. Derek was a fair and decent employer. He trusted and liked his partners, so I had to back off. He didn't need me giving him grief about the way he ran his company. *So let it go*, I told myself. Derek would make sure that Lark was gone as soon as he could possibly arrange it.

He pulled into our underground garage and parked the Bentley in our space. Then he leaned over, stroked my hair, and gave me a warm, slow kiss.

"Are you sure you have to go to work?" I asked.

"Yes. But I'll be home early." He kissed my forehead. "Let's walk down to Pietro's later and get a pizza."

I clutched his arm. "I love you so much."

He laughed. "You love pizza."

"And you," I insisted.

"And I love you." He released my seat belt. "Now let's go upstairs."

After Derek left for the office, I took a shower and dressed in my comfiest clothes: soft-knit yoga pants, an oversized sweater, socks, and yes, Birkenstocks. They had always been my work shoe of choice. Blame it on my commune childhood.

Staring at our big, beautiful bed, I debated between taking a nap and finishing one of my book projects. Since Derek had dutifully gone into work, I finally headed for my workshop. It wasn't all that noble a decision since I knew that if I went back to bed now, I would wake up cranky and disoriented. I appeased myself with the thought of pizza later. That would be my reward for putting in a few hours of work. And hopefully I could talk Derek into an early night.

"There's my girl," I said when Charlie came bounding after me. She wound her way around and between my feet as I walked, so I picked her up and carried her the rest of the way to the workshop. Before setting her down on the floor, I rubbed my cheek against her impossibly soft fur, then gave her a few scratches behind her ears.

"You're getting so big," I said. "Not my little kitten anymore, are you? But I love you just as much now as I did the day I met you."

She made a soft purring sound, and I knew it was her way of returning the love.

Sitting down at my worktable, I lifted the white cloth I'd used to cover and protect my work on the French-Chinese herb book I'd been cleaning for Inspector Lee's mother.

With my lack of sleep, I didn't want to tackle sewing the textblock back together and risk ruining the book. Instead, I picked up the thick pack of various Chinese-inspired-print papers that I'd brought back from Paris. I had already pulled out enough pieces to use as paste-downs and set them aside.

For the rest of the packet, I had an idea. I'd been toying with this one ever since the day in Bordeaux when Derek and I had strolled along the banks of the Gironde River.

It had been a warm, sunny day with a light breeze that sent puffy white clouds scudding across the blue sky. There were families with children playing along the river, digging in the sand, and picnicking on the rocks. And there had been a string of young boys flying kites. It had been such a beautiful, inspiring moment, and I could still see the vibrant colors of the kites dipping and soaring in the breeze and hear the cheerful sounds of children's laughter blending with the river water lapping against the shore.

I wanted to make a kite.

It wasn't smart or practical to use this beautifully hand-painted paper to make a toy, basically, that could be torn and broken by one stiff breeze. But maybe I could turn it into an art piece instead. Maybe Ian Mc-Cullough, the president of the Covington Library, would want to display it in *Books and Papers*, one of the permanent exhibits of the children's museum. After all, I would be creating it using many of the same materials I would use when I was making a book. Paper, of course; light cloth for the tail; thick, waxed linen thread for the string.

Additionally, I would need two balsa wood dowels to form the skeleton of the kite, as well as lots of adhesive. PVA would be perfect for pasting the papers together to fashion the kite itself, and then archival tape would fasten the paper to the dowels.

I spent the next hour laying the papers out on my worktable until I had enough pieces to make the large four-sided shape of a traditional kite. I wanted the seams of each piece of paper to match up so perfectly that when it was all put together, it wouldn't look like a patchwork but rather a single large sheet. Although the pack of papers contained a variety of patterns, the design I had picked out for the kite had a white background with Chinese symbols and letters and red accents. Matching the seams turned out to be fairly easy.

On my computer I pulled up a picture of a kite and stared, wondering what that actual shape was called. Was there a name for it in mathematics? A rhombus? A quadrilateral? How about a non-parallelogram? Did I care what it was called?

"No," I mumbled, and laughed at myself. I could make my kite any shape I wanted. But I was leaning toward the classic elongated diamond shape, or maybe I would stretch it out so that it was a little flatter and wider, like the shape of a bird with its wings extended.

I grabbed the half-gallon container of PVA archival glue from the cupboard and poured a decent amount into the glass bowl I used for such purposes. I found my thick, round glue brush and brought everything back to the table. Considering what else I would need for this job, I walked over to my desk and reached into the side drawer for the half bag of caramel kisses and shook out a healthy handful. It helped to keep up my strength.

For another hour I blissfully applied glue to the edges of each page and lined one up with another so that the pattern matched. I repeated the process until I had one large diamond-shaped piece, forty inches wide by fifty inches long. Up close I could see each seam clearly, but from a few feet away it really did look like one large piece of beautiful paper. *Not bad*, I thought, with a little burst of pride bubbling up inside me.

I couldn't go any further with the kite until I could get to the hardware store to buy some lightweight dowels. Meanwhile, in my limited research of kite making, I had learned that the vertical dowel was called the spine and the horizontal, smaller dowel was called the spar. It was fascinating stuff—and mindless, which was exactly what I needed after everything we'd been through the night before.

I refused to feel guilty for zoning out on the kite for the past few hours. As far as I was concerned, anything to do with paper and glue and linen thread was as critical to my bookbinding work as any book might be. And so far I was happy with the pretty look of the kite. I had a feeling Ian would really enjoy displaying it in the children's museum. But if not, I thought with a light shrug, I would hang it on our living room wall and call it art.

Feeling virtuous for having done something besides sleep the day away, I straightened up my worktable and popped one last kiss into my mouth. The kite-building project had taken up three hours of my time, and now I was truly starting to hit a wall. If I didn't lie down soon, I was afraid I might fall down.

Charlie meowed, and it was almost like an accusation.

I stared down at the pretty ball of fluff sitting in her little bed. "All right, all right, I'll make the call." I grabbed my cell phone and hit speed dial. The call went directly to Inspector Lee's voice mail. I was about to hang up when I glanced at Charlie. She was still watching me.

"Okay," I mumbled, and waited for the beep, then said, "Hi, it's Brooklyn. I didn't get a chance to talk to you earlier. I wanted to tell you that according to the other writers, Tailor had hidden at least one nanny cam in the store. So if you can find it, you might be able to get another picture of the intruder. So, you know . . . call me."

I ended the call and the exhaustion hit me again, this time like a big, fat brick to the head.

"I need some fresh air," I murmured, causing Charlie to lift her head and gaze up at me from her little bed near my desk. I walked over and gave her a couple of scratches, and when she stretched and rolled over, I rubbed her soft belly. Sitting up again, she head-butted my hand, so I obligingly scratched her ears and neck some more.

Finally, I stood and walked out of my workshop and into the living room. Charlie followed briskly, apparently under some illusion that I might feed her.

"You already ate earlier," I said. But I cleaned and refreshed her water bowl and then tossed a few yummy fish treats into her other bowl. She pounced on them like a shark attacking a school of guppies.

It was July in San Francisco, so I grabbed my lightweight windbreaker off the hook by the door and put it on, then wrapped a thin scarf around my neck. The sky was overcast and it was windy, too, perfect for a quick walk across the street to the Courtyard Shops. I was tempted to grab a piece of pie for lunch and headed for Sweetie Pies bakeshop. But mindful of my ever-tightening jeans, I decided to go the healthier route and detoured into the Rabbit Hole instead.

Once again, I consoled myself with the knowledge that we'd be having pizza for dinner.

I wandered around the Courtyard Shops, greeting everyone I saw and sipping my favorite drink, the Green Thing—a concoction made of apples, kale, spinach, peaches, mangos, bananas, and ginger. It was really, really *green*, but totally delicious, honestly, as long as I didn't look at it.

I checked in on the new owner of the shoe repair shop (the original owner had died earlier that year) and said hello to the perky new manager of the classy boutique that had moved in when the hat shop closed. Once I'd finished my drink, I tossed the cup and walked into the bookshop, stopping to breathe in the alluring scent of books, paper, and leather.

I spent a few minutes chatting with the delightful store manager, a fellow book nerd, then stayed for another hour browsing and buying. I sat down in one of the cozy corner chairs and read the first chapter of the newest thriller from one of my favorite authors. I had to buy it, of course, after reading the cliff-hanger chapter ending in which the beautiful, kick-ass cop heroine had determined that the woman whom everyone thought had jumped from her balcony twenty flights up had actually been hypnotized to think she was flying.

"It's so not fair," I muttered, closing the book and carrying it up to the checkout counter. "All she wanted to do was meet a nice guy." Instead she met the hypnotist-cyber-date serial killer.

Who didn't love a good hypno-cyber-date serial killer thriller?

Crossing the street, I headed to the door of my building. For some reason, the character in that book reminded me of Tailor. Death for him hadn't been fair, either. Had he been the one to turn off the alarm so the intruder could get in? Had he been tricked into believing that something else was going on instead of pure thievery?

I wondered how Tailor's writer friends were doing and how Owen was coping with the fact that a shooting had taken place in his store. I wondered if people would hear the news and be too scared to shop there, or if news of the murder would bring in even more crowds.

From previous experience, I was pretty certain it would be the latter effect.

I wondered if the hooded intruder would return to try to steal our book again. As soon as I saw Derek, I was going to see if he would drive me over to SPEC-TRE and retrieve it. We had promised Owen that we would leave the book on display through the end of the second weekend of his anniversary celebration, but now that Tailor had been killed and the store's safety had been breached, I doubted the festivities would continue.

*   *   *

On the way to Pietro's, I mentioned to Derek the idea of picking up the book later that evening or at least stopping by SPECTRE to see how everyone was doing after the events of last night.

"I know we should, but I'm knackered, love," he admitted as we walked hand in hand down the street. "Meetings all day, plus lunch with a new client. Didn't have a minute to relax."

"I'm pretty wiped out, too," I confessed. "I thought about taking a nap after you left for work, but I was afraid I would sleep all day and not be able to sleep tonight. So I just tried to stay busy."

"Then let's stay in tonight. We can open a bottle of wine to go with our pizza, fall asleep on the couch watching TV, and get a good night's sleep. And perhaps we can swing by SPECTRE tomorrow night."

"Yes, let's do that," I said. "We can check on the book, commiserate with Owen, and see how the kids are holding up."

I glanced up at him and met his gaze. In the early-evening light, he somehow looked even more darkly handsome and dangerous than usual. My heart stuttered in my chest.

"What is it, love?" he asked.

"It's nothing," I said, smiling. "I just like looking at you."

He stopped, tipped my chin up, and kissed me. "I like looking at you, too."

I leaned against him. "Are we going to get completely sappy and annoy all our friends?"

"Absolutely."

We both laughed and continued walking to Pietro's.

Ten minutes later, after greeting and chatting with Pietro and his staff, we paid for our fully loaded pizza and antipasto salad and walked home.

The next morning I went grocery shopping and stopped at the hardware store to buy the dowels I needed for the kite. I still hadn't heard back from Inspector Lee, so I decided I would call her again when I got home. But when I got there, Derek was home. He sat in the big red chair in the living room, staring up at the ceiling.

"This is a surprise," I said, delighted, until I noticed how unhappy he looked. "What's wrong? What happened? You never come home during the day."

He exhaled slowly. "I received a letter by overnight mail. It came to my office, but I wanted you to see it."

Given his demeanor, I was almost afraid to ask, but I did anyway. "Who is it from?"

"It's from Ned. You met him in Paris."

"Of course I remember Ned. How is he?"

Derek leaned forward and picked up the thin cardboard envelope off the coffee table. Reaching inside, he pulled out a one-page letter.

"Should I read it?" I asked.

He stared at me, and I saw that his eyes were dark and empty. And that frightened me more than anything else I'd seen.

"Derek?" I was unsure what to do or how to react in the face of his miserable expression. "What did Ned say in the letter?"

"He said," he began, then pressed his lips together for a long moment before he was able to continue. "He said that if I received this letter, it means he's dead."

*   *   *

I had to get up and walk around the room for a minute. "I can't believe it. He was such a sweet man. Did he have a heart attack?"

"He was murdered."

"What?" I stopped in my tracks. "Why? How? Why would anyone want to kill him?"

"He worked as a covert operative for over thirty years," Derek said cynically. "There are a dozen possible reasons why."

I was surprised by his sarcasm, but knew it was only because he was in pain. "Do you have any idea which one of those dozen reasons might apply to Ned?"

His gaze narrowed. "No."

I held out my hand. "Do you want me to read the letter?"

Again he inhaled, then let it out slowly. "Let me read it to you."

"Okay." But I took a moment, stretched my neck and shoulders, and tried to relax on the couch. It was impossible, so I sat forward, and with a nod to him, I said, "I'm ready."

But was I?

Derek stared at the page in his hand and began to read.

"'Dear Derek,

"'It was so good to see you in Paris and I so enjoyed meeting your lovely new wife. I wish you and Brooklyn best wishes for a long and happy life together.

"'Now for some news that will surely upset you,'" he continued, "'I apologize in advance for that. I've instructed my wife Patsy to send you this letter in the event of my death. Therefore, if you are reading these words, it means that I have been murdered.'"

I gasped. "This just doesn't seem possible. I mean, I know it must be, but it seems so wrong. We just saw him."

"I called Patsy from my office twenty minutes ago," Derek said, his tone bleak. "It's true."

I moved over and sat on the coffee table in front of him, just to be close. "Okay, go on. Unless you'd rather have me read the rest of it."

"No." He shook his head slowly. "Strangely enough, it helps to read it myself."

"Okay."

He lifted the page and continued. "'I would greatly appreciate it, Derek, if you would attempt to find my killer. Look in the book. Find a list of seven names, including my own. The seven of us on the list worked together several years ago on a top-secret op. I've recently learned that three of the people on that list are dead. Now, with my death, there are four gone, three remaining. I won't give you names or tell you more than that in this letter. The more Patsy knows, the more danger she's in.

"'Of the three still alive, two are potential victims. The third is a killer. I wish I could advise you as to which is which, but I have every confidence that you will be able to solve this deadly enigma.

"'I would ask that you not mourn me, but instead put any sorrow or anger you may feel toward solving the puzzle of my death. If nothing else, the resolution will give my dear wife and others—including you, perhaps?— a bit of closure. It may also answer some questions that have gone too long unanswered. Good luck, *mon ami*. And many thanks, old friend. I remain, yours, Ned.'"

Derek set the letter down and I reached for his hands. "I'm so sorry, Derek."

"Yes, so am I."

"What did Patsy say when you spoke to her?"

He took another deep breath and let it go. "She said that two attempts had already been made on Ned's life and that this third time they finally succeeded."

"Oh, how awful." I grimaced, but had to ask. "Did she say how he died?"

"He was strangled."

I felt sick to my stomach and didn't ask for any more details. I thought back to the kindly man I'd met in Paris and hoped that his evil killer received his just rewards. But as I flashed back to our meeting with Ned, I wondered out loud, "Do you think one of those attempts had already occurred when we saw him in Paris?"

"I don't know," he said. "But I can make an educated guess and say yes."

"I know you said that the two of you just happened to run into each other, but do you think there's a chance that Ned actually arranged it?"

He gritted his teeth, then gave me a reluctant half smile. "A very good chance."

"Wow." I sat back on the couch. "So he knew you were in Paris."

"I believe so."

"Are you being . . ." I hesitated. "Are you being *watched*?"

"Possibly." He tried to say it lightly, but it still gave me chills. Because if Derek was being watched while we were in Paris, then so was I. And I couldn't help but recall the strange man in the hooded sweatshirt watching Derek and Ned so intently. And as soon as I'd walked into his line of sight, he'd raced away.

I touched Derek's arm. "Do you remember that last day in Paris at the Bouquinistes, I mentioned that a man in a hooded sweatshirt had been staring at you and Ned?"

He didn't have to think about it long. "Yes. I've been thinking about that very thing. Ned reacted to your statement with studied nonchalance, but I recall that his shoulders froze up and his eyes were watchful. He might've known the person you were talking about."

"And he said good-bye to us pretty quickly after that," I said. "Was he trying to protect you? Or was he intending to go after the guy? Did he know he was in danger?" I waved the words away. "Of course he did."

Derek chuckled, but there was no humor in his eyes. "Of course he did."

"So you think they were following you? I mean us? Even on our honeymoon?"

"The fellow might have been following Ned, but not us. Either way, I'm sorry it upset you, darling."

"So am I. And I'm angry about Ned. But I'm angry for you, too, because . . . it's just a feeling, but I'll bet they were watching you as well." I gripped his hands. "I don't want anyone watching you."

He lifted my hands and kissed them, but said nothing.

Feeling helpless, I picked up the letter and skimmed through it. "What book do you think he's talking about?"

"I have an idea, but I'd rather have you tell me what you think."

I thought of Derek's friend Ned, the kindly man I'd met near the bookstalls overlooking the river. It had been a beautiful day and I had just found the book for

Derek in one of the first bookstalls we looked at. I'd also found the Chinese herb book for Inspector Lee's mother, but I hadn't shown Derek and Ned that book, so Ned couldn't have known about it. No, I had only shown them the copy I'd found of *The Spy Who Loved Me*. What other book would he have been talking about if not that one?

I looked at Derek. "He's talking about the James Bond book I bought for you."

"Yes. I can't imagine it's any other book."

"Right." I recalled something else and my eyes widened. "Derek, you thought someone broke into our hotel suite that night."

"Yes," he said with a ghost of a smile. "I feel rather vindicated that I was right about that."

"It was Ned."

He nodded. "It was Ned."

I stood. "We need to get the book."

Derek quickly changed into casual clothes and we raced to SPECTRE. Or we would have raced, but the ancient freight elevator in our building was even slower than usual. Maybe it was better to slow down for a moment, try to shake off the feeling of panic. It didn't work; I was still anxious, and by the time the elevator came to a stop, I wanted to jump out of my skin.

"It's going to be fine, love," Derek murmured. But when the door finally opened, we couldn't race fast enough to the Bentley.

Derek tore out of our parking garage and drove like an Indy 500 driver across the city. The car screeched around every corner and wove between the slower cars on the street.

I knew I was safe with Derek, but I didn't trust anyone else on the road. So rather than come unglued and allow anxiety to eat through my stomach wall, I closed my eyes most of the way and kept a tight hold on the grab handle over the door.

When I felt the car bounce into the parking garage, I opened my eyes, only to squeeze them shut again when Derek zoomed up another narrow ramp and zigzagged into a parking space a half second before another car pulled in.

"We made it," Derek said with a reassuring pat on my shoulder.

"Good job," I whispered, and avoided eye contact with the other car's driver until they drove on. Then I unlatched my seat belt, jumped out of the car, and grabbed Derek's hand, then we walked as quickly as we could across the busy street.

Right before we strolled into SPECTRE, Derek stopped me. "I don't want anyone to know about Ned just yet, including Owen."

"Okay." I gazed up at him. "But what if his name is on the list?"

"If that turns out to be the case, we'll alert him."

"And anyone else whose name is on there. We should probably hurry and find the list and let people know."

Derek scowled. "It's quite possible that someone else is already being targeted."

"As long as it's not you," I said, gripping his sweater. "It better not be you, Derek."

"It won't be me," he promised with a half smile. "There's no reason why my name would be on that list. Or any list, for that matter."

"But you worked some jobs with Ned, didn't you?"

Suddenly breathless at the thought, I had to gulp down some air.

"Ned and I haven't worked a case together in more than ten years. I doubt I'm on any lists, but we'll take every precaution regardless."

"Okay. Good." I blew out a breath, trying to keep the panic from seeping back in. "I won't say a word about Ned, but I've got to give Owen a reason why I need to take the book. Um, I'll just say that I have a chance to get it appraised this afternoon and I'll bring it back later tonight or tomorrow."

"You do your own book appraisals, love. You don't need to take it to an appraiser."

"Owen doesn't know that."

"Good point."

"I really hope Owen isn't on that list."

Derek took a deep breath. "He and Ned were friends."

"And Ned was the one who suggested that you visit Owen."

"Yes. It was a rather strong suggestion." Derek frowned, then thought for a moment. "It's possible that the phrase he asked me to pass on to Owen was a code."

I groaned silently. This whole secret agent thing was hurting my stomach. "What was the phrase?"

Derek shook his head. "No, it doesn't make sense. It's too outlandish."

"Really?" I said, cocking my head to stare at him. "You were all spies. How much more outlandish does it get?"

He broke into a grin. "Darling Brooklyn, you do bring things into perspective."

I threw my arms around him and held on. "Let's get this over with."

He hugged me for a long moment. "Good idea. And no mention of Ned," he reminded me.

"Got it."

With our stories straight, we walked into SPECTRE.

The book was still tucked safely inside its glass display case. I didn't know why I thought it might be gone again, but it was right there, surrounded by lethal weapons and silly string.

Owen came bounding across the floor. "Derek! Brooklyn!"

I gave him a hug and Derek shook his hand.

"Sorry we couldn't make it in before now," I said. "I know you're all going through a lot of grief."

"We are," he said.

"We'll try to come by tomorrow for a longer visit."

"Thank you. It's a sad time for everyone, but we're all in it together and that's a comfort."

"Are you canceling the anniversary celebration?" I asked.

"Frankly, I considered it," he said. "But Tailor's writer friends and the other salespeople were adamant that he would want the store to stay open and keep celebrating. Even his mother agreed." Owen wiped away a small tear from his eye.

He would probably want us to find out who killed him, I thought, but just said, "They must know him pretty well."

"Indeed."

"We're sorry to spring this on you," Derek said, "but Brooklyn needs to take the book home for a few hours."

"What?" His expression fell. "Oh dear. Must you?"

I touched his arm. "I'll bring it back tomorrow, I

promise. But I have a chance to get it appraised by a world-famous collector."

He looked dismayed. "You're not going to sell it, are you?"

"Oh no, never. But he could be very helpful to my career. He'll only be in the city for the day, so that's why we're in such a hurry."

"Oh, then you must take it with you," Owen said. "We can replace it with another book, just for this evening."

"Thank you for understanding."

He patted my shoulder. "I'm just grateful that you were willing to loan it to us at all. You've seen the lines of people and all the interest it's generated. It's quite exciting. And Tailor would be so proud. Ian Fleming was his personal hero."

"It makes me happy to know that the book brought him some happiness. And I promise we'll bring it back in a day or so."

He beamed with pleasure. "I'll go get the key."

Chapter 10

Relief washed over me when we made it back to the car, climbed inside, and locked the doors. Safe, for the moment. I wrapped the book in the white cloth I'd brought from home and slipped it into a small bag.

"I don't want to look at it until we get home," I said, tucking the bag into the wide pocket of the door.

"I agree. We'll be able to concentrate on it without any distractions." He started the engine and moved out of the dark parking lot.

"I can finally breathe," I said.

"Were you nervous?"

"Yes." I gazed at him. "I don't know how you ever survived being a spy. The adrenaline rush alone would kill me."

"Darling, I was never a spy."

"Sure, pal." I laughed. "Save it for the writer kids."

He smiled all the way home.

Once we were inside our garage and the security gate had closed behind us, I suffered another brief flash of fear at the thought of walking through the dark garage and riding up in the painfully slow freight elevator.

"We're perfectly safe, darling," Derek said. I was

almost certain the fear hadn't shown on my face, but it seemed like Derek could read my mind sometimes.

"I know," I said. "I'm just feeling a little uneasy after hearing about Ned. And now I'm seeing assassins in every corner."

"Not to worry," he said lightly, patting my knee. "Gabriel and I have this place wired and secured to the nth degree."

"I know." There was no one better than Gabriel when it came to security in homes and businesses. And Derek was no slouch, either. "Okay. Let's go upstairs so I can examine the book and see what we're dealing with."

When we got to our place, I went into my workshop while Derek poured himself a beer. The thought of a cold beer sounded so good, my mouth watered. But I needed to keep my wits about me while I worked on *The Spy Who Loved Me*.

I set the book down on another clean white cloth. I used a lot of white cloths, I realized, especially when I was taking a book apart. They were white cotton, soft and thin, and they didn't cause any static. The white color made it easy to see each piece of a book, and when that old book was so grungy that it was falling apart or riddled with red rot, the cloth was helpful at keeping all the pieces together. When I finished for the night, I would place another cloth on top of everything to protect the book and its components from the odd insect or falling dust particle. Not that I would ever allow a dust particle to survive in here. I was a little obsessive when it came to keeping my workshop as pristine as I could get it.

But enough about those white cloths.

Derek came back into the office carrying his beer in one of the frosted glasses we kept in the freezer. He set it down on a cocktail napkin on the desk, several feet away from my worktable. He knew I didn't allow any liquids on my worktable because, duh, liquid was the natural enemy of books. And besides, it was way too easy to spill something, even when we were being careful.

"Darling, what's this?" He walked over to look at my progress on the kite.

Feeling a touch foolish, I said, "I decided to make a kite."

"Are we going to fly it on the Marina Green?"

"I don't think it would survive the wind off the bay. I was thinking maybe Ian would display it in the children's museum."

He stared at the paper, ran his finger lightly along the edges. His eyes twinkled with pleasure when he looked up and smiled at me. "How clever you are."

I laughed. "It's just a bunch of paper and glue right now."

"But you've put it together in such a pretty way."

"Thank you." I could feel myself blushing and decided to get back to the subject at hand, namely *The Spy Who Loved Me*. "I confess I didn't look through every page of the book, so I'll do that right now." I glanced up when Derek sat down across the table from me. "This could get boring."

"If I get bored, I've got my email and phone messages to keep me busy." His smile assured me he wouldn't get bored, which I appreciated.

"Okay, here we go." I picked up *The Spy Who Loved Me* and removed the dust cover first thing and set it aside. Then I checked the hinge I repaired last week. It was holding up just fine, I was happy to see.

"Looks pretty good," I said. "No more wobbling."

"You do good work," Derek said.

"Thanks," I said, grinning. "Now I'm just going to go through the pages. Hopefully, something will fall out that we didn't notice before. Something like a list of names, perhaps? Is that too much to hope for?"

"Probably," he said, his lips twisting into a smile. "But we'll hold a good thought."

"I don't want to have to check each and every page, but I'll do so if it's necessary. Right now I'm going to very gently turn the book over and fan the pages. And if you'll say your prayers and begin chanting, the list will fall out and into our hands."

He watched while I carefully fanned the pages. "Didn't you go through the book when we brought it home?"

"No. It was in such good condition, all I did was fix the loose hinge and press it overnight." I glanced up at him. "My mistake."

"In your defense, you didn't know we'd be looking for a hidden list of names."

"No, but given my predilection for finding strange things inside of books, I probably should've checked more carefully."

I searched through the book but found no loose paper or note stuck between two pages. I started to wonder if maybe the list of names had been scribbled right onto one of the pages. I hoped not, since that would devalue the book radically. But I did finally go page by page, just in case. There was nothing, no secret clues written on the pages, the flyleaf, or endpapers.

"I'm sorry, but I can't find anything within the pages. I'm going to have to take it apart."

"That's fine, darling. You know how to put it back together, right?"

I smiled. "Of course, and it'll look as good as new. But I'll have to use new endpapers and I hate having to change the essence of the book itself." I was frowning now. "What if we don't find anything? I'll have done it for nothing."

"We will find something," he said with supreme confidence.

I wanted to trust his words, but I was running out of options. There were only so many places you could hide something in a book.

I walked to my cabinet and found my X-Acto knife and returned to the worktable. The last thing I wanted to do was cut into this book, so I hesitated. I would have to make the cut along the inner hinge between the cover and the flyleaf. That was the only way to open the book up for examination. But then I would have to replace the endpapers, and that would entail changing the book just enough that it might alter its value and price. Derek wouldn't care about that, but I would.

I searched one last time, checking the heavy cloth cover to see if anything had been slipped in between it and the hard boards underneath. I checked the endpapers for any indentations. I stood the book up to study the headband, and that was when I saw the small gap where the spine cover had been pulled back ever so slightly from the textblock. It wasn't enough to be noticeable to most people, but I was getting up close and personal here. I got out my magnifying glasses and took an even closer look. *Eureka*, I thought.

"We might just get lucky," I murmured. I walked over to the cabinet and found my tweezers, then returned to the table and held the book steady while I slid the tweezers into the narrow space inside the spine. I angled the book so that the overhead light illuminated the inside space. And extracted a thin piece of microfilm.

"Hello," I said, staring at the odd bit of celluloid an inch wide and about five inches long.

"What have we here?" Derek whispered next to my ear.

I hadn't realized he'd moved so close to me. "Can you see it?"

"Yes. It's microfilm."

"Microfilm," I echoed softly. "Totally *Spy vs. Spy.*"

He shook his head in amazement. "Ned was certainly old-school."

"Do you think you can read it?"

"It's awfully small, but I can try." He thought for a moment. "I believe we might still have an old microfiche reader in the storage room at the office. I doubt something this small could be fed into it, but also it would take some time to unearth and figure out. It's such old technology, I don't trust myself to operate it competently. And I'm not about to involve anyone else at the office in something so secretive."

"No. That could put them in danger." I frowned at the thin strip. It was black against the white cloth. "There should be an app for this."

He smiled fondly and put his hand on my shoulder. "Someday there will be."

I gazed up at Derek. "I'm afraid Tailor's death really was connected to the book. I have a feeling the guy in the hoodie wasn't just an intruder. He was after the book and Tailor stood in his way, stopping him just as he was about to steal it."

"I was thinking the same thing," Derek said. "The intruder took his time going through the store and taking things, but his real purpose in being there was to steal the book."

"He has to be on that list. Why else would he try to take the book? Somehow, he found out that Ned hid that microfilm in this book."

"Which means that the same man, the hooded fellow, must have killed Ned." Derek scowled. "And I presume he's responsible for the other deaths on the list."

"So he was in Paris and now he's here?" I looked at Derek. "The guy gets around."

"I have my doubts that the two hooded characters are one and the same person."

"It's definitely a stretch," I admitted. "But how else did the guy in the store find out about the microfilm in the book unless he was in Paris with Ned?"

Derek's forehead furrowed in a frown. "Ned was a seasoned operative. I doubt that he would've said anything."

"Unless he was someone Ned trusted."

"In which case, Ned was betrayed." Derek paced around the table, considering.

"You're thinking something worse," I said, and felt my stomach turn somersaults.

Derek's eyes darkened. "Yes. He could've been tortured."

It brought real pain even to consider that horrific possibility. We sat quietly for a few minutes until I finally shook off the ugly thoughts that had risen to the surface. Derek wrapped his arm around me. "It's all right, darling."

"I hate this."

"I know." He leaned over and kissed the top of my head, and I felt such a wave of gratitude that Derek and I were on the same wavelength in so many ways.

"I have an idea," I said, returning to the original objective.

"Let's hear it."

"I have a rickety old lightbox I used to use for studying slides of rare books. Could we make that work somehow? I've got a really good magnifying glass, too."

"Let's give it a try."

I jumped down from my high chair and opened the doors to the cabinet at the far side of the room. I had to get down on my hands and knees to peer into the very bottom shelf, but sure enough, there was my old lightbox, sitting on top of my portable paper cutter. I pulled out the lightbox and set it on the table, then grabbed my most powerful magnifying glass from its drawer.

"Talk about old-school," I said with a grin.

"The old ways are often the best." He squeezed my shoulder. "Although I wouldn't thumb my nose at a digital microfilm OCR scanner right about now."

I chuckled. "Why don't we have one of those?"

"I'll have Alexa put it on the shopping list."

I laughed and switched on the lightbox. Grabbing the tweezers, I lifted the microfilm and placed it on the lighted surface. Handing Derek the magnifying glass, I said, "See if you can read that."

He took a full minute to scan the tiny piece of film, then looked up. "I'll probably wind up with a permanent squint, but it's readable."

"Yay!" I cried. "Do you want me to try and read it? I've got good eyes."

"Yes, you do." He handed me the magnifying glass. "Be my guest."

I stared long and hard at the tiny lettering. "It feels like I'm reading one of those eye charts at the optometrist's office. But I can read it." I looked up and smiled at Derek. "Shall I dictate for you?"

"Give me a minute." He went over to my desk, grabbed a pen and a notepad, and brought them to the worktable. "I'm ready. Go right ahead."

"Ned Davies." I paused to give him time to write it down.

"Next."

"Ramon Silva."

"Oh yes. I remember him quite well. Brazilian. Spoke Portuguese. Handsome devil."

"Good to know," I murmured. "Ready for the next one?"

"Yes."

"Yoon Kee Jones." I spelled it out for him.

"I've never heard of him. Or her," Derek qualified. "Can I see it?"

"Sure." I handed him the magnifying glass.

He stared for a moment, then glanced at the list he was making on the notepad. "Looks exactly the way it sounds. But I still don't know who she is."

"His or her mother might have been Chinese and their father was American." I frowned. "Or the other way around."

"One of the parents could be English," he suggested. "Jones is a very common name in England and Wales."

"Let's finish the list," I said, taking the magnifying

glass back. "Then we can talk through all these names."
Blinking a few times to clear my vision, I stared again
at the film strip. "Next name is Bettina Mayer."

"Oh, sure. She's American. Been around for years."
He thought for a moment. "I think she's a friend of
Owen's."

"Next is Malcolm Brown."

"Never heard of him," Derek murmured, writing it
down.

"Thomasina Robinson."

"Tommie," Derek said thoughtfully. "She's a friend.
I've known her for ages."

I didn't care to remind him that having his old friend
Tommie show up on this list meant that she might be
dead. Or a killer.

"The last name is Christopher Peeler."

Derek frowned as he wrote. "That name sounds
vaguely familiar. I'll have to think about it."

I had a brief moment of pure relief that Derek was
indeed not on the list. I set down the magnifying glass
and turned off the lightbox. "Okay, that's it. Let's look
at the list."

Derek pulled his chair over next to me, held up the
notepad, and read off the names. "Ned Davies. Ramon
Silva. Yoon Kee Jones. Bettina Mayer. Malcolm Brown.
Thomasina Robinson. And Christopher Peeler."

"I know you told me, but I want to make sure I have
it straight. Which of these people do you know?"

"Ned, of course, and Ramon and Tommie." He
stared at the list for another few seconds. "I've heard
of Bettina Mayer. She was with CIA for years. And as
I said, Peeler sounds familiar. But I've never heard of
Malcolm Brown or Yoon Kee Jones."

"Another problem," I said. "Except for Ned, we don't know who's alive and who's dead."

"I'll try to get photos from Harold for each of them."

I had heard him mention the name *Harold* in the past. He was apparently an old friend who now worked at Interpol, the international criminal police organization.

Derek was jotting down notes on the same page as the list. "I might recognize the others by sight rather than by their names. Especially when you consider that some of them might not be using their real names."

"Photos would definitely be helpful," I said. "I assume they were all affiliated with some kind of covert intelligence service, right? Either CIA or MI6 or Interpol or . . ." I gave Derek a quizzical look. "You know. One of the other ten thousand intelligence agencies out there."

"I'm assuming they've all been connected at some time to an agency somewhere. And some of them may have gone to work for a private company."

"Like yours."

He gave a reluctant nod. "Like mine."

"But none of those people on that list are working for you."

He smiled blandly. "I'll know for certain when I see their photographs."

"Yikes." I blew out a breath. "So how do we find out which of these seven people are alive and which are dead?"

Derek exhaled slowly before meeting my gaze. "I'll make some calls."

While Derek made calls, I distracted myself by working on the kite. Because he had worked for years with British intelligence and then later started his own highly reputable security agency, he had access to the most clandestine information in the world. He had friends in a couple dozen different intelligence services in almost every country you could think of.

He would get the answers eventually.

But meanwhile, I didn't want to listen in on the phone calls, having realized that just by contacting someone in his old office or Interpol or one of those other agencies, Derek might be putting himself in danger as well.

Despite the large number of intelligence agencies out there, the world of espionage agents and covert operatives seemed to be very small indeed. I imagined their gossip grapevine could crisscross the world in minutes. Briefly, I considered the possibility that our neighbor Alex might know some of the people on that list. She, too, had been in the "business." Was Derek stirring up some kind of hornet's nest simply by making a few phone calls and asking some questions?

"Oh God." My anxiety level had just skyrocketed.

Taking a few deep, calming breaths, I popped two caramel kisses into my mouth and got to work on the kite frame.

After measuring the length of each dowel, I pulled out my toolbox to find the right saw. But then I recalled that I'd worked with balsa wood in the past, back in college when I made a set of wooden book covers for a book arts display. I knew the wood was flimsy and could crack with the lightest pressure, so I hesitated to use my mini-hacksaw to cut the dowels.

After scratching my head for a few minutes, I realized that the best tool for cutting the lightweight balsa wood was my X-Acto knife.

Instead of sawing back and forth with the knife, I pressed it down into the wood and slowly but surely worked it through the dowel. Then I used my finest grade of sandpaper to smooth the ends.

I glued the two dowels—the spine and the spar—where they joined in the center, forming a cross. While I waited for the glue to dry, I used a big fat needle to carefully punch holes in the ends of each of the dowels where the linen thread would go through.

"I've managed to learn a few things."

I flinched at the sound of Derek's voice. I'd been so wrapped up in dowels and sandpaper, I'd lost track of where I was and what we were doing.

And now I didn't like how pale Derek's usually tanned, handsome face had turned. The kite was forgotten as I rushed across the room and wrapped my arms around his waist. "What did you hear? Tell me everything."

He held me, and for a moment we were in our own little world. I just wished we could stay there forever, insulated and safe from the scary monsters and covert operatives who were out there roaming around the real world, often carrying guns.

"It's quite a story," he said, trying for a light tone.

"I might need a glass of wine."

"Yes, you might. Excellent idea." He took my hand and we walked into the living room and over to the kitchen island. He opened a new bottle of French pinot noir and poured me a healthy glass. He was still sipping his beer.

"Let's sit." He pulled out a barstool on the kitchen side of the island, and I sat across from him on the dining room side.

"I spoke to Harold," Derek started. He took a quick

sip of beer and continued. "He's cross-checking the names with all the operations that have occurred around the world, going back ten years."

"Was it a good conversation?" I sighed, shaking my head. "And by that I mean, did he threaten to have you dragged off in chains for just mentioning those names?"

"He did not." He smiled indulgently. "It was a good conversation. I trust Harold. We were in the Navy together. I've known him for years. And he knew Ned."

"I wouldn't trust anyone right now," I muttered, then winced. "Sorry. I guess we have to trust someone or we'll never get to the bottom of this mess."

"Quite right."

"I just don't want you to get hurt." I blew out a breath I didn't realize I'd been holding. "I mean, if someone gets wind that you're asking questions, don't you think it could be dangerous?"

He reached his hand across the island to grab mine and held on. "I won't get hurt."

"You'd better not." I clutched his hand tighter. "Or I'll have to hurt you."

He grinned and took a long drink of beer. "I'm waiting for Harold to call me back, so if you want to go work on something, I'll let you know when I hear from him."

"I don't think I can concentrate on much right now." I sipped my wine. "Was Harold able to give you any information right away or will we hear everything when he calls you back?"

"He was able to give me some information, but he still has to call back with more details. He recognized six of the seven names right away. Yoon Kee Jones was a mystery at first, but then he realized that she actually went by the name Kay Jones."

"Oh. Okay." I shrugged. "Maybe Ned didn't spell it correctly."

"That's possible." He gave my hand another squeeze and then let me go. Standing, he reached for the wine bottle and poured me a second glass. Then he went to the refrigerator and got himself another bottle of beer. As he twisted off the cap, his cell phone rang. He swiped the screen and put the call on speaker.

"It's Harold," the voice said. "And I've got some answers for you."

"You're a good man." Derek reached for his notepad and pen.

"First off, Kay Jones is half Chinese, as you thought."

"It's a woman, for certain?" he asked.

"Yes. I had to go deeper into the files to track down that little fact." Harold spelled the name out for us, including two accent marks. "It's Yúnquè Jones, pronounced *Yoon Kay*."

"Got it," Derek murmured.

"She took that name when she started this op," Harold explained. "Before that, she always went by Kay Jones."

"Is that something that people do?" I asked. "Change their names for every new op?"

"Good question," Derek said. "Harold, how much do you know about this op? Did it require name changes? Was it deep cover? Did it come out of MI6?"

"No," Harold said, following Derek's questions. "It was a freelance operation, although most of the agents were former CIA or MI6. Including Yúnquè Jones."

"Was she MI6?"

"No," Harold said. "CIA."

"Can we dig any deeper on her?" Derek wondered.

Harold sighed. "I dug down as deeply as I could, but I'll try to go deeper. It'll take some time."

"What was the op?" Derek asked again.

"It took place almost six years ago. The agents were hired to protect the daughter of a powerful European potentate, along with her recalcitrant husband."

Derek flashed an amused smile. "Recalcitrant?"

"Yes," Harold said. "Apparently he was, to put it bluntly, a hound dog. And not a very bright one."

Derek raised an eyebrow. "Do we have a name for the potentate?"

Harold hesitated. "I could tell you, but—"

"You'd have to kill me." Derek chuckled. "Right. Go on."

"The king is an ally, but their country was going through some turmoil, so our State Department wanted extra protection assigned to the daughter and the hound-dog husband while they were visiting their country's consulate in San Francisco."

"Interesting," Derek murmured.

"Oh yes, positively fascinating," Harold said drolly.

I smiled. Harold sounded like a pretty fun guy. I just hoped we could trust him.

"Now fast-forward to just a few months ago," Harold said. "It has recently been speculated that the king is about to name the son-in-law as his successor."

"The hound dog?" Derek said, exchanging a quick glance with me.

It was my turn to raise an eyebrow. I wondered what the king's daughter thought about that possibility. And if it turned out to be true, was there a reason for her father's decision to bypass her? He had to know about the son-in-law's infidelity. Did he not trust his own daughter to capably rule their country? Or was he just a good old-fashioned male chauvinist pig, as my mother would say?

"Yes, the hound dog," said Harold. "Although apparently he's on his best behavior at home, but when he travels, he goes a little wild. I can probably dig deeper on this thread, too, but it seems that the son-in-law is being blackmailed."

"Ah." Derek took a drink of beer and leaned back, contemplating the possibilities. "By one of the agents?"

"We don't know that," Harold murmured.

"No, of course not."

Without thinking, I asked, "Why wouldn't the king name his daughter as successor?"

"Harold," Derek said. "That lovely voice belongs to my wife, Brooklyn."

"Sorry," I whispered to Derek. He waved away my concern.

"Pleasure to meet you, Brooklyn," Harold said. "It's a good question. The answer is that their country's law decrees that only a man can rule."

"Ah. That's so . . . modern of them."

Catching my clear sarcasm, Harold laughed. "It's too bad, really. She's a doctor and studied law at Harvard. She's a goodwill ambassador to the UN and works with the Human Rights Campaign. Her husband, on the other hand, is a pretty face. But he's male."

"Ugh."

But that wasn't answering the real question, I thought. Why was someone killing off the agents who'd been assigned to the daughter and son-in-law in San Francisco? And Harold had also said that the son-in-law was being blackmailed. Was the killer trying to get rid of a blackmailer? Or was the blackmailer the one doing the killing? And why was the son-in-law being blackmailed? Probably for being a hound dog, I thought with a sigh.

"What would you like to ask, darling?"

I looked at Derek in surprise. "Oh. Sorry. Again."

"You're thinking loudly," he said, smiling.

"Okay," I said. "Do you know why the son-in-law is being blackmailed? Is it because he's a hound dog?"

"Probably," Harold said. "The king is a good man, a family man. He's also a religious man. If he found out that his beloved son-in-law was embroiled in an affair, the king would be devastated. The son-in-law can't take a chance on losing favor with the king. So he's paying. Twice-a-month payments of twenty thousand dollars."

"If you have that much intel," Derek said, "you must know who's getting the money."

"Unfortunately, they are a lot smarter than the son-in-law," Harold said. "They've covered their tracks quite well. But we'll find them."

"Good," Derek murmured. "The sooner the better."

"I'll do some more digging," Harold said. "I know there's more buried in the file than just this surface stuff."

"I appreciate it, Harold."

"One more question?" I said.

"Of course," Harold said cheerfully.

"Do you know who on the list is dead?"

"That's a very good question," Harold said. "We can confirm that Ned Davies is dead. We can also confirm that Malcolm Brown is dead."

I frowned. "Ned said there were four dead."

"Christopher Peeler was thought to be dead," he said, "but then resurfaced in Tokyo last week."

"That must be a relief for him."

Harold chuckled. "He's gone into a safe house for the time being."

"So Ned and Malcolm for sure," I mused. "And Ned must've thought Christopher was dead when he wrote the letter."

"That complicates things," Derek murmured. "Mathematically speaking."

"According to the letter," I said, "there should be one more death."

"We've had no reports," Harold said, "other than what I've just told you. But I'll alert you the minute I hear anything."

"Thank you," I said.

He and Derek had a nice moment of small talk, with Harold sharing a cute story about his wife and baby daughter. Then he promised to call Derek as soon as he had any more information.

"Be careful, my friend," Derek said to Harold, just before they finished the call. "The only people who know these details are winding up on the endangered species list."

Chapter 11

That night, Derek was able to track down his old friend Tommie Robinson by phone. Derek put the call on speakerphone, and I listened as they spent a few minutes catching up. Then Derek told her what had happened to Ned.

After she expressed her deep sympathy and they commiserated and reminisced about Ned for another minute, Derek broke the real news.

"Ned's murder is connected to the San Francisco consulate job you worked on with him. Do you remember?"

"Of course, but that doesn't make sense," she said. "We did that job years ago. Who would care about it now?"

"It was only six years ago," he murmured. "And now, word has it that the king is planning to appoint his son-in-law to the throne."

"That knucklehead?" Tommie's laugh sounded harsh. "Honestly, Derek, he's useless. Handsome as sin, but vain and dim-witted."

"Don't sugarcoat it, Tommie," Derek said dryly.

"Sorry, but I wasn't a fan," she muttered. "He was a dangerous man, with a cruel streak that was frightening."

He sounded awful, I thought. If the king was thinking of installing him on the throne, maybe they were
two of a kind. Except that Harold had described him
as a good man who would be devastated if he found out
his son-in-law was cheating on his daughter. So either
the king wasn't paying attention or the son-in-law was
a master of deception.

"What about the daughter?" Tommie wondered.
"She was the one with all the smarts in the family."
Another pause, then she added, "Ah, just answered my
own question. The king is deliberately bypassing her
because she would show him up. She's smarter than he
is. And now, by installing that idiot son-in-law, he's
about to prove that he's even dumber than I thought."

But last night Harold had said that the king was a
good man. So what was the truth? I wondered.

"The king is supposed to be a decent man," Derek
said. "The problem is that the law in the country forbids
women to rule, so the daughter will never be queen."

Tommie swore under her breath. "God, spare me
these ridiculous medieval laws. So instead, they'll have
some psychopathic knucklehead in charge. Good luck
to ya, I say."

I couldn't blame her for being exasperated. If I had
a nickel for every psychopathic knucklehead . . .

"Word is," Derek said, "the son-in-law is being
blackmailed."

"Blackmailed?" Tommie paused to think about it.
"I guess I'm not surprised. He was always getting into
trouble. I can't imagine the king doesn't know what
kind of a man he is, but maybe the knucklehead knows
how to play him."

"Maybe," Derek murmured.

"I wonder who would blackmail him," she said. "Someone who's trying to protect the daughter? Or someone who wants to endanger the monarchy?"

"Could be either of those," Derek said. "Or it's someone who couldn't care less about the daughter or the monarchy but simply saw an opportunity to make some money off the fact that there's a dim-witted knucklehead ripe for the scalping."

"Well, yes," she said with a touch of humor in her tone. "There's that."

Derek brought the subject back to the original point. "Besides the royal guard, there were seven of you in charge of the couple's security while they were in the states and particularly in San Francisco. And now at least three of you are dead. I just don't know which three."

There was silence on the line. Derek finally said, "Tommie? Are you there?"

"Yeah, I'm here. I'm just suffering a little reality shock, I guess. When you put it like that, it's worrisome."

"Did you know the other agents working on the assignment with you?"

She snorted with impatience. "No. The powers that be were too paranoid about assassination attempts to allow us to mingle. I only fraternized with my partner. That was Ned, of course."

"Right."

"It wasn't a long assignment. About three weeks, if memory serves. Ned and I had a good time in the city."

"In San Francisco?"

"Yeah. Great town."

"Who was your contact at the agency?"

"Owen Gibbons," she said. "Good man."

I didn't know why I was taken aback, but I was. So Owen was involved in that assignment, too. Small world. And now I recalled that he had told us how he'd fallen in love with San Francisco when he'd worked here six years ago. I sighed. We hadn't made that connection.

"And you probably know that he married one of the agents working with us," Tommie continued. "Another small-world moment."

"Who did he marry?" Derek asked casually.

"Bettina Mayer."

I tried to keep my eyes from goggling.

"Did you know her?" Tommie asked.

"No," Derek managed. I could see he was as blown away as I was.

"We didn't spend much time together," Tommie said, "but she seemed pretty sharp." She took another moment to ponder the situation, then said, "So you believe one of the agents could be blackmailing the son-in-law?"

"It's possible."

"It's not me," she said blithely. "You're going to want to check my bank accounts. I can give you access." She laughed. "As if you couldn't access them all on your own anyway."

Derek chuckled. "Do you think I'd be calling if I thought you were capable of blackmail?"

"I hope not," she said. "But look, if you're calling to warn me, Derek, that's darling of you, but not necessary."

"Don't brush this off, Tommie. I want you to take precautions. Until we get to the bottom of this, your life is in danger."

"I'm perfectly safe," she insisted.

"That's what Ned thought as well," he pointed out. "Come on, Tommie, I had no trouble at all tracking you down. You're listed in the phone book, for God's sake."

"My phone number is listed, but not my address."

"I could unearth your address in five minutes," he muttered.

"Well, sure. *You* could." She sighed a little, and I knew she was growing impatient. But then, so was Derek.

"You were always the best among us," she said. "Look, don't worry about me. I appreciate your concern, and I promise to be careful."

Derek knew there was nothing else he could do to convince her to take further precautions. "If you won't leave town, I want you to call me every night for the next week. Or you can text me. We don't have to talk, just leave me a message telling me you're all right."

"So dramatic," she said fondly. "Honestly, I've missed you dreadfully. Okay, I'll do it. And keep me posted."

"I will."

Despite my fears that Derek himself might have become the target of a vicious killer and my frustration at leaving town while the murders of Ned and Tailor remained unsolved, Derek and I drove out of the city on Saturday. It was time to visit my family in Dharma, the small town in the Sonoma wine country where I grew up.

We had been planning this day trip since we returned from Paris. We had goodies to deliver to our family and friends, as well as several private messages to pass along to Robson Benedict, secretly known as Guru Bob to us kids while we were growing up.

Guru Bob had been my parents' teacher, guru, and friend for over twenty years. He was the reason my parents left San Francisco and moved to Sonoma with their six children to join his Fellowship for Spiritual Enlightenment and Higher Artistic Consciousness. I was eight years old at the time, so I couldn't say whether the commune helped my parents become more spiritual or artistic, but I do know that they were happier than they'd ever been in the city. And we kids had thrived as well.

Guru Bob had started with sixteen hundred acres of land, half of it covered in grapevines. The first thing his followers—and their children—did was plant more grapevines. I remembered that very well. Eventually we began to make wine. We moved out of our campers and built homes. We called our little community Dharma, and over the years it grew and developed into a fabulous destination spot with high-end shops, restaurants, small hotels, and a thriving winery.

These days, my father and brothers ran the winery and sat on the town council. After eschewing their worldly goods all those years ago, my parents had now become the elder statesmen—and wealthy to boot. My father thought that was a real kick in the pants.

Earlier this year, Derek's brother Dalton had moved to Dharma to be with my sister Savannah. And just last month his mother and father, Meg and John, bought a second home in Dharma and hoped to split their time between the wine country and Oxford, England. Luckily, our parents got along famously. My mother and Meg had so much in common that I sometimes wondered if maybe they were sisters separated at birth.

As we drove over the Golden Gate and into Marin County, Derek and I talked about our plans for the day.

"We need to stop at Robson's house for a few minutes," I said.

"Yes, I made an appointment for ten thirty. He's expecting us."

"You're way more organized than I am," I said, impressed.

"You're always organized," he countered. "But I have Corinne."

I smiled. "You're a lucky man. She's an angel."

"Yes, she is."

"Speaking of Corinne," I said cautiously. "How is she handling it with Lark still around?"

He shrugged and never took his eyes off the road. "She knows there's a light at the end of the tunnel, so she's managing just fine. For now."

I glanced over and saw the tension creep into his jaw. "And how are you surviving?"

He rolled his shoulders and stretched his neck side to side, trying to relax his tense muscles. "The sooner she leaves, the sooner I'll be able to breathe easier. I just don't trust the woman."

I watched him for several more seconds. "Is there something you haven't told me?"

"What do you mean?"

"I don't know how to explain it exactly," I said, keeping my gaze on him. "But it's unusual to see you showing signs of stress about work. Or else maybe you just usually hide it better than this. I know her lawyer would love to sue you, but did Lark do something else to threaten you?"

He reached over and took hold of my hand. Bringing it to his lips, he kissed my knuckles. "No, love. No threats." He turned and gave me a level look. "More like a promise."

"Excuse me?"

His lips pressed together in a thin, angry line. "She promises to make our lives a living hell if I try to get rid of her."

My hands turned into fists. I truly wanted to throttle the woman. "She actually said that to you?"

His features tightened again. "Yes, she did."

I held up my hand. "Wait. You said *our* lives. She threatened me, too?"

"Oh yes," Derek said softly, dangerously. "She doesn't like you, darling."

"I think I've mentioned that to you, so it's not a surprise." I tried to keep my tone light. "But it sounds like a really good reason to fire her."

His mouth was a thin line. "I did."

"You did?" I was shocked and thrilled all at once. "Is she gone?"

"Not yet."

"Why not?" I might've sounded a bit shrill, but good grief, would we never get rid of her?

"Because Bart got wind of what was happening and came running into my office. He insisted that I keep my word about giving her until the end of the month when the sales figures come in."

"Oh my God, she's got him wrapped around her little finger," I said in disgust. "I know he's your old friend and I've always liked him, too. But he's completely blinded by her."

My hands curled into fists again and I imagined pounding her face in. And I added a smack upside the head for Bart, too, while I was at it. And I wasn't a violent person! But Lark was driving me crazy with her arrogance.

I counted to ten, then backward down to one. "Maybe it's a good thing that we're wrapped up in this puzzle over Ned and the book and the list. It's the only thing that's distracting enough to keep me from clawing Lark's eyes out."

"Good point. We won't talk about it anymore."

But I was still so angry, my hands were beginning to shake. I had to close my eyes for a minute and will myself to chill out. If I showed up in Dharma looking tense, my mother would catch my vibe and do a karma cleanse on me. I shivered at the thought.

"I do have one question," I said.

He reached for my hand. "What is it?"

"Have you explained to Bart that I'm being threatened by this woman?"

"I have." Derek was clenching his teeth again and I felt bad about that, but I needed to know. "But he can't believe it. Bart is one of those people who only sees the good in everyone."

"He might be a danger to himself."

Derek laughed. "That's it. No more talk about 'she who must not be named.'"

"Deal." But that didn't mean I couldn't imagine kicking her bony ass right out the door of Derek's office and watching her roll down the hill and into the bay. And that possibility cheered me all the way to Sonoma.

As we drove up the driveway and parked the Bentley, my mother and father dashed out the front door and onto the porch.

"You're here!" Mom cried, jumping and waving. "Oh, I've missed you so much."

We hadn't even left the car yet. As I unbuckled my seat belt, I glanced over at Derek. "I told her we would only be here for an hour. She's making it sound like we're staying for a week."

I sort of wished we were, I thought. Especially with everything that was going on in the city. And watching my parents always made me smile. Mom wore one of her handmade tie-dyed rainbow skirts with a soft-knit sweater and ancient cowboy boots that suited her like nothing else. Dad was wearing jeans and an old rainbow T-shirt that Mom had made him eons ago. If I squinted a little, I could still see them as the adorable young Grateful Dead fans they'd been when they first met all those years ago.

"Your mother is lovely," he said kindly.

"Yes, she is. Thank you for saying so." I smiled, leaned over, and kissed him. "She's also a whack-a-doodle and you know it. Promise me you won't let her cast any spells on us."

"Promise."

We climbed out of the car to hugs and kisses and questions all the way up to the porch and into the house.

"How was the honeymoon?"

"Paris was fabulous," I said, "and Bordeaux was fantastic. We went truffle hunting and we stopped in Lyon to visit with Ariel and Pascal. And then we drove to La Croix Saint-Just to check in with Robson's relatives. And because it was so close, Derek took me over to see Oradour-sur-Glane."

Mom came up behind me and began to rub my shoulders. "Oh, sweetie. That must have been difficult."

"It's not an easy place to visit," I admitted. "But I wanted to see it, especially after we learned the true story of how Robson's family came here. And La Croix is so close, it didn't seem right to stop there and then not make the pilgrimage to Oradour-sur-Glane."

The small town had been completely decimated by the Nazis in World War II. The women and children were rounded up and led into the church, where they were attacked with tear gas and machine guns. The men were gathered together and executed. And then the town was burned to the ground.

And in a village a few miles up the road, Robson's great-grandparents worried that, because several of the brothers were part of the Resistance, the same fate would befall their town. The family escaped in the night and made the long journey across the ocean and into the United States. Since they were a family of winemakers, they settled in Sonoma with other relatives and grew grapes.

"So we brought back some family heirlooms for Robson," I said, "along with a letter from one of his aunts."

"Oh, he's going to love that," Mom said, still rubbing my back and kneading my shoulders.

I moaned with pleasure. "Mom, I'm going to give you two hours to cut that out."

Dad laughed and Mom gave my shoulders one last squeeze. "That's it for now. I've got to clean these breakfast dishes."

We stayed for an hour, talking about our trip, showing them photos on our cell phones, and asking about the latest happenings in Dharma. Finally, I asked about Derek's parents.

"You should drive by their new house," Mom said.

Dad grinned. "It's a nice one. Just up the next hill. Plenty of room for visitors."

"I'd like to see it," Derek said, then glanced at his watch. "We'd better get going. We have to be at Robson's in twenty minutes."

"Will we see you later?" Mom asked.

"We're going to try to have lunch at Arugula if you feel like joining us. After that, we're driving back to town."

"If we decide to join you, we'll call Savannah and let her know to expect us."

"Good idea," I said. "I hope we'll see you, but if not, we'll be back in a few weeks."

"And thank you for my pashmina," Mom said.

"Sorry it's such a cliché gift." I gave her a hug. "But I hope you like it."

"It's beautiful." She pushed my hair back from my face, something she'd been doing since I was a little girl. "And you're sweet to have thought of me."

"I saw it and had to buy it," I said. "That shade of blue reminded me of your eyes."

Those eyes of hers were instantly filled with tears. "You're going to make me cry."

I grinned. "Then my work here is done."

We followed Dad's directions down the hill and then up to the top of the next one, where the view for miles was of rolling green hills covered in grapevines and olive trees. Derek stopped in front of a pretty Craftsman-style home painted sage green with pale yellow trim and with a wide wraparound veranda in front. The house was two stories and was perched on the hill, surrounded by pine trees and a wide, verdant lawn. Pink and red flowers flowed from pots near the front door, which was painted a bright, shiny red.

"Mom suggested that your parents paint the door red to create good feng shui."

"That's a must-have."

"Right. Since the door is facing west, the red color will naturally attract the best chi into the house."

"Of course it will," Derek said, laughing as he checked his watch and pulled away from the curb.

I sighed happily. "It's charming."

"Yes, my parents chose well. We'll see the rest of it when everyone arrives next month."

"Gracious, come in," Robson Benedict said, opening the door and stepping aside to let us in.

Guru Bob, despite the silly childhood nickname, was a lovely, serious man with so much knowledge and goodness, I simply loved being around him and soaking up his positive energy.

He was tall, fair-haired, and handsome. Despite the gravitas he exuded, he had a good sense of humor and was as comfortable in a tie-dyed dashiki as he was in a tuxedo. He gave me a hug and pressed his hands to my cheeks. "You look wonderful." But then he took a closer look. "But something is troubling you. What is it, gracious?"

Another quirk of Robson's was that he liked to call us "gracious." When I was little, I assumed it was because he couldn't remember all of our names, but my mother assured me that it was his way of making us aware of the fact that we were actually filled with grace.

"It's the same thing that usually troubles me," I said, trying not to grumble too much.

"Come and have tea and we will talk," he said, leading the way into his beautiful living room, where we sat and enjoyed a cup of tea and delicate pastry-style cookies. I could've eaten a dozen of them, but I stopped at two.

"I brought a few things for you from La Croix Saint-Just." I put my teacup down, opened the shopping bag, and handed him the first item. "This is a letter from one of your aunts. There's also something that belonged to one of your great-uncles. I'm not sure which one, but they wrote out an explanation for you. It's in French."

He pulled the letter out and read it. "That is very heartwarming," he murmured. "She says that they received all of their belongings and it was wonderful of me to store them safely." He gazed at me, shaking his head. "We all know that this is not the true story, but I am grateful to you for going there and making sure everything arrived safely."

Last year, during the expansion of the wine caves, we discovered a treasure trove that belonged to the families back in La Croix Saint-Just. It had been hidden for decades, and when it was unearthed, plenty of devastating family secrets were also revealed. Along with a poor dead soul who had been trapped in the cave for all those years.

"Everyone was very thankful," I said. "They couldn't be happier now that they've got their family heirlooms back. It's a sweet little town. Have you been there?"

"No," Robson admitted. "But I have already made plans to visit next year."

"You'll love it. They took very good care of us."

"Yes, they did," Derek agreed. "They're quite a generous group."

"There's one more thing they sent," I said. "It's a gift for you from the entire town." I had to set the shopping bag on the carpet and lift the box out carefully.

"What is this?" he asked, staring at the box.

I smiled at his hesitation. "You can open it, but be careful. It's fragile."

He lifted the heavily wrapped object from the box and set it on the table. Then he slowly unwrapped the packing paper.

"Good heavens, what is it?" He turned it around. "It's art nouveau, definitely. Porcelain. It's beautiful."

It was delicate and dreamy, with a highly glazed lily growing the length of one side of the ten-inch-high pitcher.

"Yes. We were told it had been in the Benoit family for over a hundred years."

He blew out an unsteady breath. "They are sending a message."

"A good one, I think. They told us this was a wine jug, so perhaps the message is eat, drink, and be merry."

He was able to chuckle. "I like that."

"We hope you'll enjoy it in good health," Derek said.

Robson nodded his thanks to Derek, then turned his attention to me. "What is troubling you, gracious?"

Where to start? I thought. But I didn't want to burden him with everything that had been going on with us, so I just told him about Ned. "We recently received word that a friend died, someone we just saw in Paris a few weeks ago."

"I am so sorry," he said. "He died a violent death."

It wasn't a question. Robson just knew.

"There's more you're not telling me," he said cryptically. "Someone else has died? Or someone is in danger."

I knew Guru Bob could come across as psychic sometimes, but it still startled me to realize how insightful he was. I opened my mouth, then closed it. "Um, well, there are a few other things going on, but I don't want to trouble you with all that. You're very kind to care."

"Of course I care, and you can trouble me anytime you want," he said, and then smiled. "It pleases me to be able to talk with you. Both of you," he added, patting Derek's arm.

He walked us to the door and I gave him another hug. "Thank you for the tea and cookies."

"And thank you for the gifts from La Croix. I am grateful that you made the trip there."

"It was our pleasure," Derek said. "The people in the village were charming. We felt quite at home there."

We were about to leave when Robson's expression dimmed suddenly and he clutched Derek's arm. "Take care, Derek. There are dark forces hovering."

"Yes, there are," Derek said with deadly assurance. "And I will protect my own."

Robson let go of his arm and smiled. "Thank you for coming to visit. Have a safe trip back to the city."

When we got into the car, we looked back and saw Robson standing at the door. We all waved at each other, then Derek and I drove away.

"That was just weird," I said. But I should've been used to it. After all, my own mother was uncanny with her witches' spells, and Guru Bob was often prophetic with his words.

"Okay," I said, stretching my shoulder and neck muscles to loosen the tension I felt. "Let's shake it off and go see Gabriel."

*   *   *

Gabriel lived a mile up the hill on the other side of Mountain Ridge Road from my parents. It took almost a half hour to get there because of all the switchbacks and narrow curves on the way up, but the view from the top was glorious.

We turned onto Dragon Valley Road, pulled into Gabriel's wide driveway, and parked by the house. It was lined on one side by three gigantic satellites dishes, and they weren't there because Gabriel liked to watch a lot of TV. No, they were there because Gabriel was a security expert, and his clients around the world, including Guru Bob and all of Dharma, depended on him getting unfettered access to communications and information at all hours of the day and night.

His home was a rambling log cabin as big as a small hotel, and it included a lap pool built into the deck in back of the house.

Last year Gabriel had fallen for our friend Alex, and who could blame him? The only problem I could foresee with the relationship was that Alex tended to go for the kind of man who could be trusted to follow her lead. As a high-powered businesswoman, she spent a lot of time around men with those same high-powered qualities, and when she got home, she didn't want to deal with all that ego and the control issues.

Gabriel wasn't one of those ego guys, but he was definitely in control of every situation he stepped into. I never thought Alex would go for him, but then, how could she not? He was almost as amazing as Derek. It made me happy to realize how well they suited each other and how much in love they were.

As we got out of the car, Gabriel walked out onto

his front deck wearing a black T-shirt and faded jeans that perfectly outlined his long, lean legs and wide, muscular shoulders. His thick, dark hair was pushed back from his face and almost touched his shoulders. I had always described his looks as those of a fallen angel, but he actually had more of the devil in him, I thought. A gorgeous devil.

"Hey, babe," he said, giving me a hug. "You smell good."

"Thanks." I was surely blushing, not because of the compliment, but just because of the way he said it. He was sinfully sexy.

The two men shook hands and Derek said, "Thanks for meeting with us on short notice."

"That's what I'm here for."

The front door opened again and Alex walked out, jogged down the steps, and grabbed Derek in a tight hug. Then she walked over to me.

"Hey, girl," she said, giving me a warm hug.

"I didn't know you would be here," I said.

She smiled. "I hang out here once in a while."

I looked at the view of terraced vineyards that spread across the rolling green hills and valleys. "It's so beautiful up here."

"Yeah, it is," she said, gazing at Gabriel.

I gave her a moment, then said, "We're going to lunch at Arugula after this. Do you guys want to join us?"

Arugula was my sister Savannah's restaurant in Dharma. She was a Cordon Bleu–trained chef and her restaurant was vegetarian, but her meals were unlike any vegetarian meal I'd ever had. She had received her first Michelin star earlier this year, and her restaurant was one of the reasons San Franciscans came in droves to visit Dharma every weekend.

"That sounds like fun," she said. "If we can get in."

I grinned. "I made reservations."

"You're a smarty-pants," she said, wrapping her arm around my waist and walking me up the steps.

"Yeah, that's me."

"So, is this just a friendly visit," Alex asked, "or is something going on?"

I glanced back at Derek and Gabriel, deep in conversation across the drive. "Something's going on."

Gabriel took us into his small conference room and served us coffee and scones as if we were his clients. As we talked about the situation, I glanced around the table.

It wasn't difficult to be in a room with both Derek and Gabriel if you didn't care about breathing. One man was better looking than the other, and both were tall, dark, dangerous, and tantalizing. Gabriel had a touch of the wheeler-dealer in him, and when we first met, I frankly wasn't sure if he was a hero or a thief. But then he saved my life, and that turned him into a permanent hero for me. Turns out, he was a little of both, the classic bad boy. Derek exuded strength and polished charm from the very start. And all women were grateful when either of them walked into a room.

I found Alex staring in amazement at both men and had to grin. Clearly, she agreed with my assessment.

Gabriel and Alex listened to everything we told them about the last week, including all we knew about

Ned's murder and Tailor's murder. We talked about the list of agents who were being killed off one by one. Alex had been to SPECTRE with me and knew about the writers' group and Owen.

Gabriel leaned forward and folded his hands on the table. "Let's boil this down. But first, my sympathies to you for losing your friend in Paris, and I'm sorry for the loss of this young writer at that place, SPECTRE. But it sounds like you've got two separate problems to deal with."

"I'm not sure about that." I took a sip of the dark, rich coffee Gabriel had made, and I sighed happily.

Derek said, "Brooklyn's right. There appears to be a connection, but it's tenuous."

"Here's the thing," I began, "Tailor was killed when he interrupted the intruder who was trying to steal our book. And that was the book that Ned planted the microfilm in."

"Ah," Gabriel murmured. "The microfilm with the list of agents. Yeah. Connection."

Alex had been listening to everything, and finally she nodded and turned to Derek. "So what would you like us to do?"

"Gabriel has the means to dig deeply—without detection—into the agency's records on the San Francisco consulate assignment."

Gabriel sat back in his chair. "I'm familiar with the system you have in your home. It's as good as mine. I know because I helped you set it up. You could find this same information just as easily. Why do you need me to do it?"

Derek smirked. "Did you catch the part where I mentioned *without detection*?"

Gabriel chuckled. "Sorry, I'm only on my second cup of coffee. So yeah, I get it. Happy to help."

"Seven agents on a list," I said. "At least two, possibly three—or four by now—are dead. Of the agents that are still alive, one's a killer, and one's a possible blackmailer. So we want to know a couple of things. First, who exactly on the list is dead?"

"Second," Derek continued. "Who is the blackmailer?"

"And third, who is the killer?" I asked.

"And fourth," Alex added. "*Why?*"

The lunch at Arugula was another gastronomic triumph by my sister. The only downside was that Mom and Dad couldn't make it, but they promised to visit us in the city two weeks from now.

We feasted on wild mushroom crepes, chargrilled bok choy with garlic and fennel, sweet chili dumplings, pasta with four cheeses, and a Meyer lemon and fig tart with lavender ice cream for dessert.

Every time I ate there, I was thankful that Savannah had never gone full vegan, eschewing cheese and eggs. Thus, ice cream. She cleverly paired interesting wines with each course and even suggested a special beer to go with Gabriel's deep-fried veggie tempura.

When the meal ended and Savannah came over to sit at our table, I gave her the forest green cashmere beret. She held it and stared at it for several long seconds. "Wow, thank you."

"I thought of you when I saw it," I told her. It wasn't really a white lie, because as soon as I got home from Paris, I did think of her and how good she would look in it. "I hope you love it."

"I do love it," she said, leaning in to give me a one-arm hug. "But it's too special to wear in the kitchen. I'll wear it whenever we go out."

"Good." I was just happy the beret was going to a good home.

A few minutes later we walked out the back door to the parking lot and there were hugs all around.

"Thanks for your help," I said when Gabriel hugged me.

"Anytime, babe," he murmured in my ear. "We'll see you Tuesday night."

"You will?" I asked.

"Yeah." He gave me a wicked grin. "We're all going shopping at SPECTRE."

Chapter 12

Derek and I spent Sunday afternoon at the ball game. I tried to tune out the ugly horror of the murders that had occurred, along with my profound fear that Derek could be in danger from a vicious killer.

It helped that the sky was crystalline blue with breezy white clouds. Sailboats floated on the sparkling water of the bay as seen from the amazing box seats Derek had wangled from Corinne. She was in charge of the company's season tickets and she guarded them with an iron fist, only doling them out to very important clients and vendors. The fact that she was willing to give the boss those seats for a change made us very lucky ducks indeed.

It also helped to be outside with thousands of happy baseball fans cheering for our team.

A couple of hot dogs, one order of cheesy nachos, and two beers helped, too.

And hey, the Giants won! So we walked home, flushed with victory and stuffed with pride. And hot dogs. And I realized when we reached our apartment building that I hadn't thought about cold-blooded murder for four long hours. That was a victory, too.

*   *   *

Monday, after Derek left for work, I finished the kite. After the glue had dried completely and the frame felt sturdy enough, I held it up to the studio window. Morning sunlight poured into the room and illuminated the lovely Chinese-inspired-print paper from behind, giving it the appearance of a stained glass window. I actually felt tears gather in my eyes, it was so beautiful. Maybe it was my own vanity, and maybe I would be the only one who thought so, but I hoped that Ian would agree that this fine-looking kite would be a perfect addition to the paper exhibit at the children's museum.

As soon as the Covington Library opened, I called him to talk about the kite.

"You're back," he said. "How was the honeymoon?"

I was still happy to answer any and all questions about the honeymoon, but I had a feeling it might get old pretty soon. Sometimes it felt like their question was code for *Hey, how about all that hot sex in Paris?* Or maybe it was just me. I was the one who needed to get over it, I thought with a sigh.

"I have four hundred pictures to show you," I said cheerfully. "It was fabulous because it was Paris. So, you know, it was all about breakfast in bed, and sex, the Eiffel Tower, more sex, more food, museums, sex, blah-blah-blah, rinse, and repeat."

He laughed as I knew he would. "Sounds like you're a little tired of answering that question."

"You know me too well," I said with a chuckle.

Ian and I had been friends for years and were once even engaged to each other for six months before we both came to our senses and called it off.

"We really did have the best time ever," I said, then changed the subject, telling him about the kite. And he went crazy.

"I want to see it. Now. We're revamping one corner of the kids' museum and it sounds perfect for our needs." He paused for a moment. "If it works, we might rethink a few other pieces and turn yours into the centerpiece for the new display."

"I'll bring it in today or later. I really hope you love it."

"If you made it, I'll love it."

"You're so sweet," I said fondly.

"I know," he said, and I could see him smirking through the phone lines.

"You're going to want to light it from behind," I added. "It's really pretty."

"Bring it in and we'll play with it."

Ian loved the kite. I brought it to him on Monday afternoon, and he had his assistant curators scurrying around, rearranging an entire display of Legos built to resemble a giant book, as well as two dozen papier-mâché skulls for their annual Day of the Dead celebration next fall, all in order to accommodate the kite.

Ian frowned. "I'm not sure this is going to work. I had an image of something completely different."

"Oh." I was truly disappointed. "Well, thanks anyway for taking a look at it."

"Whoa," he said. "Not at all what I meant. The kite stays. All this other stuff can be arranged elsewhere." He moved around the display floor. "I just meant that we need to find more of a spotlight for the kite, instead of just sticking it on a platform."

"Maybe we can hang it up above everything," one of the curators, a blond woman, said.

The other assistant, a really young guy, nodded. "Yeah, like it's flying in the sky."

"Excellent, both of you," Ian said, and the two assistants gave him wide, adoring smiles. "We'll put it up in that corner," Ian agreed, pointing. "So it looms above everything."

"And so it's out of the reach of little grabby hands," another assistant added.

"Very good point," Ian murmured.

I nodded in approval. "It'll be easier to light it up there, too."

"I want it lit so that it catches the eye no matter where you are in the room," Ian said. "And I want the tail to be suspended with wire so it really does appear to be flying."

"It's going to be awesome," the blond curator said.

The other one frowned in contemplation. "Everyone who sees it is going to want to make a kite. We'll start a trend."

I had already thought about that. "If you'd like, I could make up a flyer or brochure on kite making. Maybe you could offer a class for the kids."

Ian clutched his heart. "You are divine."

I laughed and gave him a hug. "I know."

When Derek arrived home Monday evening, I greeted him at the door with a kiss and a new plan of action. "I think it's time to take the book back to SPECTRE."

He pulled me into his arms and kissed me more thoroughly, then we walked into the kitchen, where he removed a bottle of cabernet from the wine fridge.

"Are you sure you want to take the chance? The intruder could return anytime and try again."

I walked over to the dining room table and picked up the book. "Here it is. Tell me what you think."

He put down the corkscrew and examined the book. Shaking his head, he began to smile. "Obviously, that's a different book."

"It's obvious to you and me," I countered. "Especially if you hold it in your hands."

I had substituted *The Spy Who Loved Me* with a bestselling novel of about the same size. I'd made a color copy of the dust jacket, trimmed it down to size, rolled it back and forth to try and soften the grain a little, and then folded and wrapped it around the fake book.

"You can feel that the paper is new and stiff," I said, taking the book back. "The dust cover is way too bright and clear. And the book itself doesn't have the flexibility of age. But in the dark, in a locked display case, you might not notice right away."

He frowned as he loosened the cork. "It could work. At first glance, anyway."

"If the killer returns to steal it again, I don't want him to see an empty display case. I want him to think he's getting the real deal. At least until the police run over and slap a pair of handcuffs on him."

He poured the wine and handed me a glass. "How did you come up with this idea? It's a good one, by the way."

"I kept wondering how we could lure the killer out into the open. And the answer is, he has to come back to the store. And the best bait to bring him back is the book."

Derek pursed his lips in thought. "How do we know he hasn't come by the store in the last few days and noticed that the book is gone?" Derek sipped his wine. "He might assume that we've already found the micro-film."

"I thought about that, too," I said with a sigh. "I don't have an answer."

"Well, let's think of one."

"Okay, but while we're thinking, we need to figure out how to ask Owen about his wife."

"Bettina Mayer," Derek said. "She could be our killer."

"It's entirely possible. How can we get Owen to bring her into the store?"

"Who's to say she hasn't been there all along?"

"Right," I said. "Wearing a hoodie and a ski mask, maybe?"

Derek chuckled. "It does seem far-fetched. But then, this entire operation seems a bit out of bounds."

"Okay, then let's return to our book quandary." I paced from the kitchen island to the dining room table and back. "Maybe Owen could post a sign near the display. It could say, THE BOOK IS BACK! or something like that. Owen doesn't know about the microfilm, so he won't be nervous about lying. And if anyone asks him, he could mention that the book's owner was a little gun-shy after the attempted robbery, but the store has beefed up security, so the owner has agreed to display it again." I sipped tentatively, knowing it was a shaky scheme. "What do you think? It's a little weak."

"It might work," Derek said. "But yes, it's iffy. The killer might've heard through the grapevine that we're already making inquiries about the names on the list."

"That's what I'm afraid of," I muttered. *Afraid?* I

was terrified that Derek might become a target. But I
didn't mention it. "We've got to figure some way to lure
him out."

"Let's go with your idea. Ask Owen to put up a sign
announcing the return of James Bond. Something simple but intriguing."

"I like that."

"If the intruder doesn't show, we're no worse off than
we were before. And if he does"—he smiled grimly—"we
get him."

Tuesday night, we met Gabriel and Alex at the Buena
Vista for an early dinner before returning the book to
SPECTRE. We were getting to be regulars at the BV,
which wasn't a bad thing—although the place did get a
little crowded with tourists sometimes. But some of the
menu items were so worth waiting for, not to mention
the Irish coffee.

In the car on the way over, I gave Inspector Lee
another call. And once again, I was sent straight to
voicemail. I told her that since I hadn't heard back from
her, I wanted her to know that we were going to SPEC-
TRE to give them back the book, although I wasn't
sure if I had already told her why we had taken it away
in the first place. And while we were there, we might
hunt down the hidden camera for her.

Without even looking, I knew Derek was rolling his
eyes.

"We'll keep you posted," I continued on her voice
mail. "Oh, and I want to tell you about Derek's friend
in Paris who was murdered and a possible connection
to Tailor's death and the book. Anyway, have a nice
evening."

When I ended the call, I turned to Derek, who was laughing.

"That might've been a little abrupt."

"Do you think so? 'There's a murder. Have a nice evening.' Nothing abrupt about that."

I shrugged. "Maybe it'll nudge her to call me back."

At the Buena Vista, Derek and I split an order of fish and chips and the four of us shared a bottle of wine. I figured I'd need a touch of liquid courage to face the search for a hidden camera at SPECTRE.

"Okay, so we're looking for a hidden camera," I said, after taking a bite of the crisp, deep-fried fish. "It could be as tiny as a thimble, you know?"

"Right," Gabriel said. "With any luck, he had it wired to a nearby receiver."

"So we look for a wire? Or a receiver?" I clearly didn't have a clue.

"It could be wireless," Derek said, "but if so, there will be a receiver nearby."

I winced. "I'm not sure what a receiver looks like."

"It could look like a Wi-Fi box, the one that comes with cable for your television. Or it could look like a little transistor radio." Gabriel grinned. "They come in all sizes, too, just like cameras."

"Just so you know," I confessed, "I'm not holding out a lot of hope that we'll find something, but I'm sick of sitting around. We've got to do something."

Alex grinned. "Right there with you, sparky."

We were greeted just inside the door by Tinker. "Hi." Then he blinked and stopped talking, struck dumb once again by Alex's presence.

Gabriel was merely amused and sympathized with

the younger man. "I'm Gabriel," he said, and shook Tinker's hand. "How you doing?"

"Okay."

"Hi, Tinker," I said, and gave him a quick hug. "Are you doing all right?"

"Pretty good. Well, to tell you the truth, it's been kind of weird around here. That detective was in earlier."

"Inspector Lee?" I asked in surprise.

"Yeah. She wanted to see the surveillance video again."

I gave Derek a quick look. "Didn't she take a copy of it with her?"

He nodded. "She did."

"Good." So at least she was on the case, even if she wasn't interested in talking to me. I wouldn't take it personally. She was a busy cop.

Tinker jumped in. "Yeah, but first she wanted me to watch it with her. She asked me a bunch of questions while we were watching. And she also wanted to see some of the coverage from earlier in the day and then some from the day after. She's thinking maybe the hooded guy has visited the store more than once or twice. And maybe he returned in disguise to try again."

"Good thinking," I murmured. Actually, Derek and I were absolutely certain the guy had come in a few times before that night to take a look around.

I observed Tinker as he spoke. "So you watched the entire video?"

"I did," he said. "Owen played it for the three of us the next day, but he wouldn't let us see the shooting itself. He just wanted us to watch the earlier part, thinking we might recognize the guy in the hood."

That was smart, I thought. "Did you?"

"No." He scowled. "He was covered from head to toe, so I couldn't tell who it was." With a shrug, he went on. "Drummer thought he looked familiar. Or rather, *she* looked familiar."

My eyes widened. "She? Drummer thinks it's a woman?"

Tinker twisted his mouth, puzzled. "I don't see it, but she thought from the way the killer walked, it could've been a girl."

"I'd like to take a look at it," Alex said with a casual smile. "Is that okay?"

"I'm sure Owen would let you, but he's not here right now." Tinker looked around, thought for a second, then gave us a sly smile. "But I've got a key to his office. I can set you up."

"That would be wonderful," Alex said. "Thanks, Teddy."

Tinker—Teddy—blushed like she had just kissed him. "Follow me."

While Alex and Gabriel viewed the surveillance video, I walked around the bookshop, looking for hidden cameras. It was kind of like looking for a needle in a haystack, and I figured I'd have just as much luck finding either. So I focused on the bookshop area, looking around for any possible hiding place that might show the glass counter area where the book had been displayed.

But frankly, even if I did find something, what would it reveal? Not much more than the store's surveillance video itself had revealed, which was nothing, as far as the identity of the killer was concerned. But I looked anyway, because I would go crazy if I didn't.

On every bookshelf, I moved the books back and forth, pretending to line them up neatly. On the wide back shelf where all the Ian Fleming books were displayed, I picked them up at random and moved them around. And found nothing. Not inside any of the books or hidden in between or behind them.

Above that shelf, on a small book rack mounted on the wall, there were more James Bond books, but these had been written by other authors. Not Ian Fleming. Rather than lined up in a row with the spines showing, these were shelved with the covers out. Randomly, I reached for *Goldeneye*—and it didn't budge. I pulled a little tighter, hoping I wouldn't yank the entire rack off the wall, and realized when it glinted in the light that the cover was damaged. Someone had cut into it.

"What the heck?" Gingerly, using both hands, I managed to pull the book off the rack. It was a paperback version of the novel that was written from the screenplay by John Gardner. The cover was green with a large black circle around the name *James Bond*. It featured a military helicopter and a handgun with a silencer attached. Under the blade of the helicopter, a small circle, less than a half inch in circumference, had been cut out of the book. And inside the circle was a camera lens.

"I found something," I whispered, and Derek came around the display case to see. "It was on that shelf up there."

I tried opening the book, but it was glued shut.

"You try to get the book open," Derek said, "and I'll look around for a receiver."

As soon as Derek walked away, I pulled out my phone and went online to my favorite book site.

"I want to know what I'm dealing with," I murmured. In the search box, I typed in *Goldeneye*, clicked on "paperback," and found a dozen copies, all worth less than ten dollars.

It was a relief to know that the book hadn't been worth much money, but I still didn't approve of anyone damaging a book. I'd have to get over it.

I pulled my key ring out of my purse and used my Swiss Army knife to cut into the book. Cutting through a few hundred pages, I finally reached the center, where I found a mini-cam the size of my thumb buried inside the book. A red light blinked, telling me that it was still recording.

Derek came back. "I didn't find a receiver."

"I did." I held the book open and showed him. "It's attached by this cable to the camera and he fitted it inside these cutout pages."

"Let's find someplace to plug in this cable."

"Should we do it here or go home?"

"Let's go home," Derek said. "I don't want Tinker or any of the other kids to see what might be on the video."

It was a good decision to view it at home.

Derek and Gabriel fiddled with the camera and cables and set up the video to view on our big screen in the living room.

"It's got audio," Gabriel said, sounding surprised.

Derek nodded. "Yes, isn't that interesting?"

"Why?" I asked.

Gabriel turned. "The type of surveillance cameras we're talking about, mainly nanny cams, don't usually include audio. It's not usually necessary if you've got a video picture memorializing the event. Also, there have been a number of lawsuits and the audio has been problematic. The cases often get thrown out on technicalities."

"That's weird," I said.

"It may be that the 'hidden' element bumps up the liability," Derek suggested.

"Ah, good to know," Alex said.

After pouring everyone a glass of wine, Derek started the playback.

The first thing we saw was Tailor in an extreme close-up, like he was taking a video selfie. It was a shock to see the young murdered writer alive and speaking into the camera.

"Tailor here," he said, his voice low as he aimed the camera at himself. "Today I'm testing the Buffalo brand mini wireless nanny cam with so-called gizmoid technology." He chuckled and shook his head. "They come up with the dumbest names for this stuff. Anyway, this baby has night vision and motion detection features, plus audio capabilities. So here goes."

Tailor aimed the lens outward and panned across the store. "I'm here at SPECTRE," he said. "I've constructed a perfect little spot to hide this mini-cam."

He held up the copy of *Goldeneye*, then opened it and set the camera into the cutout area. Everything went black, but he narrated his actions so we knew what he was doing.

"I took this book apart to dig out a place for the camera and the cable. I paid for the book, by the way." He chuckled. "Now I'm lining up the lens with the hole

I cut in the cover, and I'm going to tape the book shut and stick it back on the shelf. And then tonight we'll see how well the night vision feature works."

We heard the sound of tape being pulled from a dispenser. "I'm wrapping the book closed so it won't fall apart."

After a full minute, he said, "Okay, it's ready to go." He aimed the lens toward himself again, grinned, and waved. "I'm doing some paperwork for Owen in his office, so I'm going to watch the feed from this camera to see how it looks and sounds."

He started to walk away, then returned and stared into the lens. "And by the way, nobody better judge me for taking this book apart. I'm a huge Ian Fleming fan, so I would never destroy one of his books. Instead, I picked *Goldeneye* because not only did Fleming *not* write it, but it's not even a book. It's a *novelization*. From the movie. Can you believe it?" He said the words with so much sneering derision, I almost laughed.

"The movie wasn't that bad, though," Tailor said with a shrug. He adjusted the lens again and shoved the book onto the wall rack in the bookshop. "Okay, let's see if this works."

The video showed him walking out of the frame, then a static shot of the middle of the store from the bookshop wall. Derek pushed it into fast forward, and a few seconds later when the picture shifted, he stopped. The store was much darker and the view was grainier.

"The camera's been motion activated," Gabriel explained. "And the night vision feature just clicked on."

"There's someone in the store," Alex said. "I can see their shadow from the light coming in the front."

"I'm impressed with the clarity," Gabriel murmured.

"Can't see their face, can you?" I asked.

Alex shook her head. "Not yet."

"Wait. I can see the shadow now." It was so weird to see the shadow growing larger as the intruder sneaked farther into the store. I knew the video was taken the same night as the original surveillance video, knew this would be the same person, but from this angle it felt like a new event.

He moved toward the glass enclosure where *The Spy Who Loved Me* was on display. The guy pulled the tool from his pants pocket and began to cut into the glass. But before he could get anywhere, there was a commotion in the background, then the sound of someone running across the floor.

"Hey! What are you doing here?"

The thief whipped around, and that's when Tailor stepped into the camera shot. We could see his face clearly. My shoulders hunched in fearful anticipation, knowing what would come next.

"Get out," the hooded prowler growled. He turned and, for the briefest moment, was silhouetted in the moonlight pouring through the nearby café window.

I watched in fascination. Now we knew how Tailor had gotten into the bookshop area so quickly. He was right around the corner, in Owen's office, doing paperwork and watching the intruder on his computer.

"Stop the video," Alex cried. "Go back."

Derek instantly froze the image, then rewound it. "Say when."

Alex jumped up and pointed. "Right there. Can you play it back? Can you see it?"

"See what?" I asked.

She grinned, moved up close to the screen, and pointed. "That is the outline of a breast."

Gabriel stared at the screen, his elbows resting on his knees. "I can certainly attest to that fact."

"Maybe it's just a bulge of material," I said lamely. "You know, from his sweatshirt." But the more Derek played the video, the more I knew I was wrong. "For the love of . . ." I looked at Derek, dumbfounded. "I can't believe it."

He shook his head slowly. "Drummer Girl knew what she was talking about."

"She sure did," Alex said. "And you know, when I watched the first surveillance video, there were a few moments when I thought it could've been a woman. I wasn't positive, but you know, it was something about the way she walked. Not the whole time, but once in a while. As if she was trying to walk like a guy, but every minute or so she would forget."

"There was one moment when I wondered, too, but I blew it off," I groused. "I just assumed it was a guy."

"We still can't see her face."

Gabriel shrugged. "A hoodie and a ski mask tend to make it difficult."

"Let's keep watching," Derek said, then hit the forward arrow, and we watched the video come back to life.

On the screen, Tailor took a step closer to the intruder. "I've called the police. You can still get out before they arrive."

"You're boring me," the thief said, pulled out a gun, and shot him.

That was a woman's voice, I thought. And the "boring" line was something a woman might say, too. I hated to admit that.

But pulling out a gun and shooting a young guy like Tailor? That wasn't male or female. It was inhuman. Cold. Sickening. I'd seen the tape a few times now and it always made me woozy.

Tailor spun around, then grunted in pain and stared dumbfounded at the shooter. He pressed both hands to his stomach. "That's screwed up," he mumbled, and backed away a few steps. Then he turned and ran off toward the back of the store.

The intruder pounded her fist on the counter and began to swear under her breath.

"Do you recognize her voice?" I asked Derek.

"Pretty certain it's a woman," he murmured. "But no idea who it is."

Alex said, "She's pissed off, that's for sure."

Was it Bettina Mayer? Owen's wife? But wouldn't she know Tailor? How could she have shot him so cold-bloodedly? Owen hadn't recognized her when we all watched the video together. Or maybe he had been lying. Maybe he knew exactly what she was doing. That thought made me feel a little queasy.

The woman turned back to the locked book display, then leaned over to stare in the direction Tailor had gone. It took her another second to make up her mind where her priorities lay, then she dashed off after Tailor. And disappeared from the camera's view.

"She left the book," Alex said.

"She came in for it, but now she has a new goal. She's got to make sure the kid is dead." I rubbed my arms, still feeling chilled. "He's a loose end."

"But stealing the book was her main goal," Alex said.

I shrugged. "I guess she figured the book would still be there when she got back."

"We've seen this play out already," Gabriel said. "She comes back, but doesn't get the book."

"Right," Alex said.

"Okay, the camera might go into sleep mode here," Gabriel explained. "But her reappearance will start it recording again."

"She was gone about five minutes," I said.

"So who is she?" Alex asked.

"There are three women on the list," I said, watching Derek. "Does she look like Tommie?"

He muttered under his breath, then pressed his mouth closed in a stubborn line. Finally, resigned, he exhaled in a rush. "It could be Tommie. She's tall. I haven't seen her in years, but she used to work out like a madwoman. I remember her being a little shapelier than this woman looks, but she could've lost weight or been wearing body armor or . . . one of those bodysuits or . . . something."

"It's either got to be her," I said, "or one of the other two women on the list."

"Yúnquè or Bettina Mayer."

"I prefer to think it's one of the other two," Derek grumbled.

"I know." I rubbed his shoulders in sympathy.

"How do you spell that one?" Alex asked. "What is it? Yoonkay?"

"Close." I spelled it for her, but before I could say anything else, the picture shifted again and we all turned back to the screen.

"Here we go," Derek murmured.

The woman came jogging back to the glass display case, and unlike the view from the overhead cam that had blocked so much of her action, this shot revealed exactly what she was doing.

We watched her reach for her glass cutter and press it to the surface. But before she could cause any damage, she lifted her head and began cursing again.

"I can hear the sirens," Gabriel said.

"Yeah, the cops were responding to a silent alarm that Tailor set off."

The woman was obviously furious. She clenched her fists, then sprang into action, grabbing her shopping bag filled with the merchandise she'd stolen and disappearing from view.

Derek stopped the video. "We know from the original surveillance video that she made it out of the store and managed to escape."

He stood up, turned the lights on, and poured more wine.

"Okay," I said, feeling a little exhausted after watching that all over again. "We all agree that the book thief and Tailor's killer is a woman."

"Do you think she's also the blackmailer?" Alex asked, then yawned. "Sorry, I didn't get much sleep last night."

"It's getting late," Gabriel murmured, and wrapped his arm around her.

"I don't know if she's the blackmailer." I sipped my wine. "Now that I know the killer is a woman, I'm rethinking the identity of the blackmailer." I held up my hand. "Not that I don't think a woman is capable of blackmail, but just how much evil can one person manage?"

"Plenty," Alex stated, her eyes hard.

"I know you're right," I conceded.

Derek jogged to the kitchen and returned a few minutes later with a plate of cheese and crackers. "It's been a long while since we've eaten."

"Thanks, man," Gabriel said. He grabbed a couple of crackers and handed one to Alex.

"Where does Tommie live?" I asked.

"She's on the East Coast," Derek said, then frowned. "I don't want to believe she's involved."

"I know. Just thinking of possibilities."

"What about Bettina Mayer?" I asked.

"We need to contact Harold. Get more information."

"Or we could just ask Owen about his wife."

"Let's do that," Derek said flatly. "Because I know Tommie has nothing to do with any of this."

"But if both Bettina and Yúnquè are dead," Gabriel began.

Derek scowled. "Then my old friend Tommie just killed that innocent young man."

"It's not Tommie," I said adamantly.

He looked surprised by my statement. "How do you know?"

"Because I know you," I said firmly. "You have good instincts. And good friends." I leaned against him. "This whole situation is making you doubt yourself, and that bothers me because it's something I've never seen you do." I sighed. "We'll figure it out."

He slung his arm around my shoulders and squeezed me closer. "Thank you, love."

"I need to walk around," Alex said, pushing up from the couch. "Does anyone want water?"

"I can get it for you," I said.

She grinned and headed for the kitchen. "I can handle this."

"Gabriel, I totally forgot to ask you." I reached for a cracker. "Were you able to find out anything about the other people on the list? Who's alive and who's dead?"

"Not about the people on the list yet, but I managed to get some intel on the son-in-law. My sources tell me he was having an affair while staying at the consulate in San Francisco."

"Bingo," Alex called from the kitchen.

"An excellent reason to be blackmailed," Derek murmured.

"And not unexpected," I said. "Harold called him a hound dog and Tommie had a horrible opinion of him. I figured he screwed around everywhere he went."

"Except at home," Derek noted. "Where the king and his men probably keep a close watch on him."

Alex walked back into the room and flopped down on the couch. "So someone saw him with another woman."

"Someone on the security detail?" Gabriel suggested.

"Security agents often see everything," Derek said.

"But Tommie said that they kept them all isolated from one another," I said. "She was only familiar with her partner, Ned."

"The blackmailer could be part of the consulate staff," Alex said as she walked back into the living room.

"It feels like it all connects back to the security detail," Derek said. "I need to check back in with Tommie."

"And Harold," I added.

Alex yawned again. "Sorry, guys. I'm falling out. And I've got an early meeting in the morning."

"Let's go," Gabriel said, patting her leg before standing and pulling her up. He looked at Derek. "Keep me posted, okay?"

"You bet."

I stood and gave them both a hug. "Please walk carefully." She and Gabriel were staying at her place, so their commute was only a few yards down the hall.

They laughed as we followed them to the door. "Thanks for all your help tonight."

"We'll keep thinking," Alex said.

When we closed the door, I looked at Derek. "I just want to say this again. Your instincts are unimpeachable. You would never be friends with a cold-blooded killer, so it can't be Tommie. We have to talk to Bettina Mayer and find Yúnquè Jones."

He leaned into me. "I want to keep working, but I can't use my home system to dig too deeply." He raked his hand over his head in frustration. "I received a text from Tommie, but when I tried to call her back, there was no answer."

That wasn't good. Anyone could respond to a text. "Is it too late to call her?"

"Yes." He grimaced. "It's even later on the East Coast. We'll have to wait until tomorrow. I'll need to contact Harold as well, for an update."

I thought for a moment, then smiled up at him. "I'm going to try one thing and I'm not going to tell you what it is."

"Why not?"

"Because you'll laugh at me."

"Never," he insisted, but he was already smiling.

"Okay, let's give it a whirl." I led the way into my

workshop, sat down at my desk, and powered up my computer.

Derek sipped his wine as he paced around the room. As was often the case, it was hard to tell if he was relaxed or tense. Maybe a little of both, but I would guess that the tension was winning out. And who could blame him? We were dealing with some really dangerous people who would go to any lengths to cover their tracks, including murder.

He stopped pacing and moved up close to me. Setting his wineglass on my desk, he placed his hands on my shoulders and gently kneaded my tight muscles.

"That feels so good," I whispered, then clicked on a site and waited.

Suddenly Derek laughed. "Seriously, darling? Google?"

I shrugged. "It's my go-to for everything else. Why not this?"

I typed in *Bettina Mayer* and watched a dozen images pop up. Each was a different face. Not helpful. "There are hundreds of different Bettina Mayers on LinkedIn. And twenty-four of them are in Germany."

"We'll simply talk to Owen tomorrow and ask him about his wife."

"Yeah." But I was disappointed. My go-to search engine had failed me. "I'll try the next one." I typed in the word *Yúnquè* and hit Enter, wondering if anything would register.

But within seconds, over a dozen references for the word *Yúnquè* appeared. It only took the first entry to make my eyes boil over, but I checked three more entries, just to be certain.

"Damn it," Derek muttered, and the string of expletives that followed was not something I would ever want to repeat in polite company. But I completely agreed with every last word he said.

Yúnquè was the Chinese word for a skylark.

"Skylark?" I stared at the screen in complete disbelief. I was downright flabbergasted. "Are you kidding me?

"Lark," Derek snapped, and the word sounded worse than any obscenity I'd ever heard him say.

Chapter 13

"How can she be connected to any of this?" I asked. "She's just a salesperson in your office. I mean, she's horrible, but—"

"She used to be with the agency," Derek said tonelessly.

"Wha—huh?" My mouth opened, but I couldn't think of a word to say. I was speechless. Incredulous. All this time, all the many conversations we'd had about how annoying Lark was, and he'd never once mentioned that she used to be with the agency?

My sputtering seemed to relax him and he managed a half smile. "Most of my staff have some background in government security."

"But Lark? You never said a word. And . . . she's . . . in sales."

"I should have told you before, but it simply didn't occur to me." He poured us both another half glass of wine. "I run a security company, darling. We handle highly sensitive information every day, and our agents are often put in dangerous situations all over the world. Our salespeople are in contact with those agents, and they're actively searching for others in the security field. They have to be aware of all sorts of information and situations. And they have to be able to deal discreetly."

"So everyone in your company has a security clearance?"

"Yes."

"Okay. Wow. Good to know." I weighed this new info and nodded. "Makes sense."

"I'm calling Gabriel." Derek punched in the number and hit the speaker button. "He needs to know what we've uncovered."

Gabriel answered his phone immediately. "Yo."

"Can we use your deep-dive computer to confirm a theory we've just come up with?" Derek asked, and then told him our suspicions about Lark. His anger was back and he paced around my worktable as he spoke.

"Come on down," Gabriel said.

Derek slipped his phone into his pocket, grabbed our keys, and took my hand. We quietly jogged down to Alex's apartment to talk it out.

Gabriel sat at Alex's kitchen island, typing and clicking on his computer. Alex stood on the opposite side of the island, mixing flour and sugar.

"I thought you'd be sound asleep," I said.

"I got my second wind," she explained. "Especially when Gabriel told me what you found."

"So you're baking?" I asked in disbelief.

She shrugged. "It's my superpower."

"You have many," I said, smiling. "But your cupcakes are the most significant."

"So what's going on with that horrible woman?" she asked as she reached for the tin of baking powder.

"I just found out that Lark used to work for the agency," I grumbled.

"I never said anything about it," Derek admitted, "because it was never an issue. Most of my people have worked in government or security, including Lark. And when we did a background check on her, we were told by several high-ranking officials that she had only worked a desk."

"Then how did she land that consulate assignment six years ago?" Alex wondered.

Gabriel clicked a few more times, typed a few sentences, then stared at his computer screen and snorted. "Dude, she has a higher security clearance than some of those high-ranking officials you got references from."

"That's annoying," Derek muttered.

"It's beyond annoying," I said irately. "It's a complete—"

"Don't say it," he said quickly, holding up his hand. "You're right. It's reprehensible. I've always conducted my own background checks, but a couple of years ago I was out of the country for an extended period of time and my staff had to depend on the headhunters."

"Lesson learned," Gabriel said philosophically.

"I must point out that the headhunters we used were also vetted carefully." Derek shook his head. "But things do slip through cracks."

"If Lark has such a high security clearance, why would she bother with a sales position?" I wondered. "And why did she want to work for your company? I mean, yeah, you're the best. But what was her game plan?" I frowned. "Maybe she's being paid to obtain information. She might've arranged the whole job interview process to get close to you. That didn't work. I mean, she didn't get as close as she wanted to. But have you noticed that she's awfully close to Bart? And by the way, *that's* annoying."

"I am certain that Bart has nothing to do with any of this."

"Okay, you would know," I said, and backed off. But I still wasn't convinced of Bart's loyalties because he always supported Lark instead of Derek. Was Derek's partner having an affair with Lark? It was worth looking into, but that wasn't my job. I might mention something to Corinne, though. I tucked that thought away for later.

Derek rubbed my back, adding, "Darling, I know Bart's clean because after you said something the other day, I personally ran a deeper background check on him."

I gazed up at him. "Yeah?"

"Yeah."

I was happy to hear it, but I was still going to talk to Corinne. The woman saw everything. And a high security clearance couldn't protect Bart from a sneaky, seductive woman like Lark.

Gabriel stared at his computer screen and whistled. "Hmm. Here's something. Did you know she's the daughter of the head of security in Guangdong Province?"

I blinked a few times and shook my head. "Say what?"

"Guangdong Province borders Hong Kong," Gabriel said, sitting back and folding his arms. "It's on the coast, so it's strategically important for that and many other reasons. It's also the most populated province in China."

"So her father has a lot of power," Alex concluded.

Gabriel grinned. "Actually, it's her mother."

"Whoa," I muttered.

"Let's follow the money," Gabriel said to Derek. "Can you access your firm's accounting records?"

"Of course," Derek said.

"Expense reports?" he asked.

Derek stared at Gabriel for one long moment. Then with complete understanding, he nodded. He began pounding keys on his keyboard like a maniac, so I walked over to the kitchen island to watch Alex doing her magic with cupcakes.

The first batch of cupcakes were coming out of the oven when Derek finally looked up from the computer screen. His jaw was tight, but he was smiling. Admittedly the smile was sharklike, but there was a touch of satisfaction, too. "It just gets better and better."

"What did you find?" I asked.

He looked up at me, then glanced at Gabriel. "You won't believe this one."

"What?" I demanded, a little too sharply. "Sorry."

He chuckled. "Understandable. Anyway, I'm still piecing it together, but it appears that Lark is the one who was having an affair with the potentate's son-in-law."

No one spoke for a minute. I figured we were all in shock. I knew I was.

Finally I found my voice. "How did you find that out?"

"Follow the money," he said with a nod of appreciation to Gabriel. "Lark has been flying to Miami once a month for the past six years. She submits expense reports every month that claim she's meeting a certain client there, and she always stays at a particular hotel in Miami Beach." He glanced up from the screen. "The son-in-law's name is Kristof, by the way."

"Good to know," Alex said from the kitchen.

"I cross-referenced Kristof's name and Miami Beach and came up with several articles describing his lavish lifestyle and the time he spends doing business in Miami Beach. Then I added Lark's name to the mix. The dates are remarkably similar."

"But that could just be coincidence," I said reluctantly.

"True," he said. "But there's another set of expenses she claimed when she was wining and dining a new client from Seattle last year. At the same time, Kristof was in Seattle for meetings with Japanese investors on behalf of the king."

"Okay, okay. I'm starting to believe it."

Gabriel nudged Derek away and sat down at his computer. "I can check the timing of Kristof's flight records for other cities and give you a list. Then when you get to the office tomorrow, you can check Lark's expense reports for that time period, see if they coincide."

"They will," I said, even without more proof. I had no idea that this kind of stuff could be tracked down so easily, but I loved that Gabriel and Derek could do it. "So she's a killer, a thief, and a floozy."

"But at least she's not a blackmailer," Alex said with a twisted grin.

"Maybe not," Derek said. "But if she finds the blackmailer, she'll kill him, too."

"Maybe they're blackmailing *her* as well as Kristof," I said.

Derek stared at me. "Oh, darling. That's good."

I scowled. "You'd better make sure she's not stealing money from your company."

"Corinne has already investigated that possibility."

That little revelation gave me another reason to smile. "Go, Corinne," I said.

After another half hour of searching records, during which Alex whipped up another dozen red velvet cupcakes, Derek and I went home. But I couldn't sleep. It was all too much to take in. I had distrusted Lark from the moment I first saw her, but things had veered way off the track. She had transformed into evil personified—on a global scale.

Derek and I stayed up for another hour, debating, plotting, arguing, and planning the best way to trap a killer.

Happily we were doing it in the comfort of our warm and snuggly living room couch.

"We have to go back to what we talked about earlier," I said. "Lark doesn't know that we've found out all this stuff about her. All she knows is that she's got to get that book and find the microfilm."

"Why?" Derek asked.

I blinked and looked up at him. "What?"

"Why? Why does she need the microfilm? Is it because her name is on the list? Or does she want to find out the other names? We think she killed Tailor, but can we be sure she killed Ned?"

"No. But it makes sense." I thought about it. "Was she at work the whole time we were gone or did she take a few days off?"

"I'll have to check with Corinne."

"How did Ned wind up with the microfilm?" I wondered.

"He would've made it himself," Derek said. "He was a good photographer back in the day and had a studio and darkroom in his house."

"You did say he was old-school."

"He probably never used a digital camera in his life," Derek said with fondness. "So he typed up the list, took a photograph of it, developed the film, and snuck into our hotel room to hide it."

"Poor Ned," I whispered.

We sat in silence for a few minutes.

"It's late," Derek said.

"We can still use the book as the bait that will bring her back into the store."

"Yes. Let's sleep on it and we'll decide how to carry it off in the morning."

"Is she an American citizen?" I asked. "Could she claim diplomatic immunity or something?"

"She became an American citizen three years ago," Derek said. "But I'll have to double-check tomorrow to find out if she has dual citizenship"

"Good."

"You know," Derek said, "if we just want to skip to the chase and not involve SPECTRE or the book, we could simply have her arrested at my office."

I thought about it. "But we wouldn't have any evidence, would we? I mean, we know she killed at least one person. We saw it with our own eyes. On the video."

"We didn't see her face," he said.

"No." And just because I'd googled a name and it had translated to "skylark," it didn't make it evidence of anything. "I guess Inspector Lee could arrest her on suspicion of murder, but a decent lawyer would have her back on the street in a heartbeat."

"True enough."

"So I think we actually have to catch her sneaking into SPECTRE, breaking into the display case, and grabbing the book in her hot little hands."

"So she gets arrested for stealing a book?" He shook his head dismissively. "Not exactly a capital offense."

"*And* breaking and entering," I said haughtily. "And also, it's a very expensive book. So, you know, grand theft."

He chuckled. "I recall you paid at least seven euros."

I smacked him, but it didn't pack much of a wallop. "It's worth a lot more."

"That was rude of me." He chuckled. "I meant to say, it's a very important, very pricey book that was a gift from my beloved wife."

"You make it sound like I'm dead."

"I didn't say you were dearly departed." Derek grinned. "Though I'd like to point out that the fake book we're planning to put in the case is probably worth about fifteen dollars."

"Harrumph," I said theatrically. "Good point. But since I'm sitting in your lap and feeling very cozy, I forgive you for being snarky."

He kissed my cheek. "I think we're getting punchy. Let's get some sleep and wake up ready to kick some butt."

"We need to prime the pump," I declared the next morning after we'd both had a cup of coffee. I sat at the island counter while Derek dashed around the kitchen, preparing breakfast.

He glanced up from buttering toast. "What does that mean?"

"You know, like, you have to lead a horse to water."

He cocked his head, looking confused. "I'm going to need more information."

I tried again. "We need to scatter bread crumbs for a little mouse to follow."

"Are these metaphors?"

"Yes. Maybe not very good ones, but I was hoping you'd catch my drift."

He smiled. "Strangely enough, I do."

"And that's a beautiful thing," I said, pressing my hands to my heart.

"Isn't it?" He handed me a plate with toast and bacon and apple slices.

"Yum. Thanks." I munched on toast for a moment. "So what I'm saying is, we have to come up with a plan to get Lark to come to SPECTRE and steal the book. It has to be tonight."

"Yes, tonight would be ideal."

"And we have to prime the pump," I added.

"That still makes no sense," he said with a smile, and tore off a corner of his toast. "I'll call Inspector Lee to let her know our plan."

I frowned. Not because I didn't agree with him, but because I knew what her reaction would be. "That's not going to go over well."

"No. We've done this to her before. Come up with a plan and then ask for her help."

"True. She never seems to appreciate our hard work."

He smiled again. "I think we can convince her to go along with it this time."

"I hope you're right."

We sussed out the plan over breakfast. As scenarios

went, it wasn't the world's greatest, but it wasn't the worst. It required me to play a role, and while I'm not the best actress, I was determined to make this work.

My role required that I show up at Derek's office, and that meant that I needed to look polished and put together. Sadly, no yoga pants. No Birkenstocks. So after Derek left for work, I prepped for the role.

Once I was showered and my hair was looking good—I left it long and straight instead of pulling it back into my usual daytime ponytail—I decided on my wardrobe. I dressed in pink skinny jeans, a silky flowing pink-and-white tunic, and strappy pink high heels that I rarely wore unless I was forced.

I added a long dangly necklace studded with pink stones and gold baubles and a matching bracelet, then threw a filmy pink sweater over my shoulders.

When I stared at myself in the mirror, I smiled. I wasn't much of an authority on fashion, but I'd done okay. I looked very pink, very girly yet casual—not that it would matter to Lark. I just wanted to look nice for my husband and the people who worked for him. The ones I liked anyway.

I gave one last look at myself in the mirror and declared the outfit awesome. I felt good about it. Good enough, I hoped, to strike contempt and hatred in the heart of a certain killer/thief/floozy who would be so incensed to see me looking so good that she would be motivated instantly to carry out her own mission to steal my book.

That was a bit of a pipe dream, but I was determined to prime that pump any way I could.

I was still mixing metaphors right and left, but I was okay with that.

I grabbed my buckskin driving mocs and left the house.

When I walked into Derek's plush Nob Hill offices, the receptionist greeted me with warm enthusiasm. "Oh. Good morning, Brooklyn. Is Derek expecting you?"

"Hi, Marina. No, he's not expecting me, but I wanted to drop off some papers for him to sign. I won't be long."

"Okay. I'll let him know you're here." She pressed a button on her earphone, murmured a few words, and pressed the button again. "You can go right in. His meeting doesn't start for another ten minutes."

"Thanks, Marina."

"That's a beautiful outfit, by the way. You always look great."

"Thank you."

Driving over, I had worn my comfortable driving mocs. Then before I got out of my car, I had switched to the killer strappy heels. So now I walked very carefully across the spacious open reception area and down the hall. Derek's massive office was near the back of the building, giving him an amazing view of the city and the nearby park from the top floor of the company's stately four-story classical revival–style mansion.

I followed the wide, well-lit hall, admiring the high coffered ceilings and thick crown molding. Rounding the curve, I spotted Corinne waiting for me at the door to Derek's office.

"Hi," I said, glancing around to make sure we were alone. "You ready to do this?"

"More ready than you'll ever know," she whispered. "Derek told me everything and I still can't believe it's true."

"It's a shocker, all right."

"I checked back over the records and it's all true."

"Wow. That was fast work."

"Frankly," she said, glaring at me, "I wish I were more shocked than I am. As hard as it is to believe, it's somehow not surprising. That woman belongs behind bars."

"You've got that right."

"Let's make it happen," she said firmly, and slipped her arm through mine. "And by the way, you look adorable."

"You're so sweet to say so." I loved hearing the compliments. I wondered if maybe I should get out into the world more than I did. But no, I was happiest working at home in my Birkenstocks. You could take the girl out of the commune . . .

We walked into the large open kitchen and coffee break room, where five women sat around one of the tables on their morning break.

"Does everyone know Brooklyn, Derek's wife?" Corinne said to the table in general.

We all greeted each other cordially. I recognized one of the women from the Sales department, along with Kara from HR. Another was Shana, the word-processing supervisor. The three of them had been part of a group I'd met at the very first party I'd ever attended at Derek's office. I would never forget that they were the ones I'd overheard talking about my being Derek's "flavor of the month," a hateful term if ever there was one. And their cattiness hadn't stopped there.

I shook off the unpleasant memory and managed another smile before joining Corinne at the coffee machine. "Brooklyn dear, do you prefer decaf, regular, espresso, or latte?"

"Just regular black coffee," I said. I glanced back at the table and noticed the saleswoman texting on her phone.

"So what's new, Brooklyn?" Corinne asked in a clear voice while the coffee was dripping into a mug. "How was your weekend?"

"It was so nice. We spent Saturday in Dharma with some of my family and friends, and we had lunch at Arugula. And Sunday we went to the baseball game."

"I just love going to baseball games," Corinne said. "It's such a pretty stadium."

"The view from the box seats is spectacular," I said. "And thank you for the tickets, by the way. It was so nice to sit outside for a few hours and forget our troubles."

"I couldn't agree more," Corinne said, then whispered, "They're not *my* tickets, you know. You can have them anytime you want."

I started to smile, but just then, Lark walked into the kitchen.

I stared at Corinne, who gave me a slight nod. *Showtime.*

I coughed to clear my suddenly dry throat. "The drive up to Sonoma is so lovely. And we just adore hopping from house to house, visiting friends and having tea. And a touch of wine, of course."

I giggled. Did I sound like a pampered plaything? I hoped so. Whatever made Lark go ballistic would work for me.

"How fun," Corinne murmured, giving me a surreptitious wink.

"And then last night we went back to SPECTRE," I said, loud enough for everyone to hear.

"Don't you just adore that place?" Corinne said. "Wallace and I enjoy it so much."

"I love it, too," Kara the HR clerk piped up. "The escape room thing was a kick. I could spend all day there."

"I agree," I said, then turned back to Corinne. "Did Derek tell you that we loaned them this fabulous novel that I found in Paris? They put it on display for their anniversary celebration."

"Isn't that wonderful?" Corinne said enthusiastically. "Yes, Derek told me all about it." She lowered her voice dramatically. "But he mentioned the other day that you were afraid someone tried to steal it."

"That's right. And someone was actually murdered right there in the store."

"Good heavens." Corinne gasped and slapped her chest.

"I know. It was awful. So we brought the book home. But I've decided to take it back there this afternoon. The crowds at the store have really enjoyed seeing it."

"Aren't you worried about it?"

"No, no." I waved away my qualms. "I'm not concerned. They have it locked up in this glass case that's wired and hooked up to a security alarm, so there's no way anyone can steal it."

"I just hope it'll be safe."

I smiled. "That store is so secure, the book is probably safer there than in my house."

"That's good to know." She handed me the mug of coffee. "Here you go."

"Thank you." I took a sip of coffee. "So we'll leave the book on display through the weekend. It's fun to see all the customers lining up to get a good look at it.

They love that it's vintage James Bond. Goes right along with the whole spy theme."

"It certainly does," Corinne said with a laugh. She picked up her coffee mug. "Let's go see if Derek is available to sign those papers."

"Oh, let's." I turned to the group at the table and smiled brightly. "See you all later."

"That was fun," I said when we were safe inside Derek's office.

"You were wonderful," Corinne whispered.

I laughed. "I was kind of a dingbat, wasn't I?"

"Not at all." She chuckled. "Just a little chatty."

I glanced at Derek. He looked fantastic in a high-powered black business suit with a thousand-dollar silk tie and a crisp white shirt. I wondered, Was there any man on the planet who was handsomer and more dangerous than this guy? I doubted it.

"I think it worked," I said. "I could feel the scorn wafting from across the room."

"It was positively delicious," Corinne said, and we smiled at each other.

"We're pulling off a caper," Corinne continued, and patted her chest again. "My goodness, my heart was pounding there for a minute."

"Have a seat, Corinne," Derek said. "I'll get you some water."

She took his advice, and I sat down in the comfortable chair across from her. "Everything is going according to plan," I said. "And we couldn't have done it without you."

"It'll all be worth it when she's taken away in handcuffs," she said through clenched teeth, her irritation returning. "I'm so angry about this, I could spit. Imagine working with a killer in our midst all this time. And she was stealing from the company, claiming all those expenses when she was really just screwing around."

I laughed, a bit surprised to hear the prim and proper Corinne talking like that.

"It won't be for much longer," Derek said, patting her shoulder. "Here's your water."

"I'd better get going," I said, and gave Corinne a light hug. "Thank you again."

"No, thank you," she said with a grin. "It made my day."

Derek took hold of my arm and gave me a quick, hard kiss. "Be careful, darling."

"I promise," I said, and kissed him back. I took off down the hall and walked out to the lobby, waving to a few people I recognized.

And then I saw Lark standing at the receptionist's desk. She stared right at me, and I knew she had planted herself there to try and intimidate me one last time. It creeped me out, but I wasn't afraid of her.

"Thanks again, Marina." I waved to the receptionist, then gazed steadily at Lark. "Buh-bye."

Just before the door closed, I heard the sound of her hissing at me.

Since I was halfway across town anyway, I drove a few blocks over to Van Ness and took it all the way up to North Point. Turning right, I drove to Grant Avenue and took it the rest of the way to the Embarcadero, where I parked in the now-familiar garage across from Pier 39. I locked my car and walked cautiously down the steep, narrow drive and out to the street.

Crossing to the pier, I strolled past the flower-strewn balconies and the double-decker carousel and into SPECTRE.

When I stepped inside, Tinker waved and hurried over to meet me.

"Hey, Brooklyn, how's it going?"

"Great." I pulled the book out of my purse. "I brought the book back for the display. Is Owen around?"

"He'll be back pretty soon. He's out to lunch with his business partner."

"Oh, I remember he told us about him." I racked my mind and pulled the name out. "Richie, right?"

"Yeah, Richie Sylvestri. He doesn't come to town too often, so Owen took him out to lunch." Tinker checked his watch. "But they should be back any minute."

"I'll wait. I can browse around for a few minutes."

"That's cool." He blinked and shoved his glasses up. "Let me know if you need any help."

"Thanks, Tinker." Then I took a good look at him. "How are you doing?"

"You know." He shrugged. "It's tough. But I'm doing okay."

"I hope so." He was too young to look so tired, I thought. His eyes were red and a little puffy, but maybe he hadn't been sleeping. Maybe he had just been crying. He had watched the surveillance video more than once, and that might have been a bad idea. I knew that Owen had skipped the part where Tailor had been shot, but then Tinker had watched it again with Inspector Lee and then Alex and Gabriel. He had probably seen everything.

Watching the video had been traumatic for me, too, but I'd seen a lot of violence in my life, up close and personal. Tinker was just a kid. Okay, maybe not a kid, but he clearly wasn't used to watching a good friend get gunned down right before his eyes.

Violent death was a heavy thing to deal with at any age. I knew that from personal experience. So if Tinker was suffering from sadness and grief, it was completely understandable.

Gazing up at the small book rack hanging on the wall, I had a passing thought that there might still be other cameras hidden around the store. It didn't really matter, though, since we already knew who killed Tailor. What else was there to see?

I turned to look at more books and saw through the wall of plate glass windows at the front of the store that Owen was walking toward the door with another man. This had to be his partner Richie. He was a good-looking man, shorter than Owen, with dark hair and a well-trimmed mustache. They were having a spirited discussion, and just as they reached the door, they shook hands. Then the dark-haired man patted Owen on the back and walked away. Owen watched him for a moment, then entered the store.

"Hi, Owen," I said when he looked over and saw me.

"Brooklyn," he said, his voice positively jolly. "Don't you look sparkling? It's good to see you."

"Thank you." I couldn't help but smile. I didn't remember being called sparkling before. I liked it. "I brought the book back."

He clapped his hands together. "Excellent. Shall we put it in the display case together?"

"Yes, please."

"Let me get my keys."

I followed him into the café and waited while he

entered his office and found the big key ring with all the keys for the secure displays.

"I'm so glad you decided to bring it back," he said as he bustled out of the office and wound his way over to the center of the bookshop. "Our customers have gotten such a kick out of it."

"That makes me very happy."

"Here we go," he said as he found the right key and slipped it into the lock.

"I guess I just missed meeting your partner," I said. "Tinker told me that you had lunch with Richie Sylvestri."

"Yes," he said with a grin as he slid the glass doors apart. "He's in town for a few days of meetings. He's a busy man."

"It's nice that you had a chance to see him."

"Indeed it is." He gazed at me. "Would you like to do the honors?"

I blinked. Do the honors? It took me a moment to realize he was talking about the book. I guess I was still recovering from my dingbat moment. "Oh yes. Thanks. I'll put it in there." I pulled the fake book out of my purse and knelt down to place it on the bookstand just right. "How does that look?"

He gazed into the display. "It looks better than ever."

I gave him a big smile. "Yes, it really does."

I watched Owen lock up the case. I had worried and wondered if he would realize that it wasn't the real book, but it seemed as if he might be too distracted to notice.

"Derek was thinking that you could put up a banner near the front of the store announcing that James Bond was back."

He laughed. "That's a good idea. We'll bring in a lot

of new customers with something like that." He thought for a moment. "I think I'll add another sign for Tailor."

"Derek and I would be happy to contribute to a fund for his family."

"He lived with his mother," Owen said. "She's not a wealthy woman."

"She'll need money for his burial," I said.

Owen sniffed and blinked rapidly. "I was thinking of starting a scholarship fund in his name."

"That is a wonderful idea," I said, clutching his arm. "We would be happy to contribute."

"Good," he said, still sniffling. "Thank you."

"Of course. I miss him, too."

"Everybody does. He had a way of worming himself into your heart."

"He did." I laughed and glanced down at the fake Ian Fleming in the glass cabinet. "I remember Tailor really loved seeing this book here."

"I'm very grateful that you brought it back," he said again.

"I'm glad I could. I know it'll be perfectly safe while it's here."

"Absolutely," he said. Ready to change the subject, he said, "By the way, we've started construction on the new escape rooms. I'm wondering if you'll have time over the next week to come in and give us some of your expertise."

"Do you know what you'd like me to do?"

He frowned. "I'm a little stumped on where I might find a few hundred used books at a rock-bottom price."

I smiled. "I can put you in touch with a librarian friend of mine who's always looking for new homes for old books. She hates the thought of throwing them away."

"I would hate that, too," he said. "If you have her number, I'll be happy to give her a call."

I reached for my cell phone and a small notepad and jotted down my friend's phone number. "Here you go."

"Thank you. I'll call her this afternoon."

"And I can probably stop by sometime this week to see the Scary Library."

"Wonderful," he said cheerfully. "I hope we'll see Derek sometime soon as well."

"You will." Inspiration struck. "He was just mentioning this morning that it would be nice to have you and your wife over for dinner sometime."

"Oh." Owen touched my arm. "That is so kind of you both. But my wife passed away last year."

"Oh no, I'm so sorry," I said, truly shocked by the news. Without another thought, I wrapped my arms around him and gave him a hug. "I didn't know."

"I know," he murmured as we stepped back from each other. "That's another reason why I threw myself into making the store a success. It helps keeps my mind from dwelling on unhappy memories."

"I'm so sorry," I said again. Glancing around, I smiled. "You really have created a wonderful place here. I'm looking forward to working on the new escape room. And Derek might be willing to help out, too."

He pressed both hands together in prayer. "That would be more than I could hope for."

I laughed. "I'll make sure he comes in. And we're also excited to try out your virtual reality room."

"You should make a reservation," he advised. "That room is getting very popular."

"We will. Thank you again, Owen." I turned and walked quickly to the front door and back to my car.

*   *   *

I drove home to change into a more comfortable outfit of nice jeans and a good shirt, added a sweater and loafers, then drove over to Bay Area Book Arts, or BABA as we called it, for a meeting with Naomi, the director of the center and a good friend. I was scheduled to teach an intermediate-level bookbinding class next month, and I wanted to find out how the sign-ups were going. Also, they had recently made some changes to the formats of the classes, and I wanted to make sure I was in compliance with their new plans.

The fact that a murder or two had taken place while I had been teaching inside the artistic confines of BABA was something I chose to ignore whenever I returned to work there. It wasn't easy.

But the meeting went well. My class was almost full and BABA was thriving. I was happy to see how nicely Naomi had moved into the director's role after standing in the shadow of her domineering aunt, who had ruled the place for so many years.

My cell phone buzzed as I was turning onto Brannan Avenue and heading for home. I punched the hands-free button on my dashboard. "Hello?"

"Hello, darling," Derek said, and his captivating Oxfordshire accent echoed through the car. There were times when the situation called for him to crank up that posh upper-class tone that could intimidate and alarm the most hardened criminal. But when it was just the two of us alone, his voice softened and I could hear a whisper of the rolling hills and green meadows of his childhood landscape.

"Derek, hi." I glanced up at the cross street. "I'm only a block from home. Should be there in a minute or two. We have to talk. I spoke to Owen about his wife. She passed away last year. I didn't want to ask how it happened. Frankly, I was too shocked to say much of anything."

"So Bettina Mayer is dead," he said flatly. "I'm sorry for Owen."

"Yes. Me, too."

"Harold would've said something if he'd known about her," Derek said.

"Maybe she went by another name, too."

"Perhaps," he said. "I'll find out. Meanwhile, I wanted to let you know that I spoke with Inspector Lee."

I felt a muscle twinge in my shoulder, and instantly felt guilty. She was a friend, for goodness' sake. I sighed. Maybe so, but right now she was a cop. "I was going to call her, I swear. What's up?"

"I filled her in on our plans for this evening. She'll meet us at home around four o'clock."

I almost laughed at the formal way he'd said "our plans for the evening," but quickly realized he was being cryptic with his words. After all, he was working with a thief/killer/floozy right down the hall. And "our plans for the evening" included witnessing her steal my very expensive fake book and then waving merrily as the cops carted her off to jail for murder.

I couldn't wait.

Chapter 14

Derek got home a few minutes before Inspector Lee arrived.

I dashed over to give him a kiss, but stopped when I noticed he looked angry enough to kill someone.

"What's wrong?"

"Corinne called me in the car, soon after I spoke to you."

"What happened?"

He took a deep breath. "Lark is telling people that she and I are having an affair."

I felt my heart stop. I reeled back and pulled out a dining room chair and collapsed into it.

"You know it's not true."

"Of course I know that," I said, annoyed that he felt he had to say it.

He pulled out another chair and sat right in front of me. "She told Marina that the reason she left work for a few days while we were on our honeymoon was because I flew her to Paris to be with me. I couldn't live another day without her."

"So you were cheating on me during our honeymoon."

"That's what she said."

I gazed at him steadily. "My rage is complete. I will kill her."

"Not if I kill her first."

"Oh God." I buried my face in my hands. "When will we be rid of her?"

"Soon, love. Very soon."

The doorbell rang, but I had to sit for another moment, just breathing.

He held his hand out to me. "Come on. This will all be over soon."

"Not soon enough," I muttered, but pulled myself together, gritted my teeth, and walked to the door.

As Inspector Lee walked in, Derek's cell phone rang. He glanced at the screen. "I have to take this."

"Okay," I said.

Derek quickly shook hands with Inspector Lee. "I'll be quick."

"No problem." She turned to me and held up both hands. "I'm on duty, so no hugging, hear?"

"Okay," I said with a laugh. But then I took a good look at her. "Are you okay?"

"Yeah," she said, sounding a little harried. "I spent all last week in trial. Then we had that triple homicide gang shooting under the Bay Bridge and, well. You know."

"I get it. You're busy."

"I'll say. But I had a little free time so I'm glad to see you guys. Your voice mail messages have been entertaining."

"I'll bet," I said with another short laugh.

Since we had all missed lunch, I had put together a platter of veggies, along with olives, pickles, crackers, cheese, and salami and ham slices. And chocolate-caramel kisses, of course. Because when the discussion ran toward grand theft and murder, it was nice to have some tasty sweet and savory munchies on hand.

Derek finished his phone call and joined us at the dining room table. I took a quick look at him, saw how pale he'd become, and thought about Lark. The woman had made his life hell, and I couldn't wait to see her behind bars.

But I valiantly brushed that topic aside, and Derek and I took turns updating Inspector Lee on all that we'd learned over the past two days.

"I understand why you think this person Lark is the one who shot that kid, but—"

"I know she is," I said firmly, ignoring the niggling twist in my stomach that told me we didn't have proof beyond a doubt. But it didn't matter. Lark did it. She was sick and twisted and she had killed Tailor. It was as simple as that.

Inspector Lee looked at Derek. "And you believe she's the one who strangled your friend."

"I have no proof that Lark killed Ned Davies," he said, honest as always. "His wife, Patsy, is still awaiting the outcome of the investigation by the Paris police."

"But look," I said. "Lark was away from the office for three days during that last week we were in Paris. That would've given her time to fly over and do the job. She even told some people that she went to Paris to hook up with Derek."

"That's sleazy," she said, her lip curling in disgust.

I glanced at Derek, who scowled. But I wanted Inspector Lee to know what sort of killer/thief/floozy we were dealing with.

"Still, it's a stretch to claim that she flew all that way

just to kill your friend, then fly back." Inspector Lee was clearly skeptical. "You're moving into fictional spy-thriller territory, Brooklyn. Let's bring all that back down to earth."

"You're right." I grabbed a cracker and took an irate bite out of it. "We don't have proof. Yet. But the evidence is stacking up by the minute."

She tried desperately to hide her smirk. "You think she killed Tailor and she also tried to steal your book."

"And she'll try to steal it again tonight, now that she knows we've put it back in the display case."

"She's running out of time," Derek added.

"That's right," I said, jumping in. "She's got to find that list of names and destroy it. It not only links her to that assignment six years ago, but it's got the other agents listed, and at least one of them knows that she's connected to that assignment. And one of them is blackmailing her lover. So why not systematically kill them all and cover her bases?"

"It's a little too far-fetched to be believed."

"You need to get to know her," I grumbled. "Anyway—"

Inspector Lee held up her hand to stop me. She picked up an olive and nibbled on it for a few seconds before her eyes narrowed in on me. "I saw the video. I saw someone shoot that kid and I saw them try to steal your book."

"Exactly," I whispered. "And the microfilm was in the book. She knew it because she tortured Ned to get that information."

"Why does it always come back to a book?" she wondered, but I knew she was just giving me a little grief. "I don't believe anyone would go to all that trouble unless they were looking for something important *inside* the book."

"That's right," I said, feeling cheered that she agreed. "The list."

Janice grabbed a slice of salami and sat back in her chair. She glanced back and forth at Derek and me. "You should've called me when you found that camera with the new video."

"I did," I insisted, feeling a little defensive. "I called you a few times to let you know what we were doing. You never called back."

"Still, you should've waited for me to view it."

I frowned, trying to look contrite. "Sorry."

"I want to see it now."

"It's all set up and ready to view," Derek said.

He stood and led her over to a chair in front of the screen. "Tell me when you're ready."

"You can let it roll anytime," she said.

"I'll close the blinds first." Derek shut the blinds on the windows on either side of the TV screen. Then he picked up the remote and hit Play.

Ten minutes later, Inspector Lee stood. "You can turn it off." While Derek stopped the video and turned off the television, she walked over to the dining table and sat down.

"Should I be thanking you two for doing my job for me?" she asked with a lightness that I found highly suspicious.

"We just happened to put some of the pieces together, that's all." I held my hands up, all innocence. "As soon as we figured it out, we called you right away."

"I appreciate that," she said. "You've been busy. But now I'm going to caution you to step back." She leaned forward, glanced again from me to Derek. "Both of you."

I sucked in a breath, let it out. *Message received, loud and clear*, I thought. "I'll be happy to step back, but—"

"No buts," she barked.

"But there *is* a but," I insisted. "It's not a big *but*, but it's a very important *but* to me." I rolled my eyes, knowing I sounded like an idiot.

She peered at me, a look of false concern on her face. "You're turning pink, girl."

"I just want this really badly."

"Okay, let's hear your big but." She gave a surprised laugh. "*Big but*. Now that's funny." She waved her hands. "Anyway, go ahead."

I had to fight the urge to roll my eyes again. "I want to be there when you arrest her."

She snorted. "Is that so?"

"Hear me out," I said. "Look, this woman, Lark. She's hateful. She's never been anything but rude and contemptuous of me. It's because I'm married to Derek."

"Oh, come on."

"No, really," I said quietly. "It's just that simple. She enjoys making fun of me to other women on Derek's staff. She likes to intimidate. She hisses at me. It's weird." I breathed in deeply and exhaled, then gave Derek a quick glance. "She pulled something again today, something really awful, but I don't want to talk about it." I shook my head to clear it.

"Okay," she said, but said nothing else, apparently catching my mood.

"All that stuff about me," I continued. "It's just a sideshow. What's important is that she's a murderer and a thief and she belongs behind bars. All I ask is that you let me be there. I want to look her in the eyes when you slap those handcuffs on her. I want to blow her a big, fat kiss as you drag her svelte butt off to jail."

She raised her eyebrows. "You really hold a grudge, don't you?"

"In this case, yeah." I sniffed, rolled my shoulders, and settled back in my chair. "Other than that, I'm cool."

She laughed out loud. "Cool. Right."

"Look." I stared at the veggie platter, watched it go blurry, and huffed out a breath. "I'll stay out of your way. I'll hide in the office or in one of the back rooms. But I want to be there. Please."

Inspector Lee glanced at Derek as if she expected him to make more sense than I did. Chances were excellent that he would.

"Inspector," he began as he reached over to squeeze my hand. "I was only recently made aware of this woman's behavior toward Brooklyn, and for that alone, I would happily see her punished. But she is also responsible for the death of a very dear friend of mine, as well as the murder of the young man you saw on the video."

"Tailor," I murmured.

"She's been implicated in the murders of several other agents on that list," Derek continued. "Besides Ned Davies, there's Bettina Mayer, Malcolm Brown, and Christopher Peeler."

Implicated, I thought, but nothing had been proven. Still, I knew right down to my soul that Lark had killed those people.

Derek reached for my hand. "That phone call I took a few minutes ago was from Harold."

I gripped his hand tightly. "Is Tommie all right?"

"She's fine. I spoke with her earlier."

"Good." I breathed a sigh of relief, but then jerked my head up. "Wait. Why is Lark implicated in Bettina's death?" I glanced at Inspector Lee. "Bettina Mayer was married to Owen, the owner of the spy shop. She passed away last year."

"Her real name is Betty Morgan, by the way," Derek said. "That's why Harold didn't know about her before now."

"Ah." I couldn't blame Harold. There were too many names to keep track of.

Turning to Inspector Lee, Derek said, "She was definitely murdered. Owen found her floating in a bathtub. Her wrists were sliced open."

"Sounds like suicide to me," Inspector Lee said.

Derek's jaw clenched. "She had defensive wounds, along with skin under her fingernails. She was attacked first, then drowned. The killer slit her wrists to make it look like she took her own life."

"Oh God." I had to hold my stomach to quell the sick feeling. "Poor Owen."

"Malcolm Brown and Christopher Peeler are both now confirmed dead as well. And Ned, of course."

"I thought Christopher Peeler was safe in Japan."

"They found him yesterday," Derek said grimly. Then he turned to Inspector Lee. "Brooklyn and I have a big stake in this operation. So if you wouldn't mind, we would very much like to be on hand when you arrest Lark."

Once again, Inspector Lee glanced at Derek and then back at me. She grabbed another salami slice and took a bite. "I guess I can make that happen."

* * *

Derek drove over to SPECTRE that afternoon to meet with Owen personally. Inspector Lee was already there, going over the logistics.

The plan was for us all to arrive after the store closed at ten o'clock that night. We entered the building through the emergency entrance in back of the store, just in case Lark was monitoring the front door. And now we were waiting in Owen's office for the thief to break in and steal the book.

Owen had his computer screen angled so that we could all watch the surveillance video as we waited. Derek and I had brought plenty of chips and cookies to keep us from starving. Owen had provided coffee and drinks from the café. It was like a party, except the party guests were all really edgy and grim.

It was after midnight when things began to happen.

Inspector Lee spoke into her Bluetooth earpiece. "Copy that." She turned to the rest of us. "She's on her way. She just walked onto the pier."

That was easy, I thought. *Maybe too easy?*

Everyone in Owen's office was immediately silent. There were six of us in the room, including Owen, Derek, me, Inspector Lee, and two uniformed officers. Four more uniformed officers were stationed in the escape room lobby behind the double doors, where they would await Inspector Lee's command to move out. An unmarked police van was parked down the street. They were the ones who had alerted Inspector Lee when they observed Lark approaching.

About a minute later, I watched the computer screen as the hooded figure appeared on the first camera near the front door. My initial emotion was pure anger, but then I just shook my head. I truly had to marvel at her arrogance.

Lark walked briskly through the store, and instead of stopping to steal things as she had the last time she broke in, she moved directly to the book display. She seemed much more single-minded tonight. Taking out her glass cutter, she went right to work.

"We wait until she has the book in her hands," Inspector Lee murmured into her headset.

The two officers nodded and one said, "Yes, ma'am."

Derek murmured, "She looks different."

"I noticed," I said, staring at the screen. "I think she's wearing tighter pants. Something's changed."

It only took a few seconds for Lark to reach into the glass case and grab the book. She slipped it into the pouch of her hoodie and walked quickly out of the bookshop area and toward the front door.

"Go! Go!" Inspector Lee ordered. "Move it! And hold your fire. I don't want anyone hurt."

She and the two officers raced out of Owen's office, with Derek and me following a short distance behind.

"Police! Stop!" Inspector Lee shouted. "Hands up! Stay right where you are."

Lark ignored her commands and continued to run toward the front door. I was amazed at how fast she was. But she was no match for Inspector Lee, who took a flying leap and grabbed her from behind. I winced as I watched them land on the floor with a heavy thud and skid another ten feet before coming to a stop. Lark twisted and bucked to get Inspector Lee off her, but the inspector wasn't budging.

"Restraints," Inspector Lee yelled, holding one hand out.

Immediately one of the officers pulled handcuffs from the back of his utility belt and placed them in her hand. She quickly cuffed her prisoner, then climbed off her back and yanked her up to a standing position.

"Damn, she's strong," Inspector Lee muttered, then flipped the hoodie off Lark's head. "Let's get rid of this, too." She grabbed hold of the ski mask and yanked it up.

And exposed the intruder's face.

I gasped in astonishment. "Who in the world . . . Wait, I know you."

"What's your name?" Inspector Lee demanded.

Owen came running up behind us. "Good heavens. It's Richie!"

Richie Sylvestri, Owen's business partner, was read his rights. Inspector Lee explained to Owen that his partner would be driven to the main police department in the Hall of Justice, where he would go through the arrest process and be put into a cell overnight.

"I'll interrogate him in the morning," Inspector Lee finished.

"Call my lawyer!" Richie shouted to Owen as Richie was led off to a waiting police car by the two uniformed officers.

"I'll have to think about that," Owen said, his cheeks red with anger.

When Richie and the cops were gone, Inspector Lee turned and looked at Derek and me. She jerked her head toward the café. "Let's talk."

Derek and I exchanged a nervous glance, then followed the inspector to a table in the café.

"Sit down," she said. "Maybe you can explain what just happened."

"I'm as stunned as you are," I said. "That's not the same person who came in here the other night."

"Brooklyn's right." Derek folded his arms tightly across his chest. "I don't know what sort of game she's playing now, but Lark is the person who killed Tailor last week. Not this guy."

Owen came over looking pale and chastised. "I don't know what to say."

"Please sit down, Owen," Derek said, sounding kinder than he appeared to feel.

He sat, then gave Inspector Lee an abashed look. "I'm sorry. I'm speechless. And angry. Was I just played for a fool?"

"Owen, how long have you known Richie?" Derek asked.

"I've known him for years. We used to work together."

"At the agency?"

"Yes." He stared at his hands. "You know how it is, Derek. We don't always get close to people because, well, who knows when someone will disappear on us?" He chuckled mirthlessly. "But Richie and I shared a few assignments over the years, managed to become friends. He was always a pleasant sort."

"And when did you become business partners?"

"Just last year. It was shortly after my wife died. I had finally decided to rejoin society and ran into him at a party. He mentioned that he was looking for an investment opportunity. He explained that he had come into some money a while back, you see."

"Did he tell you where the money came from?" Derek asked.

"No. I assumed it was family money. An inheritance. You know."

Something had been tickling the back of my mind for the last half hour. "Did Richie ever go by another name while you were working with him?"

Owen swallowed. "Er, well, we all did, didn't we?"

"I didn't," Derek said easily.

"Yes, well." He stretched his neck, clearly nervous now. "It was a covert operation. And even though the assignment only lasted a few weeks, they required Richie to go deep for over a year."

"Go deep," I repeated.

"Deep cover," Derek murmured. "New look, new identity, no contact with the outside world. Tell no one."

"Got it," I said, nodding.

"What was Richie's name?" Inspector Lee asked, impatience simmering.

Thoroughly intimidated, Owen's eyes widened and he turned to Derek.

"Oh, come now, Owen." Derek patted him on the back. "It's been years. We're all retired now. What can it hurt?"

I leaned forward. "Don't you wonder why he would come in here and try to steal from his own store?"

"I do," Owen said, shaking his head. "Yes, I do." He took a long, slow breath in and out. "All right. Richie went by the name *Ramon Silva*."

It was almost two o'clock in the morning when we got home. Before leaving SPECTRE, we had managed to get Owen calmed down enough to lock up the store and walk to his car. We watched him drive off and then walked Inspector Lee to her car. Before she got in, she promised to keep us posted on the Richie/Ramon Silva interrogation tomorrow.

Once we were home, I quickly brushed my teeth and then climbed into bed with Derek, more exhausted than I'd ever felt before. But my mind was still humming with everything that had happened earlier.

"You know that Ramon, or Richie or whatever, has to be in cahoots with Lark." I punched my pillow to get more comfortable. "And I refuse to believe that Ramon is the one who shot Tailor. It had to be Lark."

"I agree," Derek said, and reached over to turn off the light.

"Ramon and Lark had to be partners in that consulate assignment," I said, yawning. "And they still are, apparently."

"Apparently," Derek murmured.

"So how do we catch her in the act?" I wondered. "Maybe we can ask Inspector Lee to bring her in for questioning."

"No more thinking," Derek crooned, pulling me close and kissing the top of my head.

"But that would tip our hand," I conceded, ignoring his words. "Lark would know that she was a suspect and she might disappear for good."

"Let's sleep on it," Derek said.

"But she already knows she's a suspect," I argued with myself. "That's why she coerced Richie into showing up at the store tonight."

Derek sighed. "That's enough. We'll have plenty of time to figure it out tomorrow morning before I leave for work."

"But if you go to the office, you'll run into Lark. And we both know she killed Tailor."

"Shh." He kissed my temple. "Sleep, love."

"Wait," I said. "Maybe Ramon Silva is the blackmailer," I said. "He had to know that Lark was having an affair with Kristof. So maybe he's been double-crossing his partner. Maybe that's how he came into so much money."

"It's all quite possible," Derek said. "Good night, darling."

I was so sleepy I couldn't keep my eyes open. But something else occurred to me. "Tommie didn't change her name for that assignment. She didn't 'go deep.'" I wiggled my fingers to indicate quotation marks—not that Derek could see my sarcasm in the dark. "And neither did Ned. Or those other two guys. The only ones who changed their names were Ramon and Lark. And Bettina. Did she have something to hide? Because Ramon and Lark sure did."

"Yes, I know."

"God, I'm tired."

Derek rubbed my back. "Sweet dreams, love."

"Sweet . . ." It was the last word I said before I drifted off to sleep.

Richie Sylvestri was released later that day after a mere two hours of interrogation by Inspector Lee.

"He owns the store," the inspector explained over my protestations. "And his lawyer was pretty slick. The guy insisted that Sylvestri did what he did because he was checking out the store's security issues, trying to see how fast the police would respond if there was a break-in."

"That's just so much baloney," I said, disgusted as I paced across my living room with the hands-free speaker switched on my cell phone.

"Yeah, we both know that," she admitted. "But they

also made a big deal out of the fact that he didn't actually steal your expensive rare book. He took the fake one."

"But that's no excuse," I griped. "His intention was to steal the real thing."

"Sorry, kiddo," Inspector Lee said. "We had to let him go."

"What about Lark?" I asked. "Any chance of dragging her into interrogation?"

"Did you want shackles with that?"

"Har har," I muttered.

She chuckled. "Sadly, it's not against the law to be a nasty bee-yotch."

"But she's a murdering psychopathic bee-yotch," I said. "She killed Tailor. You know she did." *And she hissed like a freaking snake*, I thought, but didn't say it out loud.

"We're still investigating the shooting, and as soon as we have enough evidence, we'll bring her in."

"All right." Even though her words sounded like mumbo-jumbo cop-speak, I knew I would have to be satisfied for now. Because unless there was another video that showed Lark ripping off her ski mask as she shot and killed Tailor, I was afraid there wasn't much more we could do. And Lark would be free to kill again.

I called Derek to tell him the news.

"I'm sorry, darling," he said. "Although it wasn't unexpected."

"I just wish I knew why Richie showed up last night instead of Lark." I drummed my fingers on the table. "Maybe I played it too heavy when I was in the lunch room with Corinne. Lark might've gotten a spidey sense that we were onto her."

"I did wonder about that," Derek said. "Lark is

brash and arrogant and often infuriating, but she's not stupid."

"Could you please fire her today?" I asked lightly, even though I was seething over the fact that she was still employed by his company.

"Frankly, darling, I've begun to think that the best thing that happened was that I didn't fire her."

I did a double take. "Say what?"

"If I'd fired her, we wouldn't be able to keep track of her. This way, we know where she is and what she's doing. At least for the next day or so."

"That makes a lot of sense in a really annoying way," I said. "Just please be careful around her, okay?"

"I will," he said. "Let's talk about it tonight, love. Perhaps we can come up with another plan of attack."

I spent the rest of the day working in my studio, completing several unfinished projects. Charlie kept me company, and mint-chocolate chunky chips kept me nourished. I managed to shut out all the grouchy voices in my head while I sewed the textblock for the Chinese herbal book. I also finished repairing an antique family Bible for my neighbor downstairs.

If I spared a moment to think of Lark, it was only to picture her behind bars, wearing a baggy orange jumpsuit. Ah, the joy. Otherwise, I completely avoided any thoughts of her.

When Derek arrived home that night, we sipped cabernet while he grilled filets mignons on our rooftop patio. It was a great spot, with lounge chairs, a pretty dining table with colorful umbrellas that guarded against either too much sun or too much rain, and pots and pots of flowers tumbling in brilliant colors.

I baked big fat potatoes loaded with butter, sour cream, and chives and put together a salad for a touch of healthy greens. For dessert we had Meyer lemon gelato.

We laughed and talked. He told me about his day at the office and we reminisced about Paris.

And—my favorite—we plotted the demise of Lark.

The next day I was close to finishing the Chinese herbal book for Inspector Lee's mother. The textblock was sewn, and all I had to do now was paste the new endpapers into the book so that the cover and textblock would be back together again.

Last week I had put aside several sheets from the stack of handmade paper I'd used for my kite, so I pulled those out of the drawer. They were even more beautiful than I remembered. A cherry tree spread its delicate branches across a lustrous gold background, and pale pink blossoms were embossed in random patterns along the limbs. I filled a small bowl with PVA glue and went to work, pasting the vibrant endpapers into the book.

When I was finished with the pastedowns, I admired how nicely the papers looked against the pale green cover of the book. I placed a piece of waxed paper inside the front and back covers to keep any extra glue from glopping onto the book itself. Then I set the entire finished book in the book press between two flat cloth-covered bricks and adjusted it firmly. The book would stay there overnight and be ready to go in the morning.

With my work finished for the day, I called Owen.

"Would tomorrow be a good time for me to start working on your Scary Library room?"

"Oh, Brooklyn, you're an angel," he said. "I was just going to call you. Your darling friend Beverly came through and the books have arrived. They're ready to put on the shelves anytime you are."

"Perfect," I said. "I'll be there as soon as you open tomorrow morning."

We ended the call, and then I pressed Inspector Lee's number. I had her on speed dial, of course.

When she answered, I said, "I brought you back something from Paris."

"You didn't have to get me anything," she said, a bit too coyly, I thought.

"You may recall that you threatened me," I said with a laugh. "So yeah, I did. But it's not really for you. It's for your mother."

She was silent for a long moment. "You brought my mother something? From Paris?"

"Yes. Because, well, I just happened to see it and thought she might like it."

"Brooklyn, that's so thoughtful." She sighed. "I'm going to have to be nice to you now, aren't I?"

I grinned. "Yup."

"That's really sneaky."

"I know." I chuckled. "So when are you available to meet?"

She took a minute to check her calendar. "Okay, this week is really tight because I have to be in court two days. But I have time tomorrow afternoon around four o'clock. Does that work for you?"

"That's fine with me."

"Sorry to be so stingy with my time, but you know how it is."

"I do, and it's not a problem. I'll be at SPECTRE, working in one of the new escape rooms. Would you mind swinging by there?"

"Not at all," she said. "I'll see you then."

That night, Derek and I finalized our plan over spaghetti and meatballs.

"Is Corinne set to go?" I asked as I cut into a juicy meatball.

Derek smiled across the table as he lifted his wineglass. "She's excited to do her part."

"All righty, then." I lifted my wineglass and tapped it against his. "In honor of Corinne, let's toast to a successful caper."

After Derek left for work the next morning, I got dressed and walked into my workshop, where I removed the Chinese herb book from the book press. Wrapping it in soft tissue paper, I slipped it into a small gift bag. I tossed in the Eiffel Tower key ring just for laughs.

I packed the bag inside my very businesslike briefcase along with a number of bookbinding tools and supplies and a dozen photographs I'd printed out last night.

A half hour later, I showed up at SPECTRE to get my first look at the Scary Library escape room. Owen met me at the front door and gave me a big bear hug. "I'm so pleased that you agreed to lend your expertise."

"Thank you for including me," I said. "I think it'll be fun."

He led the way to the back of the store. "And I want to thank you again for giving me Beverly's name."

"You're welcome. She must've been anxious to get rid of those books."

He grinned. "Wait until you see. There are hundreds of them." He unlocked the double doors. "You'll be in charge of them, if you don't mind."

"That's right in my wheelhouse," I said with a smile. "Derek plans to show up later, too."

"Isn't that marvelous?" he said jovially. "The Jackals are helping as well."

"Sounds like we'll have a good group."

"Oh yes," Owen said. "I believe this room will be the scariest yet."

Scarier than the Cursed Kindergarten? I seriously doubted it, but just smiled up at Owen. "That's exciting to hear."

As we walked through the escape room lobby, I heard the unmistakable sounds of construction work. Heading into the hallway, I could smell freshly sawed lumber and hear the whine of a circular power saw.

We walked into the last room on the left. There were bookshelves up against two walls. Soldier stood in the middle of the room between two sawhorses, pushing the power saw into a six-by-eight piece of wood, sawing it neatly in half. He noticed us walking into the room and immediately powered down. The earsplitting shrill abruptly stopped, and it took a few seconds to adjust my ears to the silence.

"Hi, Brooklyn," he said cheerfully. "Long time no see."

I grinned and waved. "At least a week. Good to see you."

"Beep, beep," someone said from out in the hall.

I turned and watched Tinker and Drummer Girl follow us into the room carrying an old stuffed loveseat. The faded chintz upholstery reminded me of something I once saw in my grandmother's bedroom.

Owen and I quickly moved out of their way as they scurried across the room and set it down against the third wall.

Tinker smiled at me like we were old friends—and maybe we were by now, after all we'd been through. I gave him a hug. "How are you doing?"

"Better every day," he said. "Owen hired us to work on this room, so we're all pretty busy."

"Yeah," Drummer Girl said. "We don't have the time to sit around and dwell on what happened."

"That's probably a good thing." I gave them both an encouraging smile.

"For sure," she said, then strode across the room to fluff up the couch pillows.

"I'll leave you hard workers to your tasks," Owen said. "I've got paperwork and payroll issues to deal with."

"We'll be here," Tinker said.

"Nobody warned me about all the paperwork," he grumbled, but then smiled. "It could be worse, though."

"Yeah," Drummer Girl said. "You could be in charge of feeding the sharks at Water World."

"Right," Soldier said. "Or working for the bomb squad."

Owen laughed as he walked to the door. "Thank you so much for your perspective. Be sure to call me if you need anything."

I noticed Tinker hadn't moved away yet, so I gazed at him casually. "How's everything else?"

"Well . . ." He took in a huge breath of air and exhaled slowly. "I heard from an agent who's interested in my book."

"Tinker, that's fantastic," I said.

"It is." He shook his head as though he didn't believe it was true. "He actually called me on the phone."

I broke out in a big grin. "That's impressive."

"It . . . it's completely awesome." He brushed his fingers through his hair, still looking utterly dazed. "I told him I'm going to take two weeks to do a quick rewrite and then send it in."

"That's wonderful, Tinker." I held out my arms and wrapped him in a big hug. "Good luck."

"Thanks." He blushed and stared down at his feet. "To tell you the truth, I'm pretty sure it was Derek's advice that helped hook the agent."

"Wait." It was my turn to look puzzled. "Didn't Derek just tell you to make it more thrilling?"

"Yeah." He shook his head, bewildered. "It sounds so simple, but it really made me think. I went back to chapter one and added a bunch more conflict, gave my protagonist a whole new backstory, really dark, you know? I raised the stakes and sort of beefed up the ticking-clock thing."

"Well, that's good."

"I'll say. It must've worked because the agent raved about that first chapter when he called. I think maybe it sold him on the whole book."

"I'm sure your writing sold him, too."

He grinned. "Yeah, maybe. But I owe Derek. I can't wait to tell him."

"He'll be here a little later. He's going to help us out in here."

"That's awesome." He smiled to himself, then said, "I can't wait to thank him. You know, for taking the time to help me out."

He was still blushing, so I knew it was time to change the subject. "I'm going to start loading those books onto the shelves, if anyone wants to help."

"We can all help," Soldier offered. "In between building furniture and stuff."

I smiled at him as I grabbed the box cutter from my briefcase and slit open the first box. "Cool. Thanks."

Derek arrived two hours later. He had changed out of his bazillion-dollar business suit, pristine white shirt, and elegant silk tie and into faded jeans, a lightweight black Henley, and work boots. Either way, he looked stunning and darkly sexy. And when he flashed me a quick, crooked smile, my heart went giddy-up in my chest.

Tinker told him all about the interested agent, and Derek congratulated the younger man with a slap on the back that had him blushing again.

Then Derek jumped right in, helping Tinker move lumber from the back entryway, down the hall, and into the escape room, where Soldier would saw them down to the proper lengths for bookshelves and several library tables. Since Soldier had worked as a carpenter before joining the military, he was in charge of building the furniture.

Meanwhile, I stared at the rest of the boxes stacked against the wall. There were a lot more than a few hundred books here, I thought. Probably more like a few thousand. I was going to need all the help I could get.

"Now this is scary," I muttered, then shrugged.

What the heck? Owen had said we had plenty of time to load the books onto the shelves, so all I had to do was keep going. I opened the next box and pulled out another stack of books.

I had been toting books and stacking them on the shelves for over an hour when Derek came up and touched my shoulder.

"What's up?" I asked.

"Darling," he said as he swiped the arm of his shirt across his sweaty forehead. "I'm going to drive Tinker to the hardware store to pick up more lumber, some screws, and a replacement blade for the circular saw."

I leaned in close and whispered, "I love it when you're all hot and sweaty like this."

He laughed out loud, then held out his hand. "I'll need the keys to your car. I'm not about to cart lumber around in the Bentley."

"There's my lord of the manor," I said, laughing along with him. I found my purse tucked inside my briefcase and handed him the keys. "Be careful," I said, and gave him a light kiss.

"Be back soon."

As soon as they left, Drummer Girl flopped onto the couch. "I'm starving. Who wants lunch?"

"I was thinking about one of those Italian subs from Mangia," Soldier said. "It's right on the pier."

"That sounds awesome," she said. "I'll go with you."

I reached into my purse and pulled out my wallet. "Why don't you get enough for everyone? My treat."

"All right!" Drummer said.

Soldier gave me a thumbs-up. "Works for me."

"Be back in twenty minutes," Drummer said, and

the two of them strolled out the door to pick up lunch for the crew.

"Take your time," I murmured, and continued emptying boxes and stacking books by myself. After a few minutes, I realized that I was feeling pretty hungry, too. When everyone got back, we could take a little break and eat lunch together. It would be nice.

Earlier Drummer had told me how the writers had created an origin story for the room that included a really mean librarian who put people in chains when they didn't bring their books back on time. The point of the game would be to find the missing book so the librarian wouldn't fine you and put you in chains.

I was laughing and getting creeped out all at the same time.

Once the furniture was in place, Drummer had explained, they would begin the process of turning the room into the scariest fake library possible. The lighting was important, as dark as possible while still letting people see the room. Lots of cobwebs and streaks of dust, weird old props, and some odd portraits hanging on the walls. Manacles and chains were always a fun touch for the people who didn't pay their library fines. The bookshelves and tables would be aged using dark paint and some soldering to give everything a burned-out look. I couldn't wait to see the finished room.

I was working up a bit of a sweat myself when I heard footsteps approach the doorway. I turned to greet Drummer and Soldier, but my words died unuttered when I saw Lark.

Oh, hell, I thought. Our plan had worked, almost to perfection. Earlier, Corinne and Derek had let it be known around the office that I would be working alone in an escape room at SPECTRE today—and that I had the real book with me. We had theorized that Lark would show up after work sometime this evening, but she must've slithered out of the office when nobody was watching. I felt bad, knowing that Corinne would be upset when she found out.

But I felt even worse because I really *was* completely alone back here with the snake woman. I gauged my timing. Derek and Tinker had been gone awhile. They could be back in five minutes or another half hour. Drummer and Soldier might show up sooner, and maybe their presence would force Lark to run away.

Part of me wondered why she had come here, knowing that the last time had been a trap. Was she that desperate to get the book?

She could have the book, I thought, but surprise! The microfilm was long gone. I couldn't wait to tell her.

But I really wished someone would come back from lunch or the hardware store. For now, though, I was on my own with this living horror show.

"What are you doing here?" I asked, not in a friendly way.

"You look like crap," Lark said, ignoring my question. She laughed and I watched her face contort. It was disturbing to realize it might be because she just wasn't used to laughing.

"You look like a psycho killer," I said. "And a liar. I heard you were telling people that you're having an affair with my husband. Did you really think anyone who knows you would believe that?"

"Yeah, they do," she said, stone-faced.

"You have no idea how ridiculous you are."

"I'm sure you and Derek laugh yourselves to sleep

at night telling each other stuff like that. I can't imagine you do much else in bed." She laughed at that.

It was kind of pathetic to hear her hurl insults at me. She had no idea how jealous and silly she sounded.

I was wishing desperately that I had gone to the sandwich shop with Drummer and Soldier, and I scanned the room, looking for a weapon I could grab to hurt her.

I gazed at her. "You're pitiful."

She hissed in a breath. And I mean hissed. That snake noise again. It reminded me of all the hateful things she'd said to me, and it made me want to strangle her with my bare hands. I didn't care what anyone said, the woman was really stupid, and worse, she had no sense of humor. She was vicious and cold, and those were her *best* qualities. Lark had relied on her looks to get her through life, and I hoped she died an ugly death. And how dare she spread lies about Derek and my relationship? She was clearly obsessed.

"I'm busy, Lark," I said, pretending I didn't know just how dangerous she was. "What do you want?"

"I want the book."

"Right." I forced a laugh. "You know, you've tried to steal it more than once and failed. Maybe you should think about moving on with your life."

"I want the book," she said again, her tone deadly calm.

"Why? It's just a book. There's nothing inside it."

"You don't know anything." She pulled the gun from her pocket and pointed it at me.

Okay, then. The gun changed things. Yes, she was a hideous human, but now she was an *armed* hideous human. I stared at her. Objectively speaking, she was a beautiful woman, but now she just looked dead. Her face held no expression. Her eyes were empty. And I knew that she would kill me in a heartbeat if I didn't give her the book.

I held up my hands in surrender. "The book is in my briefcase." I pointed to the bookshelf where I'd left my things. "Right over there."

"Get it," she said with a guttural growl, waving the gun as she spoke.

I walked sideways toward my purse, not daring to look away from her. I opened my briefcase and took a while to rummage through it. I had to stall for time.

"Why did you kill Tailor?" I asked.

She looked confused. "Who's Tailor?"

I wanted to slap her. "He's the guy who caught you stealing the book."

She waved her hand dismissively. "He was in my way."

I had to take a breath. Her indifference made me sick.

"Did you kill Ned Davies?" I asked.

This time she seemed pleasantly surprised that I would show an interest in her work. "Not right away," she said. "I needed to find out where he'd hidden the microfilm."

"So you . . . tortured him?"

"Maybe just a little." She shrugged. "And I threatened to kill his wife if he didn't tell me where he put it."

"I see." So just extortion, not torture. Shame on me for quibbling. "He told you where he hid the microfilm but you killed him anyway."

"He outlived his usefulness."

"That was you in the hoodie, standing on the sidewalk."

She rolled her eyes. "This is tiresome."

"Why did you kill Bettina Mayer?"

"She was a know-it-all," she said with a shrug. "She threatened to tell the royal family about me and Kristof."

I had to remember to breathe. "Why do you need the list?"

"To destroy it, of course. It's a loose end."

"How many others on that list did you kill?"

"None of your beeswax."

That was mature, I thought, then I tried another tack. "Do you think the king's son-in-law will divorce his wife and marry you?"

"He won't have to get a divorce," she said with a simpering smile. "As soon as he's installed on the throne, his wife will die in a horrible accident."

"So what's the end game?" I asked. "Is it all about the money with you, or do you just want to be queen?"

"Money, power, it's always about that, isn't it?"

"Do you love him?"

"Kristof?" She threw her head back and laughed. "He's a pig. But he's handsome and he loves me, so why not use him?"

"Why not?" And since she had just revealed all of that to me, there was no way she would let me live. I had to fight back with . . . something. I was thinking about weapons and self-defense while I pretended to look for the book and keep her occupied. Good thing I had always excelled at multitasking.

"Are you being blackmailed?" I asked.

She scowled. "How do you know all this?"

"You can learn a lot from the Internet." I glanced up from my purse. "So who is blackmailing you and your lover?"

She frowned, unsure of herself for once. "I've gotten rid of everyone but Ramon and Thomasina. I'll go after her next because she's smart enough to pull it off. Ramon isn't. But if he turns out to be the one who's blackmailing us, I'm going to be very angry."

I hadn't expected that. "I should think you'd know if it was Ramon. I thought you two were working together."

"We were, for as long as he was useful. They'll find his body in his car. And maybe the blackmailing will stop."

A chill raced up my spine. The woman was cold as granite—and not very bright. But bright or not, I knew she was already planning how she would leave my body to be found.

"The book," she said. "Now."

"Right." I took another deep breath, pulled the book from my briefcase, and flung it at her head, Frisbee style, as hard as I could.

Shocked, she ducked her head and let out a little scream.

While she was distracted, I rushed at her, balled my fist, and hit her as hard as I could right on her perfect little nose.

At that very moment, Drummer Girl walked into the room carrying a restaurant bag. She saw Lark, saw the gun, and saw me slug her.

"Hey!" she cried.

"She killed Tailor!" I shouted.

Without another thought, Drummer dropped the bag, grabbed a two-by-four, and smacked Lark in her stomach, propelling her backward into the bookshelf.

"Oww!" Lark howled. The bookshelf teetered and began to fall over.

"Look out!" I shouted, and pushed Drummer to get her out of the way. Lark was on her own.

"Stay back!" Lark shouted, waving the gun at both of us and swiping one hand under her bloody nose.

"There it goes!" Drummer cried.

Not even a second passed before Derek raced into the room. He started for Lark but jumped out of the way as the bookshelf fell. Books went everywhere as one of the shelves conked Lark in the head and knocked her unconscious.

"Do you see the gun?" I asked in a panic. The woman could wake up at any moment and start shooting.

"I've got it," Derek said calmly. He stepped between the books and the shelf itself, reached down into the mess, and came up with the gun.

"My hero," I said. "Boy, am I glad to see you!"

"I'm relieved to see you as well," Derek said. "But I believe you were your own hero." His lips twisted in a sardonic smile as he bent to kiss me.

"Actually, I was talking to Drummer," I said, and laughed.

Drummer laughed, too, and shook her head. "It felt really good to hit her. Does that make me a bad person?"

Everyone laughed. It was good to be alive.

Soldier walked in, held up another large, aromatic restaurant bag, and said, "Lunch, anyone?"

"How did you get back here so fast?" I asked Derek and Tinker after the dust had cleared. Inspector Lee had been called, and after I gave her a brief rundown of what happened, she postponed her court appearance and promised to get here as quickly as possible.

Soldier had run outside and flagged down two of the private security guards hired by the pier, so Lark was now handcuffed and under guard while we waited for the police to arrive. Meanwhile, we grabbed chairs and ate lunch in the escape room.

"After everything that's happened around here," Tinker began, "I decided to install cameras in the escape rooms." He held up his phone. "And I have an app that shows me what's going on."

"We were at the hardware store checking out the tools," Derek continued, "and Tinker thought it would be fun to watch you while you worked. He pulled out his phone and that's when we saw Lark walk in." His eyes darkened. "We raced out of the store and I drove like a hellion to get here."

"I've never been so happy to see you all," I said.

"I'm just glad we were only a mile away," Derek said. "We thought about driving out to the big-box store in Oakland, but then decided we could do that tomorrow."

I scooted my chair over and wrapped my arms around him. He pulled me even closer and I sighed with a mix of relief, happiness, and deep regret that we had lost Ned and Tailor. And all the others, of course. But on the upside, Drummer and I were alive and Lark was going to jail forever.

Inspector Lee arrived and each of us was interviewed. Despite being scared to death, I was gratified to hear Inspector Lee tell me I was right about Lark.

"I'm sorry, what did you say?" I asked, tapping my ears.

She scowled. "I said, you were right, Brooklyn."

"Ah. That never gets old," I said, and smiled with restrained delight.

"But seriously," she said. "That woman is psycho. I only talked to her for a minute or two and I've still got chills. I'm glad you're safe."

"Thanks." I blinked when I suddenly remembered. "I have something for you. I completely forgot."

"You're about to pass out," she suggested. "Let's do it tomorrow when you'll be all fresh and perky."

"That's the best idea ever."

"Right." She grinned. "I want you wide awake and fawning all over me."

"That can take be arranged," I said with a laugh. "Maybe you could come over for a glass of wine after work?"

"Sounds like a plan."

And when she actually gave me a hug, I felt my eyes burn. That's how I knew I was fading.

"Let's talk tomorrow," she said.

"I'll call you," I promised.

After the police left, I looked around at the crew. "I think I'm going to call it a day."

Derek patted my knee. "I think we should go home and open a bottle of wine."

"That, and take a long soak in the tub," I added.

Tinker stood. "I've still got some work left to do."

"Can't it wait 'til tomorrow?" I asked, frowning. "We've all been through a lot today."

"If you're staying," Soldier said, pushing his chair away from the table. "So am I."

"Good," Tinker said with a gleam in his eye. "We really need to bolt those shelves to the wall. In case of earthquakes. Or, you know, mad-dog killers."

Drummer Girl looked around the room one more

time, then gazed at Soldier. "This would be a good place to put up that great picture of Tailor you took."

"I'll blow it up and frame it," he said. "It'll be perfect in here. Tailor will know that this was the place where you brought down his killer."

There was silence for a moment, and I had to wipe away a tear.

"He would be proud of you, Drummer," Tinker said. "I am, too. We all are. You're one badass woman."

I gave her a smile. "I was thinking 'kick-ass heroine.'"

"I like it," she said, grinning, but her eyes suddenly took on a glazed look. She pulled a notepad from her pocket and started scribbling. "I need to write this down. 'Kick-ass heroine.'" She glanced up. "I think I've just worked out the turning point in my third chapter."

I laughed. "Libraries are good for that. Even if they're scary."

Recipes

HONEYMOON STUFFED FRENCH TOAST

This is the heavenly French toast that Brooklyn and Derek enjoyed on the last day of their fabulous Paris honeymoon. Perhaps they'll have it for every anniversary.

1 loaf of French bread
8 oz cream cheese, room temperature
3 tablespoons sugar
1 tablespoon orange zest
2 teaspoons vanilla
6 eggs
½ cup half-and-half
¼ teaspoon salt
¼ teaspoon cinnamon
2–4 tablespoons butter

Slice the bread 1 ½-inches thick. Then slice each piece almost in half, but not quite all the way, so the cream cheese stuffing can be added between the halves of each piece. If time permits, allow to sit out for an hour or two to dry out a little.

For the orange cream filling, combine the cream cheese, two tablespoons of sugar, orange zest, and vanilla and mix well. Pipe or spread about two tablespoons into each bread slice.

Whisk together the eggs, half-and-half, remaining sugar, salt, and cinnamon. Dip each piece of stuffed bread into the egg mixture, ensuring that both sides are saturated. Melt butter in a skillet over medium heat. Cook each piece of stuffed French toast until brown on both sides.

If desired, serve with Honey-Orange Syrup (recipe below).

HONEY-ORANGE SYRUP

¼ cup orange juice
¼ cup water
½ cup honey
1 tablespoon orange zest

Combine all ingredients in a small saucepan. Heat on medium until it reaches a gentle boil, then lower heat and continue to simmer until reduced by about half, stirring frequently.

ESCAPE ROOM SNACK MIX

However you want to describe escape rooms—bananas, nuts, delicious, an adrenaline rush, or just plain fun— this addictive snack mix has you covered!

1 18-oz box of Life cereal
2 cups peanuts
2 cups oyster crackers
¼ cup brewed coffee
6 tablespoons butter
1 teaspoon sugar
1 teaspoon salt
2 cups banana chips, broken up
*12-oz bag of mini–chocolate kisses (otherwise known
as chocolate chips—kisses are Brooklyn's favorite!)*
10-oz bag of peanut butter chips

Preheat oven to 250 degrees. Put the cereal, peanuts, and crackers in a large bowl, mix well, and set aside.

Put the coffee in a small saucepan and heat over medium. Reduce by half, then add the butter, sugar, and salt, and cook, stirring constantly, until butter is melted. Add to the cereal mixture and stir to coat thoroughly.

Spread in a roasting pan and bake for an hour, stirring every 15 minutes. Remove from oven and allow to cool completely. After it reaches room temperature, add the banana, chocolate, and peanut butter chips. Store in an airtight container.

PARMESAN CHICKEN SALAD

This salad is delicious with any vinaigrette, but my favorite is Pimento Vinaigrette (recipe follows).

½ cup butter, melted then cooled
1 teaspoon Dijon mustard
2 dashes Tabasco
4 boneless, skinless chicken breasts cut into 1-inch chunks
1 cup bread crumbs
½ cup Parmesan cheese
1 teaspoon garlic salt
½ teaspoon black pepper
6 cups salad greens
½ yellow bell pepper, diced
6 spring onions, diced
1 cup cherry tomatoes, sliced in half
½ cup pine nuts

Preheat oven to 375 degrees. Place ovenproof metal rack over two baking sheets; spray with cooking spray for easy cleanup.

Combine the melted butter, mustard, and Tabasco. Stir in the chicken chunks to coat thoroughly.

Put bread crumbs, cheese, garlic salt, and pepper into a zip-top bag. Add the chicken in small batches and coat. Place on the metal racks. If there's any remaining butter mixture, drizzle it over the chicken. Bake until chicken reaches 170 degrees, about 25 minutes.

Divide the salad greens, other vegetables, and nuts between four salad bowls. Top with chicken.

PIMENTO VINAIGRETTE

¼ cup olive oil
¼ cup red wine vinegar
2 teaspoons jarred pimentos
1 garlic clove, minced
½ teaspoon dried basil
½ teaspoon Dijon mustard
¼ teaspoon salt
⅛ teaspoon black pepper

Blend all ingredients.

QUICK & EASY WEEKNIGHT SALMON

To make this even easier and just as delicious, skip all of the sauce ingredients and just pour in a jar of Alfredo sauce. Because everything is cooked in one pot (other than the pasta), cleanup is a breeze.

1 lb farfalle (bowtie) pasta or pasta of your choice
2 tablespoons olive oil
1 lb salmon, fresh or frozen
8 oz mushrooms, prewashed and sliced
1 small onion, diced

Salt and pepper to taste
2 cloves of garlic, minced
1 cup cream or half-and-half, divided
½ cup white wine
1 tablespoon lemon juice
1 teaspoon cornstarch
2 cups baby spinach

Cook pasta according to package directions. While the water is heating, heat the oil in a large saucepan. When the oil is glistening, add salmon, mushrooms, and onions. Sprinkle liberally with salt and pepper. Stir infrequently to help everything sear a little. After four minutes, flip the salmon fillets. Cut the fillets into smaller pieces right there in the pan.

When the salmon is almost cooked through, just a little pink, add the garlic and cook until fragrant, about 30 seconds. Add ¾ cup cream, white wine, and lemon juice. Whisk cornstarch into remaining cream, then add to salmon mixture. Stir well, then add spinach and stir to combine. Simmer until pasta is done.

Before draining pasta, add one ladleful of pasta water to the salmon mixture. Drain pasta, then combine with the salmon mixture and stir well.

Keep reading for a sneak peek of

The Grim Reader

The next Bibliophile Mystery by Kate Carlisle!

"It's good to be back in Dharma," Derek said, breathing in the crisp fall air.

We stood on the balcony outside the master bedroom of the home we'd be living in for the next two weeks and took in the gorgeous scenery. I felt all of my stress dissipate as I gazed out at the green terraced hills. As far as the eye could see, thousands of sturdy grapevines grew tall and lush, their leaves turning golden brown in the autumn sun. Even from this far away, I could see the clusters of ripe fruit more than ready for the coming harvest.

"This view never gets old," I said with a happy sigh, smiling up at him.

Derek pulled me close and kissed my temple. "Beautiful."

"It's been way too long since we've been here." I rested my head on my husband's shoulder. Actually, it had only been a few months, I realized with some amazement. But so much had happened in that time, it seemed longer. First, I had attended a national librarians' convention and faced down a deadly librarian or two. Then Derek and I had gotten married and we'd flown off to honeymoon in Paris. It had been an incredibly romantic time. And then we had come home to find dangerous goons with guns, a vicious assassin, and more than one victim of cold-blooded murder.

Sudden shivers skittered across my shoulders at the memory. You would think I'd be used to finding dead bodies by now. But no, it shocks me to my very core every time.

With determination, I shook off the chills. We were in Dharma now. We could relax and enjoy our families and friends. This coming weekend was Dharma's first annual book festival, and the following week we would stay to help with the grape harvest. I took a few more deep breaths to get rid of the last of those shivers. I didn't want anything to interfere with my excitement over the upcoming book festival. There would be books everywhere—and no dead bodies!

Yes, it was good to be back in Dharma with Derek. It was good to be back in the place where my family and I had lived since I was eight years old, before there even was a town. Back then, there were only Airstream campers and tents and grapevines. I had been very unhappy that my parents had forced us to move from San Francisco out to the boondocks until I climbed down from the family van and spotted a dark-haired little girl. She defiantly clutched her bald Barbie doll and looked just as pissed off as I felt. That was Robin. We clicked instantly, and everything was okay after that.

Our parents were part of a group of Deadheads and seekers of wisdom who had followed their spiritual leader, Avatar Robson Benedict—or Guru Bob, as my siblings and I called him—to the wilds of Sonoma County, where they created the Fellowship for Spiritual Enlightenment and Higher Artistic Consciousness.

Now, of course, most members of the commune lived in beautiful homes that dotted the hills and valleys around Dharma. They worked for the winery or in the vineyards or contributed in other ways to the busy, thriving community of shops, tech firms, restaurants, and wineries scattered around Dharma. Thanks to plenty of canny advice from Guru Bob and the lucrative profit-sharing plan he'd established early on, his followers had learned to invest wisely. And now, twenty-five years later, our people were thriving and our town had become one of the most popular destination spots in the wine country.

And lately, some of Derek's family had bought homes in the area, so for me, Dharma kept getting better and better.

"Is everything out of the car?" I asked.

"Yes." Derek grinned. "Including all of your bookbinding supplies. And Charlie."

I reached out and squeezed his hand. "Thank you."

Just that morning, Derek and I had driven here from San Francisco with our cat, Charlie. The drive itself had only taken an hour, but it had taken even longer to move our clothes and essential items from the car into the house. Now it was time to take a minute and enjoy the quiet.

I felt a whisper of movement and glanced down to see Charlie winding herself around and between my legs, brushing her thick, creamy white tail against my ankles. "Well, look who ventured out of her crate."

Derek led the way back inside and I carefully closed the door behind us. The cat has been precious to both of us ever since Derek had brought her home as a surprise for me.

Footsteps sounded from behind us, and I turned to watch Annie walk into the master bedroom where we were standing.

"Does everything look okay?" she asked, giving the bedspread a minute tug to straighten it. "This room is pretty nice, isn't it?"

"It's fabulous," I said. "The whole house is amazing and the view from the balcony is wonderful."

Annie sighed and glanced around the master bedroom. "I could never bring myself to move into this room. I've replaced all the furniture and painted the walls, but it still reminds me of Abraham." Her eyes clouded, then she seemed to shake herself out of the mood. "Besides, I prefer staying on the first floor. It's easier and, you know, it suits me."

I gave her shoulder a soft squeeze. It was a long story, but basically this house had once belonged to my old bookbinding mentor Abraham Karastovsky. He'd never known he had a daughter until the last few days of his life and he had been looking forward to getting to know her. Sadly, he was killed before that could happen, and consequently, left his entire estate to me, including his sumptuous Mediterranean-style house with its amazing views, along with the equally amazing, fully stocked bookbinding workshop out beyond the pool. Plus six million dollars, but that's a whole other story.

So legally the house belonged to me, but after my family and I got to know Annie—and after the required paternity test results came in, proving that Annie was indeed Abraham's daughter—I asked the lawyers to write out a joint tenant agreement that gave half of the property to Annie. We also set up a trust that would pay Annie a generous allowance until she could determine what she wanted to do with the rest of her life.

Annie's mother—the woman who never told Annie or Abraham about their connection to each other—had passed away during that same period. So with no more attachments, Annie moved to Dharma, where she was welcomed by my mother with open arms.

After a very short time, Annie figured out exactly what she wanted to do with the rest of her life. She had taken her money and opened a cute kitchenware shop on Dharma's fashionable shopping lane. Since then, she had become an integral member of Dharma's business community, and now she was truly thriving. But I could still picture the grief-stricken Goth girl she had been when we first met.

"It's kind of you to open up your home to us, Annie," Derek said.

"Oh. Gosh, Derek, it's really no problem." Her eyelashes fluttered and she gave him a sappy smile, clearly charmed. Derek had that effect on people, especially women. It might've been his elegant British accent that did it, or maybe it was his amazing good looks. Either way, I, too, found myself charmed daily.

Derek and I followed her downstairs, with Charlie keeping up alongside us.

Annie gave us quick lessons on using the coffee-maker and the toaster oven. "You're welcome to drink my coffee and eat anything you find in the pantry or the fridge. Oh, and I have an unopened package of English muffins in the freezer if you want any of those. And cupcakes. Help yourself."

Heading back to the kitchen, Annie glanced down at the clear plastic crates I'd set on the floor near the door leading to the laundry room and the garage. It was easy to see the stacks of books and papers inside. "Looks like you're ready for the book festival."

"As ready as I'll ever be, I guess." I snapped the lid

off the top crate and surveyed the contents. "I brought along a few dozen demonstration books and a ton of bookbinding supplies, just in case."

"Probably a good thing. Your mom says you've got back-to-back presentations lined up on all three days."

I rolled my eyes. "That's what happens when your mother is cochair of the festival committee."

She leaned against the kitchen counter, folded her arms across her chest, and smiled indulgently. "Your mom's really proud of you. And it doesn't hurt that you're the book guru of the Western world."

I chuckled. "Book guru. I like that."

"It suits you," Derek said with a grin.

The first annual Dharma Book Festival was the main reason we had moved in for the next two weeks. I'd been campaigning for years to have a book fair in Dharma, had taken time to visit every bookstore owner in the wine country in hopes of convincing them to take part in the project, and now it was finally happening. It was my very own dream come true, and I had big hopes that the festival would bring lots of smart new visitors to the area. You know, the kind of visitors who liked to read books.

And yes, my mother had signed me up for at least a dozen events on all three days of the festival, but it didn't bother me one bit. I'm a bookbinder specializing in rare-book restoration. Books are my life, so why would I mind?

When the idea of putting on a book festival first came up, Mom had researched the subject with single-minded determination. She signed up for extension classes at the local college and even took several online courses. She formulated a budget, obtained a few big local sponsors, established a working timeline, and solicited a number of active local people to help form a committee.

The committee members divided up the responsibilities of contacting vendors and booking authors, presenters, and other participants. They had someone assigned to promotion and someone else working out an elaborate schedule of events and activities. Mom was relentless in her desire to put on the best festival ever.

In her research, she learned that the big trend with book festivals was to designate a classic book as the official "book of the festival." After a lot of wrangling, the Dharma festival committee had chosen *Little Women* to be that book.

The entire town and anyone planning to attend had been encouraged to read the book in anticipation of the various events and workshops that would celebrate the story and the author. The committee had invited a Louisa May Alcott scholar to take part in several panel discussions. But the biggest and most exciting event of the entire festival promised to be the one-time performance of *Little Women*, the musical.

Everyone we knew was assigned to some aspect of the musical's production, and my family members were no exception. My youngest sister London had signed up to be the director, which made sense because, frankly, she enjoyed telling people what to do. My other sister China was making all the costumes—with help from some of the ladies in town. I figured my sister Savannah would help with the catering. And then Annie, of course, had one of the starring roles. She wasn't an official Wainwright daughter, but Mom treated her like one of her own anyway.

And by the way, if you've never heard of the musical version of *Little Women*, you are not alone. It had even been performed on Broadway, and yet it was still relatively obscure. I wasn't sure why. How bad could it be?

"We're looking forward to seeing you in the musical," Derek said. "Rebecca tells us you're the real star of the show."

Derek was one of the few people in the world who called my mother Rebecca. And after hearing Derek repeat Mom's compliment, Annie practically melted and pressed her hands against her chest. "Awwww, that's so sweet."

"It's true," I confirmed. "Mom said she was blown away when she saw you sing at one of the rehearsals."

Annie actually blushed, but then waved away the compliment. "I just got lucky. They gave me a really pretty song to sing and then I get to die."

"It doesn't get better than that," I agreed.

"I know, right? But Shandi Patrick is playing Marmie, so she's the real star of the show."

I made a face. Shandi Patrick was a well-known Hollywood actress who had been living in Sonoma for a few years now and was part-owner of a local winery. Many of the locals called her "the Diva." Not because of the Hollywood connection, but because she could be a real pain in the butt. According to the town buzz, anyway. I had never met the woman.

Shandi hadn't made a movie or TV show in a long time, so I had to wonder if she could still be considered a *star* except in her own mind. The few times I'd seen her walking along the Lane, I noticed she'd been wearing a lot of spandex to accentuate her statuesque figure. Not that there was anything wrong with that. It was also a well-known fact that Shandi had a regular weekly appointment at Tangled, Dharma's premier hair salon, to touch up those gray roots of hers.

And didn't that make me sound catty? I didn't even know the woman, but I'd paid attention to the rumors.

"I'll bet she hates playing the mom," I said with a smirk.

"She wanted to be Jo," Annie admitted.

"Seriously?" I rolled my eyes. The woman had to be at least fifty years old, probably older. What made her think she could play a teenager?

"Yeah, it was a stretch, for sure," Annie said. "London ended up giving the role to Sara Janz."

"Much more age-appropriate." Sara was a high school junior and favorite babysitter for China's little girl, Hannah.

Annie nodded. "And Sara's good. Everyone is, really. Including Shandi. She's actually kind of . . . nice."

"I'm glad." I smiled. If Shandi was being nice to Annie, I might consider changing my opinion of her. "Sounds like you're having fun with it."

"I am. It's a lot of hard work, but I love it."

"Well, we can't wait to see it," I said.

Annie glanced around the room for one last check, then grabbed her tote bag and purse. "I'd better get going. I'll probably see you around town, but definitely at the festival."

As soon as Annie left, I checked my wristwatch. "I told Dad I might be able to pick up Mom from her committee meeting. I think it'll be fun to surprise her. Do you want to come with me or would you rather go visit your parents first?"

Derek's parents and mine had become such good friends that the Stones had finally bought a home nearby. They planned to come out here twice a year and stay for a few months each time.

"We'll see my parents later this afternoon," he said, wrapping his arms around me. "I'll come with you now."

"Good." I breathed him in for a long moment, then gazed up into his dark blue eyes. "The committee is meeting at the town hall, so if you want, we can park at the far end of the Lane and take a nice walk, see what's new and exciting."

"Sounds like a plan."

We found a parking space on Shakespeare Lane—more casually known as the Lane—a few blocks south of Arugula, my sister Savannah's gourmet veggie restaurant, and headed north toward the town hall. The weather had cooled off and I zipped up my jacket to stay cozy.

Derek reached over and pulled my arm through his. "Come over here and we'll keep each other warm."

"What a good idea."

"The Lane looks especially festive today," he remarked.

"People pull out all the stops for the Harvest. It's everyone's favorite season."

The shops and cafes had been festooned in their best fall colors. Wreaths, garlands, and tiny twinkle lights decorated doorways, and the windows gleamed in the cool sunlight. It was nice to see so many people I recognized. Even the strangers we passed were friendly enough to nod a greeting.

And every single shop window displayed a poster for the upcoming book festival and the *Little Women* musical to be performed on the last evening.

"I'm so happy we're here," I said to Derek, as we continued walking.

"I am as well," he said. "It's lovely to recognize more faces each time I return."

"We'll have to invite Gabriel over for dinner," I said. "I've missed him."

"I spoke to him yesterday. He's already invited himself."

"He would." The thought of seeing Gabriel again cheered me right up. "He can bring the wine."

We continued chatting about this and that as we walked the rest of the way to the town hall.

I checked my watch as we entered the building. It was three forty-five. Perfect timing, I thought. Dad had mentioned that the festival committee meeting usually wrapped up by four o'clock, so Derek and I could sit in the back of the room and watch and listen to the conversation until Mom was ready to leave. I just hoped that, since we were planning to surprise Mom, she didn't interrupt the meeting to make a fuss over us.

We walked across the empty main hall. We had used this space last year for an unusual installation of photographs of art and artifacts found in one of our wine caves. Recently the photographs had been moved to a smaller space inside the town hall to make room for the musical being performed on the last night of the book festival.

"I'm not sure which room the committee members are using," I said, my voice echoing in the large space. We entered the hallway that led to several meeting rooms, and that's when we heard a loud argument.

"I believe we can figure this out," Derek murmured.

"Yeah, no kidding." But I frowned at the vitriolic tone of the conversation. "That voice is definitely my mom's."

Derek hustled us toward the door that was open a crack and we slipped inside. Mom didn't even notice us as we sat down in two of the chairs that lined the back wall.

And I realized that the main reason Mom hadn't noticed us entering the room was that some big guy was standing right in front of her. His fist was raised and he was shouting at her.

I stood and took one step forward, but Derek stopped me. "Wait."

"You incompetent twit," the man bellowed. "This festival will be a complete failure and it'll be all your fault."

"What the hell?" I muttered, and shot a glance at Derek, who also stood. I read his body language easily: *Ready to kill.*

But Mom wasn't cowed.

"That's beyond ridiculous," she said, standing her ground. "This is going to be the most successful event the county's ever seen."

"Not if I can't be there." He was so close that I knew she could feel his breath. It made my skin crawl. "My company is on the verge of taking over this whole valley. I've already bought up six wineries and I'm not done yet."

"Well, you're done here," Mom said.

"The media will expect me to be there," he continued. "Everyone knows my name. You're a fool if you shut me out."

I didn't have a clue what this was all about, but I was seriously going to tackle that guy if he didn't back off. Nobody raises a fist to my mother and lives to talk about it. Sure, I knew she could handle whatever came her way, but she didn't have to handle it alone.

The man turned and glared at Conrad Schmidt, the cochairman of the committee. I'd known Conrad for years. "And you, Schmidt. You're nothing but a thief and a liar."

Conrad stood. "Really, Mr. Banyan, you should go."

Banyan brushed him off. He turned back to my mother and wagged his finger in her face. "I know you're the real troublemaker here, and I'll make sure you pay for this."

"Time for you to leave, Mr. Banyan."

"Oh, but I will," he said, his tone threatening. "Don't cross me, lady. You've got a happy little family here. Be a real shame if something happened to one of them."

Mom gasped. "You're going to be sorry you said that."

Incensed and ready to pounce, I took a step forward. Derek grabbed the back of my sweater to stop me. "Your mother is handling this berk just fine."

I turned on him. "Did you hear what that *berk* said?"

"Yes, love."

I was breathing fire, but Derek's sharp, steady gaze calmed me down. Sort of. I also appreciated his use of the British slang word for *twit* or *idiot*. Banyan was both.

So, for Derek, I compromised. I stayed right where I was and shouted at Banyan, "Get outta here, you jerk!"

Banyan whipped around and sneered at me, then glanced back at Mom. "Can't fight your own battles, I guess."

Mom ignored that comment. "If you threaten me or my family again, I'll have you arrested."

"Ooh," he taunted. "I'm so afraid of the Mayberry police force."

She fisted her hands on her hips. "Just leave, Mr. Banyan."

"Oh, I'm going," he shouted to everyone. "But you won't stop me for long. I'll win this one."

Conrad bared his teeth. "Over my dead body."

Banyan leaned in to Conrad and murmured softly, "Be careful what you wish for." Then he turned and stormed out of the room.